the Monsters of Templeton

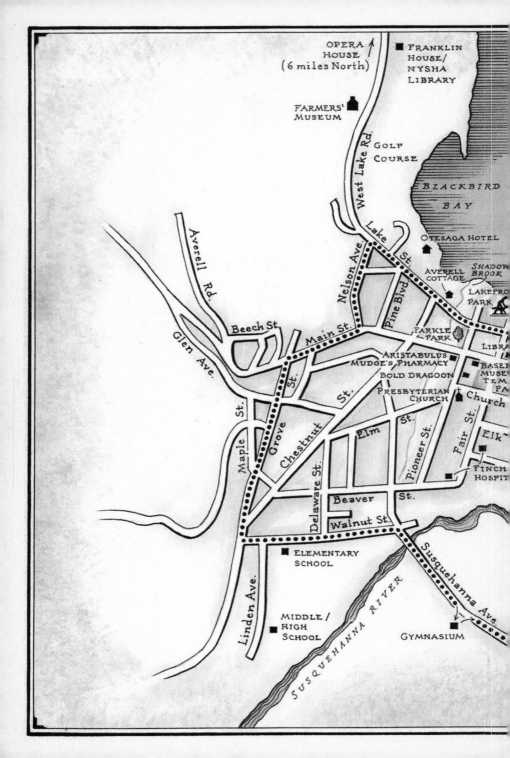

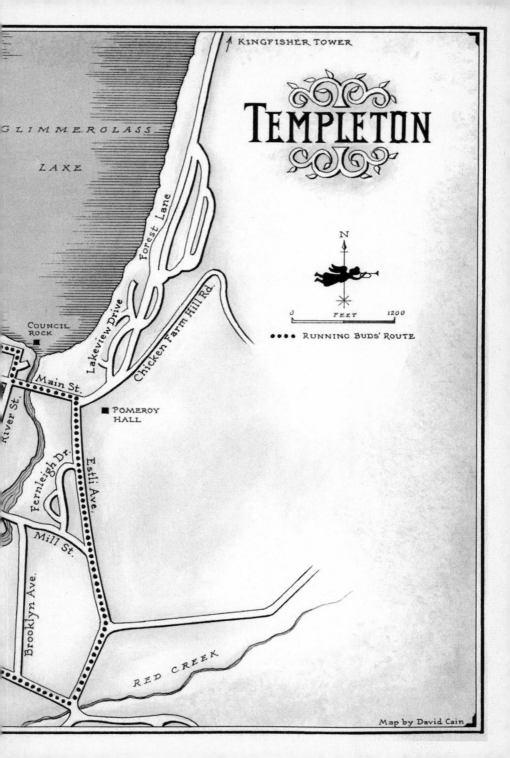

the **M**onsters
of **T**empleton

Lauren Groff

V
VOICE

Hyperion • New York

ISBN-13: 978-0-7394-9916-0

Design by Guenet Abraham
Illustrations by Beth White
Map by David Cain

For my parents, Gerald and Jeannine Groff

"Ah, my friend, 'tis true!" cried old Natty
Bumppo, slapping his knee. *"A man cannot know
hisself if he don't know where he come from."*
—JACOB FRANKLIN TEMPLE,
The Pilgrims of Templeton

*Who can open the doors of his face? His teeth are
terrible round about . . . By his neesings a light
doth shine, and his eyes are like the eyelids of the
morning . . . He maketh a path to shine after him;
one would think the deep to be hoary. Upon earth
there is not his like, who is made without fear.
He beholdeth all high things: he is a king over
all the children of pride.*
—THE KING JAMES BIBLE,
Job 41: 14, 18, 32–34

This is a story of creation.
—MARMADUKE TEMPLE,
Tales of the American Wilderness, 1797

Author's Note

*An interesting fiction . . . however paradoxical the
assertion may appear . . . addresses our love of
truth—not the mere love of facts expressed by true
names and dates, but the love of that higher truth,
the truth of nature and of principles, which is a
primitive law of the human mind.*
—JAMES FENIMORE COOPER, from *Early
Critical Essays*, 1820–1822

ONE WINTER WHEN I was an adult and very far from my hometown, I'd awaken every night, heartsore, haunted by my dreams of
my calm little lake. I missed my village the way I'd miss a person.
This book came from that long, dark winter; I wanted to write a
love story for Cooperstown.

I began as a diligent student, reading many books about the
town's history and as much of James Fenimore Cooper's work as I
could stomach, because one cannot write about Cooperstown
without writing about Fenimore Cooper. But a curious thing happened: the more I knew, the more the facts drifted from their
moorings. They began shaping themselves into stories in my head,
taking over. Dates switched, babies were born who never actually
existed, historical figures grew new personalities and began to do
frightening things. I slowly began to notice that I wasn't writing
about Cooperstown anymore, but rather a slantwise version of the
original.

I panicked; luckily James Fenimore Cooper was there to save me. In his novel *The Pioneers* he wrote about Cooperstown, too, and his facts also went a little awry, so he decided to rechristen his town Templeton, New York. I relaxed and followed his lead.

That's about the time his characters knocked on the door and joined the party. In walked Marmaduke Temple and Natty Bumppo. In walked Chingachgook and Chief Uncas and Cora Munro. Remarkable Pettibones even made an appearance, though she changed her last name to the funnier Prettybones in the intervening centuries. Their arrival made sense: I had grown up with these characters almost as if they were real people, and they formed the myth of my town in my head. They belonged very firmly in my Templeton.

In the end, fiction is the craft of telling truth through lies. I ended up with a different sort of story about my town than the one I had begun. This story saw history as malleable and tried for a different kind of truth about my little village on the lake, one filled with all the mystery and magic that I was surrounded by in my childhood. Myths like Abner Doubleday and the monster in the lake and Leatherstocking and all the many things that go bump in the night are things that we natives, by nature of belonging to the town, have come to feel are true pieces of our story. My Templeton is to Cooperstown as a shadow is to the tree that spawned it; an outline that takes texture from the ground it falls on.

Of course, all characters from the book are, for the most part, invented, and characteristics shared with real living inhabitants of Cooperstown are accidental, unless I have told the models otherwise. People from history have been modified beyond all recognition. I only hope that the town itself, a place I love with all my heart, has not been.

Contents

the
Monsters
of Templeton

Homecoming

THE DAY I returned to Templeton steeped in disgrace, the fifty-foot corpse of a monster surfaced in Lake Glimmerglass. It was one of those strange purple dawns that color July there, when the bowl made by the hills fills with a thick fog and even the songbirds sing timorously, unsure of day or night.

The fog was still deep when Dr. Cluny found the monster on his morning row. I imagine how it went: the slide of the scull's knife across the lake, the oar heads casting rings on the water, the red bow light pulsing into the dark. Then, sudden, looming over the doctor's shoulder, an island where there had never before been an island, the vast belly of the dead beast. Gliding backward, the old doctor couldn't see it. He neared; the bow-ball of his boat pushed into the rubbery flesh like a finger into a balloon; the pressure of boat versus skin reached a tensile limit without piercing anything; the boat checked its bow-ward motion, and jerked to stern. The doctor turned, but he was prepared only for the possible, and didn't at first know what was before him. When he saw the large and terrible eye still milking over with death, the good doctor blinked. And then he fainted.

When Dr. Cluny came to, the dawn had thinned, the water was shot with bars of light, and he found himself rowing around and around the bellied-up beast, weeping. In his mouth there was the sweet burn of horehound candy, the exact savor of his long-ago childhood. Only when a seagull landed upon the flat chin of the leviathan and bent to steal a taste did Dr. Cluny return to himself; only then did he skid back over the water to the awakening town, shouting his news.

"Miracle," he called. "Miracle. Come, quick, see."

AT THAT PRECISE moment, I was idling in the park across the street from Averell Cottage, my childhood home. For at least an hour, I had been standing in the depression that the town flooded in winter to make a skating rink, gathering what courage I could. The fog veiled my grand, awkward house, with its original cottage from 1793, one wing from Victorian 1890, and another from the tasteless 1970s, turning the whole into something more coherent, almost beautiful. In my delirium, I thought I could see my mother inside with a few lifetimes of family antiques and the gentle ghost that lived in my childhood room, all traced like bones on an X-ray, delicate as chalk.

I felt the world around me creak and strain, snapping apart, fiber by fiber, like a rope pulled too tautly.

Back near Buffalo I had had a glimpse of myself in a rest-stop bathroom, and was horrified to find myself transformed into a stranger in rumpled, dirty clothing, my once-pretty face bloated and red with crying jags. I was drawn, thin, welted with the bites of a thousand Alaskan blackflies. My hair, shorn in April, was now growing out in weird brown tufts. I looked like some little chick, starving, molting, kicked out of the nest for late-discovered freakishness.

As the night thinned around me, I leaned over and retched. And I still hadn't moved when, down Lake Street, there came a muffled trampling sound. I knew before I saw them that the sounds were from the Running Buds, a small, dear band of middle-aged men who jog around the streets of Templeton every morning, in all weather, in ice, in rain, in this fine-pelted fog. When the Buds came nearer, I could hear gentle talking, some spitting, some wheezing over their footsteps. They moved out of the dark and into the glow of the single streetlamp on Lake Street, and seeing me in the park in my little depression, seeing, perhaps, something familiar about me but not quite recognizing who I was at that distance, all six of them raised their hands in my direction. I waved back and watched their thick bodies disappear down the street.

I FOUND MY feet crossing the street, heading up the driveway, passing through the garage doorway, and I opened the door to the mudroom to the smells of straw and dust and bitter orange, the smells of home. I almost turned around, returned to the car, waited for day. I hadn't seen my mother in more than a year: I couldn't afford the trip home, and, for the first time since I'd left, she hadn't offered to pay. Instead, though, I came in as silently as I could, hoping to have a few good hours of sleep before awakening her. I placed my shoes beside her white nursing clogs, and went through the mudroom, then the kitchen.

But although I had expected Vi to be sleeping, she was sitting at the kitchen table with the *Freeman's Journal* spread before her, her profile reflected in the great plate glass door that looked out over the two-acre lawn, the lake, the hills. She must have had a night shift, because her feet were in an enamel bowl filled with hot water, her eyes closed, her face hanging above her tea as if she were trying to steam her features off. They were slipping that way, anyhow: at forty-six, my mother had the worn, pouchy skin of a woman who had done far too many drugs at far too young an age. Her shoulders were slumped, and the zipper in the back of her skirt was open, revealing a swatch of red cotton underwear and a muffin-top of flesh above it.

From my position in the kitchen door, my mother looked old. If I weren't already holding the pieces together with both squeezed hands, this sight would have broken my heart.

I must have moved or swallowed, because Vi turned her head and looked at me. Her eyes narrowed, she blinked and heaved a sigh, and passed a hand over her face. "Goddamn flashbacks," she muttered.

I snorted.

She looked at me again, her forehead creasing. "No. You're not a flashback, Willie. Are you?"

"Not this time. Apparently," I said, coming over to her and kissing her on the part in her hair. She smelled antiseptic from the hospital, but, deeper, there was her own smell, something birdlike, like warm and dusty wings. She squeezed my hand, flushing.

"You look horrible. What in the world are you doing home?" she said.

"Oh, boy." I sighed, and had to look away, at the thinning curls of fog on the lake. When I looked back, the smile had fallen off her face.

"What. The heck. Are you. Doing home?" she said, again, still squeezing, but harder with each word until the bones in my hand were crushing one another.

"Jesus," I gasped.

"Well," she said, "if you're in trouble, you'd better be praying." It was only then that I saw the crude cross of raw iron that hung heavily between her breasts, as if my mother had gone to the Farmers' Museum up the road and blacksmithed her own crucifix out of two hobnails. I nudged the cross with my free hand and frowned.

"Vi?" I said. "Oh, don't *tell* me you've become a Jesus freak. You're a hippie, for God's sake. Remember? Organized religion equals bad?"

She released my hand, and tugged the cross away. "That," she said, "is none of your business." For a long moment, though, Vi couldn't look at me.

"Vi," I said, "be serious. What's going on?"

My mother sighed and said, "People change, Willie."

"*You* don't," I said.

"You should be glad I do," she said. She dropped her eyes, not yet remembering that I was standing there in her house when I should have been under the twenty-four-hour dazzle of an Alaskan tundra. I should have been blowing lichen off definitive proof that human culture existed there over thirty-five thousand years ago, some incisor embedded deep in the ground, some tool still glistening with seal grease, intact from the deep freezer of the steppe. I should have been under the aegis of Dr. Primus Dwyer, PhD, Barton P. Thrasher

Professor in the Sciences at Stanford University, where in a few short months I was supposed to finish my PhD dissertation, and graduate, heading toward a life of impossible luminescence.

When I told my mother in my sophomore year that I wanted to focus my furious ambitions in archaeology, she looked bitterly disappointed for a moment. "Oh, Willie," she'd said then. "There is nothing left in this world for you to discover, honey. Why look backward when you can look forward?" I talked for hours then, of the intensity of wonder when you blew away the dust and found an ancient skull in your hand, when you held the flint knives and saw the chisel marks made by long-dead hands. Like so many people who have long ago burnt through all of their own passion, my mother recognized mine, and longed for it. Archaeology would take me into the great world, into deserts and tundras, as far away from Templeton as I believed she had always wanted me to be. By now, her ego and a good portion of what inheritance she had left were invested in this dream: me as intrepid explorer of bone and potsherds, tunneling into the vastness of prehistory. Now, in the lightening dawn, she looked at me. A motorboat was speeding across the lake at top throttle, and its whine rose even to us, set two acres back on glowing, overgrown lawn.

"Oh, Willie," said my mother now. "Are you in trouble," and it was a statement, not a question.

"Vi?" I said. "I messed up big-time."

"Of course," she said. "Why else would you find yourself in Templeton? You can hardly stand to come back once a year for Christmas."

"Goddamn it, Vi," I said, and I sat down in one of the kitchen chairs and rested my head on the table.

My mother looked at me and then sighed. "Willie," she said. "I'm sorry. I'm so tired. Tell me now what happened so I can get some sleep, and we'll deal with it later."

I looked at her, then had to look down at the table. I traced designs in the waxy residue of its surface. And then I told her one version of the story, vastly abridged.

"Well, Vi," I said. "It looks like I'm pregnant. And it's maybe Dr. Primus Dwyer's."

My mother held her fingers over her mouth. "Oh, heaven help us," she said.

"I'm sorry," I said. "But, Vi, there's more." I said it in one exhale, in a great whoosh. I told her that I also tried to run over his wife with a bush plane, and she was the dean of students, and it was probable that charges of attempted manslaughter would prevent me from returning to Stanford again. I held my breath and waited for the knuckled sting of the back of her hand. Despite Vi's hippie mores, it was not uncommon in my childhood for us to get to this point in our battles, panting and narrow-eyed, stalemated across the table. And once or twice, for my greatest sins, she did send her hand across to settle it all with a smack.

But she didn't hit me now, and it was so silent I could hear the two-hundred-year-old grandfather clock in the dining room as the pendulum clicked, clicked, clicked. When I looked up, Vi was shaking her head. "I can't believe it," she said, pushing her tea farther from her with one finger. "I raised you to be exceptional, and here you are, a fuckup. Like your stupid fuckup mother." Her face wobbled and grew red.

I tried to touch her arm, but she snatched it away, as if mere contact with me could burn her. "I'm going to take a few pills," she said, standing. "I'm going to sleep for as long as I can sleep. And when I wake up, we're dealing with this." She moved heavily to the door. With her back still toward me, she paused. "And oh, Willie, your hair. You had such beautiful hair," she said and moved away. I could hear her footsteps on every creaking floorboard in the old house, up the grand front stairway, far away over the hall and into the master bedroom.

Only in recent years did such coolness arise between Vi and me. When I was little, I would play cribbage and euchre with my young mother until midnight, laughing so hard I never wanted to go to the few sleepovers and birthday parties I was invited to. My mother and I held an odd relationship with the town, as we were the last remnants of its founder, Marmaduke Temple, and direct descendants of the great novelist Jacob Franklin Temple, whose novels we read every year in high school, whose link to me would actually make a college professor burst into tears when I confessed it. But we were too poor and my mother was young, unmarried, and too weird with her macramé and loud politics, and so when we left the safety of our eccentric house, it always felt like Vi and me against the world. I remember vividly when I was ten or so—which would have made my mother my age, twenty-eight—listening outside her door as she wept for hours after being slighted in the grocery store, that one memory standing in for many. I dreamt at night of being so big I could march down Main Street, grinding our enemies under my furious ogre's feet.

Alone now in the dawn, I drank the rest of my mother's tea to melt the block of ice in my gut. Vi was wrong: I did want to come home. Templeton was to me like a less-important limb, something inherently mine, something I took for granted. My own tiny, lovely village with great old mansions and a glorious lake, my own grand little hamlet where everyone knows your name, but with elaborate little frills that made it unlike anywhere else: the baseball museum, the Opera, the hospital that had vast arms extending into the rest of upstate, an odd mix of Podunk and cosmopolitan. I came back when I had to, to feel safe, to recharge; I just hadn't had to in so long.

For a while I sat alone at the table, watching the crows fall into the vegetable garden, pecking at the heirloom vegetables that thrived every year under Vi's benign neglect. Then the motorboat that had gone out before zipped back, and soon more motorboats were roaring out into the lake like a vee of geese. Curious, I slid open the glass door and went onto the porch, in the warming dawn. From where I stood, the hills around Lake Glimmerglass looked like the haunch end of a sleeping lion, smooth and pelted. I watched until the motorboats came back into sight, collectively straining to pull something pale behind them, something enormous and glinting in the new sun.

And that's how I found myself running barefoot over the cold grass down to Lakefront Park, even as weary as I was at that moment. I went past our pool, now so thick with algae that it had become a frog pond, plunking with a thousand belly flops of terror when I passed. I went down the stretch of lawn, across the concrete bridge over Shadow Brook, trespassed over Mrs. Harriman's backyard until I stood in the road at Lakefront Park, and watched the motorboats coast in.

I stood under the bronze statue of the Mohican, the best known of the characters by our town novelist, Jacob Franklin Temple, and, slowly, others gathered around me, people from my childhood who nodded at me in recognition, startled by the great change in my appearance, struck silent by the solemnity of the moment. Somehow, none of us was surprised. Templeton is a town of accreted myth: that baseball was invented here; that a petrified giant, ten feet tall and pockmarked with age, was disinterred from under the old mill—a hoax; that ghosts lived among us. And we had been prepared for this day by the myths we'd always heard about a lake monster, the childhood tales around campfires in the summer camps on the lake, the small rumors filtered down. The town crazy, Piddle Smalley, would stand on a bench in Farkle Park wearing his pants backward—urine-soaked, which is why we called him Piddle—and shout about the rain-swollen April day when he stood on the Susquehanna bridge, staring down into the fat river, and something immense passed by, grinning its black teeth up at him. He'd shriek at the end of his story *Glimmey, Glimmey, Glimmey,* as if in invocation.

Most of Templeton was watching as the motorboats cut their engines and glided in. The *Chief Uncas* tourist boat groaned in the waves against the dock. The Running Buds climbed out with great gravitas, old joints creaking, and secured the beast's tethers to the iron hitches in the walls at the lake's edge. And in those brief minutes before the baseball tourists in town heard of our miracle and came running with their vulgar cameras and shouts and poses, before the news trucks drove ninety miles per hour from Oneonta, Utica, Albany, there, in the long, peaceful quiet, we had a few moments to consider our monster.

In that brief time, we were able to see it in its entirety. The beast was huge, a heavy cream color that darkened to lemon in places, and was floating on its back. It looked like a carp grown enormous, with a carp's fat belly and round eye, but with a long, articulated neck like a ballet dancer's, and four finned legs, plump as a frog's. The ropes of the motorboat had cut into its skin, and the wounds were open to the day, still oozing dark, thick blood. I stepped forward to touch the beast, then everyone else did. When I placed my hand upon its belly, I felt its porous skin, its hairs as small and delicate as the ones on my own arms, but thicker, as if the beast were covered in peach fuzz. And, though I had expected the early sun to have warmed it, the monster burned cold, as if its very core was made of the ice some said still existed at the bottom of our glacial lake.

It was somehow clear, even then, that the monster had been lonely. The folds above its eye made the old face look wistful, and it emanated such a strong sense of solitude that each human standing in the park that day felt miles from the others, though we were shoulder-to-shoulder, touching. Later, we would hear that when the divers couldn't reach the bottom of our lake, they called in deep-sea pods to search for another beast like the one that surfaced that day. We would hear that, scour as they might, they couldn't find another beast like ours, only detritus: rusted tractors and plastic buoys, and even an antique phonograph. They found a yellow-painted phaeton in its entirety, the bones of a small spaniel inside. They also found dozens of human skeletons, drowned or dumped corpses, arranged side-by-side in some trick of current or metaphysics, on a shallow shelf near Kingfisher Tower, beside Judith's Point.

That morning, before I drew my hand away from the monster, I felt an overwhelming sadness, a sudden memory of one time in high school when I slipped to the country club docks at midnight with my friends, and, giggling, naked, we went into the dark star-stippled water, and swam to the middle of the lake. We treaded water there in the blackness, all of us fallen silent in the feeling of swimming in such perfect space. I looked up and began to spin. The stars streaked circular above me, my body was wrapped in the warm black, my hands had disappeared, my stomach was no longer, I was only a head, a pair of eyes. As I touched the beast I remembered how, even on that long-ago night, I could feel a tremendous thing moving in the depths below me, something vast and white and singing.

Marmaduke Temple
CIRCA 1800, *the Gilbert Stuart portrait*
that now hangs in the Franklin House Museum

2

Marmaduke Temple

AN EXCERPT FROM *Tales of the American Wilderness,* 1797

In the spring of 1785 I left my family in New Jersey and traveled into the vast and melancholy wilderness of New York to survey and lay my name on the place that has since made my fortune and renown. It was a wondrous time, after the revolution, and in our young country, a man such as I, a once-unlettered maker of puncheon and barrel, could build himself from nothing and become great. The journey was difficult and the land still frozen, and I was alone in those parts still trod by bloodthirsty natives. I felt all the eyes of the forest upon me and slept with a knife in my hand.

When at last I reached the edge of my land, I left my horse behind me to crop grass in a green and rich valley and struggled wearily up a great mountain to look upon a place yet untouched by man. The forest was quiet and I passed over the strange orange mushrooms, over the gnarled roots. All was dark at first, and the trees cast a midday twilight upon me. Then there was a rift in the darkness, a cliff where the trees dropped a hundred feet from the mountain's lip, and there I stepped into the light.

Below me the lake was cupped in its hills, shimmering like a plate of glass. Three hawks circled in the pale sky and the hills arched with pines. From my perch I watched a mother bear and her cubs emerge near the river's mouth to drink at the lake. There was no wind in this desolate New York wilderness, and all was calm.

Suddenly before me rose a vision of ghostly buildings on the edge of the lake, a true city of spires and rooftops, a phantom bustle in the streets, smoke. I sank to my knees in the strange ferns. On the lip of the lake wavered the city I was to build, Templeton, a place of impossible importance pressed upon that virgin land, a great metropolis like Philadelphia, or London. And when my eyes lifted to the hills, I saw that they were covered in good things: heifers, orchards, vineyards, fields of wheat. I would carve a great civilization from this savage place. I would build a city, myself, from nothing.

I must have been there for hours on that cliff's edge, for when I came back to myself my knees ached. My vision had at last been blown by the wind into tendrils of dust and smoke and I had begun to see stranger visions, a huge billowing of something white and struggling in the water, something surrounded by a darkening stain before it sank again. I was later sure it was a cloud reflected in the glassy lake, but at the time this new vision filled my heart with a horrid thrill, and when I stood, I was weak and suddenly cold, shaking as if with an ague. I stood and moved back into the dark forest. Only in the cool embrace of the trees did I remember the glorious first vision I'd had, Templeton, rich with crops and industry. As I slipped over the damp humus I vowed I would return and stamp my will on the wild place, the image of my own hand. I would call the mountain where I had had my first taste of Templeton, Mount Vision, and the glassy lake upon which I looked, Lake Glimmerglass. And as I walked, I believed myself to be an Adam setting foot in a new Eden, sinless and wild-eyed, my sinews still stiff with creation.

Vivienne Upton
*As a child, in the middle of a recitation for all of her father's
historian friends. And later, as a young hippie.*

3

Vivienne, Bright and Beautiful

A GIRL WAS in the sun on a shuddering bus, a rash of acne across her cheekbones. Her polyester dress had been dyed black in the ladies' room sink of some midwestern terminal, and the dye job was clearly quick and recent: the orange flowers were still bursting across the fabric, though now a cindered color, and there were black marks like bruises wherever the dress touched her skin. The dress didn't really touch much of her skin, however, as it was both a halter top and a mini-mini skirt, and the girl shouldn't really have been wearing it, as she was both far too plump for it and goosebumped, having traveled from a mild San Francisco February into an upstate New York ice storm. Of course, she didn't really feel the cold, having popped a very nice pill only a few hours earlier, and was deep in a voluptuous, openmouthed sleep.

The farmwife who boarded outside Erie, Pennsylvania, stared at the sleeping girl indignantly, chewing her own upper gum. At last she heaved out "hippie," having brooded on the word like a hen on an egg for two hundred miles. Now that it was delivered of her, she fell asleep herself, in a position mirroring the young girl's own.

The girl was, of course, Vivienne, my mother. It was early 1973, and she was seventeen years old, returning home to Templeton. She would always feel this wild girl was the truest of any of the people she had already been: adored daughter, bourgeois priss, rebel, runaway, dope-fiend San Francisco hippie; or all the people she would later be: mother, nurse, religious fanatic, prematurely old woman. Vivienne was a human onion, and when I came home at twenty-eight years old on the day the monster died, I was afraid that the Baptist freak she had peeled down to was her true, acrid, tear-inducing core.

But then she was only a girl, though a highly medicated one. A tin peace medallion patted and patted her braless chest with every jerk of the bus, as if in sympathy for her new orphanhood. Both of her parents, she knew hazily, had somehow expired, but she knew little about how or why, and it hadn't really occurred to her that they were gone. When Vivienne opened her eyes next, it was to behold the white buildings of Templeton at the end of the lake, huddling there like a flock of geese, ready to hiss. She was so innocent she didn't realize the town would soon turn on her. *That girl has gone too far*, the gossips would say. *Just look at her.* She was dangerous, they felt, a one-woman protest march, just tempting their children into pot and sex and sit-ins by the mere unkempt look of her, those hairy legs, those bloodshot eyes.

Vi as yet had no idea of this imminent betrayal: Templeton was her town, she felt. She was related to the tremendous Marmaduke Temple, a direct descendant of both the great man and his great novelist son, Jacob Franklin Temple. She thought of the town as her ancestral seat, even though she also had a vague idea that, as a hippie, she wasn't supposed to believe in all that jazz anymore.

Poor Vivienne. When she disembarked from the bus by the old railroad depot and dragged the (stolen) blue suitcase to the curb, she didn't realize that there would be nobody to pick her up. She sat there for an hour, quaking with cold, sure she had told her father to come for her when the bus pulled in. At last, she remembered the car accident and the terrible telephone call during a party, when she thought for a long time that the attorney trying to tell her of her parents' death was a friend playing a practical joke.

Then the new orphan in her flimsy California dress dragged the suitcase behind her all the way down the lacquered ice on Main Street, past the courthouse, past the Civil War memorial, under the one blinking yellow yield light on Chestnut, all the way to Averell Cottage, where there were no lights, no warmth, nothing to greet her but even more silence.

She saw the note from the lawyer by the telephone but was too tired to read it. And it was only when she wearily climbed the stairs to where there were twin dips in the mattress where her parents had lain for so many years that she understood what had happened. That though this felt trippy, it was actual unsleepoffable reality. When she awoke in the morning in their bed, her parents were still gone, and she had missed their funeral by a day.

The next day Vivienne walked about with her head thick, as if overstuffed with wool, feeling for the first time like an orphan. But she didn't cry then, and wouldn't cry until years later, when, chopping a tomato still warm from the garden, she would put down her knife and go upstairs to the bed and weep and wail for three days straight, not even getting up when her four-year-old daughter stood in the doorway, sucking her finger, bringing up boxes of cereal and pushing the little o's one by one into her mother's wet red face. At the end of which time, Vi would dry her eyes, pick the three dried tomato seeds off her chin, and go back downstairs to restart the gazpacho she was making when she had her little breakdown.

The official story of my grandparents' deaths went like this: George and Phoebe Upton (née Tipton) died together by automobile. The obituary said that they were speeding too fast over East Lake Road when they hit an icy skid and roared off a thirty-foot precipice onto soft ice, which they cracked through. Knocked out from the crash, they drowned in the wintry water. George was the town historian, PhD Yale, working out of the New York State Historical Association library. This library was in the vast fieldstone farmhouse called Franklin Manor that George had, perhaps not unrelatedly, donated to NYSHA; although it was built by Jacob Franklin Temple and had been passed through the generations, it was so vast and expensive that George couldn't carry it with his limited means.

George was not a man to care about lost fortunes, but his tremulous little wife, Phoebe, often started her sentences with a sigh and, "When we were rich . . ." As in "When we were rich, the butcher *always* let us pay with credit," and "When we were rich, we knew the Roosevelts," though that was an outright fib: it was George's parents who had known the Roosevelts. In town, it was commonly assumed the family had lost its fortune in the great crash of '29, though it was more due to George's absentminded mismanagement than anything else.

As George often said, he couldn't care less for filthy lucre. He was strange: prematurely antique, stern, smelling of musty books and cattails. Vi never once had a hug from him. But she understood him, she always said: he was raised by his grandmother, whose sole enthusiasm was the orphanage where the old folks' home, Pomeroy Hall, is now, and Vi often wondered if he felt less like her kin and more like one of her orphans. His own mother had drowned in the lake when George was tiny, and after that he never saw his father, who, crippled with grief, moved to Manhattan and only sent a check and a terse note to the boy every month. Still, George was happy enough, in his way, Vi told me. He, she found out when she returned to Templeton, had a private obsession that had taken up all his attention.

That morning Vi found herself sitting, shivering, in the lawyer's office, glimpsing the idea that her father's passion for his work was deeper than she had imagined. In fact, the lawyer intimated, its souring was perhaps what led her phlegmatic father to send the Cadillac spinning over the brink.

"Ahem. Your father," he said gently, "was perhaps too, well, *susceptible* to criticism?"

To this, Vivienne could only say, "Hell, yeah," remembering the way her square daddy-o would freak out even at the slightest criticism of the Republican Party, Templeton, or his own uneven bowties. The lawyer smiled with great unction at the girl. Chauncey Todd was an old friend of her family's, a man who had a habit of drawling over words he wanted to emphasize. He was also a breast-ogler, addressing her two great sagging boobs as if he were primarily sorry for their loss—of possible support, perhaps—and only secondarily for the girl's they were attached to. He wondered if what they said was true, and those hippie girls really were as *loose* as they were said to be.

"Vivienne," he said hesitantly toward her nipples. "You have, ahem, perhaps heard of your father's *book*?"

"Nah," said Vivienne, giving her chest a gleeful little shake to make the old man sweat. "He wrote a book? Wow."

In fact, she did know of the book, having received it in the mail with the fifty-dollar check she got every month from her parents. She even sent a rare note of congratulations, read three chapters, and then used it to prop up a wobbly leg on her bedside table. She simply forgot. The pot she smoked every day upon awakening, after eating, before bed, tended to make her forgetful.

And so the lawyer refreshed her memory. The book was eight years in the making, he reminded her: her father had begun it long before Vivienne turned rebellious and left town for "freer *waters*." The book, he said, was about Marmaduke Temple and a shameful secret he had. This secret affected Vivienne herself, her mother's family, as well as the view of Marmaduke Temple in the eyes of American historians everywhere. The lawyer paused, then, for effect.

"And what was the secret?" Vivienne asked, interested despite herself.

The lawyer cleared his throat; rhetorical drum-rolling. "Your father proposed that your mother's old Templeton family, the *Averells*," he said, "are the descendants of Marmaduke Temple and a *slave* girl he owned named *Hetty*." And he sat back, and looked up at her face for the first time all morning to see her reaction. There had been such tremendous outrage on all fronts since the book came out that the lawyer was expecting sudden shock to flit over my mother's face.

But a dazed smile burst out, instead. "Cool," said Vivienne, "I'm a Negro."

In the time it took Chauncey Todd to digest this idea, the slow crunch of Vivienne's mental machinery had brought her to a different place. Her face grew grave and disappointed. "Wait a second," she said. "If my father was related to old Marmaduke and my mom was too, that's incest, right? I mean, I'm a product of incest?" She felt this was a great tragedy. *That explains it*, she said to herself, though it was not quite clear what about herself had now been explained.

Chauncey Todd dragged a hand over his bewildered face and sighed at the breasts. "Now, Vivi*enne*," he said. "We're talking perhaps *five* generations here. Your parents were only *slightly* related."

"Ah," she said. "Right." She waited for a while, and then frowned again. "So, what's the problem?"

Chauncey Todd felt as if he were on a merry-go-round spinning out of control. He squeezed his eyes shut. And, thus safe against my mother's magnificent though untethered bosoms, he explained as calmly as he could that Marmaduke Temple was perhaps the archetypal American, the first self-made man; that he, a Quaker, had slaves was scandal enough; and far worse, that he, a married man, had relations with his slaves—scandalous! It made everyone very uncomfortable. It shattered the idol that was Marmaduke Temple. He was not the man everyone had thought he was. After twenty minutes of impassioned speech, Chauncey Todd was panting, surprised at his own zeal, pleased with his eloquence. When he opened his eyes, Vivienne was gazing at him with more bewilderment.

"So?" she said at last. "Like, he was a human being, right? Nobody is saying he was a god or anything. Human beings do shitty things sometimes. Oh well. We're over it. I don't see what the big deal is."

"Well," said Chauncey Todd, "you are in the minority, here. The *extreme* minority. All of Templeton was *greatly* upset, I'll have you know. And so was the nation's historical community. Your father was berated for such speculative history. There was even talk of taking away his job at NYSHA. I, for one, as his confidant, know that he couldn't bear the idea, and that he was *bewildered* with all of the negative press. He, like you, couldn't understand what the *brouhaha*, if you will, was about. The poor, blind man," he said soulfully, shaking his head, "had no idea what hit him. And so I do believe that perhaps your parents' accident was *not* an accident."

"You know, Mr. Chauncey Todd," said my young mother. "I don't think so. I mean, it's not like the relations were ever a secret or anything. My mother and grandmother always said they were related to Marmaduke Temple through something illegitimate. Like, they used to make this joke about it. They were always so proud of it. But they said they couldn't prove it. I mean, all my daddy did was prove it, right? It doesn't change the facts. I mean, it's history. Like, what's history, but the facts we find out later, right? I don't know, it's like I'm getting all deep now."

For a while, there was a silence between them in the dusty, walnut-paneled room. Chauncey Todd went to the window and looked down onto Main Street, where a small pack of young male joggers was going by, their thighs a skim-milk blue under their tiny shorts. "Health *nuts*," he said with disdain. He turned back around, gave the breasts a doleful stare, then sat down again. "I suppose, Vivienne," he said, "we should carry on and finish our business for today. Now, for the *will*," he said, and pulled the document from a folder.

This was when Vivienne learned that almost everything her parents had was gone. Edgewater, the brick mansion built by her great-great-great granduncle Richard, the rent of which supported her family for years, would have to be sold for tax purposes. The Gilbert Stuart oil painting of a fleshy Marmaduke Temple and the smirking painting of novelist Jacob Franklin Temple had to be taken off the walls of Averell Cottage and sold to NYSHA to cover the funeral expenses. Almost the entire library of first-edition Jacob Franklin Temple books would have to be sold off to pay other bills, though she should feel free to keep one of each book as a family memento, Jacob having been in the habit of keeping five copies of his own editions on hand at any time. The jewels of her great-great-grandmother, Charlotte Franklin Temple, would be sold, though Vi would keep the pocket watch inscribed to the authoress from her dear father. George had already donated to NYSHA all of the valuable papers: Marmaduke's maps and letters and Jacob's notes of admiration from the likes of Edgar Allan Poe and Samuel Morse and General Lafayette, etc. Vi would get the family Bible, Marmaduke's wife's prayer book, the large collection of baseball memorabilia collected by her father's father—Asterisk "Sy" Upton, the longtime baseball commissioner. The only furniture she could keep was the furniture already in Averell Cottage. She had about fifteen thousand dollars in the bank when all was said and done, a gift from her grandfather at her birth, all that remained of Marmaduke's millions.

"The good news," said Chauncey Todd, "is that you get to keep *Averell Cot*tage. Your mother had held it in trust for you *all* this time."

Vivienne stared forlornly at the lawyer, who was sitting back and pinching the bridge of his nose. On her long bus trip across the country, she had come to the secret resolution to sell off everything, take the money, and buy a sweet, wisteria-covered house in Carmel-by-the-Sea that overlooked the ocean. She would be a poet: words, she always told me when I was growing up, burned her fingertips from her late teens until her twenties. Years later, she would read my clumsy high school essays and rearrange the words with great innate skill until they tripped lightly across the page. On the bus home, she had imagined in detail the long life she would live in the cottage by the sea, how she wouldn't have to ever work again. We all have our theories about why people react the way they do, especially when they're acting eccentric; mine is that those daydreams of Carmel-by-the-Sea were how she staved off the sorrow ticking at her from inside, the incomprehensible loss of both her parents at once.

Now, in Chauncey Todd's office, it looked as if she would have to stay for a little while to get ramshackle Averell Cottage back into shape, and then try to sell it. Even then, she would probably only have enough money for a decade or so in a smaller place than the one she longed for, and then she would have to get a job, if she weren't a famous poet already.

The lawyer looked at her pale face with its burning carbuncles of acne, and felt a tiny mewling movement of pity in his breast. "It is not *much*," he said, not unkindly. "But it can be a good life if you manage it well."

"Good. Fantastic," she said. And Chauncey Todd, unaccustomed to the sarcasm of the next generation, took her at her word, and beamed her bosoms a tender smile. In response, Vi took her left breast in hand and shook it at him for a good-bye, then trudged home in her scandalous dress and cork shoes, the ratty zigzag of her part lowered into the lake wind.

At home, she stood looking out the parlor window at the lake. Snow devils were whirling around on the ice, and the pines were spiked with white on the hills. Vivienne thought of old Marmaduke Temple boffing his slave, and laughed.

Then, standing there at the window, she surprised herself. At one time, she had been a princess, an obedient Shirley Temple in patent-leather shoes and pink organza dresses. At one time, she declaimed to crowds of historians perched on the seats of antique parlor chairs, who sent streams of pipe smoke at her as they shouted "Hooray!" If she had done well with her declamations, her father would briefly press his hand against her cheek as he escorted her up to bed. "My girl," he would say. "My brilliant girl." Now watching the winter out of Averell Cottage's windows, words she remembered from when she was little just bubbled up from nowhere. "*In the spring of 1785 I left my family in New Jersey and traveled into the vast and melancholy wilderness,*" she said aloud in a sort of half-murmur, "*. . . all was dark at first, and the trees cast a midday twilight upon me. Then there was a rift in the darkness, a cliff where the trees dropped a hundred feet from the mountain's lip, and there I stepped into the light . . . There was no wind in this desolate New York wilderness, and all was calm. Suddenly before me rose a vision of ghostly buildings on the edge of the lake, a true city of spires and rooftops, a phantom bustle in the streets, smoke. I sank to my knees in the strange ferns.*"

The words of the man in question, Marmaduke Temple, at the epiphanic moment when he first laid eyes upon the place where he would build Templeton. This great, calm, heroic, rational man, now exposed as a base slave owner and philanderer among the unpaid help. What a lark!

For a second, Vi considered the stern portrait of Marmaduke over the mantelpiece. "I like you better now that I know that about you, old guy," she said, and laughed. Something about her laughter, how it echoed and echoed in the cold house, cracked her up even more, and she gasped, her ribs hurt, she peed herself a little. But then she stopped, positive that there was a moment when the face of the man in the portrait twitched into a smirk and a wink. A little complicit grimace.

Vivienne gazed at the portrait, amazed, and then considered. She had seen stranger things, though those visions were usually induced by fun substances. But also, as a child, she often saw a ghost moving through Averell Cottage. To Vi, the ghost took the form of a giant quivering dove that left great misty feathers strewn about the house. A wink in oil paint was not outside the realm of possibility. She gave the portrait a little grin, winked back. Then she felt sick and ran to the bathroom to heave up her breakfast of canned pineapple, all she could find in the kitchen cabinets that wasn't tinned pork or Jell-O. She had been feeling sick in the mornings. Her navel had swollen a little. Last month, she didn't get a period.

VIVIENNE, IT SEEMED, was pregnant.

The story of my conception was one I knew from long before I could even speak: Vi's eyes would always light up with joy and nostalgia when she described how she lived in San Francisco, in a commune, in what she liked to describe as "an experiment in free love," though to me it always sounded like rented love, albeit rented cheaply. There having been four men but only three women in this commune, Vi never went to bed alone; and, as there were also always yogis and painters and sitar players and organic yogurt makers staying over, everyone, of course, was cordially invited to take part in the love fests.

She was only seventeen, she always said, sighing. What did she know about precautions? Vi awoke over the next month with vomit already in her mouth, and felt lethargic and heavy and sick. Even before they injected the bunny with her urine and watched it die, Vivienne knew.

On the day of the pregnancy test, Vi sat in her paper hospital gown, feet growing cold on the floor. The nurse, a girl three grades older than Vi in high school, was blushing. "I'm sorry," she said. "You're pregnant, Miss Upton," and she could not look Vi in the eye.

Enter: me. Wilhelmina Sunshine Upton, called a hippie-dippie "Sunshine" until I was two and already stubborn and refused to answer to that name.

The moment Vi was told by that soft little nurse that she was pregnant, she knew she had to stay in Templeton. In the vague swamp that was my mother's brain, she knew that she couldn't kick the drugs if she returned to San Francisco, and that it would be almost impossible to find more in Templeton. Her heart was good, and she didn't want to retard her little cooking baby. Also, if she were going to go back to San Francisco, she would have no idea which of the commune's men had fathered her child; before I was born, any one of the four (plus) could have been my true father. When I was born, however, more than ten and a half long months after she came home—I was even pigheaded in the womb, she always said in explanation—she had pared my fathers down to three: she was fairly certain when she saw my pink skin that it wasn't the black man. This was what she told me later, even when I was two years old, and couldn't imagine what sex was. She was frank, my mother, always. And, until I understood the mechanics of the act, I loved the idea of having three fathers: if one was good, imagine being blessed with three!

I was once sent home from kindergarten for making this boast. Mrs. Parrot squinted down at me with pity as she pinned the note onto my jacket, and gave me a pat on the head. When my mother unpinned the note in our old Volvo, she chortled, then at home pasted it into my baby album. *Dear Ms. Upton*, it read. *Wilhelmina bragged today of having three fathers, for which I send her home as chastizement. Be wary of speaking of your promiscous past before impressionable kids. Little pictures have big ears. Mrs. P.*

"Can't even spell, that wench," my mother said as she applied glue to the back of the note, tears of laughter dampening her cheeks.

But at the moment she greeted the little pulsing me in the hospital, hands spread over her midsection, Vi knew she would stay to raise her child in a healthy way, far from hedonistic temptation. She would be a good mother in Templeton, she decided; I would grow up safely there.

To be frank, this part of the story always sounded a little fishy to me, but I could never figure out why. I just swallowed it. And, until I visited San Francisco later, I was grateful to have been raised in my small and beautiful town. Then, when I saw that gorgeous, gilded city under the fog, I regretted Templeton and its tiny ways, its subservience to the baseball tourists that came in hordes every year, its lack of even a decent movie theater. I regretted San Francisco's transvestites in their lovely clothes, the cafés, the furniture stores with imported Indonesian furniture; I thought I would have been a different person, a better one, had I only been raised in a larger place. Like a fish, I thought, I would have grown to fit my bowl.

Vivienne would probably have understood my desire for a larger childhood, had she thought about it at the time when she came home to Templeton for good. She may even have convinced herself to return to San Francisco, to give her child a larger life. But in the slow-warming spring that year, she was pregnant, poor, scared, jittery from coming off drugs, incapable of too much thought. It is easy to imagine the loneliness, the feeling of worthlessness from her lack of education, the solitude, the way the town turned on her. How she was even more isolated by her grand old house and her simultaneous poverty. As I grew, I would have a pool that my country-clubbing grandparents had put in, two in-town acres, a lake to play in all summer long, a short walk to the bakery or General Store. I would have enormous privilege. And yet I would have to pick my clothes out of a bin in the basement of the Presbyterian

Church and during hard times run into the Great American grocery store to buy our cheese with food stamps. I would be Willie Upton, related to all those famous people, pet of every history teacher I ever met, the student NYSHA hired as a receptionist every summer and trotted out to show visiting writers, but also a girl who dressed in the bathroom stall during gym class, ashamed to let anyone see the state of her underwear.

This, too, Vivienne saw as constructive, however; her favorite pedagogical tool was the old carrot-on-a-stick-plus-a-dash-of-the-spurs method. "Nothing," she always said, "can be learned if you don't work a little at it," and so every (pagan) Christmas of ours, I had to smooth all the wrapping paper into reusable squares and roll the ribbons up into little nubbins before I was allowed to play with my toys, which were, for the most part, handcrafted wooden ducks from retired Vermont maple trees and puppets made by Guatemalan victims of domestic violence and other things of that ilk. Once, even, when I was six and learning to read big words by reading Anne Sexton's *Transformations* aloud, I stumbled on *penultimate*. I sighed and blew the bangs off my head and said, "I can't do it."

Vi smiled unperturbed over her knitting, and said, "Sure you can, Sunshine."

I threw the book across the room. "No," I said. "I can't."

My mother pursed her lips, stood, went to the kitchen, made a whole plateful of whole-wheat graham crackers with natural peanut butter and local honey, and came back. She slowly began eating one with little moans of delight until I stood and reached for one, but then she held the plate away, and opened the book and put it back in my lap.

I knew what she was doing; I refused to read the word; no way in heck would I read it; that big fat scheming meanie. And so I watched Vi as she chewed on the snack, fluttering her eyelids and licking her fingers and muttering, "Oh, this is the best snack I've ever had," until she only had one left and I couldn't take it anymore and I spat out many different versions of it; *pee-null-time-ate*, *penu-liti-mat-ay*, *puh-newl-too-mat*, until I hit it, and she smiled and handed me the cracker and I gobbled it down greedily.

She was right, though; it *was* the best snack I'd ever had. In those years, though I did chafe against her will, Vi was always right. I couldn't imagine her being wrong; in those first years my mother was my only friend, and I hers. But when I was at last off to kindergarten, she went to nursing school in Oneonta and took a job at Finch Hospital in town, and then her world suddenly expanded. Then she had friends, women who sat with her over coffee cake, rubbing their arches, complaining. Once in a while, in high school, I suspected a few of these women to be more than friends, especially the ones who were in Averell Cottage bright and early on a Saturday morning to eat my mother's omelets and watch cartoons with me. There would be something about their broad hips, their hungry, bitten mouths, the smiles on their faces when they didn't think I was watching, which would make me suspect things before I could even understand them. When my mother later called herself a pan-sexual when she was drunk and I was sixteen years old, it would be clear, then, like a period at the end of a very long sentence.

That was Vivienne's life in the years after I was born. She was a critical care nurse, soothing the last days of the hopeless cases with a depth of gentleness that I rarely saw from her but knew was in there, somewhere. And in the months before I myself returned to Templeton an outcast, she awoke some days grateful that she ever survived the 1970s. On others, she felt as if she had wasted everything; she had always poured so much of herself into me that she was afraid there was none left for her anymore. When she began her long walk toward Jesus, she prayed hours upon hours of fervent prayer trying to protect me from the terrible pitfalls she saw on my path. She sat at the kitchen table, head bent, trying to will me into success, deep into the night. She imprecated, she begged. At some point the prayer clicked, and she understood such a wispy thing as faith.

And on some nights on the opposite side of the country, I paused over my esoteric texts in a kitchen in San Francisco, and looked up, as if I had heard something. The enormous, pulsing world seemed so treacherous at that moment, sirens bursting up the streets toward danger, toward death, everything in turmoil. During the winter after the attack on New York City, the country was grim, gray, a wobble away from a headlong fall into apocalypse. The world as I knew it was always just about to end; we were fragile; I was fragile. It would take just a nudge for my own self to free-fall.

Perhaps with all this in mind one can understand why Vivienne reacted the way she did on the day of the monster, the day I returned. There were the strange parallels there: the pregnancy, the singlehood, the ambition suddenly curtailed. A return to Templeton in disgrace. Her own ambition lopped off, yet again, like a tulip beheaded by a stick. How she must have looked up at me that morning, as I stood there, twenty-eight years old and filthy from my trip, skinny, hair shorn, heartsore, miserable, eyes swollen from too much crying. How she must have seen only a failure, nothing like the elegant success she had always wanted me to be. A waste of all those years, squeezing herself dry. And how I must have been hateful to her, just about then.

George Franklin Temple Upton (Vivienne's father)
1935.

At two years old, with orphan girls at Pomeroy Hall. See how they're dressed in antiquated clothing, long out of style. This was by design: his grandmother, Hannah Clarke Temple, who raised George, was the director of the orphanage. She thought such dress made potential parents for her orphans harken back to their own childhoods, and be more ready to adopt.

WHAT WILLIE UPTON ALWAYS UNDERSTOOD
✤ ABOUT HER FAMILY ✤

Hetty Averell *(slave)* ← Marmaduke Temple → Elizabeth Temple *(wife)*

{ (Lots of generations, a few she'd heard of dimly; the great-grand-mother with the orphanage, the baseball commissioner, the novelist, etc.)

Phoebe Tipton ———— m. 1951 ———— George Franklin
1923-1973 Temple Upton
1933-1973

Vivienne Upton
1955-
(plus any one of three hippies in a San Francisco commune)

Willie "Sunshine" Upton
1973-

4

The Running Buds (Big Tom, Little Thom, Johann, Sol, Doug, Frankie) Speak

WE RUN; WE like to run; we have run together for twenty-nine years now; we will run until we can run no more. Until our hips click and shatter apart, until our lungs revolt and bleed. Until we pass from middle age into old age, as we once passed from youth into middle age. Running. In the winter, we run, through the soft snow, slipping over the ice. In the Templeton summer, soft as chamois, glowing from within, we run. We run in the morning, when the beauty of our town gives us pause. When it is ours and ours alone, the tourists still tunneling into their dreams of baseball, of Clydesdales, of golf. Oh, the beauty of the town, oh the sunrise over the town as we crest the hill by the gym all spread before us like a feast, our hospital with its fingerlike smokestack, beyond, the lake like a chip of serpentine, and the baseball museum, and the Farmers' Museum, and the hills, and in the foggy hollow, our houses, fanned across the town, where, inside, our families sleep, peaceful. But we, the Running Buds, are together, moving, we behold this as we have beheld it for twenty-nine summers, twenty-nine winters, twenty-nine springs and falls.

There is sometimes no conversation but companionable spitting, and sometimes we talk of our families, of our problems.

How Big Tom's middle child worries him, hanging with those meth-heads at the Sugar Shack in Fly Creek.

Of Sol's wife troubles, on his third wife and still no children of his own, the marriage souring as we speak.

Of Little Thom's thrombosis.

Of Doug's war with the IRS. Of Doug's many affairs.

Of Johann's daughter suddenly a lesbian, seems a disease now, all these pretty young girls with shorn heads.

Of our joke-man, Frankie, and his parents' passing. His jokes are now bitter, making us take them as we take black coffee: wincing, grimacing, swallowing fast.

Oh, we know such things about one another, such dark things, even when we haven't spoken them. There is something in the rhythm of the run that tells them, something that spreads our sorrows into the heads of the others and gives us some solace, though unspoken. We know of the affairs, we know of the desires, we know what we know, and we will never tell. And we are the kings of this town as we run, we own this town, some of us have owned it for generations; we, alone awake as everyone else sleeps, we guard the town with our daily circuit. With our footsteps, with our jokes, with our farts. We are sentries, keeping the place pristine, keeping the danger at bay: together, running, we keep the town safe.

We were the first ones to hear poor Dr. Cluny's calls in that foggy dawn, we on our run, we changed our course to reach him, we believed him. We threw off the ropes of our own motorboats, we sped over the wakening water out to see. There it was, massive and white, beautiful, beautiful, so beautiful. Doug wouldn't admit it, but it made him weep. It made more than Doug weep; Sol might have felt a rending in him, Frankie might have thought of his parents and coughed to keep from sobbing. Big Tom, Little Thom, Johann, all blink-blinking. It was as if a dear and secret part of us had disappeared, as if we saw our own old age, and we were alone on a dock, in a camping chair, fishing, stiff and unable to move, there, in the fog, alone.

We were the ones to go back for the other boats. We were the ones to tie the ropes to the tail, and begin our slow pull back. We tied the great beast up to the boulders under the statue of Natty Bumppo and his dog, or Chingachgook and his dog, we don't exactly know which is depicted in the bronze of that strange statue; we were the ones to awaken Dr. Zuckerman at the Biological Field Station, we were the ones to call the National Guard.

Then, when we had done so, we put our hands upon the freezing cold monster, our monster. And this is what we felt: vertigo, an icicle through our strong hearts, our long-lost childhoods. Sunshine in a field and crickets and the sweet tealeaf stink of a new ball mitt and a rock glinting with mica and a chaw of bubblegum wrapping its sweet sweet tendrils down our throats and the warm breeze up our shorts and the low vibrato of lake loons and the sun and the sun and the warm sun and this is what we felt; the sun.

5

Secrets of a Tiny Town

UP SURFACED THE monster, and after the monster there came the crowd.

From Main Street they came with their bags of baseball paraphernalia, with their country club rackets, with their cameras. In the brightening July morning, they milled and they gasped, they sipped their coffee, they shuffled in their slippers, and some, sensing the history of the moment, wept, and others saw them weeping and wept louder. In the amassing group, I lost the lassitude that touching the monster had given me. Anyone could have been in the crowd: high school sweethearts gone paunchy and Republican; girls from my soccer team I'd have difficulty recognizing; old doctors who knew too much about my vital functions. When I saw my elementary school principal, a bald little elf of a man, come toward me with his arms outstretched and great teary tracks down his face, about to shout *Willie! You're home!*, I turned and fled back over the neighbor's property, over the Shadow Brook bridge, up the hill and onto the cool orange shag carpet of the 1970s wing of Averell Cottage. I couldn't bear to face them, not yet.

In a city, any city, one can be anonymous; this is the blessing of cities. In Templeton, our tiny hamlet, I was Willie Upton; Scion of the Great Temple Family; Track and Soccer Star; Homecoming Queen; Local Girl Made Good; Soon to Be Great Disappointment to All. I leaned against the cool glass pane until my heart stopped leaping about my chest like a goosed frog. Until I dragged myself, step by step, across the length of the house, up the creaking stairs, past the hallway plastered with portraits of my many, many ancestors, and up into my girlhood room. The bedroom was part of the original cottage and had also been my mother's as a girl. It hadn't been redecorated since. The walls were a dusky rose behind the framed needlepoint pieces but a pale lavender in places touched by the sun. The peonies on the curtains were only faint shadows now. There was a huge four-poster bed and a princess rotary phone. After I went to graduate school, the posters I had taped up on the door and closets were taken down, my stuffed animals placed neatly in the antique bassinet in the corner, my books ordered on the shelves, my trophies packed in some box lost in some corner of the attic. Now frosting everything was a half-inch of dust. I could hear the noise of the crowd begin to swell and rise down at Lakefront Park, and pulled my blinds down against the day.

In the forgiving darkness, I sat on the bed and kicked off my shoes, and when I looked up, I saw something pulsing gently in the corner. It was the Averell Cottage ghost, I knew. To my mother it had looked like a bird; to me, a washed-out inkstain, a violet shadow so vague and shy that it was only perceivable indirectly, like a leftover halo from gazing at a bare bulb too long, an enigma that dissolves whenever you try to fix on it.

"Hello," I said, going perfectly still, looking at my knees. "It's nice to see you again."

I saw, or felt, the ghost inch closer, looming darker in my periphery.

"So, I'm back for a while," I said. "If that's okay with you."

In answer, it grew lighter, from violet to purple to periwinkle to pink and slipped, still pulsing, away.

It was a good ghost. I had lived with it until I left for college, awakening often in the middle of the night to see a quick dark slippage from my sight, as if it sat in vigil over my sleep. I sensed its oblique presence grow swollen and dark if I lied on the phone or slammed my door or screamed at my mother, or even picked my nose. It loved hygiene, the ghost, hated sweat and spit and bile, all the bad humors of the body. The only time I ever felt threatened by it was once, during high school, when I snuck a would-be suitor up the back stairwell and into my room because I had grown tired of my virginity, and wanted it to go away. Then, the ghost burst into a tremendous bruise-colored mass at the edges of our sight, and fading in its center to invisibility, it swelled so big it filled the room, pushing both of us up against the wall, sucking out our breath, making the boy freak and escape outside again. By school on Monday, a lock of his hair had turned white and he stopped talking to girls completely, and eventually, in college, he came blazing out of the closet in full Eurotrash regalia.

For a moment, I felt I was alone, and then, even with my eyes closed, I felt the ghost slipping back in, intangible. "I guess you can tell," I said, opening my eyes. "I'm very, very sad."

A pause; a pulse. "It's about a boy," I said. "Well. A man." I waited; a darker ring emerged. "I hate him," I said. The ghost came closer, then, a moist, dark air, that smelled of anise and the cool violet smell of shadows. I grew very tired and lay back on the pillow.

"But it's not just me, you know. The whole world's sad," I said. "It's like a virus. It's going to end badly. Glaciers melting, ozone depleted. Terrorists blowing up buildings, nuclear rods infecting the aqueducts. Influenza hopping from the pigeons to the humans, killing millions. Billions. People rotting in the street. The sun bursting open, shattering us eight minutes later. If not that, starvation. Cannibalism. Freakish mutated babies with eyeballs in their navels. It's a terrible place to bring a child into," I said. "This world. It is terrible. Just terrible."

I thought of my best friend, Clarissa, home in San Francisco. Her sick body curled under a sheet, her boyfriend, Sully, stroking her face, putting her to sleep. I thought of calling her, but my limbs were too heavy to move. I thought of the monster, then of the Lump in my gut, dividing and dividing and dividing itself, then of Primus Dwyer. And then I remembered the long sweep of upstate New York through my windshield in the dark of that morning, the hunchbacked barns falling into themselves, the deer darting startled through the dark. How—after those forty straight hours of driving, after the late hallucinations of Primus Dwyer sitting there beside me, grinning, his round glasses glinting—when I rounded the bend at the Farmers' Museum and saw my tiny little town clumped in the dark there, a perfect model town (so sweet, so good), I felt something essential in me dissolve and begin to fade away.

My eyes closed then, despite myself. "I'm supposed to be in Alaska. I'm supposed to be searching for the first human on this continent." I sighed and said with great effort, "I'm not supposed to be in Templeton." And then I was asleep.

I HAD HAD a dream about Primus Dwyer and awoke with the hard-bitten landscape of Alaska vibrating in my mind. A softer light was coming through my shades, and I lifted them to find twilight and a red-striped tent poking above the trees down in Lakefront Park. It was there, I thought, to protect the monster from the July sun. My shower with its hot water, with the soap and shampoo, almost made me cry with relief, and when I emerged and saw myself in the fogged mirror, I saw that I looked better. Still skinny, still lost-seeming. But my face had de-puffed and my eyes had emerged above my cheekbones, and, even then, the small imp of vanity chuckled in my ear. I did not look bad, it told me; I was still a pretty girl. And even my navel, where I pressed my hands and felt a pulse through my skin, was still flat.

I found a huge old tee shirt, and went downstairs. My mother turned from the kitchen counter with a raw chicken breast in her hands, and smiled uncertainly at me. "She's up," she said, her voice rough, as if she'd just awoken herself. "Sleeping Beauty. You were out for thirty-six hours. I had to hold a mirror above you to make sure you were breathing."

"Was I?" I said.

"Barely," she said. She stuffed the breast with a heady mixture of cilantro, feta, jalapeños. "You've missed all the hoopla. It's very exciting." She nodded toward the television, where on the screen a newscaster was flushed with excitement, gibbering on mute and gesturing toward the monster rotting on camera, its delicate hand curled on its chest—a large, yellow, lumpy thing looking not unlike a half-submerged ball of butter. Behind him was the bronze statue of the Mohican and his dog. Lakefront Park. My mother smiled, expectant.

"Oh. You mean the monster," I said. "I know. I was there when they brought it in."

Vi looked surprised, then frowned, as if I'd refused a gift she'd put a great deal of thought into, and turned back to her chicken breasts, arranging them in pink, gelatinous mounds on the tray. Her iron cross clinked against the counter. I watched as a new newscaster began interviewing a scientist: DR. HERMAN KWAN, the banner read below him, WORLD-FAMOUS VERTEBRATE BIOLOGIST. I turned up the volume.

"The world," the newscaster said, biting into his words as if they were crackers, "is waiting with bated breath—no pun intended, baited, ha—to know what, exactly, the people of Templeton, New York, towed in yesterday morning from Lake Glimmerglass. What can you tell us, Dr. Kwan?"

"I don't, well," said the biologist, straightening and restraightening his glasses with his thumb. He was sweating under the limelight, great bags of wet darkening the armpits of his shirt. "To be perfectly honest, I don't think we're able to say, yet. To say, really. It's just. Well, beautiful. The most beautiful thing I have ever seen," and here he blinked rapidly with emotion. "It is an historic day."

"Historic?" said the newscaster to the camera, crunching, crunching. "Dr. Kwan, please explain to our viewers why?"

"Well, Peter, we haven't had a discovery of this magnitude. Well, since fishermen caught a new species of coelacanth off the coast of Sulawesi in Indonesia. 1938. A living dinosaur. An animal that had totally disappeared off the fossil record for eighty million years. Then we found it again! But, then again, this discovery in Lake Glimmerglass might be far greater than even that. We have simply no idea as yet what the animal. Well, even what it is. It may be a new species entirely. It may not even *have* a fossil record!" And the biologist gave a bark of a laugh.

"That's truly incredible, incredible. Professor Kwan, some of our viewers would like to know if this find is possibly 'the missing link.' What do you believe?" said the newscaster with great gravity.

The biologist seemed to struggle with this, and his mouth worked for a moment as he thought.

In the silence, my mother said, almost so low that I didn't hear her, "Sunshine, I have something I need to tell you."

I waited, but she said nothing more, and the biologist finally spluttered to life. "Sorry?" he said. "But the missing link between what and what?"

"Oh," the newscaster said, struggling. "Between fish and, I suppose, well . . . nonfish?"

The biologist wiped his forehead, and a rose of moisture bloomed upon his chest. "Well, I don't know what that means. But maybe. It's far too early to tell," he said.

Then the newscaster said thank you, the camera cut away, and another reporter came on to interview the mayor of our town, a portly fellow with a penchant for ornamental canes and too-short shorts, a man with a voice so stentorious it seemed to boom up from the earth beneath his feet. "We in Templeton," he was saying, "have always had a myth about a monster that lived in Lake Glimmerglass, Glimmey we called it. For a long time, the stories have scared the bejeepers out of summer campers around their campfires as they spun their yarns above the s'mores and hot dogs, as they sat on the lakeside during those halcyon days of—" and here my mother turned off the television, her hands still truffled with feta cheese.

"Wilhelmina Sunshine Upton, I *said* I had something to tell you," she said.

"Jesus," I said. "I've been waiting for about three minutes for you to finish your sentence."

"Don't take His name in vain," she said.

I sighed. "Vi," I said. "Just because you believe in all that God stuff doesn't mean you have to censor me, does it?"

"My house," she said. "My rules." She sat down at the table, bringing with her a waft of cheese and raw meat. "That's rule number one. Rule number two is that until we pull you out of this mess you've gotten yourself into, you're not just sitting around, moping all day. You hear me?"

"I hear you," I muttered. I played with the pollen from a vase of tiger lilies that sat, bold and cloying, on the table.

"You're getting yourself a project. Go do some work for NYSHA. I'm sure the Native American Museum would like some more potsherds or something. Dig up stuff, who knows. Or docent.

Or get a job at the Baseball Museum. Or wear a nineteenth-century dress and learn the art of broom-making at the Farmers' Museum. God knows there's enough history around here to satisfy you until you can go back to Stanford."

"Vi," I said. "I hate disappointing you. I really do. But I really don't think going back is going to be an option."

"We'll see about that," she said, and squinted at me. "In the meantime, you're doing something. Worse comes to worst, you'll be a candy striper. I'll make you mop up diarrhea all day. I think I'd like that." She grinned, and her face looked briefly youthful again. "A little atonement is always good."

"I love you, Vi, but I'll never wipe up diarrhea for you. Ever," I said.

"Well, if you're living with me I'm afraid you'll have no choice." She sighed at me, and she rubbed her forehead, her mouth stretched into a down-curved string. "Willie, I just can't believe this. I can't. I mean, I wanted so much for you, I wanted you to do all the things I couldn't ever do because I was never as smart or beautiful as you. I ran away when I was fifteen because my mother tried to send me to *finishing* school for heaven's sakes. I tried to do my best. Yet, here we are."

"You did beautifully, Vi," I said, and then found I couldn't say anything more.

There was a painful rubbery silence then, when the noise of the crowd down at the park burbled up to the house and a few chirps from the frog-pool began to rise and the grandfather clock ticked and ticked in the dining room. My mother said, "Well, I'd like to hear the full story sometime, when you're ready to tell me. Maybe I can help. And it is always cathartic to confess one's sins."

I looked down at my hands. I saw a brief flash; the red glow of the tent on my sleeping bag, the whorls of hair on Primus Dwyer's arm, the empty flask of whiskey. I shuddered. "I don't think I can tell you, Vi," I said. "It's bad. Really bad."

"Oh," she said. "Of course you think that now. It'll get better. You'll see." She patted my hand, leaving cheese flakes on my fingers. "I hate to see you like this, Willie. All your vim gone. All your spice. It makes me so sad."

"I know," I said. "My vim's frozen into a little ball in the middle of the Alaskan tundra."

"Ha," she said, her face briefly filled with a soft kind of light.

"Well, in the meantime, welcome home. Anyway," she said, taking a deep breath and closing her eyes, "I said I had something to tell you, and I do. I've been putting it off for a while now, and perhaps this is not the best time to tell you. But every day I don't tell you the whole truth is a day I lie to you." She was clutching her cross in her greasy fingers, and gazing at me with such intensity I felt myself grow hot and nervous.

"What?" I said. "What is it? Just say it."

"Give me a minute, Willie. This is very difficult."

"Oh, God," I said. "Gosh. This is going to be bad, isn't it."

"Well," she said. "Depends on how you look at it. First I must say that I am sorry, Willie, for having lied to you for such a long time. Are you ready?"

"No," I said.

"All right," she said. "Here goes. Willie, I lied to you about having three fathers. You only have one, and he lives in Templeton, and he is a prominent citizen, and he has a family of his own. And I don't know if he knows you're alive. Well, I'm pretty sure he knows you're alive, but maybe not his part in . . . well, the making of you. His role in making you, I mean. I'm pretty sure he has no idea that you're his child. Just as you have no idea he's your father. Sperm donor. Whatever."

I blinked at her.

The anxiety drained out of her face, and a slow look of wonder grew across it. "It feels so good," she said, smiling beatifically, "to tell the Truth at long last."

"Oh. My. God," I said.

"I warned you," she said. "His name never in vain. Rule Number One."

"Fuck," I said.

"Better," she said.

"Fuck fuck fuck fuck fuck fuck," I said.

"I understand," she said.

I turned in my chair to face the glass window and look out onto the lake, the hills. Outside, bats swirled and dipped over the pool-pond and a mallard slid into the water from his butt, like an old lady in a green bathing cap out for a crepuscular dip. "Do I know," I said at last, "do I know this man who is supposed to be my father?"

My mother considered, then said, "Maybe." I could hear the sup-pressed smile in her voice. She was thinking, perhaps, that this was going better than she thought it would.

I said, "Who is he?"

"Ah, that," she said. "That I can't tell you."

I turned back around and glared at her. "Can't?" I said. "Don't want to, you mean."

"Yes," she said. "That's right. It wouldn't be fair to him."

"Fair?" I said. "Fair?"

The vase of tiger lilies, when it hit the wall, didn't shatter as I had expected it to, but rather hit with a thump, and then thumped again on the floor. A little water fell out, but the lilies stayed in the vase. It was not at all the act of destruction I needed. "Wouldn't be fair?" I thundered at my mother, my knuckles on the table. "Fair?"

My mother closed her eyes and held the crucifix with two hands. When she opened them again, she was smiling. She said, "There you are, Willie. I knew you were in there somewhere." She gazed upon me with tenderlovingkindness. There was the stink of burn-ing martyr in the air.

"Don't you dare go all saintly on me," I said. "Don't you even dare, Vi. You are a terrible, terrible hypocrite. I have a *father* in Tem-pleton whom I may actually know, and you kept this from me for twenty-eight years. Twenty-eight years, you let me believe I was the product of mad fornication in some orgiastic hippie love-fest? And you're not *telling* me now who he is? You have *got* to be fucking kidding me. And to tell me now of all times. *Now*, of all times?"

"I told you I was sorry about that," she said. Her hands made darting, mothlike motions around the wet loaf of her braid.

"Vi," I said. "Didn't you think? What if I dated his son? You never knew half of the people I dated in high school. Oh my God. What if I dated *him*?"

And my goddamn mother actually had the nerve to laugh. "You never," she said, "were in the habit of dating old men until you went to college."

"You horrible woman," I said.

"I'm sorry," she said. "I couldn't resist. It's not funny. I know. Willie, it's not that big a deal. I promise."

"Who is he?" I said.

"You know I can't tell you that."

"Who is he?"

"Sorry, nope."

"What if I guess?"

"You won't."

"I will."

"No," she said. "And even if you do, I can't confirm it."

"So I do know him," I said.

"Maybe."

"Give me a clue."

"No."

"What about the no-lying policy? What about no secrets?"

"For my own lies. For my own secrets."

"Vivienne Goddamn Upton, give me a clue now. Call it penance for your lifelong lying to your only child about her goddamn paternity. Call it an indulgence or Hail Mary or whatever the hell you need to call it."

"No. And I'm born-again Baptist, not Catholic," she said. "And stop saying the Lord's name in vain."

"Give me a goddamn clue now and I'll stop saying Jesus goddamn Christ's name in vain forever and goddamn ever."

"Fine," she said. "Okay. One clue. Doesn't matter, since you'll never find any documentation, and he only told me once, and it's just a rumor. So you can have your clue, but it won't help. So there."

"Goddamn Jesus Christ fucking tell me."

"All right," she said. "Know how we're related to Marmaduke Temple through both the Uptons and the Averells?"

"Yes, of course," I said.

"Well, he claimed he was related to Marmaduke, too. Through some sort of liaison at some point in the past. But I'm not going to tell you what he told me, the details, just that you, Willie Upton, are the product of *three* lines of ancestry from Marmaduke Temple. Three. It's pretty amazing."

My mother's face was magenta, and she was panting a bit. There was a long, taut moment between us, and then I watched as her eyes rounded, her mouth pursed, and she slumped back into her chair, watching me, realizing now what she had done. I could feel a smile growing across my face; this secret must have burnt in her for twenty-eight years, must have roiled and rocked my mother with its pressure. I always knew she was prouder about her heritage than she ever would admit. When I was little the thought of her family was a comfort to her, a vital source of her strength, the reason she was able to stay in Templeton. And now, she'd released her secret and was watching it dance like a demon away from her.

"Uh-oh," she said. She began to blink rapidly.

"Oh-ho-ho-ho," I said back.

My mother's hands went a little white around the knuckles. "Willie," she said. "There is no way you'll be able to figure it out from that. Right?" she said.

"Dearest Vivienne," I said. "You forget that I'm a researcher. It's what I *do*."

"Please," she said. "Don't."

"Vi," I said, "you're in no position to ask favors of me. At all. Maybe ever again."

"Oh, glory," she said. "You're not going to let it go, are you?"

"Stubborn heart," I said. "Long memory. Bad mix."

"Oh, no, no, no. Oh, what have I done?" she said into her cupped hands.

"Exactly. What *have* you done? Rather, the question is *who*, right?" I said. I felt tired. I stretched my arms above my head and, like that, could feel a beating in my belly, a little hungry pulse. "Well, Vi," I said, "I think I've found my project. Rule Number Two, wasn't it? That I have to have a project? It's a good one. Difficult, but I'm feeling confident."

My mother rose, muttering to herself, and returned to the chicken breasts and the rest of dinner, stealing little worried glances at me from time to time. As she washed the lettuce from the garden, I went out to the porch and stood in the deepening shadows. The moon was apricot above the haunches of the hills and a big band at the country club hooted its music as soft as an owl across the water. All around me Templeton seemed to crouch and hold its breath. There must have been a candlelit vigil of some sort down at the park's edge by the monster, because the tent was lit by a gentle, living glow. And, as the night gathered and thickened all around me, I imagined the body of the monster floating, ringed by this quiet light, lapped on all sides by the many hungry wavelets.

WHAT WILLIE UPTON UNDERSTOOD
ABOUT HER FAMILY, REVISED

Hetty Averell *(slave)* ← **Marmaduke Temple** → **Elizabeth Temple** *(wife)*

}(Lots of generations,
a few she'd heard of
dimly; the great-grand-
mother with the
orphanage, the baseball
commissioner, the
novelist, etc.)

Phoebe Tipton —————— m. 1951 —————— **George Franklin**
1923-1973   **Temple Upton**
                                                              1933-1973

Vivienne Upton   *Apparently not any man from a hippie*
1955-   *orgy, but, rather, some Templeton man*
                               whom Vi has, unbelievably, been hiding
                               from Willie all her freaking life.
                                                  ?-

Willie "Sunshine" Upton
1973-

6

The Wolf at the Door

IT TOOK ME a few hours after dinner to gather the nerve to call
Clarissa. I wasn't afraid of awakening her; she was in San Francisco,
and it was not yet dark out there. I wasn't even afraid that she
would be furious with me, which she would be, for what I had
done to fall into the terrible dark hole where I found myself.
Rather, I was afraid because I had been gone for two months, and
there had been no telephones out in the windswept Alaskan wilderness, and though I had had a few beautiful long letters from her,
I hadn't spoken to her all this time. I was afraid because I could
always tell immediately from her voice how she was doing, and I
didn't think I could bear to hear if she weren't doing well that day.
If, in her voice, I detected more weakness than should be expected
from a sick thirty-year-old girl, I wouldn't be able to handle it, not
in the state I was in. I sat on my bed with the princess telephone in
my lap and watched it, unmoving, for a long while.

• • •

CLARISSA AND I had met at our small liberal arts college on the first day of fall semester my freshman year, when I arrived twenty minutes early to the French class I was hoping to get into, on the creaky top floor of an old observatory. I opened the door, to my dismay, into an apparent tête-à-tête between the professor and a girl I imagined was his daughter. She had corkscrew blonde hair and the birdlike bone structure of a dancer, and her clothes were bright and mismatched, reds and pinks and plaids and paisleys, all mixed up. From the door, I believed she was ten, no older. They were speaking together but turned as I came in.

And then the little girl said in a surprisingly deep and throaty voice, "Holy crap. Scared the pants off me. Well, come on in, and make yourself at home." The professor grinned at her, tickled.

It was only when I approached and saw the girl's quick and mischievous eyes, and the way she held herself, that I knew that she was far older than I had at first imagined. "This is Professor Serget, and I'm Clarissa Evans," she said. "We were talking about George Sand. A minor writer, in my opinion, but we're reading *Indiana* this semester. Yet again," and she twinkled at the professor, who gave a little chortle. Then Clarissa smiled kindly at me and said, "And you're a freshman. Come sit next to me and I'll let you crib my notes."

Instead, though, I sat opposite her and scowled. "Willie Upton," I said as coldly as I could manage. "I'm sure I can hold my own."

She nodded and her face lit up. "Aha," she crowed as the door opened and other students began to trickle in, "spunk! Now that's what I like to see," and she winked at me.

Clarissa's ideas were excellent but her French reprehensible, and even the professor couldn't help but swallow a grin when she opened her mouth and in her incongruous voice started attacking something new. When I walked home from the class that day, she walked beside me. We must have looked ridiculous, I with my lanky height and tiny little Clarissa, like an egret striding alongside a chain-smoking parakeet.

From then on, and even though she was a junior, we did everything together. I took higher-level classes with Clarissa, ate meals at the dining hall with her and her friends, all quick-witted types. I even moved into her suite when one of her dorm mates was kicked out for selling pot. Clarissa amazed me: she could do endless keg stands and quote Nietzsche; she could hike for eight hours without complaint and give a better manicure than a beautician; she left red lipstick rings around her cigarettes, and scattered the stubs behind her like flower petals. She walked away from nastiness, from gossip, but loved her friends so much she mimicked them endlessly, and you always felt pleased she was making fun of *you*. She had the worst taste in jokes, was the most puntastic person I'd ever met, had the unique talent to always make me laugh and wince simultaneously; when she at last snagged a guy she liked, Sully Bird, she grinned at me, saying *one Bird in the hand*, and left me to supply the rest. As the coxswain for the men's crew team she made herself heard up and down the river, shouting at her boys, "Come on, you bitches, *pull*," and, because she was Clarissa, they pulled. They would win for her at Little Threes; they'd place second that year at the Head of the Charles.

The day I was going back to Templeton for Thanksgiving, I went by Clarissa's room with my knapsack, ready to leave. I saw her on her bed, reading. Her room was a sty, and there was no evidence of packing. "Clarissa," I said, "when're you taking off?"

She didn't take her eyes off the page. "I'm not," she said. "I'm staying here."

"You can't stay here for Thanksgiving," I said. "That's ridiculous."

"Sure I can," she said. "I *like* the international foods potluck. Who knew you could have poppadom and lingonberries all at the same time. Delectable."

"Good God, girl," I said. "That's it. You're coming back to Templeton with me."

It took great force, but in the end, she came. As we drove, I could tell that Clarissa was startled at the traces of poverty and decay in upstate New York, the dying barns like whale ribs sticking out of the frosty ground, the trailers hugging the highway, the ghost towns of battered Victorian houses. I could see she had begun to question her choice of coming to Templeton, picturing cat-piss-soaked couches, probably, and shivering all night from a damp draft from the window. If there was one thing that irritated me about Clarissa, it was her skewed concept of money, that she would spend a hundred dollars on highlights for her hair and only eat Belgian chocolate. And so I encouraged her dismay, telling her that my cousin BillyBob (who didn't exist) would want to take us out on his snowmobile; explaining that we called my grandmother (who also didn't exist) Genesee Ginny because she cracked open her first can of beer at nine in the morning and kept up the pace all day, to not worry if she found her passed out somewhere on the floor, just to roll her over so that she's on her side in case she vomits. All of upstate New York was dying, I told Clarissa. I told her what my friends and I called towns up there: Syracuse was Sorry-excuse. Rochester was Rot-and-fester. Albany was All-banal. Oneonta was Oh-I-don't-wanna.

Clarissa was pale and her forehead was creased by the time we rounded the lake, but when we came into Templeton, with its great old mansions and sparkling streets, with its crowds of happy tourists, she brightened. "This," she said, turning to me with wonder in her face, "is like a town in a snow globe. This is a perfect place."

"Well. It's pretty nice," I said.

"No," she said, and her voice was severe. "It's perfect."

That week, Clarissa and my mother got along swimmingly, so much so that Vi often stayed up with us late into the night over cookies and wine, and laughed and laughed, more than I'd ever heard her laugh in my life. It was a prematurely snowy Thanksgiving, and while my mother worked one night, Clarissa and I went to a candle-light festival at the Farmers' Museum, where the snowbanks were carved into cups and held flickering votives, so that the snow was lit from within by golden orbs of light. The upwafting wind smelled of woodsmoke and the fresh snow-smell and wassail cider and even the clean sweat of the Clydesdales who trotted us around from place to place in sleighs. The sounds of their harness bells mixed with the fiddlers in Sherman's Tavern, where there was a dance of sorts going on, and the laughing shrieks of the kids having a snowball fight in the darkening commons.

Clarissa stood with me on the steps of the pharmacist's, looking out at the old-fashioned village in its soft dusk. In the small, close house we had just smelled the mingled smells of a thousand herbs; feverfew and yew and bee balm and willow-bark aspirin; we palpated the phrenological head; we watched the fat black leeches crawl on the glass of their jar. Aristabulus Mudge, moonlighting from his modern pharmacy in town, watched us good-humoredly, cocking his head above his hunchback like a parrot and slipping us free lavender sachets for our sock drawers.

"Here ye are, Willie Temple," he said to me, our little ritual.

"Willie *Upton*," I said, pretending irritation, as usual.

"Whatever you say," he said, and gave me the same wink as always.

Walking outside, Clarissa sighed. "I really feel," she said, "like a colonial woman. Isn't that strange?"

I looked at her expensive duck boots, three-hundred-dollar jeans, and grinned.

But then I said what I had been thinking about, which was just as strange. I said that when we as a society ran out of oil, the hobby-horse of my econ professor that fall, when all social structure broke down and we could no longer supply ourselves with goods in the way we had developed, I felt comforted that all we had to do was go to the Farmers' Museum to learn all those forgotten, essential arts. "It's a self-contained world," I said to Clarissa, so excited I couldn't see the face she was making. "There's a whole body of forgotten knowledge here. They make everything: shoes, barrels, wheels, brooms, linens. We can learn animal husbandry and herbal medicine, you name it. Like a little backup generator of culture we've got here. When all of civilization ends, we can just come to Templeton."

It was only after I delivered my little speech that I looked at Clarissa and saw the fury on her face. "Why do you always have to ruin things like that," she said, and she leapt into the snowdrift beside the porch and went wading off, the little red pompoms on her hat waggling furiously at me.

When it was time for us to head back to school, my mother took Clarissa's little face in her hands and peered down into it.

"There is a room here for you whenever you need one," she said.

"Vi," I said, horrified. "Clarissa's got her own family."

Vi didn't look at me but rather kissed Clarissa on the forehead. And she said something so softly I could not quite hear it, that sounded like "Well, an orphan knows an orphan."

Later, in the car, as we passed into Massachusetts, I stared out at the glittering icy road. "Clarissa," I said. "Want to tell me what that all was about? What Vi said?"

And she said nothing at first, for at least fifteen miles. And then she lit a cigarette, even though it was forbidden in my car, blew the smoke out a crack in the window, and said, "She was right." Staring out her passenger window, she told me that she'd been the only child of aging professors, the child of their old age, the center of their attention. And then, when she was almost sixteen, they went on a family trip to Norway, and her father pulled the rented Volvo to the side of Goblin's Pass to get a picture. As her parents stood on the brink admiring the view, she climbed behind a tree to take a tinkle.

When she emerged, they were gone. The camera was placed at the edge of the fjord. The last picture was their two faces, smiling before the crevasse, taken by her father from an arm's length.

"Mom? Dad?" Clarissa called out uncertainly, and nobody ever answered her. She began to scream, louder and louder, and the echo that returned and returned was distant and mocking.

When the rocks below were searched, nothing was found. When she went back to the house in Connecticut, nothing was missing. She had their life insurance policies, she sold the house and most of the furniture, she had plenty of money. But her parents were the only children of only children, and so she had nowhere to go on holidays, she said.

Then she turned to me as we pulled into the parking lot behind the dorms. "You fucking tell anyone, and I kill you, okay?" she said. "Dead. An extremely painful and tragic death, understand? Garroting. Possible flaying involved, if I'm pissed enough." Parked there, we watched a boy trying to stuff an enormous duffel through the door of the dorm, his breath in the cold rising like a furze around his head.

"All right," I said at last. "Why?"

"I'm nobody's pity case," she said, and gave me a little pinch on the arm. "Ever. Not even yours. Head case, maybe," she said, and smiled weakly at her joke.

Clarissa had graduated, ended up as a journalist, though her career choice at first surprised me. But there was something about her smallness, her huge personality, her bright clothing and wickedly innocent ways that led people to confide in her. She was very good at what she did. She had a fiancé, Sullivan Bird, who was clever and kind and funny, and though I at first had a hard time accepting that a nonpervert would want to be with someone who looked as if she were a twelve-year-old girl, in the end, I was sold. Sully Bird was an architect, had a face soft as a koala bear's, and the first time he'd met her at a concert, he'd followed Clarissa around all night, looking dazzled, saying, "Please, just go out with me. Please," all unspoken rules about not looking utterly pathetic to an unknown love-object thrown to the wind. She laughed; she caved; and to the surprise of both of us, she found out how kind and gentle Sully was, and had been with him for five years. True, that past winter, things were rocky between them, blowing up once in a bar (the jukebox blaring "Love Me Tender," the tang of mojitos in my mouth), an argument that seemed to come from nowhere and that devolved quickly into ad hominem attacks. In between Sully's charges of "snob," "superficial," "egoist," "brute," and Clarissa's of "sap," "weakling," "intellectual pansy," "*conservative*," people cowered and ran for cover. All our friends dissolved away.

"I can't marry that man," wailed Clarissa in the taxi home after I had wrestled her away. "He doesn't *know* me." Their separation lasted a week, and then they were back together as if nothing had happened, cracking each other up with their saucy little impersonations of their friends, doing their choreographed, impromptu swing moves on the street corners. Still, maybe I imagined it, but I felt a little hesitation, a little chill there where I hadn't felt any before. I suspected sometimes that when she was gone for the weekend on "assignment," that she was visiting Templeton and my mother, staying in the room on the second floor of the 1970s wing that we called "Clarissa's Room." I never mentioned it, though. Everyone deserves a little comfort.

And then, out of nowhere, at the age of twenty-nine, my Clarissa found herself sick.

One night in late February, Clarissa and I went to a gallery opening for one of our friends from school. Heather was a sculptor, and already getting famous, though back when we first met her she was a plump poli-sci major who had dreamt all her life of running a think tank. Now she was splinter-thin on her diet of raw foods, sleek in her artfully deconstructed cotton dresses, and she made lush three-dimensional body parts from organic matter, great astounding breasts and bellies and penises crafted of leaves and seeds and braided grasses. We were barely in the door with champagne flutes in our hands when Clarissa sighed and rubbed her head. "I'm so tired, Willie," she'd said. "God, I've never been this tired in my life." I wasn't really listening: I was trying to find Heather to compliment her on her opening, and Clarissa had been whining about being tired for almost three months, which I thought was because she had been working hard on her current huge story about a crooked Berkeley cop. I took a step away from Clarissa and heard a little *oof*, and when I turned back, she was sitting on the granite pedestal of two billowy golden ass cheeks woven from some ripe straw. *Ex(flax)* was its title. Clarissa was pale and shaking her head.

"Whoa," I said, kneeling. When I put my hand on her arm she felt hot. "You okay?"

"I don't know," said Clarissa. "I think so. Vi thinks I'm just anemic. It'll be all right; I'm eating lots of beef."

"Wait a second," I said. "You were worried enough to call Vi?"

She shrugged. "Well," she said, "I mean I've never felt like this before. And check this out; this popped out three days ago," and Clarissa pulled her bottom lip down from her gum and showed me a livid red pustule the size of a quarter.

"That's so disgusting," I said.

She gave me a wicked little smile. "That's what Sully said." Then she stretched her arms and tossed her entire glass of champagne back and stood. "I'll be okay. Let's find Heather and skeedaddle," she said. "I need to go to bed."

I didn't see Clarissa all the next week, but when we met up for brunch on Sunday, she seemed tinier than she already was and was blinking rapidly in the bright light slanting into the café. She also had a strange red rash across her face that looked so perfectly delineated it seemed almost fake. I gave Clarissa a hug, and without sitting down, I said, "Don't order anything. I'm taking you to the doctor. Right now," I said.

"Don't bother," she said. "I went to my dermatologist Friday and he said he thought it was my face wash."

"You went to your *dermatologist*?" I said. "Clarissa, what if it's . . . ," but Clarissa waved her tiny hand and coughed juicily and quieted me. "I just want my pain au chocolat," she said. "I just want a huge vat of coffee and my best friend to make me laugh and then I will go home and take a hot bath and finish my story that was due three days ago and then I want to go to bed. Sorry, Willie," she said. "But everybody's been annoying me about this, and I've had enough."

"Fine," I said, sitting down. "You tiny little fascist."

"My body," she said, "my fascia," and her laugh sounded so

much like the old Clarissa's that I smiled, too, hoping, and ordered my omelet.

Clarissa disappeared for a few weeks after that. I called but she never answered or returned my calls. All the times I stopped by her apartment, though, nobody ever answered the buzzer, and so I assumed she was better, out interviewing people for one of her stories. One night, I went on a date with an amazingly geeky law student to a little tapas place in Menlo Park, and after an hour was jittery with boredom. I loved Sully for calling; I answered my phone, rudely, at the table. But there was worry in Sully's soft voice when he said, "Willie? Clarissa's acting strange. How soon do you think you can get here?"

"Twenty minutes," I said, then smiled at my date as he tipped his wineglass up into the air and extended his tongue to lap up the very last drops. "Strike that," I said. "Eighteen."

When I arrived at their apartment, Clarissa was bug-eyed and standing atop their glass coffee table in a tank top with no underwear on. There were strange raised rashes on her arms and legs, now, in addition to the red masklike one on her face, and in her hands were fronds from the great potted palm tree that was her pride, the only thing, she ever said, she could keep alive. She was shaking them rhythmically at the ground, breathing something that sounded like gibberish to me.

"Clarissa?" I said, but she didn't hear me, so I stepped closer and whispered in her ear. "Clarissa? What are you doing, honey?"

"Ants," she breathed between incantations. "Armies of ants trying to climb on me."

I turned to Sully and threw him my keys. "Pull the car up," I said. "Now," and I wrestled Clarissa off the table and forced her into underwear and a skirt and slippers, and carried her shouting over my shoulder into the car, where Sully sat at the wheel, white-knuckled, his face looking as if he had been slapped repeatedly.

At the hospital they didn't make us wait long. The weary attending came out of Clarissa's room and held our hands with her two moist, fat ones. "I'm sorry to tell you," she said, "but it seems pretty clear to me that your friend has an advanced case of lupus erythematosus. The rashes, the psychosis, the joint-swelling, the fever, all parts of the disease. Two weeks more and she would have had total system failure. Even now, it's attacked her kidneys and the lining of the lungs. Her brain, too." Sully crumpled into a chair, and put his head in his hands.

"Lupus, right? That's okay, right?" I said. "It's not a horrible disease. It's not like AIDS or anything. Right? It's curable."

"It's *not* curable," said the doctor. "And it *is* an autoimmune disease. But with steroids and antipsychotics and antidepressants and maybe even some advanced treatments we can talk about later, your friend can live a healthy life. It'll take her a year or so of total rest, though, until she recovers to the point when she can go back to work. I want to put her on a clinical trial, monoclonal antibodies. Expensive, but she's perfect for it."

"Not possible," said Sully. "She's a journalist. She's one of the greats. Or will be. She's totally driven."

"Not only possible," said the attending. "But absolutely necessary. If you'll excuse me, I have to go check on my other patients," she said, and scurried off.

Sully had put his head between his legs and now was breathing deeply. Great wings of sweat had feathered over his back. "It's okay, Sully," I said. "I can hold down the fort if you need to go."

"No," he said and wiped his face, smiling a shaky smile. "You're not her only friend, you know."

"I know," I said, and squeezed his hand, but there was still a little something in that hospital hallway, a dark, hard button, between us, and I couldn't understand it.

When Clarissa awoke in the afternoon, sane and furious (*Where the hell am I*, she growled), I was the one to tell her about her disease. Sully had gone home to gather some things for her stay in the hospital, and in the meantime I had charmed a medical student into using his laptop to do some research.

So I told Clarissa many people lived happily with lupus for years, that the word came from the rash across her face; *lupus*, in Latin, meant "wolf," and the way it spread had reminded oldtime physicians of a wolf's muzzle. I said it was also a constellation and another name for a fish, a luce or a pike; I said the first citation in the *Oxford English Dictionary* was circa 1400 from *Lanfranc's Cirurg.*, whatever that was, and recited it in my bad Chaucerian accent: *Summen clepen it cancrum, & summen lupum.*

"But it's definitely not cancrum," I said. "Lupum we can fight."

"Oh, so it's a *good* life-threatening condition," she said grimly, tiny in her sheets, her curls wild around her head. "Hooray, lupus!"

I told her about what she was likely to feel, the joint pain, the fatigue, the course of treatment options. About the famous people who'd had it: Flannery O'Connor (*A good disease is* not *hard to find*, Clarissa had punned then, her face lighting up), and perhaps even Jack London (*Jesus, that's ironic,* she'd said. *Wolves.*). I said that it was an inherited disease and asked her if anybody had died unexpectedly in her family history.

"Other than my parents maybe-maybe-not falling off Norwegian fjords? No," she'd said. Then, "Yes. My nana just up and died when she was forty." I looked at Clarissa, who rubbed her eyes wearily. "She had rashes, too," she said, softly. "And arthritis."

I told her, cringing now, that she wasn't allowed to go back to work until she was healthy. It was a measure of her sickness that she didn't fight what I said. She put her head back against her pillow, and closed her eyes, and I assumed she was asleep and left.

She was in the hospital for a month, until her infection left her kidneys and brain, until her pleurisy subsided. I filled her apartment with vases of purple lupine—a macabre joke—and she laughed with tears in her eyes when she saw the flowers. On the day she went home, I sat with her, watching movies, until she turned and told me that she knew the class I had to teach was in an hour and if I booked it I could get to Stanford with time to make photocopies. She told me all she wanted to do was to sleep, and Sully would be home in a few hours, anyway.

"No," I said. "I'm staying here."

"Yes," she said, and fixed me with one beady eye and began saying puns so fast it was all I could do to gather my stuff to get away. "A dyslexic man walks into a bra," she said. "What do you call cheese that isn't yours? Nacho cheese," she said, and escorted me down the elevator. I gave Clarissa a kiss on the head as I climbed into my car. "This is retarded," she said, sneaking a cigarette on the street, and blowing the smoke in my direction. "I was supposed to get lung cancer, not lupus, of all things. I'm crabby, not wolfish."

"Christ, Clarissa," I said. "That was lame."

"I'm just getting my groove back," she said, and shrugged.

In April, the day before Clarissa was to start her very expensive monoclonal antibody therapy, we were sitting in her breakfast nook when she put down her coffee. "Oh, hell. Let's just do it," she said.

"I'm in," I said. "Whatever it is. Let's do what?"

"Shave it. Shave it all off. Go to our favorite place and shave my hair down to the scalp. Why the heck not."

"Why do you want to do that?" I said, stunned.

She looked at me and frowned and said, "Because I *can*, Willie. I've always wanted to and never had the guts. Now I have the guts. Plus," she said, "my hair's falling out," and showed me a little clump of curls in her hand.

"All right," I said, and we gathered our things and went out. We went to the tulip garden in Golden Gate Park, and sat there in the heavy ocean wind, and I cut all of those gorgeous twisted curls from Clarissa's head, and they sprang and bobbled there on the ground. I ran the shaver over her head and put on lotion until her pale scalp glistened. And then, as she was rubbing her hands over her new pate, as her eyes closed and she began to look sick among all those red-gold tulips, I reached up and snipped a long swatch of hair down the center of my own head. When Clarissa opened her eyes, I was wearing a reverse Mohawk, my dark long hair falling on the sides and back, and a great gap where I had once had my part.

She looked horrified, and then began to giggle. "You would do that?" she said. "You would do that for me?"

I grinned and snipped off some more. Clarissa, cackling, shaved my head.

When we walked back over Golden Gate, past the golf course, past the bison, the wind licked over our bald heads, and we held hands. And in that city of permissiveness, people grinned at us, mistaking us for what we weren't. A bare-chested Rollerblader circled and circled us as we walked, and said, gliding splay-legged around us, throwing his arms out, "Oh, I adore this town. Hand in hand in the springtime," he sang. "Two baldy ladies in love."

THE NIGHT AFTER I came home to Templeton, I called Clarissa out of force of habit. Only after her phone began to ring did I realize that I had dialed, the phone was to my ear, and I was calling. Before I could reach for the hook to hang up, though, there was Clarissa's throaty dark voice saying, "I was watching a movie, so whoever this is, it had better be good."

She didn't sound good, but she sounded better than I had feared, weak but lively. I smiled, despite myself. I took a deep sigh. "Oh," I said. "Oh, don't you fret, Clarissa-cakes. It's good."

AFTER SHE STOPPED yodeling with joy that I was home and shouting at me for being home and not calling her right away, I told her the full story.

She had known already about Dr. Primus Dwyer, that he was my seminar professor when I first came to graduate school, that he was a big name, that when I got him as a thesis, then dissertation, advisor, I was thrilled. If anyone at Stanford could help me in the field, he could.

But she didn't know that we all called him, in hemidemisemireverence, "Mr. Toad." It fit, with his plaid waistcoats and beer belly, with his pocket watch and British accent, with his shining nose and unfortunate weak chin. He also had a new red VW bug, and every time we saw him heading down Memorial Drive in it, someone or another would chant, *Ladyboy, ladyboy, drive away home; your nose is afire and your chin is all gone.* It was cruel, perhaps, but we blamed his wife for dressing him like that. She was razor thin, all bone and black cashmere, the dean of students, and renowned for her jealousy. He reputedly wasn't allowed to close his door when he had conferences with his female advisees, and it was all because of her. The Castrating Bitch, we called her.

But Primus Dwyer we loved because he was funny and sweet and brilliant. We loved his half-poetic, half-pretentious take on archaeology. *Imagine human history,* he said on the first day of our graduate seminar, gesturing as was his wont in great, grandiose sweeps, *as palimpsest upon palimpsest. The deeper you scratch, the more layers you reveal.* And we hoped without a great deal of hope that he would like us, too, because he had a huge grant for a government dig up in Alaska with some Harvard guys, and they were about to find something big, everyone was sure.

Every year in May, Mr. Toad and The Castrating Bitch had a party up in their posh house in Los Altos Hills to celebrate the summer vacation. The party was when he always announced the graduate student he was going to take with him to Alaska for the summer to help with the dig. Everyone always prayed to be the honored student because, frankly, his projects were immediate career kindling, but he had never once selected a girl, and we all knew it was because of She Who Must Be Obeyed. But their house was gorgeous, all glass and boxy furniture and views of Redwood City and Atherton and the Bay at their feet like an offering. We went for the catered food and free liquor.

That year, all of the department was there, and most of the administration. There were caterers in tuxedos, the pool lit up in turquoise in the night, the glimmering lights of the Bay below. But that day, I had decided not to go. The party was right after Clarissa found she had lupus, and my hair was shorn close to my head; I had stopped running because there was something wrong with my knee and had gained about ten pounds since winter; that evening, I sat too late at my wheel after pottery class, and I was dressed in my filthy clothes, ripped jeans and a flannel shirt, loose and torn and filthy with clay. I looked horrible, not festive. Plus, I knew with utter certainty that this year the chosen student was going to be a boy, as usual.

And then, just as my pottery teacher left me alone in the studio, and I was spinning a vase on the wheel, I imagined people in their slinky dresses and suits ringing the Dwyers' doorbell. I sat there, watching my lumpy concoction swirl around and around and found myself wanting to be at the party more than any other place in the world. I washed my hands and my face, and put a clean tunic over my pants, hoping both that it covered the clay stains and that I looked bohemian and chic and not like the pigeon-coddling bag lady I felt like.

I made it to the party just as Primus Dwyer was clinking the wineglass in his hand, standing atop the diving board and wobbling around quite a bit. . . . *This year,* he was saying, *the graduate students I am taking to Alaska will be* (and here he paused and cleared his throat) *John Beardsley and Wilhelmina Upton.* I was in the midst of downing a glass of white wine like a shot, and froze. I saw The Castrating Bitch's eyes narrow; I saw her put her fists on her hips. But when I stepped forward, as everyone slapped my back, I saw her consider me; my pudgy face, my shorn hair, my messy clothing; I saw her relax. I almost saw her call me a dyke in her head. I frowned at her. She saw and gave me a little simper.

. . . we have two graduate assistants this year, Primus Dwyer was explaining, *because this year is the year we will find what we have come close to finding for so long.*

Hooray! shouted everyone around the pool.

Hooray, I whispered into my wine, weak in the knees, all trembly.

On the day that I met them at the airport, of course, I wore the femmest outfit I could find. I wore lots of makeup and a little pink minidress and high heels. I found the rest of the group just about to go through Security, and Dwyer and his wife having an emotional good-bye. For once, he wasn't dressed like a Victorian bachelor; he was wearing normal clothes, though he did look like a Geographic Society explorer in his matching khaki zip-off pants and button-down shirt and metal-toed boots. John Beardsley smirked at my outfit, then slid through the metal detector. Dwyer and his wife extracted themselves, and that's when they saw me.

He did a double-take, and looked away from the long stretch of my bare legs. His wife frowned, very hard. But there was no time, and then I went through. Dwyer followed, and there may have been the tiniest note of panic in his wife's voice as she called out behind us, "Good *luck!* Be *good!*"

We had a tight, cramped flight from SFO to Salt Lake City, a tiny bag of peanuts, one miserly lime soda. But after we were in the air from Utah to Alaska, John and I deep in our separate books, the flight attendant came and told us that there was an empty seat in first class, and Primus Dwyer had charmed her into offering it to one of us. John and I thumb-wrestled. I won. I went up, and there was Primus Dwyer resting behind an eyeshade, so I settled into the comfy chair and began to watch a movie.

Halfway through, he tapped my shoulder and proffered a fresh chocolate chip cookie in the tentative way one would offer a peanut to a zoo animal. So I paused my movie, and we began to speak. We talked about the project. In summary, it's a good assumption that native North American peoples came to North America from Siberia, via the Bering Strait. Our project was to push back the time frame when they'd arrived: though the lower climates have evidence that people were there 33,000 years before the present era, the oldest sites in Alaska date back only to maybe 14,000 years before the present era. This discrepancy is troublesome. Primus

Dwyer and the Harvard boys were digging a site near Cape Espenberg that they were almost positive dated back to about 25,000 BCE,
or before the common era. In the realm of human prehistory, if we
found proof of human existence there that early, it would be an
enormous discovery.

By the time we'd moved on to lighter topics, the doctor and I
had begun to do a strange dance, flirting without seeming to admit
that we were flirting, having a grand time, whispering because everyone around us was sleeping, even the flight attendant on her little
seat in the front. It felt not unlike a sleepover party. I noticed for the
first time that he had dimples, which surprised me, because I have always been a sucker for dimples. I didn't see the shiny red nose anymore, or the chinlessness. I was charmed. But I thought it was quite
innocent until the very moment he looked at me, and slid his hand
onto my thigh and raised an eyebrow.

I had two choices then. One: I could have very politely placed
his hand on the armrest between us, and continued my sentence,
and we would have had a very nice trip together, and I would have
become an honorary man for the summer, and become good buddies with all the Harvard boys, and when we returned the conquer-
ing heroes in the autumn, they, feeling brotherly, would have done
everything in their power to help me along in my career.

Two: I could have raised an eyebrow back. I could have slipped
into the spacious first-class bathroom and waited for the scratch at
the door. We could have then been very naughty, laughing and
shushing one another, my pink dress going up, his khaki pants going down, and suddenly, in the midst of the lighthearted little mis-
chief, I could look up to find a serious, sweet look on his face, and a
kiss that wasn't so light and silly anymore. In the podlike bathroom,
the engines droning on around us and the ranks of businessmen
snoozing out beyond the door, I could have looked up to an expression on the last face I ever expected to see it on, and find myself
beginning to fall, and heavily.

THIS IS WHERE Clarissa interrupted to say in a muted voice, "You,
Willie Upton, are a big, fat fool."

There was a long pause then, and I think we were both thinking
of how it wasn't, perhaps, uncharacteristic for me to have made what

was so clearly the wrong decision. First, I had a thing for authority
figures: there was the photography professor in college, balding, al-
coholic. In the darkroom, under the red bulb, watching the grizzled
face of a woman I had snapped on the street emerge in the chem-
istry bath, the professor had come up behind me, and put his hands
on my stomach, and our weird fling lasted for two semesters, until he
was fired for a DWI. Then there was my weakness for funny guys,
boys who'd gone to clown college or who were obsessed with im-
provisational comedy; a man who made me laugh was exponentially
sexier to me. And then there was the eentsy little promiscuity problem, the months I'd swear off boys, entirely, and then in one night
have such a frenzy of flirtation that I would take one into the bathroom at a party, and then take another home with me. I was not
promiscuous, I think; just sexually bipolar.

Then I told Clarissa how, when Primus and I emerged from the
bathroom, the entire plane was still asleep, as if under a spell. How
it could have been awkward between us then, but instead he held
my hand under the armrest and fell asleep, mouth open like a little
boy. And he was gentle and sweet on the difficult trip, from Anchorage to Nome, from Nome to Cape Espenberg, from Cape Espenberg out in the Land Rovers, then on the hike all the way out to
our site. He bought me coffee whenever we waited, and I'd catch
him gazing at me, a little smile on his lips, from time to time.

And so it happened again. And then again and again and again.
Nearly every night in my little separate tent, in sleeping bags zipped
together against the chill of the ground. Even on days it was too
cold for me to take a bath, it happened.

It was a kind of insanity: there we were in that impossible, beautiful place, with the sun shining all the time. All those migratory
birds spinning about us, stunning colors in the bare and impressionable landscape. Our dig was going well, the camaraderie good between us and the Harvard guys, and even the food was excellent,
one of the Harvard grad students having been a chef before he gave
it all up for academia. The work was excruciatingly hard, and it felt
nice, at the end of a long day, just to be soft with someone. And in
the sun, he lost his pallor. With the work, he grew harder and fit,
and a scruff covered his weak chin, and all of a sudden, Primus
Dwyer was really gorgeous, and not just to me. One of the Harvard
grad students, a macho gay man, began calling him "Dr. To-die-

for." I lost my extra weight, and lost even more, so that my muscles were tight against my skin, and my tan dark. I knew I looked good, too. And as there is very little fucking on the tundra that can go unnoticed, it was inevitable, perhaps, that the others knew what was happening. The Harvard guys all knew Primus Dwyer's wife, of course; she had been around for a long time. They tended to look beyond my face when they addressed me.

The time when I was supposed to get my period came, and then went again. I thought: *no worries, happens all the time, just the change in diet.* And then the time for it came and went the second time, and I began to feel nauseated.

But just as I began to feel sick, we found the spearhead. And then, one day later, we found the skeleton. Pre-Clovis, both. Our osteologist guy was dancing around: he was almost positive, just by looking at the teeth, that the skeleton was of close Siberian ancestry: John was our biofact guy and said the seeds in the stomach area were from some plant he was almost certain was extinct at least 22,000 years ago up there. The Harvard principal investigator had called for a bush plane, and we were waiting in the Land Rover at the strip to say good-bye to him, because he was off to Nome and then Anchorage, to the university, to radiocarbon-date some things.

We were just fooling around, talking about a pickup game of Wiffle ball, when there was the sound of an engine over the wind, and we all prepared to say good luck to the Harvard PI off to Anchorage. Over the horizon, the little speck of the plane turned into a big speck, and it touched down and taxied. The pilot slid out of the plane, props still spinning hard, but his face was pale and pinched. He crossed over to the passenger side and opened the door.

Out slid The Castrating Bitch.

She marched her bony ass straight up to me. By that time, the good Doctor Primus Dwyer had taken his arm off my shoulders and sidled away. His wife took her cold hand out of her mitten, pulled the sleeve up on her puffy winter coat—unnecessary in that weather—and smacked me across the cheek. My mouth dropped open, and she went over to her husband and dragged him away from the rest of us, hissing.

I watched them move off. My cheek began to burn. The Harvard guys and John were watching, amazed.

That's when I went a little crazy. I went right up to the bush plane and slammed the door and somehow put it in gear, and began driving after Primus Dwyer and his wife. He turned around and his eyes went round, and then he sprang out of the way, pulling his wife with him.

Imagine a bush plane roaring out across the tundra, spinning about, revving up. Two small figures running away from it, hand-in-hand. The plane beginning to accelerate toward the figures, and then, when they split up, turning toward the smaller figure, the skinny one, bearing down on the screaming, running lady in the puffy down jacket. Then the pilot, goddamn gutsy, swinging up into the cockpit, and swerving the plane at the last minute. He took one look at my face, then pushed the plane full throttle, lifting us up off the ground.

He took me all the way back to Nome because, he said, he was scared what I would have done if I had stayed. I caught a flight to Fairbanks and from Fairbanks a flight to San Francisco. All paid for on a credit card I'd found in the black Gucci pocketbook in the front of the plane, still warm from Dwyer's wife's hands. The cockpit was still sweet with the perfume she'd sprayed on herself only moments before she slid from the plane.

I touched down at the San Francisco airport, shaking so badly I could barely walk. I had no luggage and took a taxi to Stanford, the palm trees like a military line down Memorial Drive, the buildings pink as heaven. I sweated in my Alaska clothing as I loaded my car with everything that was important to me. And then I set off on my drive. I had had no sleep, was crying, going ninety miles an hour for the most part. I only stopped for gas and the bathroom, once to try to wash myself and change into a tee shirt and shorts. I ate nothing and could see very little by the time I crossed through Erie. A vision of Primus Dwyer sometimes sat in the seat beside me, the way I knew him best, tan and handsome, in his explorer's kit. He said nothing, just smiled. Still furious, I pretended not to see him.

I arrived in Templeton in the dark before dawn and parked my car before the post office, where it still was sitting by the time I talked to Clarissa. I was afraid that my mother would hear me arrive and come out with a hatchet. I stood staring at Averell Cottage for an hour or so, working up the nerve to go inside.

And then I told Clarissa about the monster dying, how I touched it and felt the black of the lake, infinite depth. The monster's death, I told her, just went to show that everything, everything, everything was falling apart.

THERE WAS AN excruciatingly long pause, then, and I could almost hear Clarissa thinking. My story had taken hours; it was deep night in San Francisco, and the city was quiet in the receiver. At last, she said, "Well. Your life's a mess, that's true. Then again, it's not that bad. You're in Templeton, at least. So put yourself back together. Heal, yadda yadda, come back home to San Francisco."

"I'll try," I said. "But, wait, there's more."

"There cannot be more," said Clarissa.

"Oh, but there is," I said. "The lovely and sane Vivienne Upton, who is, amazingly, now a Jesus freak . . ."

". . . I *know*," said Clarissa, "what's *that* all about?"

"Hold up. How do you know?" I said. "What?"

"Oh," said Clarissa, her voice vague, "we talk all the time. Not since you've come home, though, come to think of it."

I paused and let this sink in. "Well," I said. "Your new best friend Vivienne Upton had the gall to tell me at dinner that my entire life is predicated on a despicable lie. And she had to tell me because Jesus hates liars. So get this, ready?"

"No," said Clarissa. "But you're going to tell me anyway."

"Sure am," I said. "Remember that story Vi told you that Thanksgiving about how I was supposed to come from wild sex with three hippies in a commune? Well, that's not exactly true. In fact, I come from one man. And he is a Templeton man. And he has another family. And I know him and he knows me. And he has no idea that I'm his. And Vi isn't telling me who he is, but I squeezed and squeezed until she gave me one hint, which was that he apparently told her in passing that he was descended from Marmaduke Temple through some illegitimate channel or other. So of the four hundred eligible men of an appropriate age in Templeton, I am supposed to weed out the one who is my father, based on a tiny little rumor."

"Wait. Why doesn't Vi just tell you?"

"Oh, that," I said. "Vi explicitly forbade me to find out who he is."

"Then why do you want to find him?" I could hear the smile in her voice.

"So that I can figure out if I've gotten any horrendous genetic problems from him. And then kill him for not being there while I was growing up."

Clarissa tried to muffle it, but couldn't, and I had to suffer through long, jagged squawks of delight. At last she stopped and came back on the phone. "Oh, Willie," she said. "I haven't laughed that hard in months."

"I'm glad to hear my life amuses you," I said.

"It's not that," said Clarissa. "It's just that Vi's a nut. That she would think it preferable to tell you that you were a love child of hippie sluttishness, rather than the kid of some respectable guy in town. What a trip she is."

"Yeah, yeah," I said. "It's all fun and games until it's your life. But the question I have for you, Clarissa, is this: what do I do? What do I do now?"

"About what?" she said.

"Everything," I said.

To her credit, Clarissa thought long and hard about this one. I could hear the door of the closet open where she sat so as not to disturb Sully when he was sleeping, and then his sleepy, muffled voice. I could hear her answer, soothingly, "Soon, soon," and then Clarissa came back on the phone.

"Sully's mad, Willie," she said. "Says I need my sleep more than anything and that I only have two more minutes before he cuts the wire. So here's what I have to say. About Dwyer, you're just going to have to wait. Same goes for Stanford, which I kind of think is going to end up all right, since sleeping with students is still pretty bad, and I'm sure the Dwyers don't want to have a scandal on their hands. About your dad: is there any way that you're going to get Vi to just tell you who he was?"

"Nope," I said.

"Well, did Vi say that it was old Marmaduke Temple himself who had the illegitimate child?"

I thought hard. "No," I said.

"So it could be anyone from the family. To be honest, it usually is close to the more recent end, because I think things like infidelity tend to be forgotten over time. Plus, there has to be a lot more doc- umentation with the more recent ancestors than there would be with the older ones. Begin only a few generations up from you, and then, if you find nothing, work your way back in time. I'd guess your great-grandparents were the culprits, if I had to. Or, that sexy beast of a Jacob Franklin Temple. Looks the type," she said.

"All right," I said. "That's not a bad plan."

"Now about the baby," she said, and her voice took on a wistful tone that I didn't remember Clarissa ever using in her life. It was only later, when I awoke with a startle in the middle of the night, that I remembered the talk she'd had with the genetics counselor at the hospital, how when she came out her face was pale and pinched. She wouldn't answer when I asked her what he'd said, until, at home, she put a pillow over her face and muttered, *No baby for me. If it doesn't kill me, my genes will kill it*, and refused to say any more. Now she said, "Are you sure? I mean, about the baby? Did you take a test?"

I remembered being sick to death on the hard-baked shoulder of a Nebraska road. I remembered the pulse in my gut at dinner that evening. "I'm sure," I said.

"Do you want it?" she said.

"Oh, Clarissa," I said. "I don't know. I don't know. Why bring another child into our messed . . ."

She sighed into the receiver and said, "Spare me, Willie. Just tell me the truth. Do you want it?"

"I don't know," I said. I thought of the Lump, growing as we spoke.

"Well, that's something I just can't fix right now," she said. "I'm sorry, Willie. I've got an appointment in the morning, and I'm so, so tired, honey. Plus Sully. He's standing here, ready to rip the phone from my hands."

"Oh, God," I said. "I'm so sorry. I'm the worst friend ever. How are you doing? I can't believe I didn't ask."

"Oh, fine, fine," she said. "Everything's going great, don't worry. I need to go," she said. "Love you, kid. Everything will look better in the morning," and she was gone.

Remarkable Prettybones

Done in 1814, this charcoal drawing is so fine that it is virtually indistinguishable from a photograph. Remarkable was, apparently, very vain about the drawing, proclaiming that she "never looked quite so lovely since she was a young girlie, dandled on all gents' knees."

Remarkable Prettybones

I COME TO Templeton in the early times, 1786, when all was terrible rough and hard. I was once a marvelous fair woman with my black eyes and good bosoms, but all that had withered away with my thirtieth year, long before our troubles, before our voyage to America. And I once had silver and a grand house with great windows and fine linens, I did; I once was a lady of my town, almost quite a lady. But we lost it all and come over from Ireland, the Captain and I, when he had troubles with his ships. They said he stole, hundreds and hundreds, from the owners. Not my Captain Prettybones. Base slander and nonsense.

Still his reputation was quite ruined and we set off on a clipper pushing to the new land. But Boston was not the town I'd imagined, not some sort of airy, golden place; and it was filthy, with muck knee-deep and a terrible hanging smoke and poor little Irish urchins dying with their big bloated bellies, as though they couldn't die equal home on the green swards of Ireland. My Captain staggering home at night with his pockets emptied; picked, he said, by the bad grasping women on the street, though I smelled their smells on his clothing, on his skin, under the rum and dirt. And so the day I heard of this new place, this Templeton where they were practically giving away land, and though it be in the heart of the savage country, I come running home over the streets and packed our belongings, and when my Captain staggered back in, stinking that night, I rapped him over the head with an andiron. He woke on the back of a mule thirty miles from Boston, roaring.

The voyage was hard into the wilderness, the boatman who took us up the Mohawk crooked, but the Captain had stopped his fuss by Cherry Valley and sat, cowed, at last. We come into Templeton, and it did near steal my heart away, it did, the piteousness, the four frame houses and filth and pigs rooting in the muck and smoke hanging over the town from where the men were burning their plots for potash, burning great old trees to nubs. Immediate, we sought out the great Marmaduke Temple. He was in a bit of a house that later became Sherman's Hotel and Tavern. He had his big muddy boots on the desk, in all his papers, men queued up near down to the lake, but I being a lady pushed to the front and got the deed straight off. Though he had terrible nicked and horny hands from work, not like a gentleman at all, I thought Marmaduke Temple stunning handsome with his bulgy blue eyes and his red hair, with his deep voice and kindly Quaker speech. Captain Prettybones teased me af-terwards how it seemed I had an admirer, but No, said I, He's a man who knows how to behave to ladies, and fixed the Captain with the old stink-eye, and he said naught more to me about it. In two months, we had our little building on the new Second Street, and Captain Prettybones, he'd become a shoemaker, though he never had a chance to make a single boot. In building, he'd put a nail through his thumb, and didn't tell me of it. By the time I seen it, it was large and red and had a jagged black wound with slime drip-ping from it. The red reached plain up his arm in long streaks and I knew it was a terror. I ran and fetched Aristabulus Mudge from his new apothecary. Mudge undid the bandages, saw the streaks reach-ing toward the heart. Closed the door and said to make the poor Captain comfortable, there was naught to do. And he was right, for in a night Captain Prettybones left me a widow, no money, a useless shoemaker shop, and I knowing only how to be a lady, how to run a household, striding about with keys at my waist.

So I sate that night to vigil over the cold body of my Captain and thought where to turn my poor self. Duke Temple, I knew, ate only what his valet cooked for him, and the valet spent his day with the horses, blew his nose on his sleeve. The little house of Duke's was filthy, with the men missing the spittoons and dragging in their mud and lice and filthy hands. The smell alone would curdle cream. So after I buried my husband in the new cemetery, I went directly to Duke's house and jostled through the lines of men to the front. There were no women in town then save the Widow Crogan, who owned the Eagle Hotel, and the men allowed me to shove them a little then, for the mere touch of a woman's hand was distant to them and they longed for it, even from a woman with charms faded as my own. I marched straight to Duke, who bent over his desk like a boy over a matchbox, and said, Master Duke, my husband, he's gone. Just this morning, said I, did I bury my Captain Prettybones.

Duke looked up over his map and rubbed his temple. Oh, Mrs. Prettybones, he said, I heard the news this morning. I am so very sorry for thy loss.

Yes, said I. It is a tragedy. And then I go on to relate all that I had come from, the fine house with its silver and linens, then the slander, and at last my piteous state. By the end of my sorrowful tale, I was weeping freely into my kerchief and flatter myself to say that even Himself had a tear in his fine blue eye.

Well, well, dear Mrs. Prettybones, he exclaimed at the end of my story, agitated to standing. Whatever can I do for thee, he said.

Thank you kindly, Mr. Temple, I say. I should like to become your housekeeper in the absence of your beautiful and charming wife.

I said this though I did not know my mistress then, but thought that a man such as Duke could not have a wife who was less than spirited and lovely. Imagine my surprise when I at last met Elizabeth Temple! A dear heart to be sure, but a brown little sparrow, and plain and so easily managed. So odd a couple as Duke and she has never been seen the world over, truly. And though I was but a mere higher servant, sometimes I did think it was a shame he had not a spouse who was quite worthy of him, as capable and quick as he.

But in that moment, on the day of my mourning, Duke blinked

and let out a roar of laughter that shook the very beams. What a clever idea, he said. Fine, my dear Mrs. Prettybones. Thou shalt be my housekeeper. When canst thee commence?

Now, said I, bold as a magpie. We may talk pay over supper, said I.

Good, good, he said, sitting down. I am eager to eat a woman's cooking again.

And that was how I found myself a fine living in the little town on a lake. Duke Temple gave me succor in my time of need, and I ran his household from that little house that is now Sherman's Hotel, to the great, beautiful Temple Manor that the big, brooding slave Mingo built for Duke.

To be sure, all that time I had only been slightly bothered that Master Duke went off to the pubs like a common man, not like a gentleman at all. A mushroom gentleman, they called him, a gentleman sprung up overnight from the dung, though I grew furious when I heard it and the joker went off with such a ringing in his ear he might never hear again. Also there was always talk of the little girlies Duke looked upon too favorably, such nasty gossip. The chargirl at the Eagle. The cobbler's daughter, Trixie. Even talk of Rosamond Phinney, the belle, though she was just a slip of a girl at the time, that merciless flirt. The only comfort is to think that when a man was great as Himself there would always be talk.

But when Hetty came, I admit it was marvelous difficult. I almost considered leaving the day Duke showed up with the three slaves for me to manage. Mingo was all right, though soft in the head, I suspected, but he fished and built beautifully and did not look at me at all, let alone with the lust I locked my door against. And Cuff, such a darling little Delaware Indian boy, brought up by a minister and his wife, taught to read and write, and then sold off by the parish when the minister and wife died, a common slave. That poor boy was like a child to me, until the day he ran off with a traveling preacher man. I never had more regretted the unformed children I lost from my womb until the day Cuff ran off.

But that black and saucy Hetty was another matter, indeed. I saw she was only out to seduce with her beautiful round face and coral necklace of scars around her throat, and as I was once a pretty girl like Hetty, I knew all the tricks. I kept her busy, cooking and collecting honey and plucking the pears and putting up preserves. I will grant, she was marvelous clean, obsessed, truly, over the last speck of dirt or dust. I had never seen a window gleam the way she could make it gleam or sheets so white as the ones on the beds. But I did not keep her busy enough, in the end, sad to say. I'll admit, when I saw a special roundness when there should be nothing round at all, I had my suspicions, I did, and am proud to have acted upon them. And on the day my mistress come wrath-wracked into town, near bursting with child herself, and stepped from the carriage, all greasy from her travels, and circled Hetty and saw how rotten the girl was to the core, she threw her out into the street and I laughed and laughed to myself. But Hetty was a cat, landing on her feet, and she married that tanner Jedediah Averell, and he became a rich man. She, though black, almost quite a lady, and I could hardly stand it.

But most terrible of all was the day that came dark and heavy over the lake when that Guvnor of hers was born. I looked out the Manor window and saw Midwife Bledsoe scurrying down the road in the rain, and I knew Hetty's labor come. And I'd admit to a great and sinful fury, and so after tea, after changing our little Jacob and singing him to sleep, I put on my own bonnet and cape and took a basket with some provisions and went down to the tanner's on the lake and marched in and went up the stairs where the stink of birth was, all metal and sweat, and went right in, and peeled the swaddling from the child and looked down and saw the red hair, the skin the color of cream tea, the bulgy blue eyes, one drifting off to the side. I put down the basket and covered the baby up again and put him back in the arms of Hetty, who was watching me with a smile flashing under her lips, not on her lips, but under, and went back into the rain. And this I tell as the truth; that even on the day my own Captain Prettybones left me behind in this sorrowful world a widow, I had not felt a cleaving so terrible within me. And though I bless his sinning heart in my prayers, I could not look at Marmaduke the same way again, no, never did I look at him the same again, no.

Queen and Crane

BETTER THAN AN alarm clock, the Running Buds. I awoke in the gray dawn when they were still a half a mile away, their footsteps reverberating over the Susquehanna bridge. By the time I found an old pair of running shoes, a suitable tee shirt, and a pair of track shorts (loose black polyester, the shameful Templeton mascot of a "Redskin" in orange on the left thigh), they had already gone a half a mile more. When I emerged onto Lake Street, I could trace their passage in the dew-damp footprints on the asphalt.

In light of my love life, it is perhaps a little sad to admit that I chased those six middle-aged men halfway across town. On my infrequent trips home, I had grown used to joining at least a small part of their runs, springing out of bed when I heard them nearing, catching up to them as quickly as I could. The truth was that other than Vi they were the only friends I had anymore when I returned home to Templeton: my friends in high school were the smart kids, and the smart kids never came home, barely even gracing the village for holidays. After college, my former friends and I lost touch, and the only way I knew what was going on in their lives—their medical residencies, marriages, articles, children—was through Vi, or more frequently, the Buds. The Buds were the town gossips, the watchdogs, the caretakers. And even back when I was in high school, they made a point of going to as many of my soccer games and track meets as possible. This was partially, I'm sure, because high school sports were the only excitement in town when the air crisped into fall and the tourists disappeared. But it was partially, too, because they adopted me, in their way. Every Fourth of July, they invited me to picnics with their families, and I went without Vi, who was always working. I was taken as a babysitter on family vacations to Disney World and Hilton Head, I was escorted to a celebratory dinner by all six when I won the Daughters of the American Revolution essay contest. They paid for a backpacking trip to Europe for my graduation from college. When Vi said I couldn't accept it, it was too much, they were so sad and pleaded so eloquently that she let me take it.

Templeton was crystalline in the predawn that morning. The Buds had gone up Lake Street, past the great brick Otesaga Hotel, a grande dame sunning herself on the water; they turned left up Nelson, past the tennis courts. Right up Main Street, passing the courthouse and florist, crossing the railroad, turning left down Winter Street. Now, I approached them from behind. From two hundred yards away, I could hear them, the low murmur of their voices and the slap of their old feet against the ground. From a hundred feet away, I could smell them, the sweat deep in the fabric of their running clothes, the little poots they made when they thought the others wouldn't notice.

They were:

Johann Neumann, the father of Laura, a girl in my class. Every time Johann went home to Germany, he came back with fat tubes of marzipan for me, and he taught me, over the course of one frustrating summer, how to play tennis.

Bearlike Tom Irving, who sold used cars and gave me my cruddy hatchback nearly for free, and who, when I was eight and walking home from school, sobbing about how mean the other kids were to me, sat down on a bench and put his arm around me and let me cry until I was all cried out.

Tiny Thomas Peters, my pediatrician, so small I could look him in
the eye when I was ten, whom my mother called whenever something went wrong with Averell Cottage, because he was as good
with houses as he was with children and cheerfully fixed anything.

Sol Falconer, about whom there was always a great deal of gossip, as he'd had three wives, and he was rich and childless, and
who, because I'd asked him, let me have my tenth birthday party
at his house, with his huge pool, and, because he didn't know any
better, had it catered. His family was a long-standing one, all the
men named Sol Falconer, and when some people bridled at his
money, they called him Sol Falconer the Filth, instead of Sol Falconer the Fifth.

Frank Phinney, whose family had owned the *Freeman's Journal* forever and who gave me my first internship in college, writing captions
for photographs, a man who wouldn't stop telling knock-knock jokes
until they were like tickle-torture, fun that was *so* not fun.

And last, Doug Jones, my high school English teacher, not unlike
an aging Jim Morrison, who always had giggling girls staying after
school for help with Shakespeare. He cast me as Desdemona in the
school play, and when I babysat his three sweet little girls, he'd coach
me on my lines. "No, no, Willie. Say it with *feeling!*" he'd shout, and
his daughters would chortle like a little chorus of songbirds.

As I approached, I grinned at their oblivious backs, feeling a great
upwelling of affection. At the moment, Doug Jones was saying,
". . . just jealous because she always turned to me when she was asking questions, weren't you, Big Tom? I thought you were about to
seize up on camera."

To which the rest of the men guffawed, and Tom Irving said,
"Hilarious, Dougie, hi-lar-i-ous. True, though. I never thought
when I went on the *Daybreak!* show I'd have to play second fiddle
to you dorkuses."

Then Johann said, in his little German accent, "That Katie Doyle
really vas a vhippersnapper, vasn't she? Much prettier in person.
Much prettier."

It took me a moment, but I realized they were talking about an
interview they must have done for a national morning talk show,
probably something to do with their role in discovering the monster. I was about to step up next to them and ask them about it,

already savoring the *Heyyy!* they always shouted, when a garbage
truck briefly pushed between us, and, when the driver nodded down
at me, I was seized by a horrific thought. I stopped running alto-
gether and watched the Buds pull away down the street.

It was possible, I'd thought, that any man in town could have
been my father. The garbageman, for instance; the Running Buds.
Or Dr. Cluny, the sculler who had found the monster. Or my elementary school principal, or the rotund little mayor, or the post-
man, or the dry cleaning guy at Kepler's. The baseball museum
director, the baker at Schneider's Bakery, John-John the mechanic
at Dwight's. Dwight. Dwight's mentally retarded twin brother,
Derek. My track coach, my orthodontist, any of the three mute ancient men who played chess all summer in Temple Park. Mr. Clapp
the mortician, the pastor at the Presbyterian Church, the Catholic
priest, the railroad magnate, the biologist at the Biological Field
Station, the town librarian, my friends' fathers, oh God, anyone,
any man, could, actually, have been my father. Aristabulus Mudge,
even! A man invoked at third-grade sleepovers in the hushed and
daring tone one used for the devil himself, a man who *looked* like
the devil himself, all horny calluses and shining pickled-looking
skin, a crooked-backed, hollow-cheeked man with eyes set so deep
in his sockets no one had ever seen their whites, he who once
walked into a cloud of butterflies and made them fall dead like
dropped pennies in his wake, even *he* could have been my father,
even *Aristabulus Mudge* could have been the man who wormed his
way into and out of my life in the zip of a zipper and a hiss of relief. I felt my heart slip out of rhythm, and thought, in my melo-
drama, that I would die of this grief.

But my heart, of course, started up again, and at the end of the
street the Running Buds turned left to go back up toward the gym.
I felt sick. I felt like the birdie in that terrible children's book by
P. D. Eastman, the one that wanders around and asks everything—
the cow, the dog, the airplane—"Are you my mother?" I gagged
into the gutter and stood up, still feeling ill.

I was now by the elementary school, a squat brick Lego of a
building. I would run back to town by Walnut Street, then Chestnut, sidle down Main, and pick up my car from where I stashed it,
opposite the baseball museum and next to the post office. I would

drive it up into the driveway and drag inside Averell Cottage all of my clothes and books, everything that made home comfortable. And there I would rot until either the Lump came out or Primus Dwyer called, and not, I vowed, until then. Until I talked to Primus Dwyer, I wouldn't decide anything on the Lump, and there was no way I could call him myself. I didn't let myself think of what would happen if he never called me.

And I had to pick up the car without running into anyone I knew, which happened every time I came home. The last time I was in Templeton, two years earlier, I had stopped to pick up some groceries at the Great American for Vi, and saw a girl who was in my graduating class. She was staring at the granola, paying no attention to her three children in the cart. They were horrifying, with thyroidal eyes and snotty noses. And then Cheri turned her head and saw me, and for at least five minutes I was in acute discomfort, Cheri latching on to me as if we had been best friends, showing off her children for my admiration, talking about getting together for a beer sometime. I was so uncomfortable I forgot what I was supposed to pick up and practically ran home. I later drove all the way out to the Price Chopper in Hartwick so I wouldn't have to return to the Great American and risk seeing her still there, with her glassy eyes and the changelings throwing handfuls of sugar cereal into the aisles. When I thought of Cheri, even standing there beside her in the grocery store under the Muzak and fluorescents, I thought of her in bed, sweating and grunting, making more of those frightening children of hers. Some people you just look at and see *sex*.

That morning I jogged to Main, jittery and furtive. Schneider's Bakery was pumping its old-fashioned doughnut smell into the street, and with the waft came layers of memory. There, the dollhouse furniture store owned by the parents of a rock star, now a baseball card store. There, the candy shop that sold gourmet jellybeans. There, the baseball cap store that only sold caps from minorleague teams, a place where I worked for a summer so that even now I could list a few off the top of my head: Louisville Bats, Toledo Mud Hens, Montgomery Biscuits, Tulsa Drillers, Batavia Muckdogs, Lansing Lugnuts. I ran down the street, beyond Cartwright Field, and there were no cars out yet, no traffic on the street. Farkle Park,

where Santa's house sat in winter, and where the high school druggies sat in summer and played with their hackeysacks or ballsacks all
day. Mudge's Pharmacy in the copper-clad corner building. Then
Pioneer Street and the Smithy building, the Bold Dragoon, an ancient pub, crouching beside it. Augur's Books. Druper's General
Store. The great baseball museum with a crowd of enthusiasts already out in force, waiting beside the velvet ropes to ooh over balls
and bats. It was all there, unchanging, save for a few more baseball-
related stores every year, a couple fewer interesting small-town
places for the locals.

This, too, had been a change. In the past, the tourists had never
really taken up much of our attention: they held no part in the social strata of Templeton: they existed in our periphery, essential but
unimportant. Since the hospital came in 1918, the doctors had
made up the highest base, filling the town with money and brains,
running the country club, opening up galleries. The only rung
above them held our few millionaires: the ambassador, the railroad
magnate, the wonderful wealthy woman who made sure there were
flowers everywhere, the Falconers with their beery fortune, not to
mention both sides of my family until we lost it all. Below the doctors were the other white-collar people: hospital administrators,
attorneys, librarians, and below them the farmers, who used to be
important, but with the decline of the New York dairy heifer were
now associated with malt liquor and bonfires and hickishness. Below them the random townies who filled the Bold Dragoon on
weekends. When the new Opera House opened in 1986, we reluctantly opened ranks for the Opera visitors with their couture
gowns and Mercedes, but even they were eventually shunted off to
Springfield on the other side of the lake. When the Park of Dreams
opened in a cow field in Hartwick Seminary, south of town, we
thought that a few Little Leaguers wouldn't be able to change the
topography of the town that much. We didn't expect that they
would bring their parents, and that the parents (cheesy, loud people
with cellulite under their shorts and minivans soaped up with TEM-
PLETON OR BUST! and CHESTERTON CHARGERS ARE #1!) would demand
cheap restaurants and a better grocery store and plasticky chain ho-
tels and miniature golf. We had no idea that the Park of Dreams
would expand to hold eight teams of Little Leaguers every week

throughout the summer, 1,200 screaming baseball brats per week, plus about 600 of their awful parents. Though we tried to keep them relegated to Hartwick Seminary, three miles south of Templeton proper, we didn't know that such demand would transform the face of the town. The sewing store, the dollhouse store, the toy store, even Farm and Home would become stores that merely slutted themselves to baseball. Now, nearly every store was brimming with memorabilia or bats. The tourists were getting hard to ignore.

And there, in a crowd of stinking young boys in jerseys talking excitedly about Ty Cobb and Babe Ruth, was my hatchback in front of the post office. Stuffed to the gills with books and clothes, the bumper precariously near the ground. And there was a tow truck backing its beeping rear end into my poor little car, like the automotive prelude to a humping.

I moved fast, thankful that I'd left the keys in the ignition. In Templeton, even on Main Street where the tourists congregated, everyone leaves the keys in the ignition, either from mass stupidity or an inbred honor code. Now I slid in and reversed as the tow truck was backing into my car, keeping a coy three-foot gap between us for a hundred feet until I hit Fair Street at the end of the block. At which time, the tow truck stopped, the driver hopped out and walked back to my car. He was a tall man with a potbelly and slouching walk, wearing a Carhartt jumpsuit with the top half rolled down to his waist. He beamed under his hunting cap, an orange the color of a scream.

"You ain't going to let me haul your ass away, are you?" he called.

I stuck my head out the window and said, "No, sir. I'm doing a U-ey right here in Temple Park, and hauling my own ass elsewhere, okay?"

By now, his head was in my window, and a moment later, I felt the deep and sinking recognition. Zeke Felcher. Oh, Lord.

"Well," he said, grinning down at me, "if it isn't Miss Queenie, 1991."

I cringed: I had been at one point the world's most eccentric choice for a homecoming queen, having been both nerd and jock, but never quite a beauty. I am tall and thin, true, but only pretty, and even back then I was politically correct, superfeminist, more prone to picketing Miss America than entering it. Yet, when I found myself that day on the football field being crowned in the wet, cold mud, my hypocrite's heart rejoiced.

And Zeke Felcher, the man in my window, had been my homecoming king.

"Holy shit," I said. "Felcher, is that you?"

"Well, don't you look a sight," he said. I frowned, but a sight to Felcher must have been a good thing, because he then whistled his chewing tobaccoey breath into my face and said, "I always knew you'd end up a hottie, Willie. Now come on out and give your king a hug."

That is how I found myself on the corner of Main and Fair, pressed against the beer belly of a man I'd tried very hard to ignore in high school. He had been gorgeous then, with a soccer player's body and green eyes and a head full of blond curls, but also with a bad reputation for kissing and telling. At least in high school I'd had enough sense to stay away from the rotten ones.

"Damn," he said, releasing me, running his fingers through my short hair. "I like this look on you. What are you doing home?"

"Oh," I said, looking away. "Finishing my dissertation. Needed a little peace and quiet."

"That's right," he said. "I always forgot you were a smart one, with your degrees and all. Only college I went to was the School of Life. School of Hard Knocks. Teaches you more than any damn hoity-toity private liberal arts nonsense."

"Ah," I said, feeling weakened by the cliché he'd become, "how true."

He said, "But my two boys, they'll be like you. Brilliant little guys."

"Kids?" I said. "Christ, Felcher. Are you married now? I had no idea."

"Nah," he said. "I'm not married. Don't believe in it."

There was a queer little moment between us, I now looking at Felcher with full focus for the first time, he gazing at me with narrowed eyes. "What," I said, "what don't you believe in?"

His mouth twisted a little, and his hick accent fell away when he said, "Oh, the hegemony. The institution itself is both corrupt and exclusionary." Then he snorted to see the look on my face and said, "Don't look so surprised, Willie U. You aren't the only one to get over fifteen hundred on your SATs. Just because I stayed home in Templeton doesn't mean I'm stupid as all that."

"No," I said. "That's not what I was thinking at all."

"Oh, yes it was," he said. "But I forgive you."

There was, again, a long silence as I looked at my shoes and he smirked. And then I stuttered, for the sake of saying something, "Well, who is it you're *not* married to, then?"

Now he was the one to look down, and he frowned and kicked at a little crack in the asphalt. "Melanie?" he said. "Mel Potter? But we don't see each other much. Share the kids, that's all."

"Oh, Mel," I said. She had always been the ringleader of his personal set of groupies, with great boulders for breasts and a pretty teddy-bear face. "Neat. Well," I said. "We should get together for a beer or something sometime. But I kind of have to get back home because my mother's making me breakfast and everything."

"Already?" he said, and his face fell, a little. "All right, then."

He looked so oddly crestfallen that I put a little flirtation in my voice and touched his shoulder when I said, "So, what do I have to do to liberate my car?"

He took off the orange cap, smiling again, and scratched his scalp. His curls were gone now, and his forehead had expanded into the center of his crown, where the honey hair began, though darker, after all these years. "Well, I don't know," he said. "You were a bad girl, Queenie. Parked illegally for over forty-eight hours. I just don't know."

I pouted a little, and he laughed and said, "Tell you what. Make good on your offer for a beer, and I'll let you go scot-free. How's that for a deal?"

"Sounds good," I said, sliding into my car. "Thanks, Felcher. Owe you one."

"Anything for my girl," he said, closing my car door for me gently. Then, leaning in my window, he said, "And, Willie, nobody calls me Felcher anymore. Who knew, but Felcher's quite the dirty term. Call me Zeke, or Ezekiel. My buddies call me Zeke."

"Zeke," I said. "Ezekiel. Sounds funny, but okay."

"All right, then," he said, and slapped the top of my car as if it were the rear of a horse and I were a cowgirl off to rope the yearlings. I did my U-turn in the Temple Park and sped away, down toward the slate blue of the lake. I was already halfway home before I started to laugh: in high school we had called him Felcher as a sort of incantation against his charm and impossible good looks, as a way to bring him down a little into the realm of mere mortals. We had no weapons against him other than his name, a reputed sexual penchant whereby a person sucks semen from a rectum with a straw. Ten years after high school, he had fallen so far all by himself that it wasn't necessary to call him Felcher. Now he was among the mortals, and we felt safe enough to give him back his name. Ezekiel. I couldn't stop laughing until I parked in the driveway of the house.

VI WENT TO work in the morning, and by afternoon, I had grown tired of spying on the monster's tent from my room. A crane had arrived to transport the dead beast somewhere, but nothing was happening yet to lift it. From where I stood in the open window, I could hear the low murmur of the crowd, the soft-drink hawkers, the newscasters practicing their lines.

I stepped out into the hallway, where my mother had constructed a sort of gallery of ancestors. It began downstairs, where, vivid and huge against the wall, was a copy of the Gilbert Stuart painting of Marmaduke, with his stern look, red hair, large chin. Opposite, above the middle steps of the stairwell, was his little wife, Elizabeth, a brittle, dried-up thing. At the top of the stairs the great novelist Jacob Franklin Temple beamed down beneficently. And then, all along the hallway that led to my room, there were dozens of drawings, etchings, photographs of later ancestors, until it ended with my section opposite my door. There were only two photographs of my mother: one of her as a little girl in a frilly dress, another with her as a long-haired semihippie.

Seeing her there, smiling in the faded oranges of pictures from the 1970s, I pressed my arms tight to my navel, and said to the Lump, "Just look at all your crazy ancestors."

One step closer to the stairwell, and there were my grandparents on their wedding day. My grandfather, who was only eighteen at the time, looked skeletal in his suit. His wife, Phoebe Tipton, an old maid at twenty-eight, looked peckish with her enormous nose, absent chin, and round little body. They were, frankly, unattractive. And they looked so petrified, so stiff in their wedding clothing, that it was clear to me that neither could have been anything but a virgin. They must have danced the dirty dance once, to produce my mother, and then stopped with a sigh of relief. As neither person was, I was sure, the illegitimate source of my father, I took another step toward the stairwell to look at my great-grandparents.

My grandmother's—Phoebe Tipton's—parents were no more encouraging than she was. Claudia Starkweather and Chuck Tipton both clutched Bibles. Claudia was sallow, skinny, with Phoebe's enormous nose and absent chin; Chuck Tipton was immense and very stupid-looking. Claudia was the descendant of Marmaduke, through Hetty, but she didn't look capable of the imagination an affair requires.

"No," I said to the Lump. "Forget it. It's not her."

I moved on to my grandfather's parents, as Sarah Franklin Temple was a legitimate descendant of Marmaduke. There, I began to grin, because my grandfather's parents, Sarah Franklin Temple and Asterisk "Sy" Upton, were both beautiful. Sarah was a gorgeous brunette, fair-skinned, clear-eyed; her husband, Sy, was sturdily handsome with a rakish grin. I found it easy to believe that Sarah could have screwed around, had a child in some convent or somewhere, then hidden the evidence, and come back to town only to marry the first man to ask her. Looking at her beautiful face, I thought I saw hidden depth, a secretiveness I wasn't expecting.

So I took down the picture of my great-grandmother and great-grandfather in some windy locale, shaking the hands of Eleanor and Franklin Delano Roosevelt. I kissed them both. Even though Sy had been the baseball commissioner for years and years, my mother had given most of his documents to the New York State Historical Association—NYSHA—instead of the baseball museum, which sparked, at the time, a great uproar. But at least it served to let me know where I would find out more. I doubted Sarah would have much documentation and was prepared to search through her husband's life to find some kind of evidence about some kind of infidelity. An unexplained raw enmity toward some boorish young man in town. A mean-spirited anonymous letter sent to the unsuspecting husband. Something like that, some small nugget that would mean nothing to anyone else but would mean the world to me.

I was so excited, I forgot my resolution to rot at home until

Primus called. I gathered a notebook and a pen and hurried down the hall, past the older ancestors, past Jacob and Elizabeth and Marmaduke, out the grand Dutch door and onto Lake Street again.

THE CANTED TRIANGLES of the hops poles at the Farmers' Museum, the nineteenth-century village crouched in the middle, the waft of manure; the golf course's long, hilly sward of green to my right and the country club with its tennis *thwacks* and a school of sailboats setting off into the lake. At last, there was the pillared stone mansion, Franklin House, which thirty-five years ago belonged to my family but was now a museum. For a moment, I imagined ghostly hacks and landaus clipping up the long driveway to the house, with garlands around the pillars and windows bright-lit for a ball. The library was a more modest stone building off to the side. I stood outside for a moment gathering my courage. And then, brazen, I went into the cool dim hall.

There was an old woman at a desk who bore a remarkable resemblance to a goat, with her skinny jaw and tufts of white hair on her chin, but she was snoozing into her own chest. Before her was a sign that read: GENERAL PUBLIC: $5.00. NEW YORK STATE HISTORICAL SOCIETY MEMBERS AND GRADUATE STUDENTS IN HISTORY: FREE. I thought of my prehistoric man on his crossing over the icy Bering Strait, my careful hours on my knees dislodging grains of tundra dirt. I signed in as a history graduate student and set to work, sending skittering through the stacks for me a skinny, mustached librarian who blushed furiously when I asked him a question.

Many hours later, I was still at the oaken tables in the library when the sun slipped below the hills and cast the lake in shadow. Around me were huge stacks of books, boxes of microfilm, master's theses, my notebook filled with my scribbles. I had found out nothing, nothing, save that Sy Upton had come to Templeton in 1935 on a month-long scouting trip for the future baseball museum. But he fell in love with Sarah Franklin Temple and stayed. That's all my grandfather, George Upton, wrote about his parents in the slim book that caused such a scandal and may or may not have led to his death.

Now the pert librarian was standing before me, fingering his bow tie and pushing a little leather-bound book with his finger. "Miss Upton," he said. "I must go home very soon, I am very sorry to say." And he did look sorry; he had been so helpful all day, charging through the library to find yet another source, flipping through microfilm for evidence, his pencil-thin mustache a-quivering. I had told him that I was starting a dissertation on "the migration of baseball to Templeton," beginning in 1935, and was using Sy as a case study. It was such a stupid premise, but I couldn't think of another, and the librarian seemed to swallow it whole. The little goatwoman at the front would open her eyes once in a while and shake her head at us, putter around, and then fall back asleep in the same position.

"Oh," I said. "I'm so sorry. Let me put these things back," but he waved me away.

"It'll wait till tomorrow. There aren't too many visitors here in the summer, you know," he said. "And you may need them again. Doesn't seem as if you got that much done."

I stretched my arms above my head and yawned. "I didn't," I admitted. "I'll be back tomorrow. And if I'm going to be seeing that much of you, I should know your name."

He blushed and said, "Peter Lieder," and held out his hand for me to shake.

But I was far too surprised to do so and just stood gazing at him until he dropped his hand in confusion. "Not," I said, "Peter-Lieder-Pudding-and-Pie?"

"Well," he said, "in fact, yes."

"Holy shit," I said. Peter Lieder was four years older than I was in high school, and quite porky at the time. Probably over three hundred pounds during his senior year, and the best musician we had in school: oboe, flute, saxophone, tuba, trumpet, drum, violin, Peter Lieder could play them all. The Peter Lieder I knew could have gobbled up this fey little man with his fries. "You're Peter Lieder?" I said. "I'm so sorry I didn't recognize you all day. I feel like a jerk."

But the new Peter Lieder beamed at me. "Oh, Miss Upton, don't worry about it. I'm not the same person, clearly. Nobody has called me Peter-Lieder-Pudding-and-Pie for years. A thyroid problem! Who'd have thought? And after the gastric stapling, too. Such a pity."

"Oh, God," I said. "Wow. But don't call me Miss Upton. I'm Willie, Peter."

"All right, Willie," he said, flushed with pleasure. He cleared his throat and then said, "Now, I know you're mainly interested in your great-grandfather Sy, but I found this all the way back in Special Collections. Looks like it's the journal of Sarah Franklin Temple, his wife, you know. Your, well, great-grandma. About the time that Sy came to town. I thought perhaps there was some information in there. Insight or two. Worth a try. Interesting stuff, from what I can tell. Smith girl, prolific writer. Nobody has ever really read them— they're just sitting there awaiting the day that Sy gets a biographer."

"Oh," I said, my heart doing a joyful shimmy in my chest. "Thanks. Can I take this home tonight?"

His face pinched tiny with regret. "So sorry," he said. "Special Collections stay here."

"Please?" I said. "Just one night?"

"Miss Upton—" he began.

"Willie," I said.

"Willie," he said, "I'm so sorry, no."

"Pretty please?" I tried again.

He looked troubled, then peered around in the gloomy shadows. "All right," he whispered, peering around for the goat-woman, who was in the back with a cart and a few books. "Seeing as it's you. And your family. I shouldn't do this, but all right." Then he looked at me with large eyes and gave a curious giggle as I stood and slid the book into my bag.

"I'll bring it back tomorrow," I said. "Thanks so much, Peter Lieder," and then, fast, I was out the door before he changed his mind. Outside in the uprush of rose smell from the bushes by the door, I imagined the little librarian in the door behind me, in growing distress, frowning and rubbing his hands together like a chipmunk.

I DIDN'T SEE it until I entered the house that night and went up to my room. But there it was, framed in the twilight in a window, surreal and vivid: the monster in midair, suspended by the crane. Its neck was thrust backward so that its head tilted toward the east mountains, its arms and legs were drooping toward the ground, the great, delicate tail one long comma, looking tattered and unlovely out of the water. Like this, the buttery belly was exposed to the sky, and the monster, though huge, looked vulnerable. Water poured from the body back into the lake like long silvery strings in the dusk.

And then with a great mechanical groan, the crane pivoted the body until it was over the double-rigger flatbed truck that was to transport it, and began lowering it down. On the wind up from the lake there swept a new smell, both fishy and vegetative, a darkly rotting stink. When I looked away from the window, I felt the ghost there, an ethereal midnight blue, clenching. Angry, I could tell. I remembered the cold touch of the monster; I remembered its great sadness, which was apparent even in its corpse, and I understood the ghost's fury.

With the monster now out of the lake, something had ended, I knew. Sadness fell over me like a velvety curtain and I pressed the Lump, feeling a pulse there.

When I was small and easily wounded, books were my carapace. If I were recalled to my hurts in the middle of a book, they somehow mattered less. My corporeal life was slight; the dazzling one in my head was what really mattered. Returning to books was coming home.

So, as I heard my mother move downstairs making dinner that night, I sat on the bed with my angry ghost and picked up Sarah Franklin Temple's journal and began to read. She was a fresh college graduate when the volume began and her words were so strange that I became lost in them. Vi had to call me three times to come downstairs. At last she came up herself to take the book out of my hands.

I looked up, eager, thrilled. "Your grandmother," I said, "was a total nut job."

"Willie," she said, suppressing a smile. "I'm so glad you're pouring yourself into your quest. But even great scholars need food."

"Vi?" I said. "Weren't you ever curious about them? Sy and Sarah? The glamour of your grandparents? Never?"

She blinked at me, seeming trapped for a second before she dropped her eyes to the little book in her hands. "A little," she said. "They were so . . . removed. Like celebrities. I asked my great-grandmother about them, but she was bats then, and who knows whether the things she said were real. And I could never ask my father. He always seemed so stern when it came to her. I don't

know. I'm still maybe that obedient little girl at heart, I guess."
Then she gave a rallying sigh and said in her economical way,
"Doesn't matter. I'll hear it all from you, I'm sure. But now our
casserole is getting cold and it's late and I have my prayer group tomorrow that I still have to bake cookies for."

"Ugh. Baptist cookies. Locusts and wild honey, I'm guessing," I
said, reaching a little, because my mother seemed so sad.

"Nope," she said, giving me a little weary smile. "But they must
be dunked to find salivation."

"Hardee-har. You sound like Clarissa," I said, but I actually did
giggle a little.

Vi held my hand all the way down the stairs, and turned to me at
the bottom. "Despite everything," she said, her jowls gently wobbling, "Sunshine, I'm so glad you're home."

WHAT WILLIE UPTON UNDERSTOOD
❊ ABOUT HER FAMILY, REVISED AGAIN ❊

Hetty Averell *(slave)* ⟵ Marmaduke Temple ⟶ Elizabeth Temple *(wife)*

{ Jacob
Franklin
Temple,
etc.

Claudia Starkweather
1888-1923
m. Chuck Tipton
1887-1948

Sarah Franklin Temple
1913-1933
m. Asterisk "Sy" Upton
(baseball commissioner)
1895-1953

Phoebe Tipton —————— m. 1951 —————— George Franklin
1923-1973   Temple Upton
                                             1933-1973

Vivienne Upton
1955-
(Random Templeton Man) ——————

Willie "Sunshine" Upton
1973-

Sarah Franklin Temple Upton
*Her graduation photograph from the
Emma Willard School, taken in 1927*

*Sy and Sarah in a canoe on Glimmerglass Lake, with
Hannah holding an orphan in her lap.* CIRCA 1932.

9

Sarah Franklin Temple Upton, from Her Journal,

Abridged

Today I arrived, and the boxed-up soul of mine is at last set free. Manhattan, the mere word's a song . . . a good idea of my father's to send me here for the summer, although my brothers seem to believe I am to be married. "How in the world," they must have been thinking, "did we allow our lovely sister to graduate from college unmarried?" . . . how little they know me! I will accept no bourgeois striver, no paycheck-whore, no infernal attorney, editor, bachelor they're so intent on introducing me to, I will have an artist, I will be the wife of a genius, or I will be a fierce spinster, dedicated to intellect . . .

. . . Today Manhattan is no longer glitz and dazzle. There is dirt, men in business suits selling things nobody wants,

newspapers flying, rats with their beady eyes, breadlines. I
feel sick. I rifle through the papers and find a story of
famine forming behind those few tense lines . . . women in
the Ukraine on broomstick legs, their children with balloons
for bellies, one gust of wind and they'll all float away . . .
and all the while, my brothers serve caviar on delicate ivory
spoons. These nights, I dream of Templeton, Lake
Glimmerglass, my lake like ice on the tongue . . .

. . . two weeks here, and already this place makes me
sick; already I have seen my private people on the street-
corners, holes where their eyes should be . . . I am
afraid . . . words beating behind my tongue like flies at a
window . . . inappropriate, curious words, sometimes they
slip out, my brothers and their wives looking at me silkily,
then at each other . . . Not the needles again! I cannot go
back to the hospital . . . Smith cured me, I thought, only
one episode, there, only two weeks insane in four
years . . . all that hockey, all those teas, all that
menstruation and thinking . . . I was safe there. I am not
safe, here, at all.

. . . sick, my brothers are sending me home. This place
infects me. Templeton my smooth little pill . . . such
images I have. Such voices, that high voice, the little girl's,
so naughty, talking to me, all the time now. How I hate
her . . . the train is empty, Albany a small, spangled
fish . . . this train is all brown velvet . . . the train slows, I
am in Templeton, oh. Templeton, Templeton, the train
says, slowing down. The lake, the blue, is an embrace.

. . . Father picking me up in his wretched old car . . .
"a rich man, darling, should never show his wealth in
a time of such misery" . . . gesturing toward the
shantytown beside the railroad . . . "There are poor
people everywhere, Sarah, even here" . . . Father is so old!
So worn! Seventy-three and tottery. Mother has grown
snappish, busy with the Orphanage, feeding the people in

the shantytown, rather skinny in her forties, though still
quite fine . . . "Hello, my dear, you look beautiful as
always, I'm afraid you will find our circumstances
reduced. Your father is over-generous, you see, and we can
only keep a gardener and a housegirl now. Little Sally,
from the Orphanage" . . . I do not like this Little Sally,
mute girl, knobby face, wild hair . . . Father, closing the
door behind us in his study. Over the mantel, Marmaduke
Temple, and on the mantel old Cartwright's baseball.
Ratty thing of twine, curious my father holds such stock
in it. Everyone knows baseball is an ancient sport . . . the
Mills Commission all balderdash, bought by the Spalding
Corporation, baseball manufacturers, to grow an
American myth . . . baseball wasn't invented in
Templeton or anywhere else, it developed, like plants
develop, out of other things . . .

Father looking weary, rubbing his eyes . . . "Sarah, I am
afraid I have bad news. We are not as rich as we once
were. The Crash was not good for us. Also, I have seen
how Templeton was about to spiral downwards, invested
much of my money in the town . . . The Hospital I built
for my good friend, Imogene Finch, the gymnasium on
Main, the electric streetlights I have put in, the Civil War
Memorial near the Knox School for Girls, the tennis
courts . . . Now, that work-initiative I have, Kingfisher
Tower . . . they are calling it 'Temple's Folly' . . . a great,
stone castle on the lake with a red tile roof . . . the men, I
am afraid, are taking advantage of me. I have seen red tile
roofs on a number of outhouses in this town . . . Oh,
Sarah, Sarah, what can I do? I am afraid, my girl, that
Templeton is dying."

Dying! He told me then of what I couldn't have
known: Prohibition killing the great Falconer hop-fields
all over the county—what remained had caught blight in
the early twenties and nowadays trickled to nothing—the
piano factory burnt down, the Phinney Printers moved

to Rochester, the mercantile factory in Hartwick
abandoned, the glove factory dead in Fly Creek. There
were the dairy farms now, and that was about it for
Templeton. People were poor, and getting poorer, he
said . . .

. . . my walk today . . . paint flaking from houses,
shutters swinging . . . gardens overrun with weeds,
squashes in old flower-patches . . . the streets rough, great
potholes, horses again . . . horses! In the Modern Era!
Lumps of manure everywhere! . . . a small urchin,
running by barefoot, in rags, grinning and holding a
pathetic little trout, still flapping, the boy so happy that he
would eat tonight . . . houses abandoned . . . Main Street
filled with empty storefronts, like vacant eyes . . . yes, my
father was right, there is death here . . . even that shrill
little girl in my head silent since I arrived . . . as if even
she were frightened . . .

. . . what can I do? The five days since my father told
me, the certainty that I *must* do something in me. What can
I do? My brain is only suited for literary analyses, not for
such mundane and essential problems as this! It is surely my
father's job to revive Templeton, but I fear he is too old.
And if Smith taught me anything, it is that women are as
capable as men, if not more so. I must save the town, it is
repeated in my head, a refrain, a Greek Chorus! I must save
the town! I have thought of my French class . . . Jeanne
D'Arc . . . La Pucelle . . . divine, inspired, leading her men
into battle like a winged thing . . . I think of her . . . but I
am no Saint, no genius, I am a girl who knows too much
to know anything at all . . .

. . . today motored out to Kingfisher Tower with my
father . . . Point Judith . . . the Tower is less pitiable than I
had imagined and far more sad . . . local fieldstone, it
seems to burst organically from the lakeside until it
explodes in decidedly unorganic red at the roof-level . . .

not lovely, but a fine monument of my father . . . smacks a bit of *droit de seigneur*, true, changing the entire landscape of the lake on a Temple's whim. I liked it, for all that it is awkward and unfinished . . . as my father talked to the men (all ten stopping work to chat with him), I found myself gazing at the lake. I had dreamt of it so often when I was away . . . a fine marbled green . . . the ducks landing joyfully, summer campers far away on their tiny sailboats, sweep of wind across the surface . . . but then something very strange happened. In the center of the lake, about a mile away, I was sure I had seen one vast *thing* surface for a moment, and then duck back in . . . must have been some great bubble of gas escaping from some subterranean vein under Glimmerglass . . . my own eyes tricking me. Then, Father still talking, I looked into the water below, and saw a head emerge from the grassy weeds . . . saw a body take form in the jagged lake-stone . . . a smiling little Indian, loincloth, *not* one of my private people, a *ghost*. A ghost! He pressed to the surface of the water as if pressed to glass, and I kneeled on the rocks . . . put my ear near the water to hear what he was saying . . . but my father's hand on my shoulder, I looked up . . . looked down again, and the little Indian was gone . . .

. . . tonight, that man from my childhood has returned to me, that man's voice in my head again, bassy, barrel-chested, archaic. He silences the shrill little girl. He speaks in thees and thous, like a one-man Bible. *Thou must save Templeton*, he says. How? I shout back in my head. *Thou must save Templeton*, he only repeats. *Thou must save Templeton. Thou must save Templeton. Thou must. Thou must. Thou must.*

. . . spent all morning at Council Rock, peering down, trying to see the Indian again . . . someone else began to appear . . . wild gray hair in the lake-lap, bulbous, screaming face, ancient clothing, a book—Bible?—in

hand . . . Just as this frightening person appeared, there
was a claxon. I turned around and saw a golden Cadillac,
an impossibly beautiful car, sliding around the bend . . .
who would honk a horn at a young woman? So
improper! And who in Templeton would buy such an
ostentatious car? Someone I knew, perhaps? Dr. Finch?
The Falconers, with their residual beery fortune? Nobody
I know could be so vulgar.

Oh, joy! My father's feet beating a tattoo of happiness on
the floorboards below . . . old man sprightly . . . here's what
happened: I can no longer sleep (much too energetic for
sleep), and this morning set off to do the shopping with my
little basket, in an old silk dress, much too tight across my
bust . . . down Main Street, I walked. Then I saw The Car.
The golden Cadillac from the day before, sitting in front of
Augur's Books, a man inside, reading the paper. I was . . .
furious. I have never before been so furious, it rose in me,
suddenly . . . "Your mother would be ashamed of you,
blaring your horn at a young woman you don't know," I
said . . . one corner of the newspaper down, two, revealing
blue eyes, a grinning face, rocky jaw, lips like a woman's . . .
handsome, I suppose . . . he said, "I'm so sorry! You looked
so lovely my hand slipped! Forgive me!" . . . only speaks in
expostulation, like a race-track announcer . . . loud! . . . just
as sudden, my fury turned to embarrassment. I hurried
away, but soon found the car idling—on the wrong side of
the road—beside me.

I stopped. "What do you want?" . . . but he leapt out
of the car, came to me, put his lips on my hand. My
stomach almost overturned then . . . paid me so many
compliments, my head spun . . . in the compliments, I
heard him say, "I am so sorry Templeton won't do for
our purposes, and that I must leave in an hour or so.
Else, I would have been glad to have the opportunity to
know you much, much better." . . . I ignored the
insolence, asked why Templeton wouldn't do . . . "Oh!

It's too small and isolated for our initiative. I'm the vice
president of the American National Baseball League, you
see. We have a major project in mind, and I am driving
about the Northeast in my car to see if I can find a proper
locale" . . . Initiative! I thought . . . something like
hallelujas in my head, the deep bassoon voice of the
Thou must save Templeton man, shouting *Huzzah!*
Huzzah? . . . I looked at the Cadillac man. "What is
your name?" I said . . . "Asterisk Upton, but ladies as
beautiful as you may call me Sy. And your name is,
Miss? . . ." the early morning twinkling in his eyes.
Asterisk Upton is a strange name for such an everyday
man. I decided I would call him Sy . . . realized he was
looking at me curiously . . . he smelled of good
tobacco . . .

"Temple," I said . . . he flushed, as if with pleasure,
saying, "As in Jacob Franklin Temple?" . . . "Yes. I am his
great-granddaughter." . . . "I owe your ancestor my life.
I almost dropped out of school at twelve to work, then
found a ratty copy of one of your great-grandfather's
novels . . ." He nattered on as I led him back to
Edgewater . . . Left Sy in the hall, went into my father's
office, told him everything . . . Sy surely wondering why
he was in this house, looking at me quizzically as I came
out. Those blue eyes on my face like a burn . . .

. . . two hours, they were in there, two . . . I saw my
father escort him down the drive, shake his hand . . .
Father ran back in, fleet as a young boy, burst into my
room . . . Sy had to explore more towns for the baseball
museum the league wanted to build—to help build the
Myth of Baseball—but my father convinced him to keep
Templeton in the running . . . to come back at the end of
July, and we'll have for him an offer he'd find most
attractive . . . "Sarah, darling, it looks as if you've quite
bewitched the man. He kept asking questions about
you" . . . my father grinning . . . "Sarah, darling, I am sure

that if you wished, you could have an offer from Mr.
Upton soon. He is a good man, growing rich, and it seems
that if he fulfills his duties on this visit, he will soon be
Baseball Commissioner . . ." . . . "But he is vulgar," I
cried, "that terrible booming laugh, those exclamatory
statements!" . . . "Ah, my darling, it will be difficult for
you to find a husband who is good enough for you" . . .
laughing, my father ran out to the bank . . . I ran to the
water closet, and heaved up the small breakfast I managed
before dawn. And, now, as I write, that golden Cadillac
has circled our block eight times: Fair to Main, Main to
River, River to Lake, Lake to Fair, around and around and
around. Now it is gone.

   . . . days pass, days pass, dark then light, Templeton
glowing in the fog, the brilliance of noon . . . the little
shrill girl is back, makes me want to bludgeon my head
with a carpet beater until she's out . . . so many ghosts in
the water I see now, every day I go down, press my ear
close to the water until I drench the small hairs on the
lobe . . . beseeching, mournful. The men have bloated
skin, and the women's hair has come loose and floats
cloudlike behind them, sunnies and pumpkinseed-fish
scattered in it . . . a man with my father's face, wrists
blooming roses of blood . . . two brothers with frosted
lashes and lips, ice skates on their feet, pounding at the
surface as if it were glass . . . small Indian girl who looks
at me with serene and unforgiving eyes as she floats,
naked, bruises like plums on her thighs . . . soldier in olive
drab, the stumps of his legs looking tender as a baby's
skin . . . young men in boater-hats, young women in tight
waists and bellish skirts from before the Civil War . . .
summer-camp children with crude leather bracelets on
their wrists . . . fat old ice fisherman . . . parachutist from
my childhood, the man who leapt from the plane at the
County Fair, but hit water, not land, whose chute settled
on the lake like a flower, filled with the water, dragged
him under before the boats could reach him. Yes: every

day I see more of them, the drowned ones. It is perhaps
not madness: they are so clear, and I am not terrified by
them. Is it? I don't know . . .

. . . families up at the station, with their filthy children! A
few days ago, I took all the girls to Standish's for new
undergarments and dresses and socks and shoes . . . they
pouted when I refused to buy them the pretty patent
leather shoes with bows on them, opting for the sensible
loafers . . . but the boys . . . little gentlemanly marvels, and I
couldn't resist buying them baseballs . . . now the girls think
I am their enemy. Their mothers, too . . . all in a clump
today, with their bags and hats . . . assuming I was about to
take *them* into town and buy *them* clothing . . . how angry I
was. Such presumption! . . . I dropped off the food I'd
brought, nodded, made small-talk for a moment with Mrs.
Burgess . . . very pointedly, she said, "I'm sorry I'm sniffling
so, Miss Temple. I have a terrible cold, and I find I've run
entirely out of handkerchiefs." . . . "Well, I shall bring you a
packet tomorrow." And I went straight home. I do fear
returning, for the anger of women is a frightful thing. The
little girl mocks and mocks me; my private people have
begun moving into the shadows of the house. I escape
them in the conservatory, though half the glass is broken
out . . . they daren't go to a place so bright . . .

. . . Kingfisher Tower was finished yesterday . . . a brass
band, watermelons . . . another postcard from Mr. Upton
today, a queer photo of a man and woman dancing, he
dipping her low. First, Springfield (a cow with a
"Welcome to Springfield" sign), then Concord (a terrible
drawing of "The Shot Heard Around the World"), now
Boston (and the dancers). All so cheery and without
return address, hinting rather crudely that the only charm
he has seen on his trip has been in Templeton . . . Father
puts them by my plate . . . I read every letter twice
through, before I pick up the postcard and skim it then
fling it away . . .

Father solidified the deal with the bank and not a
moment too soon . . . This is our deal: We rent the land
for the museum to the league and build it on our own
dime . . . we pay over three hundred thousand dollars to
the league for the honor (a bribe—my word!) . . . Now
Sy is back, Sy drove back directly into Edgewater's drive,
his golden car all caked with dirt . . . seersucker suit wet
with sweat . . . apologetic . . . didn't explain why he
didn't take time to wash or deliver his things to the hotel,
but the way he looked at me, it was clear. My mother
nudged me forward to take his hand, cold like ice in his
hot hand . . . sick, sick, I could barely control my
stomach . . . Father delicately scheduling a lunchtime
conference, giving Sy time to bathe . . . Now, Sy has
returned. Holding such a tremendous bouquet of flowers
from the florist's that he hid his head behind the roses and
trailed a group of urchins . . . I scolded them for not
wearing shoes . . . "Boys, where are those shoes I bought
for you? Don't you know walking barefoot can give you
diseases?" . . . Aw-shucks shufflings, "Oh, Miss Temple,
we was saving them for school" . . . broke my heart . . .
and all the time, Sy waiting behind his flowers, his face
beet-red, until I took the vulgar display from him, trying
to smile.

Such an awkward lunch! Roses huge in the middle of
the table. Orphan Sally serving sullenly. Sy's booming
voice telling stories about the towns he was in, my mother
captivated. So captivated she didn't speed off to the
Orphanage at the end of lunch, as has been her wont to do
since I returned home . . . Sy barely touched a thing . . .
neither did I . . . every time I went to take a bite, I felt
those *asterisk* eyes boring into the part in my hair.

The men disappeared into the study at the end, and
here I am, writing. Waiting to see if my town will be
saved. The voices in my skull are silent, thank goodness.
The ghosts and others have hidden themselves . . . Oh,

my! Just now I can see my father walking Sy down the end of the drive. Is that a slump in my father's shoulders? It is, I fear. Sy is shaking his hand, speaking earnestly. My father is smiling, but tightly and nods now, and clasps Sy's shoulder. They are parting. I must run downstairs to see what is the matter.

Disaster: Manhattan has far outbid us . . . more than a million dollars, and an entire city block dedicated to the museum. It is *The Center of the World*, says Sy. We are *A Very Tiny Village in the Middle of Nowhere*. This will *Make Sy's Career*. Hateful common, vulgar man. I fear my father is weeping behind his door, but I daren't go in. My mother's face has grown pale, and she has stalked off to the Orphanage. Little Sally is beheading daisies on the drive . . . couldn't be more eloquent if she could speak . . . I will go for a walk to calm myself, to see if I can chase these shrieking voices from my head . . .

. . . more disaster! . . . I stood on Council Rock, trying to summon one of my friends from the water, and felt a gaze at my back. I turned around, and there he was, Mr. Upton, watching me . . . such fury—I have never felt this before—seems to have come from someone else, greater and much more angry than I ever have been . . . I leapt from the rock and crashed through the water, staining my skirts dark, weeds clinging to my legs . . . I ran at him, but I think he thought it was in a different passion than the one I felt, because he caught me in his arms and kissed me . . . those womanly lips on mine . . . all the while I was flailing, I was trying to kick him, I was a wild thing . . . he pushed me down, he pushed up my skirts, I do think something terrible would have happened, but I was so maddened I broke away . . . ran home, he running behind me . . . "Sarah, goddamnit, stop it, I have to talk to you! Sarah, stop, your father has already agreed!" . . . I ran into the house. I saw from behind my curtain in my room as he stood in the lawn, cradling my shoes in his hands

like birds. He put them down carefully in the rose-bed,
stalked away . . . my stomach, sour . . . my head filled
with so many voices, the little girl, the biblical man . . .
my heart broken, for Templeton, my dying town . . .

My father's manners are made of iron—he had invited
Mr. Upton to dinner . . . not a pleasant affair. My mother
and I were barely civil: I never looked at him. I just
wanted the bastard whoreson gone. My father, the old
gentleman, chatted amiably, though Mr. Upton had aged
him ten years this day. I had dressed for the occasion, in
my best emerald dress, raw silk, the color of my eyes. I
was as beautiful as I could be . . . a petty thing to do, to
be sure, to show him what he's losing by choosing
Manhattan over our small and lovely Templeton . . . Mr.
Upton seeming to plead with me via the claketing of his
knife and fork . . . again, neither of us ate a thing . . . At
the end of dessert, I steamed out, and Mr. Upton—such
a tasteless man—ran after me, took my arm in the
hallway . . . hissing, "All's not lost, Sarah, don't be a fool.
You can still save your town if you like," turning around,
leaving me there, in the hallway, as he went back into the
dining room. My knees were knocked from me. I sat hard
in a chair. And I listened, there, as my father, bound by
good taste . . . not understanding . . . was kind to this
terrible man . . . my mother, won by what she saw as a
romantic display for her beloved, beautiful, insane (thus
unmarriageable) daughter . . . even my common-sensical,
pure-hearted mother . . . had begun to talk pleasantly
with him again.

It is growing late. It is eleven o'clock. I have been
pacing, in my room. Over all the voices, the stentorian
man booms and booms. *Thou must, thou must, thou must.*
Booms and booms. The Methodist Church bell rings, as
does the Presbyterian. I have not taken off my dress. I have
vomited time and again until my stomach is squeezed raw
and my throat burns. I have brushed my teeth until my

gums bleed. I have put my hair into a severe knot at my neck, but the curls insist on coming out. Yes, I will go.

It is over . . . it is all over. That is all I can write for now.

. . . I did it, but I don't understand it . . . not that night two weeks ago. Not I who slipped my shoes on, and crept down the curved stairs of Edgewater. Not I who came out into the fresh, green-smelling night, and stole to the end of the drive, and ran, fleet as my legs could carry me, down Fair, Lake, past Lakefront Park, Averell Cottage, up Chestnut Street. I wasn't the one who stole into the Motor Inn so quietly the snoozing desk clerk didn't awaken, or scanned the keys behind his head for the one that was missing, number nine, or stole up the stairs and stood before the door, stalwart, brave. No knocking before I went in . . . Mr. Upton, though he had freshly shaven for me, must not have believed his luck, because he dropped the cigarette, and the ashes skittered across the carpet . . . we stood before one another like this for a long time . . . he moved forward, grinning . . . but I stopped him, hand against his shirt, feeling the heart beat hard in my hand . . . "Not yet. You will choose Templeton, yes?" . . . "Yes, oh, yes. Yes, Sarah, yes." I put my face up to his, to be kissed, but he put his hand on my lips . . . "Not yet . . . you will marry me, yes?" Grinning, a dimple in his cheek. A slow overturning inside me . . . the man in my head said *Yes, thou shalt marry this man, my sparrow* . . . the me who wasn't me said, "Yes."

And I was not sick, not the way I had imagined . . . scooped me up and undressed me, button by button . . . there was heat there . . . and more . . . and the two Sarahs battled with herself, the one disgusted, the other avid . . . even for the pain, there was a great deal of pain . . . my lipstick smeared on his face . . . awoke to see him gazing at me in the dawn light, moving a curl back behind my

ear . . . it is true . . . he does love me . . . I have seen him
so often in company since, Templeton's prettiest girls all
around, dressed up as much as they can . . . and his eyes
never leave my face . . .

. . . but even then, I knew I would be filled with this
new person until the wedding, this warm person with
happiness inside of her . . . and then that person would
leave me, even then I knew this . . . I will be cold, and sad
again after this . . . until the wedding, I will see no more
of my private people, hear nothing more, the words in my
mouth will be appropriate and good, and no more ghosts
will rise in the water . . . I knew we would be married in
Kingfisher Tower on Point Judith in the autumn, and the
maple leaves will swirl in the water, gold, and red, and
green . . . we will be married and I already have a child in
me, growing, I am certain, I can feel this . . . Templeton
will already have been revitalized, my father's coffers
emptied, but soon to be refilled with rent from the
Baseball Museum . . . I will be married on that Autumn
day, and the woman who possesses me even now, the happy
girl who cannot stop kissing this handsome man . . . the
girl who that morning a week ago walked back to
Edgewater, sore as the first time she ever rode Western
(why did I ever try to ride Western?), walking back in the
sweet, dim dawn with him, hand in hand, in the early
fog . . . who sat with him, giggling, at the breakfast table
until her parents awoke and came down . . . who surprised
her parents with her happiness, with her sanity that
morning . . . this girl will leave on my wedding day . . . this
was not the man I was meant to marry, not the genius, not
the artist . . . I will feel his vulgarity keenly, and he won't
know why I spurn him, but will only want me more.

And I know that soon after the wedding, the voices
will return, slowly. The child I have in me already will be
born, maybe more. And the ghosts in the lake will rise
and follow me, calling, until the day . . . when I will be

too weak to resist, and I will walk into the lake . . . until then, though, there is Sy, the solidity of him . . . yes, and though it won't last, this morning, writing here, Sy snoring in my bed behind me and I, just about to awaken him so that he can sneak from the house and back to the hotel . . . right now, right now, I am strange. It is strange. This life is strange. For now, only for now, I am happy.

Hannah Clarke, years before she married Henry Franklin Temple.

She is pictured in Baden-Baden, on a grand European tour with her mother (right). In about a week, while they're touring Luzerne, she will meet an Italian waiter at the hotel and will steal out with him for what she believes to be an innocent midnight boat ride. Unfortunately, he had other plans; he kidnapped her, and she was rescued three days later in Vienna, an episode that never failed to send her into terrific fits of giggles, even up to her ninth decade of life.

Leavings: Or, What Is Left Behind

ALL THAT NIGHT, I read three hundred pages of wildness in my great-grandmother's tight sepia script, and in the morning it was as if Templeton had fallen under an enchantment.

As I sat there, stunned, watching the distant sunrise rub the dark from the sky, I felt almost as if Sarah's Templeton were layered atop my own; as if a sheet of tracing paper had settled upon the rooftops of my village, and on it was a detailed drawing of a simpler Templeton. Some houses, some stores, some streets I knew had disappeared, and fields and copses and other buildings took their place; paint flaked off the oldest buildings, layer by layer; great trees contracted until they were tiny saplings and then seeds; old men spun younger and firmer until they shrank rapidly and weren't even a glimmer in an eye. I could feel the pull of the ghosts in the lake, knew that if I looked out onto the lawn those terrible private people of whom Sarah spoke would be standing there, in military lines all the way down the lawn, all looking up into my window, deep holes for eyes.

But then, at the base of Lakefront Park, a truck rumbled to life and shattered the spell. The truck coughed, and then the brakes squealed off. The monster, I realized, had begun to move.

I ran down the hall of my ancestors, feeling their many little eyes upon my back. I opened the door and flew onto the front lawn. All down Lake Street, Templetonians were hurrying out of their doors, slippers missing, bathrobes flapping, hair mussed. The truck came into view, turned left onto Lake Street, roaring. It straightened itself out and began to speed up.

In silence, we watched as the monster drew near. We looked at the tarp that covered the corpse, how, in the wind, one corner opened to reveal a delicate hand curled on its chest. We did not speak to one another, we did not acknowledge we were standing there, neighbors, watching; that we, just by watching, were made complicit in giving the great beast up for study. And we did not breathe in the murky dank rot but held our breath to watch until the truck passed us and pulled away. We watched until the monster was too far down the street to see. Some of us leapt into cars to follow.

In the silent cortege of cars behind the departing Glimmey, there were no tourists, no summer visitors, only native Templetonians. And I saw that one of the escorts was Ezekiel Felcher. His tow truck glowed yellow, and he was inside, singing to himself, holding his hat to his heart.

I turned to go back inside to find Vi standing on the flagstone porch, clutching her batik robe around her. "It feels strange this morning," she said, studiously not looking at me. "Templeton. It seems a little emptier, perhaps. I think."

I only nodded at her and went in.

THAT MORNING, BEFORE going to bed to sleep off my long night, I sat at the old farmhouse table with Vi. She bowed her head over her cornflakes and said a long, silent prayer, and when she looked up and sprinkled sugar on her cereal, I said, "Vi. That's really not so good for you. Extra sugar." I looked at her mound of a belly, the great twin bergs of her breasts and said, "You never had that stuff when I was growing up. And as a nurse you should know better."

She frowned and put the spoon down. "Not your business."

"I want my mother to be healthy. It is my business."

"I am forty-six years old, Williekins," she said. "I suffered through organic peanut butter and tofu for far too long when you were little, and by golly, if I want my cereal to be a little sweet in my middle age, it'll be a little sweet." Her face had flushed and she was looking fierce.

"Wait," I said, beginning to laugh, "I always thought you did all that organic vegetarian stuff because you *liked* it."

"Oh, my goodness, no," she said. "No, no. I did it for you. For your health."

"For me?" I said. "For me? It was for me that you handed out apples on Halloween? That the first time I tasted a glazed cruller at Petra Tanner's I almost puked? That you'd said I was allergic to processed sugar, and when people brought in birthday cupcakes in kindergarten, I had to sit there eating carrot sticks while everyone else chomped into cake? That was for *me*?"

She gave a little humph and said nothing.

"Well, thanks so much," I said. But somehow the Lump made itself present again, a little twisting twinge in my gut, and I no longer wanted to follow the path of my argument to its end. Instead, I said, "It must've been painful for you, too. Sign of an excellent mother."

"Damn tooting," she said and dug into her cereal with vigor.

"Anyway," I said, "I just wanted to run this by you. My progress, I mean, on the father front. Or lack thereof. But you said you wanted to know last night, so here goes." I took a deep breath, and she looked at me with interest. "One," I said, testing her. "My father is not the product of any extramarital shenanigans on the part of your parents. He's not, say, a half-brother, in any way."

She stopped chewing and cocked her head and said, "No. I did not sleep with my brother, Willie, thank you very much."

"Right," I said. "I thought that'd be a little odd. And, two: your mother's parents didn't have anything to do with it either. At least Claudia Starkweather, Hetty the slave's great-great-granddaughter, didn't. I'm just basing that on a hunch from her wedding photograph. Your grandparents didn't seem the type. They seemed. Well, celibate."

Vi blinked and said, "I'm guessing you're doing this backward. Most recent ancestors to least recent, correct? You've ruled out my parents, so on to my grandparents?"

"Yes," I said. "Clarissa told me that's what she'd do. I thought it was smart."

My mother nodded slowly and said, as if she were very, very distant from me, "She's a clever girl, my Clarissa."

"Am I right, though? Can you tell me if Claudia Starkweather was the source of the illegitimacy?"

"She wasn't the source," she said, still musing. "Nope, she wasn't."

"Okay. And so I looked at the other side of the family, your dad's parents, Sy and Sarah. So, here I'm making an assumption that whatever happened there must've been adultery, because she seemed pretty virginal before Sy. Frigid, almost. But, I don't really think there was adultery, of course; nothing that easy. Though I did find out some pretty crazy stuff, Vi. Apparently, Sarah was insane. Schizophrenic, I'd say—she saw ghosts and heard voices and things like that. And she bartered herself away to Sy because Templeton was really suffering in the Depression and he wouldn't let the baseball museum come to town unless she married him."

"Oh, my," said Vi. "So the rumors are true, then."

"Yup," I said.

My mother clicked her tongue and put her spoon down. "I hate that," she said, "though, if you think about it, that's not so different from what traditional marriage was supposed to be. Women like cattle to be given from one man to another. Disgusting, really."

I looked at the woman before me, suddenly feeling warm; the old Vi was still in there with the new religious freak. When I was little, she'd wear inflammatory tee shirts to PTA meetings that said A WOMAN NEEDS A MAN LIKE A FISH NEEDS A FISHHOOK and SCREW PHYLLIS SCHLAFLY. PLEASE, SOMEBODY, SCREW HER. There was one time, during a movie at the grand stone library—we went to every free, educational event in town when I was a child—when the camera panned over a sleeping San Francisco, wreathed in fog, and I saw Vi's eyes fill and threaten to overspill with tears. I felt longing rolling off her in waves, and knew, at that moment, at barely seven years old, that she would have been much, much happier in a larger place, somewhere cosmopolitan, surrounded by people like her. I sat in the dark and held my breath and prayed to whatever secular god I believed in then for the welling in my mother's eyes to not become actual tears, to stay where they were, because if they did, I would know that she was giving up more than she could bear to give up so that I could be raised in Templeton. I watched, in terrible suspense, but they didn't spill. At the last minute, she looked at me in the darkness, and smiled, and when she looked back at the screen her eyes had dried. Now, this morning, I watched her metal cross swing and swing, and, remembering the hippie of my youth, said, "Vi, how do you reconcile your old feminism with your new Christianity?"

" 'I am large, I contain multitudes.' " She laughed at my expression and said, "I read, too, Sunshine." I smiled at her. When I was little, she'd have a line for everything: on watching boys jump off the docks at Fairy Springs, she'd blink and say: " 'How the boys/with dare and with downdolphinry and bellbright bodies huddling out/are earth-world, airworld, waterworld, thorough hurled, all by turn and turn about.' Hopkins." Or, walking home on a dark winter's night from a school play, my mother would see Cartwright Field glinting in the pale light and mutter, " 'Studded with stars in ball and crown, the Stadium is an adastrium,' " and take my hand and squeeze it, saying, "Marianne Moore." Now, as she stood to rinse out her bowl, my mother still looked pleased at herself for quoting Whitman.

"Vi?" I said. "Sarah's journal cuts off really suddenly. Just after she gets engaged to Sy. Do you have any idea what happened to her? You said you'd asked your great-grandmother and she might've been bats, but what did she say?"

"Well," my mother said. "As far as I know, after she gets engaged, she gets married. She has my father, and he comes out a month prematurely. And then, when he's two months old, she does a Virginia Woolf, walks into the lake with rocks in her pockets. Drowns, of course. When I was a stupid kid, about nine, I think, I asked my great-grandmother, Sarah's mother, about her. Hannah Clarke Temple. I'd seen that picture of Sarah upstairs, the one from her graduation, and thought she was so gorgeous. My great-grandmother was this wrinkled old dowager who wore huge pearls like hen's eggs around her neck and glared at everyone and tried to hit at dogs and birds and small children with her cane. For a minute I thought she was going to brain me, but instead she just spoke long and fast, in this little whisper, and said she'd never seen her daughter so happy, never, not even as a little girl, than when she was engaged to Sy. She was a beam of light, her dark, sad daughter. And then, as soon as my father was born, it was as if a switch went off. She fell darker and darker, until she seemed buried under this thick, velvety cloud of sadness. And my great-grandmother knew it was coming and that nothing she did could stop it."

"Why?" I said. "How did she know?"

"The housemaid had found a list of all the people who had ever died in the lake in Sarah's room, that's how," said Vi. "They found it when she came home after she spent the summer with her half-brothers in Manhattan. Sarah had done her research. My great-grandmother was horrified. Burnt the thing. Sad," Vi said. "For a long time I thought it'd make a good poem."

My mother stood and washed out her bowl. She seemed buoyant now, breezy. "I'd love to chat some more, I really would, but I'm off to ease the dying," she said. "Search long and hard today, and discover all you can. I'm here if you want to talk tonight." She moved toward the door, then turned around with a new idea, her fleshy face folded in delight. "And unless you want to pay rent for the rest of the summer, sweetpea, you really have to get going on your chores. The house needs a dusting. Maybe a vacuum. It should only take an hour or two. Have at it." And then, chuckling, she was gone.

IN THE MIDST of dusting that afternoon, my eyes still glued at the corners with sleep, I realized that my mother had been looting the attic. When she had first come back to Templeton and found herself pregnant, an orphan, in charge of a huge house, she'd been irritated with the overstuffed nature of her mother's taste and had packed all the tchotchkes and other unnecessary things away. The Averell Cottage of my childhood was spare, almost spartan, every shelf of the corner cupboard and every surface of the furniture bare, nothing on the mantels. She had taken away all the unnecessary furniture and most of the pictures, too. Had she had a choice of where to live, I believe my mother would have been most happy in a light-filled glass box, with blond Scandinavian furniture and slate floors. A house not unlike Primus Dwyer's, in fact.

Now, though, in the time I'd been away from Templeton, a little over two years, *things* had appeared. A little bronze model of the Mohican and dog statue in Lakefront Park on the formal parlor's mantel;

ancient china and colored glassware in the corner cupboard in the dining room; many more old oils on the walls; everything presided over by a cunningly executed little horse on wheels on the vast dining room table, a cheeky-looking, very old toy. I lifted it from the table and held it in my hands. It was heavy, actual horsehair over a carved wooden frame, with bright glass eyes under the dust and a perfect little bridle and saddle set.

I looked the horse in the eye. "What," I said, "could Vi have meant by digging you up, little one?" And then I looked around the room, noting the new ferns in their antique willowware pots, the unnecessary sideboard, the paintings. The room felt, for the first time, comfortable and complete, as if Vi had reluctantly given in to the necessity of living in Templeton and had allowed herself to admit that she wasn't going anywhere.

"Aha," I said aloud. "I see my mother has decided to stay in Templeton."

But it wasn't until I came home that evening, exhausted after a fruitless trip to the library and little Peter Lieder's bright eagerness, that I began to understand the change. All day I had been looking into Sarah's half-brothers as the possible source of my father but had found no evidence that they ever came back to Templeton after they were sent off to private school. There were boarding school bills that Sarah's father, Henry, had paid, with extra charges for boarding over holidays and the summers; there were pleading letters in Henry's quiet, kind voice, asking his sons to forgive him for having married Hannah so soon after their mother, Monique, had died of an aneurysm, and to urge them to come and meet their sweet new sister.

"My boys," Henry had admonished in one letter. "There is nothing more important than family. Do not take out your anger with me on your new stepmother or your sister."

The boys, aged eleven and thirteen when their mother died, never did come to terms again with their father, and only reluctantly met their sister at her high school graduation from Emma Willard, when they were both married attorneys in Manhattan. Since they never lived in Templeton, or even visited the place, it was easy to rule them out as possible father-sources. But still, I felt sad for old Henry, Sarah's father, who died brokenhearted, with all his children already dead or turned against him.

On the long walk home, I began brooding over my other troubles. When I was in the house, my heart would race every other hour, sure that the telephone was ringing and Primus Dwyer was calling me. I was wrong—the phone never rang, and every other hour, the ache I felt that he hadn't yet called deepened. And the Lump was gathering weight in my gut, omnipresent, though I knew that at two months it was barely an eraser head, still splitting and splitting into nondiscernable parts. That evening as I walked into Averell Cottage, I was sunk in such a bog of my own thoughts that I ignored the pile of homely kicked-off shoes and walked right into the trap.

I first became aware of the air having changed—there was a slight coolness to it, a sense of damp wool. And then I heard the voice, a deep bass and yet unctuous, singsonglike—like an oiled bassoon.

". . . oh, let us pray now," it was saying, "for she who is the child of our dear sister in Christ, Vivienne Upton, let us pray for her in this trying time in her life; not that her hardships fade and she lives a life free of them, for all men must have hardship; but rather that she learns from her travails, and that she feels the gentle grace of God's bosom, through the gift of the light of Christ . . ."

By that time, my stunned eyes were able to understand what they were seeing in the living room. A circle of people in dull clothing, hands held, heads bent, all lit golden from the last sun. A pillowy white mess of a preacher, his gelled comb-over flapping like a hand as he prayed. My mother at the head of the circle, looking up at me, inscrutable. And everyone sitting in my living room was wearing the same heavy iron cross.

"What," I said, interrupting the minister's deep drone, "in the hell do you all think you're doing?"

One old lady looked up at me, and though she had the sweet round cheeks of a grandma, a grandma's marshmallowy hair, the fury in her expression was searing.

But nobody else opened their eyes and the minister didn't stop, but, rather, hurried up so that his words elided; "and-keep-her-from-the-devil-and-give-her-strength-to-withstand-temptation-and-give-her-peace-in-the-name-of-Christ-our-Lord-Amen."

"Amen," said everyone, and looked up at me, beaming, save for Vi, who was gazing at her knees, avoiding me now.

"Vi?" I said. "What in the hell is this?"

The skim-milk minister rose to his feet and folded his fat white hands across his belly. "Wilhelmina," he said, "we were giving you a gift. A prayer for your time of trouble, for your everlasting soul."

"Oh, screw my everlasting soul," I said.

One old lady gasped; one old man clucked and said, "Devil got your tongue, missy."

"Screw the devil," I said. "You don't come into someone's house and ambush them with prayers, not if they don't believe in all that crap. You just don't. This is insane."

"Willie," my mother snapped. "You're being rude."

"Rude?" I said, puffed and self-righteous. "Me? Well, Vivienne, I'm sorry, but rude is telling the whole town that your daughter's a fuckup, Vivienne. Rude is forcing someone to be the beneficiary of a religion she finds insulting and the basis of everything that has gone wrong with the world. Vi, *you* were rude. You were the rude one. Not me."

"Wilhelmina," boomed the minister, pointing at me. "That is your mother you are addressing, and she deserves your respect. You should be ashamed."

I stared at him so darkly that a hint of a flush came over his pasty face. "You," I said, "are the one who should be ashamed. You are a nasty con artist. Now get your cult out of my house," and I spun and slammed the door to the dining room, and then I slammed the door from the parlor to the hall, and then I slammed the door at the top of the stairs, and then I slammed the door of my room.

I forgot for a moment that I was twenty-eight; I felt thirteen again, wild and hormonal. I pitched the stuffed animals from the bassinet against the wall, one by one, where on impact they puffed out seventeen years of dust. When the Bible-beaters lingered in leaving, I punched my pillow so hard my hand seized up for a few days. Out of the corner of my eye, I caught sight of myself in the mirror, and for the first time I saw that I was flushed prettily, back to my flashing, good-looking self. The stupidity of vanity at such a time. So silly. I gave a little low laugh.

It was unfortunate that my mother chose that moment to storm into my room. "Oh," she said. "I'm so glad you find it hilarious to humiliate your mother in front of her friends."

"Please," I said. "You insane person. Of course you're the put-upon one, aren't you. When you've told the whole town that I slept with a married professor and have been visited with punishment for my adultery in the form of some godless heathen bastard. I should be apologizing to you, right?"

"Actually, yes. They were only being kind. And I never told anyone why you're here."

"Right. Out of nowhere, they felt compelled to say a prayer for me in my time of need. Because they had no idea I was in trouble."

A ripple of—what was it? impatience? mirth?—came over Vi's face. "Reverend John Melkovitch is a very spiritual man," she said. "I'm sure he figured it out all by himself."

I turned away from my mother, then, toward the flat lake. Although it was a fine, hot day, nobody was out; there were no motorboats, no Jet Skis, no swimmers at Fairy Springs or the country club that I could see. The lake seemed lackluster, moody.

"And about that Reverend Milky, anyway," I said. "What a total creep. So bland and nasty. You can tell from a mile away he's just a total phony. I'm disappointed in your choice of spiritual guides, Vi. As if you couldn't choose some yogi or monk or anything more suited to who you are. I mean, a Christian Coalitioner! Probably doesn't believe in Social Security or women's rights. Probably thinks the best people I know are going to hell just because they don't see the world in the same, narrow, revisionist sort of way that assholes like that do. I'm afraid you've been taken in, there, Vivienne. I'm afraid for you, really afraid."

There was a long silence then and when my mother spoke, she was close to my ear and her voice was very low. "Well, that's a shame," she said. "Because he's more than my minister, Willie. We've been dating for about nine months. Seriously. Just so you know."

I was too stunned to say anything, and so she just turned triumphantly and stomped out the door. There, she said in her martyr's voice, "Dinner will be at seven, Sunshine. *Tomates farcis*, your favorite," and then she went out the door.

"Reverend Milky is *so* not your taste," I called out, but she just heaved an enormous sigh and clomped down the stairs.

• • •

WHEN I CALLED Clarissa and the answering machine picked up, *Hey, it's Clarissa Evans and Sullivan Bird. Be brief but nice,* I put on my best Nancy Drew voice, a WASPy chirp.

"The Mystery of the Miraculous Christian Transformation is suddenly revealed; call for your exciting new installment of Willie Upton, girl detective. I'll be up all night doing genealogical questing and praying for a phone call from a certain dark, handsome Brit, so call at any time, and don't be offended if I am at first disappointed. Love you both. Bye."

I was lighthearted, almost ditzy, but when I hung up, I felt wrung out. And when I went downstairs for dinner, I ate my tomatoes before my mother even finished her prayer and took my glass of milk upstairs, to be alone. I had come home to become a child again. I was sick, heartbroken, worn down, teetering between either abortion or unplanned motherhood, and my mother was allowing me to act like a child. I was carrying on like a teenager, all hormones and grief. Though I was furious with her, there was a little tired piece of me that was grateful, relieved.

11

Hetty Averell

MOST TIMES, I can look at a man and see if I can run him. Most times I can, even ones who don't look like any woman could. See it straight out in Duke. That day in Philadelphia he's buying slaves to make Templeton, in the stinking slavehouse. Big, silent Mingo to help build things. Cuff, the Indian boy, to write for Duke. Duke can't spell, and Cuff, he writes like the brightest angels in the sky.

Duke goes to the door with those two behind him. I put my eyes on him, I like his looks. Red hair under all that powder. Tall, built like a bull. Good, dark clothes like Quaker clothes, but I know he's no real Quaker because no Quaker buys slaves. So I burn my eyes on him. He feels it. Turns around, slow-slow, looks at me. Got my shirt off and the men are examining my breasts and teeth and they are beautiful and my skin is shining like water. I am eighteen or twenty then and a beautiful girl. I'm not vain, it's a truth. Already have two babies though they left back in Jamaica. I come at age ten, eleven from Africa to Jamaica, eighteen, twenty from Jamaica to

Philadelphia. They sell me for having a long tongue but that is all lies. Truth is, my master, MacAdam, I run him easy. Make him a rich man. When he dies Widow MacAdam don't like me, puts a hot poker around my neck, one by one, makes me a pink necklace on my skin. Hate her then, but can't say I blame her, running her man like I done.

That day, Duke don't want to buy slaves but don't have a choice, no good dentured servants anywhere. All is sickly, none have any skills. So he comes to the stinking slavehouse but not ready to buy humans, gets sick, almost leaves. But then he sees Cuff almost took by an evil-looking man. Duke sees the evil clear, that fat man licking those red lips at the pretty Indian boy. So Duke buys him. Has a son Cuff's age, and I think it is because of Richard he buys Cuff. Then he sees Mingo, sees how he does good woodwork, buys him too. Thinking, I'm already a slaveowner, might as well get a house out of it. When he's about to go, I burn my eyes on him. Turn him around. We look at each other and there's a flash between us. He buys me.

Expect he's lonely. Missus Temple, she refuses to come to Templeton, all rough as it is then. She has a life in Burlington, books and company and music and her father. Tell the truth, expect Missus don't want Templeton at all. So many years Duke tries to get her to come and she says No. No, no, no. She's afraid. But he's lonely and works too much. Remarkable Prettybones the housekeeper can't cook a whit, burns the porridge, burns the ham. I call her Remarkable Uglybones, that witch. I come and start to cook and Duke begins to get fatter again. Looks happier. I feel his eyes on me all day long.

Duke is a good man, I'll grant. Struggles. Don't touch me, not for a long time. And if he don't touch me, I can't run him, works that way. Magic like that. And in the beginning, Duke, he's so busy he don't even have time to touch me, selling land faster than a man could breathe, out all day surveying, riding to Albany, riding to Philadelphia, riding to his family in Burlington. But I run the house good. Cook good food, make a beautiful house. I like things neat-neat, clean as a Sunday morning. Mingo, he builds Temple Manor almost by his lonesome, huge and stone with a yellow roof. But I am the one to make it nice, the whitewash, the curtains, the varnish, though Remarkable takes the credit, that ugly skinny toad. I do the cooking, and even in famine with all the Templeton babies screaming for food, we always have food. I buy our meat from Davey up the hill, and Mingo, he catches fish. I catch fish with Mingo, too, but the one time I go with him in his little boat I seen a huge, bad thing deep in the water, and Mingo puts his hand on my leg and it is all I can do to fight him off and not tip into the water for whatever it is down deep, ready to eat me alive. Never again do I go, never again. Just because we're both dark doesn't mean I'm meant for Mingo I tell him. He leaves me be after that.

Even though I fill her belly, Remarkable is not my friend. She stares at me, suspicious. Brings that little angel Cuff on her side and makes him hate me, too. For some time, Cuff and me was friends, taught me to read a little. Words like *water, apple, snake, horse*. But Remarkable, she gets her hands on him, changes him. It hurts but I got a mean streak so I call him Little Poof. Your breakfast is ready, Little Poof. Go fetch some water, Little Poof. Turns out I tell the truth, cause a few years later he runs off with a traveling preacher-man and turns out to be a little poof, after all.

The day comes we move into the Manor. My room's off the kitchen, and I know it's coming. Duke is hungry, starving for it. Think may well be me as anyone, certainly won't be Remarkable Uglybones, and anyways I can run him if it's me. I oil my limbs, set the taper ready. There's a knock on the door. I open and see Duke falling over himself, trembling, pale as a mealybug. I bring him in.

Tell the truth, I don't like it. Never have. What I do like is the running. Making men do what I want. That, I like.

I run Duke so gentle he don't see it. Need to do it that way for the menfolk think themselves bigger than anybody and you can't threaten their bigness. I get him to make changes to Templeton, move the market to Second Street, not First, build the courthouse, build the icehouse down by the lake. For years I run him. The town is a big success. Marmaduke gets rich, then richer. Richest.

The day Jedediah Averell come into town on a donkey I see him, sweeping the porch, I see him, I take a long look at him. Not much to look at, all hunched and ugly, but I see the iron in his back, the strength of him and I say, Hetty, that man there's going to *be* something. And I say, Hetty, you can run that man. Know it first look. Later Averell watches me wherever I go and I feel his eyes on me and I smile. I wait on him, though. Bide my time.

Though I'm careful, go to Aristabulus Mudge every month for herbs, I get with child. Bad news. Remarkable, she sees it immediate. She works on Cuff, and one day he puts my news in a letter Duke dictates for Missus Temple. Duke never reads the letters Cuff writes, account that Cuff is perfect in his writing, so he doesn't know what's in it. Duke signs his name, sends them off. He misses the mention of me, and I don't even think Missus Temple even knows of me before that letter. And she's in Burlington, she's with child, too, with Jacob, and she reads this. Goes a little crazed, sets off that very day with her big son Richard, even though she's eight months gone with a child that kicks her day in, day out. Hops into a carriage and off she goes, like a madwoman. Jostling for weeks over those pitted roads in hired hacks and wagons, sleeping on flea-bitten mattresses, chewing gristle and hardtack. She, a porcelain cup. A wonder she don't break.

I know the Missus's carriage is coming from a mile away, somehow, put on my pretty pink calico, tie my hair back. And she comes into the drive, her little face pale, round in surprise at the big house. First time she's seen it, and I don't know what she's thinking all these years, maybe we live in the trees like the bears. But Duke, he comes running out of the house, joyous, shouting, and Richard, he jumps out to hug him, only fourteen and already so hairy, and Missus Temple, she pries herself out, fat with her baby, but so very tiny. I'm twice near as big as her. She's a little wren. Could break in my fingers like a twig, though I never would do it to her. I pity her, somehow.

And I pity her still, even after she looks at me, eyes burning. Even after she walks around me in one circle, two, three. Even after she says, Marmaduke, I don't want no slave in the house, though she don't say it about Mingo or Cuff, just me. She says, Marmaduke, I don't want no slave in my house. I am a Quaker, she says. Get rid of her. Today, get rid of this ugly wench today. And still I am not angry with her although I am *not* an ugly wench and she knows it, too.

So that day after my chores I slip up to see Duke in his study. Missus Temple collapsed, sleeps for two days entire, I'll hear. Duke's near to crying. Oh, Hetty, I'm so very sorry, he says. In the dark, with one taper, he looks older than he is.

I sit beside him. I say, Duke, no matter. You go on and give me to that tanner on Front Street, that Jedediah Averell. You'll see. He's a good man, he'll marry me, even if I am black. I say, Oh, and Duke, careful. I say, Duke, take a look at the boy I am to have in a few months. You'll see someone in him you love dear.

Duke, he's both happy and sad, wants to set me up with my very own inn in Albany so that I can have his son. But I say no. No, Duke, Templeton's mine, my own place. I have moved enough in this hard life. I'll be nobody's slave in a week, I'll be a wife. In one week, you'll see. A wife.

Next day I go to Averell with all my things tied in an apron. Knock at the door. He's working in the tannery in the back by the lake, and the terrible strong smell there has made his eyes water. He looks up with his water-eyes, turns red. I say to him, Judge Temple is giving me to you. I'm yours, I say. I say this and smile in his eyes.

In a week, I run him. In two I'm a married woman. The day my son comes, five months too soon for Jedediah, he holds the big boy in his arms. He looks into the pale face, the red hair. He sees the one eyeball gone untied in the boy's head. How it wanders, and maybe Jedediah thinks of his own hunchback and maybe he loves the boy for the eyeball before loving him for who he is. And I see that Jedediah don't care if the boy's not his, or if he does, he don't even think it to himself. Instead, he tries to name him. All night, trying out names. Adam, says he, Aaron. Methuselah, says he. Jesus, says he, laughing. At last, I'm tired out. Midwife Bledsoe, she's cleaned up and gone, Remarkable's come and gone, left gifts, probably poisoned, and I have the baby in my arms. I say, oh Jedediah. What's bigger than big. Bigger than anyone in this little town. President, I say. Emperor. Governor.

My husband looks at me, smiles. Says, Guvnor, that's a good name. We'll name him Guvnor, and that's what he writes in the fat Bible. *Guvnor Averell, Born The twentythird Of January, 1790.*

Later, when Guvnor grows, I am careful-careful. I tell him my own mother was made with child by her redhead master, though it is not true, though she is an African lady and my father is an African man with two round black cheeks and I remember both in the dust and heat, she in her wrap, he chewing something and smiling at me. I tell Guvnor a redhead skips from grandfather to child always. I tell him he is so smart because I am so smart and he is finer than anyone in this town, than anybody in the world. He is a good boy, he is so laughing and strong, so brave, nobody teases him for his dark skin.

I do not know if he finds anything out, or how, if he does. But I do know that one day, when he is ten, he comes home and he does not look at me anymore. He does not embrace me. His face folds in anger. And that is the day he begins to save his coins, to buy up land. And my own mother's heart is cleft in two, cause that is the day I lose my son. Gone from me, he is that day, gone from me, my boy, for good.

Cowboy Faces

THE WEEK AFTER the monster left, Templeton slipped into August. We all dreamt of the beast, its long-fingered hands, its delicate neck. We imagined ourselves lodged in its ancient brain, saw the dark water before us as it swam so fast in the cold depths. The leaf-thin shimmy of the moon through all that water. The glacier still slowly melting at the bottom of the lake, glowing phosphorescent blue. Those who loved Templeton felt the monster's loss like a phantom limb, still aching.

No wonder, then, that over our hamlet there had fallen a blue-gray pall, even on the hottest, sunniest days. Even on the days when the tourists were loud and thick on Main Street, we scooped the ice cream, we watered the ferns on the lampposts, we sold the caps and balls and bats in a sort of fuzzy dream state. In the fine old hospital, Vi found the sick less crabby, more misty, dying more quietly than they used to, fighting less against the dark tide of death. Pomeroy Hall—once an orphanage, now an old-person home—stank less of incontinence and smelled more of the air coming up from the lake. In every open window there were old people, sniffing the wind to try to smell the change they sensed in their bones.

That week, we heard nothing about the monster from the authorities. There was a long, puzzled silence. The newspapers with their wild speculations about the beast's origins: "The World's Last Dinosaur" and "Scientist Says: The Missing Link?" and "The Fish from Mars!" began to move on to other matters. There was war in sad and gray parts of the world. There was a virus killing people on cruise ships. There was an adopted woman meeting her birth mother for the first time, pulling her car into the parking lot where the mother stood, weeping, when a semi ran over her and killed her. The ordinary rot of the world. When I read about these things that week, I sometimes found my hands stealing over my still-flat navel, as if covering the eyes of the Lump, keeping it safe. On nights when I couldn't sleep and the ghost ringed my room in a haze, I imagined the Lump as a spinning nucleus, splitting and splitting in red cell-corpuscles, until it resembled nothing more than a halved pomegranate. This put me off fruit for some time.

Every night, I checked the answering machine, hoping to hear the soft round sounds of Primus Dwyer's accent, even if all he said was "hello" and hung up. Every night, I stood listening to the frog pool's rising chorus after the tape beeped off, feeling empty.

I had avoided Ezekiel Felcher twice that week, once in line at the Farmers' Museum café, as I was waiting for lunch and he was chatting up a townie I didn't recognize at the register; once as he was towing a van plastered with Phillies paraphernalia, hooting to himself with joy. He, I took it from the bobble-headed toy on the dash, was a Pittsburgh Pirates fan. And I was growing fond of Peter Lieder and the caprine sleeping woman because I spent most of my day in the library looking for—and rejecting—ancestors. Claudia Starkweather's mother and aunt were my next targets, but Ruth and Leah Peck had been sent off to wealthy relatives in New York City when they were ten and eight, respectively. Only Ruth returned, and she returned only when her own daughter Claudia—my great-grandmother—was eighteen and ready to marry. By then, Ruth was already an old widow, devoted to her weeds. Ruth and Leah Peck were the daughters of Guvnor

Averell's second daughter, Cinnamon, the products of her fifth and final marriage.

"Just checking," I had said to Vi. "But Ruth and Leah Peck weren't the source of my father, were they?"

"Who and Who Who?" she said.

"I didn't think so," I said.

Ruth and Leah were on the Averell side; their compeer on the Temple side was Henry Franklin Temple, Sarah's father. But he seemed a quiet, sober soul, and though you can never tell about ancestors, I had a strong feeling that he would never have committed adultery. For a few days, however, I did believe in his guilt; I was charged with energy and a feeling I was coming close to the secret when I learned that Henry had set up Finch Hospital in Templeton for his old friend Isadora H. Finch, the first lady-doctor in upstate New York. After much searching, however, I discovered that Isadora lived in a "Boston marriage" with a woman she had met when she was thirteen and a student at Miss Porter's all-girls school. Everyone called the woman she lived with "mannish," and I found a letter addressed by her to Isadora, affectionately calling her "my wife." My suspicions died at that moment.

It was a hot day when I moved to the next generation up, on both sides. Ruth and Leah's mother was Cinnamon Averell Stokes Starkweather Sturgis Graves Peck, Hetty's granddaughter, five times a widow. And Henry's adoptive mother was Charlotte Franklin Temple. She was a spinster who never had children of her own, and had seven sisters, all of whom dispersed elsewhere when they were married, young. Charlotte was the only one left in town, the daughter of Jacob Franklin Temple and a minor literary figure herself; I relished the idea of digging up mud on such an exemplary virgin, finding some secret pregnancy that she hid with her money and influence. She was the one to start Pomeroy Orphanage. The little brown mouse in her watercolor was the first lady of the town from the time her father died and almost into the twentieth century.

I had just dug into my books and was absentmindedly chewing on a pen when Peter Lieder came by with the squeaky cart and guffawed. I looked up, frowning. His Adam's apple danced a jig above his bow tie.

"That's a great look, Willie Upton," he said. "Vampire-Slash-Angel-of-Death. Very à la mode."

"Huh?" I said.

"Here," he said and took out a foldable pocket mirror, and the fact that fey Peter Lieder actually carried around a pocket mirror startled me more than his comment. But when I looked into the mirror and saw that the pen I was chewing had exploded over my face, even dripping under my chin and onto my neck, and my teeth and tongue were stained, and that I, in my ignorance, had smeared the black ink all over my cheeks and forehead, I understood.

"Oh, yes," I said. "It's a medical condition. Unfortunate, really. Sometimes my cynicism about this big ugly world of ours builds up pressure and bursts all over me. Nothing I can do. Sorry."

"Oh," said Peter Lieder. "I, too, suffer from explosapenitis."

"Really?" I said. "And what do you do about it?"

Peter gave a little glance around the hot library, and I saw with him the way with each pass the rotating fan lifted the wisps of the ancient woman's hair, then returned them to their places. I saw two unfortunate houseflies beating against the window in panicky parabolas. I saw the dark and cool-looking lake outside.

He turned to me and raised an eyebrow. "I usually wash it off," he said. "Lake water does the trick beautifully."

I looked at him with narrowed eyes and then I, too, raised an eyebrow.

He gave a shrug. I shrugged back.

He nodded and stepped back into the stacks, where the old woman couldn't see him. He walked off toward the back entrance, and in about ten seconds, I saw him emerge in the window and break into a run down the long green sweep of lawn toward the shore. It was so incongruous—his starving chicken run, the way his legs almost tangled each other—that I laughed. Then I too hurried out the door, and tossed off my shoes and let my own legs loose and free, so fast that I caught up to Peter and passed him in a moment, and had a few seconds to cool my feet in the shallows as he panted down the hill. He had already untied his bow tie and was taking off his shoes. He stripped down to a black Speedo, and then ran clumsily into the water, diving in and swimming out a bit.

"Peter," I said, "what in the heck are you doing with a Speedo under your clothes?"

"I swim every day at lunch," he shouted, spitting water at me.

"Up until the first ice, and then it gets too cold for me. Only thing that makes my job bearable."

"Ah," I said, looking at the water with regret. "Well, I don't have a bathing suit."

He swam closer and said, "You have a bra on? And underwear?"

"Yup," I said. "I do indeed. But they're white. Unfortunately."

"So what," he said.

"White goes transparent when it's wet," I said.

Peter Lieder dove under, and when he came up, he was grinning. He smoothed the moisture out of his caterpillar mustache, then said, to my enormous surprise, "Well, Willie, it looks like today is my lucky day."

THE LAKE FELT cool and hospitable on my skin, the sky unfolded itself wide open, almost daring a person to look for evil omens lurking over the hilltops. And yet, when we walked up the long green lawn toward the library, as Peter Lieder shook water out of his ear and I held my shirt out so I wouldn't have a wet bikini stamped on the cotton, I said, "It was odd, wasn't it, Peter? The lake, I mean. I have never wanted to get out of it so fast in my life. Maybe it's just me."

"It's a fact," Peter said. "Not just you. Any other year in August, you'd have water-skiers so thick out there they're almost murdering one another. Clotheslines, collisions, you name it. Not this year. Nobody out there. There's something creepy now about the lake, at least after Glimmey died." He gave a little sigh and said, rather abruptly, "Not that we know that Glimmey was a bad monster, or anything, and I don't remember anybody coming up out of the lake with bite marks all over, you know? But he could've been. He could've eaten babies, for all we know. And all those times we went swimming, there he was, looking at our little tiny legs, salivating. And so though the lake looks all pretty and simple and almost blank now that Glimmey's gone, there's still some sort of menace, I think, just lurking there. It's very, very scary."

I stopped walking, feeling worse.

"Peter," I said. "This is terrible. The world is falling apart faster than we can catch up, and the one place, the one place in the world where it's not supposed to fall apart seems to be rotting, too. I come home to Templeton because it's the only place in the world that never changes, and I mean *never*, never changes, and here's this half-dead lake. I always thought, hey, if the ice caps melt and all the cities of the world are swallowed up, Templeton will be fine. We'd be able to make do. Plant vegetables. Bunker up, sit it out, whatever. But it doesn't seem right anymore. Does it?"

I felt like weeping; I felt hyperbolic; I felt as if all the shadows of the earth had just fallen over Templeton. Peter put his hand on my shoulder and made me turn to him. "That is totally psychotic, Willie," he said with admiration. I looked up into his face, and it was cracked into a wide smile, the mustache broken in the middle like a twig. "You're kidding, right?"

"Well," I said. "No, I wasn't."

"Ha," he said, and it was less of a laugh than a phonetic recitation of the word. We had reached the back entry now and were standing by the door, where, in the glass, the lake was traced very faintly. "You're a romantic, you know. I never thought you'd be a romantic. Always thought you'd be hard-boiled somehow. Listen, everything changes, Willie, whether we want it to or not. I mean, look," he said, gesturing vaguely across the lake at the hills bristling with pines. "See that hill? Before this area was settled, that was all huge, old-growth hardwood. Maples, ash, oak. Not so many pines to speak of. A century later it was all hops, not a single tree. I mean, at one point," he said, warming to his subject, turning pink, "there were passenger pigeons in the Northeast, these spectacular, gentle black and white birds who'd flock in the millions, all at once. In a few years, they were completely exterminated. Now the only pigeon you're going to see is one of those," and he pointed to a mottled bird plucking at a crushed Styrofoam cup on the grass. "You get what I mean?" he said.

"I see your point, Peter—" I said, and was about to say more when he interrupted me.

"Willie, all I'm saying is that worrying about it isn't going to fix anything. The only thing we can do is keep on with our own small thing and try hard to be good and to make life better, and know that if it all ends tomorrow that we were at least happy."

"Bullshit," I said. "Not only is that a cliché, you're a lotus-eating hedonist."

"If that weren't redundant, it might be true," he said. "Listen, this may sound presumptuous and everything, but don't give up on living your life, Willie. I have hope for you yet. Tell me: what is the one thing in the world that you'd be overjoyed to have, right now, even if you were to die in the middle of experiencing it?"

The first thing in my head was a vision, Primus Dwyer smiling down at me in the soft red light of our tent on the tundra, the terns outside screaming and screaming. The second were words, which shocked even me as they pulsed into my head: *the Lump*, I thought, then chased the thought away. It was only with the third thing that bubbled up in my mind that I spoke. "A frigid martini, dirty, with very excellent vodka," I said, dreamily.

Peter Lieder's eyes flashed, and he gave a shrug of his skinny shoulders. "That was not what I was thinking," he said, "but that's definitely second best. I am taking you out tonight, Willie Upton, and you can't say no. Bold Dragoon. Ten o'clock. I'll see you there."

Before he could finish his sentence, the door swung open under his hand and the tiny old woman stood in the doorway, tottering, her cirrose protrusions on her chin still quivering from the violent updraft.

"You," she said, shaking her finger at Peter Lieder. "Get your bony behind back to work. If I didn't watch you like a hawk, like a dang hawk, you'd be out gallivanting all day with pretty young ladies, wouldn't you? You would. Now stop your gawping and get going," and Peter hightailed it inside, so fast I barely saw the tracery of the wet Speedo on his khakis. The old woman held the door for me, frowning malevolently.

"In, miss," she said. And she began muttering so low that I couldn't understand what she was saying. She followed me back inside and stood near my table, still muttering until I stood and stacked the books in a neat pile, and called it a day, happy to escape from the old goat-woman's gloomy little presence.

I CAME IN that evening exhausted, expecting to smell the rich smells of Vi's cooking or at least to see her out at the grill on the back porch, flipping shish kebabs with her tongs. But the house was empty, and on the counter there was a note for me.

Sunshine, it read. *I'm at "Reverend Milky's" as you see fit to call him. Real name's John Melkovitch, in the phone book—I'm staying over.*

There's cereal, or you could make yourself some eggs or leftovers. Clarissa called. Love you.—Vi

I chuckled when I read the note and touched my navel. "Looks like someone's a hypocrite," I said. "Sex before marriage. *Très* taboo." And then I noticed my hand on my gut and said to the Lump, "Why am I talking to you? You're not even a person," and sat down to eat some cold stuffed chicken from the Tupperware.

I turned on the television, and in thirty seconds realized why I hated television. I turned off the television and stood up to do 500 jumping jacks, since I hadn't exercised after the day I realized any man in town could have been my father, and stayed home to avoid the Running Buds; I was too afraid of literally running into them again. At 341, I thought I heard the phone ring, and ran over to it, but the dial tone only beeped, vague and impersonal, in my ear. I came back to the couch, flipped through one of my mother's knitting books, and promptly fell asleep.

IT WAS DARK when I awoke, the moon screwed crisp as a bolt in the sky. And because the clock on the VCR was already flashing 10:21, and because I don't believe I had ever been late in my life, I was thrown into a panic and didn't have time to pause and reflect. I didn't think that I probably shouldn't drink, or that I should call Clarissa back or even take the time to consider an outfit, and instead just threw on whatever I had at hand. That turned out well enough; I wore a short old hippie dress of Vi's, tucked my lake-stiffened hair up under a red silk kerchief, threw a couple of gold hoops in my ears and a coat of some lipstick I had on the old vanity, and stepped back to see the effect. It was far better than I had imagined; I looked like some expensive designer's idea of gypsy fashion. I put on a pair of ancient espadrilles and was out the door before 10:25.

The Bold Dragoon was the oldest bar in Templeton, built in the earliest days of Marmaduke Temple's settlement. The innkeeper had come at a time when there were still few people in Templeton, and built the little wooden structure with his own hands, even painting the sign that still hung up there in the lake wind. There was a curling fire-breathing dragon and the words *The Bold Dragoon* in neat script above. In those days of limited literacy, nobody caught that the word *dragon* was misspelled, not even Marmaduke, since he had taught himself how to read, and couldn't spell worth a whit. When the first attorney came into town and stopped on his spavined mare to read the sign, he threw his head back and laughed and laughed until he drew a crowd.

"Pray tell wot's so amusin', sir," said the little badger of an innkeeper, reddening under the insult.

"A dragoon," sputtered the attorney, "is a knight, my good man, *not* a dragon."

With that, the innkeeper pushed out into the crowd with a pot of paint, stood on the vast shoulders of a settler named Solomon Falconer, and drew a hasty but handsome knight in armor spearing the dragon from below. It was that glossily restored, eerie-looking sign flapping in the lake wind that I strode under on my way into the pub. On Friday, the young people took over this pub as their own. The rest of the week, it was a Harley hangout, and Pioneer Street bristled with motorcycles all the way up the hill toward the elegant Presbyterian Church. Just outside the door, hearing the bone-crunching bass of music, I stopped to take a deep breath, to steel myself, and then I went into the pub with its smoke-lacquered beams and glistening original floorboards.

The music did not spin to a stop; not every person in the place turned to look when I entered. But enough people did pause for a moment and peer to see who I was that a palpable hush fell over the place. And then Peter Lieder was by my side, grinning in his dorky way, and I had a shot glass full of some dark liquid in my hand, and then my mouth was washed with a strong, sweet taste of liquor and my throat convulsed with heat.

"Willie," said Peter, his breath already spiked, "to be honest, I didn't think you were coming."

"Peter, to be honest, I took a nap and almost slept straight through." I put the glass down on a table nearby and smiled at him.

"To be honest," Peter Lieder said, and it was here that I noticed that he was without his little bow tie and he was dressed in a pink Polo shirt underneath a yellow sweater and that one could see where his shirt sleeves ended and his skin began. He looked as yuppie as a person who was not a yuppie but wanted to look like a yuppie could look. "To be honest," he said again, putting a possessive hand on my shoulder, "Willie, you are one hot cookie."

"Oh, Jesus," I said. "Peter, no offense, but I thought this was a pity date, on your part. I'm not in any state to want to be pawed at tonight, okay?"

"Pawed at?" said Peter, smiling painfully. His mustache twitched like a living thing. "Surely I'm far more suave than that."

I must have looked doubtful because Peter reared back, offended. And then, just as he was about to open his mouth and say something, just as I was cringing in preparation, a voice said "Who, Peter?" in my ear. "He gets all the ladies, just you wait and see." My heart rose in gratitude then fell again when I turned and saw Ezekiel Felcher in a wrinkled dress shirt and khakis. He even smelled like the trope of the guy who stayed home—Old Spice. Strong.

"Felcher," I said. "Ezekiel. Lovely to see you out tonight."

"Lovely," he said, "to see the lovely Willie Upton. I see you're here to repay me my beer."

Peter was watching, and he winked at me before I could respond. "Drink's on me, tonight," he said, over the roar of the jukebox. "You'll be all right with this guy if I go get us some, Willie? You'll tell me if he tries anything he shouldn't?"

"I'll be fine," I said. "Thanks." He turned around and went dancing toward the bar, swinging his girlish hips.

"That was nice of you, Ezekiel," I said when we were alone. "This is so weird, but for some reason I always thought Peter Lieder was gay."

"You're kidding," he said. "Pete? No way. I wasn't joking. He really does get all the girls. In a town this size, if a guy buys a girl flowers and makes her breakfast and calls her throughout the day to tell her he was thinking of her, he gets the reputation for being a good guy. When a guy has the reputation for being a good guy, he becomes a popular date. Even the girls who made fun of Pete when he was so huge, even *they* love him."

"And you?" I said.

"He's okay, I guess. We're buddies," he said, taking a sip of his beer.

"I meant, what is your reputation like?" I said.

"Oh," he said. "I made some big mistakes early and so nobody thinks I'm a good guy. Mel and all. My little boys, you know. But I do pretty well. I still have my mojo. You'll see," and he said this with his old knee-shattering smile.

No I won't, I thought, but he was already leading me through the crowd to a table, and on the way I was stopped by some girls I recognized vaguely. Susanna? Hillary? Erica? Joanne? Some of them said hi, looking in an irritated way somewhere past my left ear; some threw their arms around my neck and jabbered, but I couldn't catch what they were saying, so I only grinned and nodded and let Felcher pull me through.

When we were settled in the curved booth in the corner of the room, he lifted his shirt and prodded the little bundt cake around his belly button. "See this?" he said. "This is going to be gone in one month. I'm running in the mornings. Up to about four miles today. Not bad, right?" And he smiled shyly in my direction.

"Great. But why?" I said. "What's come over you?"

He looked at me slyly and said, "You."

"What?" I said with alarm. "Don't do anything because of me."

"No," he said. "I mean, you came back and looked so good it put me to shame. I thought, heck, that Willie Upton has her shit together. You know? She almost has a PhD, for God's sakes, and she looks even better than she did in high school, with her chic hairdo, and I thought, *Zeke, in comparison to Queenie over there, you're mud.* And I don't like feeling like mud, you know. Not in comparison to anybody."

"Ha," I said. "Funny you think I have my shit together."

Felcher leaned toward me, and those green eyes of his sparkled with some of their old charm. "Is that why you're home? Tell me about it. Just sit back and relax and tell old Dr. Felcher what's wrong, honey."

It was the *honey* that got me, as unexpected endearments always did. I felt an overwhelming pressure behind my eyes, and had to look down at my hands in order to keep everything from spilling. And in that moment of pause, Peter Lieder returned, and set down a tray full of shots.

"Zeke and I," said Peter, sliding into the bench beside me. "We're going to teach you how to drink like a Templetonian, aren't we, Zeke?"

"That is correct," said Felcher, and something curious then passed between the two boys, something charged that I didn't really want to understand. I took a shot and knocked it back without even wincing.

"One," I said, glad that Peter hadn't noticed my distress. "I am a Templetonian. I am, in fact, *the* Templetonian." I took another little glass and shot it and said, "And two: I already know how to drink." It was only after the second that I realized it was whiskey.

Felcher gave a little whistle under his breath and said, "Damn."

"Game's on, then," said Peter. "Cowboy Faces. Everyone knows the rules?"

"Take a shot and pretend it didn't hurt. Make your face as stoic as possible," said Zeke and put one back so deadpan that it looked as if he had drunk water.

"Agreed," said Peter, and he took a shot, and his nostrils flared and there was a little tension around his chin, and Felcher and I agreed Peter had no points for that round, as his Cowboy Face was pretty horrendous.

Somewhere on the fifth shot or so, Felcher put his hand on my bare knee and I let him keep it there. My knee was cold, I reasoned, and he was just warming it up. Somewhere around the seventh shot, Peter Lieder saw the hand on my knee and gave us both a curious look. "Gotta go potty," he said, then weaved his way through the crowd.

Alone now with Felcher, my head swimming with alcohol, I looked up into the bar and saw that life was not as bad as I had feared. Bobbie Jean LaMarck was dancing beside the jukebox to some male-hating country music song, Felcher was telling some story about duck hunting in my ear, and I had forgotten momentarily about my own problems. I was feeling sleepy and sweet. When Peter came back to the table, he did so with a small, plump girl on his arm, clearly a tourist. She wore a backward baseball cap and had thick bars of mascara on her cheeks from blinking before it had dried. "Guys," Peter said. "Meet Heather. Such a cutie, isn't she?"

"Adorable," said Felcher, dryly. "How old are you, sweetheart?"

She twinkled. "Eighteen?" she said, looking at Peter for confirmation.

"Hear that? Eighteen. Great age, great," said Peter. "We're going for a little walk down to the lake. I was telling her all about Glimmey and everything. The monster. She was so interested."

"It's sooo cool? A monster! Wow! Plus?" said the girl. "It's so romantic tonight? With all the flowers? And the moon?"

"Bye, honey," I said. "Be careful. A suave one, our Peter-Lieder-Pudding-and-Pie."

"Sure thing?" she said, and she giggled and followed Peter Lieder out the door and into the night. Felcher and I watched from inside the bar as, on the sidewalk, Peter took off his yellow sweater and tucked it over her shoulders. She beamed up at him.

"Damn," I said to Felcher. "Peter Lieder really does get the girls."

"Told you so," he said, and then buried his nose on my shoulder. "You smell so good, Willie Upton," he said. "What perfume you use? Makes me want to eat you up."

"Soap," I said. I pulled my knee from under his hand. "I'm going home."

"What?" he said. "Already? It's only eleven thirty."

"Oh, well. I'm drunk enough to find you attractive."

"Ouch," he said, looking blurry and hurt.

"Sorry," I said.

He gave me his most charming grin and said, "Does that mean I get to come home with you?"

"No way," I said.

"Why not," he said, and a little whine had crept into his voice.

"Because," I said, "you're not married to someone with whom you've had two kids, Felcher. Sorry. No offense. We'll just be good friends."

"Can't I walk you home at least?"

"Nope," I said. "It's two blocks. And guess what? I don't want to be seen leaving with you. Sorry if that's harsh."

He seemed to shrink a little in his seat and turned away from me. "Such a meanie, Queenie. Always were," he said. And then I went out, calling out good-bye to a group of girls who, I imagined, watched me wryly, seeing me leave alone when I could have been with that stud Zeke Felcher.

The night had cooled, and goose bumps came out on my arms. Across the street, the Pitt Hotel was filled with another set of Friday-night clientele, the town's old boozers, men who had come to this mecca of baseball and never learned how to leave. I hoped to God that the man who was my father wasn't one of the sad old men in there, his belly straining against his shirt, his nose red and glossy with grease. The remaining news trucks from Glimmey's appearance were lined along Main Street in front of the gourmet sandwich shop and the art gallery. The flag at the crossroads of Main and Pioneer flapped against its pole, clang-clanging, and at the foot of Pioneer the lake spread dark and beautiful. I wanted to go out in the oily dark and feel the whiskery light of the stars on the surface beside me; I wanted to tread water back to the time when I was the little high school know-it-all, eager to go out into the wider world, sure of my ability to conquer it. But passing Farkle Park, I turned my ankle on the curb and cursed and bent down to take one espadrille off. Hobbling this way home made me feel like Quasimodo, though, so I took the other one off, too, and swung them in my hands.

"Anyone attacks me," I said aloud, "I got some nunchucks." I imagined the face of Primus Dwyer on the lightpole at the corner of Pioneer and Lake, and swung my nunchuck-espadrilles at him, so loose in my muscles now that I only connected once. The shoe smacked against the pole at the precise altitude of a man's gonads.

That's when Ezekiel Felcher stepped in front of me and took the shoes from my hands.

I saw him wobble a bit before me. "You snuck up behind me," I said. "You. I told you to stay back there. At the whatever. Drinking place."

"Oh, honey," he said. "Looks like you *do* need some help getting home." He took my arm rather gently and put it over his strong shoulders.

"Don't oh honey me," I said, though I leaned against him. "Makes me want to cry. My house is like right there. I can see it. Right there. Lights right there. I can make it all by myself."

"Well," he said, "you still have to cross a road. Don't want to see you getting smushed by a car at the last minute."

"Okay," I said. "But nobody saw you. You know, leave after me. Right? At the bar?"

He sighed and said, "No, Willie, nobody saw me leave. I went out the back door because I respected your wishes. Embarrassing as it would be to be seen leaving with me."

"Hell, yes," I said. "You're a total whore. No offense. But what you did in high school? So mean. Kiss and tell. Ruined reputations. Everybody always crying, and still you got girls to go out with you. Don't know how, Felch. I never wanted to go out with you."

He frowned a little and said, "Is that why you refused to dance with me at the homecoming dance, Queenie? Hurt my feelings a lot, you know." By now, we had crossed the street, and the driveway was still warm on my feet from the light of the day.

"Yup," I said. "Though I had a crush on you, big-time. Everybody did. I's one of the only ones never did anything about it. Smart. Back then, at least. Not now. Nohow. I'm a dumb fuck now. My mom even says so. And she's never been the brightest bulb on the block. In the pack. Whatever."

We were in the garage by then. It was cool, and the familiar smell of home came rising up, the straw and dust, the bitter orange. I felt relaxed, but so very tired. The stretch between the mudroom door and my room seemed enormous, a marathon.

"I," said Felcher, "*always* had a crush on you. And I don't think you ever could be dumb, Queenie."

And then his big man's body was leaning against mine, pressing my body into the door. And his breath was near my face, then his face was near my face, then his lips near my lips and he was kissing me. My lips were numb, but even so, it was true what they said: Felch was a *killer* kisser. Lips soft and full. Tongue just forceful enough. I closed my eyes because everything was swimming before me and in the dark of my eyelids, I forgot where I was; Templeton fell away, Averell Cottage fell away, the long, strange day fell away, and there I was nowhere but inside my skin, and I was warming up, warming perceptibly under his hands and his mouth, hands down the length of my bare thighs, the door hard on my back, and in the solitude of the moment, the dreamlike strangeness of it, I forgot that Ezekiel Felcher even existed and a thought flashed through my mind of Primus Dwyer, and it was as if he were there before me, as if I had imagined him in Ezekiel's place, and I felt the hands slide up now into my underwear, and they were Primus's, and I felt the weight of the belly and it was Primus's, and I felt my skirt rise up and my underwear slide down and heard the merry jingle of the belt buckle falling against the concrete, and they were all, somehow, Primus's. They were his arms now boosting me up against the door, his hips my legs went around. It was his silky erection sliding across my thigh now—but—no—it was *not* his— and my hand fumbled back and turned the doorknob, and we crashed down onto the hard linoleum of the mudroom. I looked up into Felcher's face.

"No," I said, and pulled myself away.

"Oh, God," he said. "I'm so sorry." He turned, and hesitated, and, his back to me, said, "I'm such an asshole, Willie, such a total asshole. Comes over me and I always think with the wrong head."

"Go," I said.

He went, his footsteps quick and loud down the driveway. Somewhere in me, I hoped I would never have to see Felcher again. I didn't look up when he stood and fled, and I shut the door hard with my foot. But also, somewhere very close to my skin, I hoped he would come back. I sat in the dark for quite some time, waiting for that small knock on the door that didn't, in the end, come.

WHEN I CAME back to myself, I realized I was holding my navel in two hands. "Oh my God," I said to the Lump. "I forgot about you. I am so sorry."

I needed water: I needed fat. And after I had fried up two eggs and drunk a half a gallon of water, I saw my mother's note again and needed Clarissa. I dialed, and as the phone rang on the other end, I felt tears of self-pity, the stupid story about Felcher rise up like so many bubbles to my eyes and mouth.

But Sully was the one who answered, voice curt in the night. "Hey, Sully-Sully," I said. "Clarissa up?"

And though I counted Sully as one of my closest friends, one who came over to play our Thursday Scrabble game even when Clarissa was off on assignment, he gave a little hiss. He said, "Oh, fuck off, Willie. It's goddamn eleven at night. Try to think of some-one other than yourself for once," and he hung up.

I stared at the receiver, shaking, and slowly put it back. Almost immediately, it rang again. I picked it up, but it was Clarissa, and it took me a few beats to understand what she was saying. Her voice was grim. ". . . don't pay any attention to him," she was saying. "He's under a lot of stress. I'm not feeling so good, Willie, so I can't talk too much, but I didn't want you to be upset."

"Whatever," I said. "He's an ass."

Clarissa's voice changed now and she said lightly, as if she were smiling, "You drunk, Willie? You drunk-dialing me?" In the background, I could hear a new burst of Sully's cursing.

"Well," I said. "I'm sorry. I guess I'm a shitty friend."

"No," she said. "But untimely. I was asleep. We'll talk tomorrow, okay?"

"Okay, yes," I said. "You sick again, Clarissa?"

"We'll talk tomorrow, honey. Drink some water and go to bed."

"Love you," I said.

"Sleep tight," she said, and was gone.

I HAD ALREADY changed into my pajamas, had brushed my teeth and washed my face when the phone in my bedroom rang once more. I felt sober, old, and went to pick it up. "Hello?" I said, tentative.

"Willie," hissed Sully. "Here's the deal. Old friend nephritis is back. Clarissa is so sick. I know that things are all messed up in your life, but, Willie, where are you? You're her best friend, but instead of being here, taking care of her, you're interrupting the only deep sleep she's been able to get in about a week with a stupid drunken phone call, and you've been gone all summer, and you're freaking her out, and the last thing Clarissa needs right now is to be freaked out. She has enough on her plate already. I know you're having some kind of existential crisis and everything, and you've just pretty much collapsed into a big puddle, and I'm really, really sorry to hear that, Willie, I really am, but, God, could you be any more selfish? And remember at the hospital you *said* you'd help me. You did say that. And here we are, and you're not."

"Oh, God, Sully," I said. "Where are you?"

He paused and then said, "On the balcony. Clarissa's asleep again. I made her take a few more pills. This is so insane, Willie. Who ever heard of a thirty-year-old woman dying of lupus? I'm not even clear on what the hell lupus is, anyway. Why the hell did it decide Clarissa was a good candidate? This is so freaking confusing."

"I know," I said. I imagined Sully in the cold San Francisco summer night, the Coit Tower bright and phallic beside him, his thinning hair whipping in the wind. "Sullivan, I promise you I am so, so sorry about running away from this." Then I heard again what he had said, and said, "Wait. Who said anything about dying? She's not dying, is she?"

"Well," he said, "that's what happens when the infection spreads into the organs."

"Oh, shit," I breathed.

"Yes," he said. "Luckily nothing irreversible has happened yet, but if she keeps refusing her therapy, it will. She's been going to this Chinese quack woman who's giving her herbs. Listen, when you talk tomorrow, can you please, please talk some reason into the girl? She won't listen to me. There's nothing I can do. There's nothing I can do." Sully's breath was coming out in short jags, and I wondered if he was crying.

It was only then that I thought of Sully's last months, waking up to Clarissa's sickness, working fifteen hours a day at a firm he hated, coming home on the bus at dark, knowing that Clarissa was still there, still sick, needing his patience. Needing him to make what food she could eat, to deal with her, querulous and pouty from forced rest, when she had never been querulous or pouty in their entire lives together. I had one bright image of him in the elevator to their apartment, eyes closed, hair askew, rain slicking his sparse hair to the skull. His one brief moment of peace. Then he had to step into the hall, pause before the apartment, open the door, when all he really wanted was a glass of wine and a little bit of kindness for himself.

"Should I take a plane?" I said.

"What?" he said.

"I'll drive to Albany right now. I'll take the first plane I can find. I'll be there tomorrow morning."

Sully paused, and I heard his breath in the receiver. He cleared his throat. "You know," he said. "I don't need you tomorrow, just really soon. Willie, it'd mean so much to me if you could call Clarissa in the morning and see what she says. I mean, I'm just relieved that you're willing to come. Thank you." He thought some more and said, "Tell you what. If you work on her and convince her to go to her real doctors, do her psychotherapy and antibody therapy as well as whatever homeopathic shit she wants to do, I can hold out a while longer. But can you please, please, please come back whenever I need you? And, if you can, try to call every day. You have no idea how lonely it is. You'd think from the way her friends are acting that lupus is contagious. The people from the paper? Gone. Once in a while, someone stops by with flowers, but they're always lilies, and Clarissa says lilies are for corpses, and throws them out the window. She'd never tell you because she knows you're having your own problems, Willie. But I think Clarissa's really sad."

I listened for a moment to the wind in the receiver, the nighttime life of San Francisco, the constant traffic, the distant sirens, the low rumble of a plane overhead. I began to feel again the way I felt just before I left for Alaska; that every step I took was one breath more than that fragile, fault-ridden city could handle. Those months, I had to close my eyes sometimes, fight the rising panicked urge to get out fast, or see that whole beautiful city just crumble under the knuckle of some great and angry god. Sully made a noise, and I remembered he was there.

"Oh, Sully," I said, "this is so incredibly hard for you, isn't it."

There was another long pause, and I listened as Sully's breathing slowed. "I needed that," he said, at long last. "Just to feel, I don't know. Understood."

"We'll whup this lupus thing," I said. "Just watch."

He laughed and said, "I needed that, too. A little bit of feist in my life. Good to have you on board again, Willie."

"Good to be back, Sully," I said. "I'll call Clarissa tomorrow." And then the phone clicked. The ghost, which had been pulsing in the corner of my sight, listening to my conversation, faded until it was nothing, and from my window I watched the soapy blue-black fog skulk over the lake and up the lawn.

13

The Running Buds (Big Tom, Little Thom, Johann, Sol, Doug, Frankie) Speak Again

WE HAVE RUN though the dark orange days of July, run through the summer mornings soft as mouse fur, through the drizzle, through the baking heat, through the scent of wakening gardenia, under the wisteria draped on the covered bridge. By now we have run ourselves plumb into August, though this year has been hard on us. After the monster, the summer splintered apart. When we are together, we hold ourselves together, our old feet tapping on the Templeton pavement, our old hearts pounding in time. This is called solace, our morning run. When we have finished our coffee at the Cartwright Café, we drive away from one another, drive our old bones home to the messes we have made of our lives.

Big Tom's meth-head kid is gone, run off. Two years ago, she was the hard-nosed captain of the debate team with purple-framed glasses and a dimpled smile. We do not know where she went, though we have looked, contacted the papers, searched all of upstate New York. Together, we made up the flyers, that black-and-white picture, the girl changed, we are sure, from that dear goofy girl in replicate from Tom's office photocopier.

Little Thom's heart has been acting up again, and he had to take a moment when he was leading grand rounds in the hospital to step into a supply closet and press down. He was pale and shaking when he came out. We tell him he should not run, but he looks at us. *I'd rather die running*, he says, and we let him run because we would rather die running, too.

Johann's daughter's not talking to him because of something he did when he was drunk after the Clarke girl's wedding. Johann called his daughter in Memphis and said, in his slurred German accent, *Honey, just so you know you didn't ruin my life by being a dyke. I dought you did, but you vill grow out of it, and get married and seddle down and haff kids. Just so you know, I luff you anyvays.*

Yikes! we said when we heard this on our morning run the next day, and he looked at us mournfully, hungover, wincing.

It's dat bad? he said. He didn't know, honestly.

Oh, Johann. It's that bad, we said.

Sol's third wife, the spinning instructor at the gym, has delivered the divorce papers to him via her new boyfriend's sleek Harley. The kicker? *Failure to provide children in the marriage*: three marriages, three aging wombs, each time this the reason to find someone new. Alone of all of us, Sol has no children. He is silent when we talk of ours, all in college and beyond, sad-faced even when Big Tom talks of his meth-head girl. We see him blinking behind his sunglasses, we feel the weight of his silence. We sense he would take even Big Tom's druggie at this point, he would take trouble, he would take a kid who hated him, like Johann's girl. He would take anything, we believe.

Doug's possibly facing prison time for nonpayment of overdue taxes. Sol has offered to help him out (the only time we ever really realize he's so rich), but Doug scoffs: he'll fight them to the end, he says. Whose end? we want to say, but don't. He has a new girlfriend that his wife maybe knows about, an eighteen-year-old hostess at the wax museum who is paid to draw men inside the cool waxy place with her killer boobs and smile, to bring them inside that mausoleum where Mickey Mantle and Babe Ruth begin to melt when the generator goes out. We are troubled more than he is by both jail and jailbait. He doesn't think he will go to jail. He doesn't think his wife knows about the girl. We feel certain about both, and shiver.

And, to top it off, Frankie has lost twenty pounds after his parents' death, and his skin hangs loose and yellowing on him. He swings through manic to depressed five times a day. Yesterday, he told a joke so long and incoherent Johann had to interrupt with his own joke to save Frankie some face. After that, we ran silently back and didn't linger over our coffee at the Cartwright Café as we usually do.

Templeton has become sad, we think. Templeton feels dark this summer. We have not had time to relax at the country club. We have not had time to play much golf. Crazy Piddle Smalley began foaming at the mouth and touched himself in front of a young girl, and his parents were forced to lock him in his room until his new meds kicked in. Secretly, in our deepest of our deep hearts, we think it is the monster's fault. As soon as it died, our lives spiraled down.

Even still, we run. We have not reached our average of 57.92 years without knowing that you run through it, and it hurts and you run through it some more, and if it hurts worse, you run through it even more, and when you finish, you will have broken through. In the end, when you are done, and stretching, and your heartbeat slows, and your sweat dries, if you've run through the hard part, you will remember no pain.

Davey Shipman (aka Leatherstocking, Natty Bumppo, Hawkeye, etc.)

I WOKE OLD on the morning of the pigeons. Joints hot, brain aching. Looked out over the gutted land, the charred stumps, the lake brown with mud. Long ago I felt it were my own kin, but it hadn't been kin for a while. I should have left long before, pressed into the truer wilderness in the West, for I hated the settlers and their wasty ways. For their part, the settlers were confounded by me, a white hunter living like an Indian, past his prime, though still fearsome. Once, boys threw rocks from afar, calling me Ol' Stinkstockings, and though I could have picked them off with my rifle in a second, easy as crows on a branch, I only growled at them. They lit away quick enough, never did do it again. As for me, I hung on to the land like a snapper whose severed head still bites, naught else to do with its waning life.

Boiling coffee, I turned to Sagamore in his red blanket, and was not surprised to see he looked as I felt, weary to the marrow. He groaned as he stood, then looked shamed about it. I knew what he felt, though, pretended not to hear. Mornings like those, I could hardly remember we were young once, that I was just eleven when his family took me in after I run off from my own. My father was an Anglican preacher, godly during the day and a devil at night, whipped me until I preferred the dark woods and whatever would eat me there. Half-starved, I stumbled one day into a Delaware camp and found a better family. Sagamore my blood brother, taking me hunting and fishing, teaching me such joy. But by the time Duke came to the lake, the Delaware were mostly dead, and last I heard of my father, he was rich, owned a gin mill, brought a preacher over to his church all the way from England. That's how it went, the gentle ones died quiet while the mean ones thrived. Sickened me unto death all my life.

As my old friend took his morning piss down by the pines, I sawed off some meat and threw it in the kettle for a stew. Then we lit our pipes, spat. As Sagamore and me sat over our coffee, we scented the smoke of another parcel of forests on the wind, destruction, the particular blight of Marmaduke Temple. We'd lived together for years, and I knew what Sagamore was thinking. How it had only been a few years since we'd first seen Duke stumbling through the forest, muttering like an idiot or the war-mad soldiers from the French wars who once stood outside the forts, half-naked, begging, stumps bared. One even exposed his swollen genitals, three flesh-pumpkins, for he couldn't fit in trousers, and refused a dress: mad, plain as day. Duke that day staggering up the mountainside had the same stars in his eyes. We had stood, Sagamore and me, in the trees, a doe bleeding between us. Watched the giant stumble, fretting, up the hill. A man such as him, in his fine clothes, was so unbefitting in the woods that we gaped. We laughed, thinking we'd seen his tail.

But, like idiot hunters, we fell into our own traps. A man living in a place that doesn't change doesn't expect it ever will. This land, this lake, has shaken off all past tries at taming it, so we thought it always would. Long before us were the native tribes, the Iroquois, the six great nations of Haudenosaunee, who used this lake as a summer camp, planted beans and squash and maize in the riverbottom land. They still did when I came upon the lake as a stripling, and saw such beauty I thought my heart forgot how to beat. The land *was* me, slid into me, tongue-and-groove. And so I came back to this lake, kept coming back, even after the Mohawks met at the Council Rock and decided to join the French. A bad bet. They lost everything when the English won.

After the French war I made my cabin high above the lake, and for a time I was alone. Then I watched as Moses the Mohican set up his rough little academy on the southmost morsel of lakeland. But that winter was hard. He hadn't stocked enough. When the ice thawed, some students were dead, some eaten. Moses never seen again. Probably eaten.

Then came the couple like animals in heat. A man and a woman, she lovely to look upon. I laughed, watching them, for they believed themselves unseen in such wilderness. Alone. Couldn't look beyond one another to see the string of my smoke on the hill. Began walking about naked until one day there was a sudden blizzarding wind from the north and they were out gathering firewood, naked as babes, and lost their way. Froze in a solid blue block, laced together, forty feet from their cabin. Come spring, I buried them, still entwined, at the river's lip.

And I watched from my cabin as another came, a mean German Lutheran minister. Hartwick. Espoused a free community, all vegetables and cold baths. Crossed his fingers at me as if I were the devil, just for the meat I hung in my smokehouse. His followers left one by one, and I watched. When they were all gone, he went to the lake and read the Bible to the fishes at high voice, in a great fury. I saw him peer down, see something, startle. Fell in and drowned. When I rowed out to find him, his body was gone. I think the great lake-beast took him, the one the Haudenosaunee call Old Sad Spirit in their tongue.

After him, during the revolution, came a troop of one hundred men under General Clinton, frozen in for the winter, beset by hostile natives. Rebels. Decided to build a dam on the river, let it carry them to Pennsylvania, come spring. I had Sagamore staying with me then. He'd broken with his son, Uncas, for marrying Colonel Munro's daughter, Cora. Though brave, though she fought off many a Huron, Magua among them, she was not Delaware, unlike the squaw Sagamore had wanted for a daughter. She was white with a little brown within. So Sagamore, old fool, unblessed his son.

Sagamore and me lived together in our old badger's hut, and watched the soldiers, too old to join another fight. Once, in war, I'd leave a Huron corpse to rot for every mile I'd go. But with the rebel effort against England, I just watched the men from my cabin. They shot my deer and frightened away the smarter beasts. Drank, cursed, did unspeakable things to each other in the blaze of bonfires. The lake pushed up until it lapped on my door. When they broke the dam down, they spun so fast downstream they could see Indian villages frozen under the water, like leaves in ice. Teepees still up. Dogs moving their legs. Babies nested on the backs of squaws. Fires not yet quenched, still burning under the water the boats crested on.

The end of it all was Duke Temple. Self-proclaimed first man to set foot on this land. Parceling up land as if serving a pie to his settlers. Tickling the hotel's scullery maids in the pantry, I'd seen him, murmuring to the shoemaker's daughter. He, a married man, taking what wasn't his. And his settlers weren't any better. They come, money-mad, greedy, eat their mothers if it'd earn them a penny or two. Though that's a mite close to home; that first hard winter, horrid and long, there were people starving everywhere. In the far reaches of the county, cottages were found with skeletons enlaced in the beds, the bones of the baby in the kettle. But beyond that winter, it grew easier, and in later days, they only ate up the trees, all the fish from the lake, all the deer from the woods.

Only good thing Duke brought was his kind son Richard and frailish wife Elizabeth, who sent up to our hut a kilderkin of whiskey every Christmas, without fail, who once met me on the street and pressed my hand. When I pressed it back, it trembled in my own, so soft and delicate. Touched my very heart, it did.

So it was a surprise when, on the morning of the pigeons, I stepped from our hut to carve some more meat for the stew, and come upon the man himself. I thought he was a leftover dream, for it was not unknown to me to see him in them. I'd be gutting a dream-carp and its bulgy eye would turn to me, and I'd see I was gutting Duke. I'd be wrestling with a catamount and it'd roar and become Duke. I'd be with a woman and she'd turn to dust under my hand and I'd realize it was Duke's wife Elizabeth, and then he'd step from the shadows with my trusty long-barrel gun in his hand.

That morning, I thought he was a dream until he turned and I saw road mud upon his face.

Duke had been inspecting the buck I'd killed the day before. Shipman, he boomed. He was angry. His fleshy face was red, his great shoulders drawn up to his ears. What, he roared, did I tell thee about killing my deer?

I don't believe I killed yer deer, Duke, said I. He thought me stupid, a mere squatter that he allowed on his land, so it behooved me sometimes to act such. And it be an honor, Duke, said I, to see the great man himself. Ye normally send your bootlicker lawyer Kent Peck or Richard to talk yer poaching talk to me.

Usually this was true. Peck I sent scuttling with a volley from my good old long-barreled rifle. Richard, Duke's big hairy son, was a good soul, and so I'd serve him some venison stew, and he'd warn me, mildly, and pay the remittance from his own pocket.

But Duke was having none of it. My land, he said. My deer.

Nobody's land. My shot, I said. My deer.

Now, though, Sagamore emerged from the hut, his face creased. Hear that? he said in Delaware, and I listened but said no. What is it? I said, but Duke had lost his angry face and was nodding respectfully to my friend. How do you do, Chief Chingachgook, he said, which was what the whites called Sagamore. Though I hated the man, I liked him a small bit for greeting my old friend with respect.

But Sagamore ignored him. He turned to me, his face softened almost into a smile. Pigeons, he said, and he laughed.

Then I heard it, the far whirring. I saw the black mass crest the far hill and then Sagamore and I began to run down into the town. Every dozen years, they came, a blessing, the passenger pigeons, in the tens of thousands. In that moment we were young hunters again, stalking Hurons, though we brought no weapons to kill these beautiful birds. Behind us, Duke shouted, What, in . . . and then seemed to understand, for his great bootsteps came crashing behind us, nearly catching us when we crossed the Susquehanna.

Then the pigeons burst into town, the wind from their wings blowing shingles off houses, bringing sheets from the lines. The blue sky drowned in orange and black feathers. The women ran indoors, arms above their heads to shield their bonnets from scat.

Boys and men ran to the fields by the lake, faces shining with glee. Whatever they threw brought down a bird. Sticks, stones, shoes, brooms, butter churns, toy soldiers, planes, lathes, rolling pins. Men shot once and dropped three beasts. A strange-looking boy with a wandering eye waved a scythe in the air, and when he pulled it down, he'd pierced six birds in their still-fluttering breasts. Clothes and faces were splattered with blood and waste. Remarkable Prettybones, Duke's housekeeper, swooped like an old bat, catching birds in her bare hands, breaking their necks, stuffing them in floursacks. The old Clinton cannon, the Cricket, was dragged out. With a boom rolling off the hills and a great huzzah, a buckshot of old nails exploded the brains of a thousand pigeons.

When the great mass of birds flew back over the hills like a black mist, there were pigeons knee-deep, some sobbing like babes. The settlers, glutted, left them there to suffer.

I had watched this all, sick to death. I couldn't move. The pigeons had come, every few years, falling on the land like a prayer. For the first time, they had been welcomed with a massacre. I crushed the head of a bloody bird beneath my boot to put it out of its misery, and anger rose dark and strong in me. The waste. The needless pain.

Duke was the one who allowed this, the massacre. He had laughed and laughed. He had suggested the cannon. He had carried his smallest child, pinch-faced four-year-old Jacob, on his shoulders. The boy was big-eyed, bloodied, flushed, and smiling.

There was a terrible pain in my chest, and my old friend Sagamore had sunk to his knees, gasping. Across the quieted killing fields, Duke saw Sagamore kneeling and the joy fell from his face. He let Jacob down, sent him into Remarkable's skirts. He approached. I took one step forward and kept my eye on my old friend's tomahawk. Despite what I felt for Duke Temple, despite that I could have killed him just then, I saw his sweet, weakly little wife Elizabeth in my mind's eye, and I kept my hand from my rifle.

Duke came toward us and bowed his head. Chief Chingachgook, he began, but Sagamore looked at him with such heat Duke stopped. You may have the buck you shot, Davey, said Duke, but when that did not soften my old friend's face, he said, And may I offer you some money in recompen—

I quieted him with a violent motion. We're leaving, I said. Tonight. I had decided that instant. We're going, I said, to live with Sagamore's son, Uncas, in the westy wilderness of this state.

Sagamore looked at me, and though he did not like English he understood it. It was perhaps with relief that he nodded. I did not know then what I knew later, about Uncas and Cora, about Noname, their beautiful daughter. And when I turned to Duke, I did not know we'd return. I said a thing then that perhaps I should not have said.

I looked up into Duke Temple's great, broad face and cursed him, I said, and may your town and your family be cursed, Duke Temple, for seven generations, for all your sins. Then Sagamore stood and we walked away together. I remembered enough from those long Sundays of my childhood, my father raging on the pulpit, my tailbone aching from the hard pew, that nothing in this good world could have stirred me to look back.

15

Vivienne's Superhero Side

I HAD ABOUT four hours of sleep before the passing tourist trolley rolled by on Lake Street, and the guide's voice infiltrated my dreams, saying . . . *off to the left here is Averell Cottage, where in Marmaduke Temple's time there was a tannery* . . . I rolled to the telephone to dial Clarissa before my eyes even opened, and when I moved, my brain felt like a small pickled beast sloshing in the jar of my skull. My friend picked up the phone on the first ring, saying, "What," her voice already tight and angry.

"Clarissa," I said, but that was apparently the starting pistol; Clarissa was off to the races. "Oh, Willie, you are freaking dead," she said. "Dead. *Don't* you *ever* go behind my back and decide what's best for me without talking to me first, ever again. Jesus *Christ.* I woke up this morning, and Sully's like, 'Don't worry, Willie's coming soon, we talked last night and she promised' and I just about went ballistic on his ass." There was the sound of a door slamming on Clarissa's end, and I could imagine Sully, red-faced in fury, stalking out of the apartment building. "Don't you think," she said, "that if I *wanted* you to come I would have *asked* you to come? Didn't you stop to think that the last thing I need right now is to babysit someone even more of a wreck than *I* am right now? Don't you think that what I need is some freaking peace and quiet? What gives you the right to *think* for me? That's all I want to know. What gives you the fucking right?"

It was not easy for me to be quiet through her harangue, but the image of Clarissa before my eyes, tiny, pale, her little face knotted in fury, only made me say through clenched teeth, "Being your best friend, just maybe? Relieving Sully, who's about to have a break-down, maybe? Or maybe the fact that you need me?"

"I don't need you," she said. "I'm doing fine."

"Right," I sneered. "*Homeopathy.* I'm coming today. You can't stop me." I swung my legs out of the bed but was instantly so dizzy I had to lie back again.

When Clarissa let out her breath it was in a long, slow hiss. "Wilhelmina Upton," she said, "I love you very much. You're my best friend. But, dammit, if you insist on coming back to San Francisco in the state you're in right now, I'll be forced to tell Vi something that you probably don't want her to know. If you know what I mean. Miss *Audiodidact.*"

My stomach roiled even more at this, my head throbbed, my tongue felt sickly furred. "You wouldn't," I said.

"I would," said Clarissa, grimly.

"You wouldn't," I said again, but I knew she would. The only thing I could never tell Vi was a thing only Clarissa knew about: how, in college, in lieu of having to tell my mother about a tuition hike that wasn't covered by my scholarship, plus credit card debt rapidly deepening by dint of mere proximity to spendthrift Clarissa, I began a small side-business called Audiodidact in "academic paper transcription." This meant that slackers with enough money to af-ford my prices would hand me a microcassette on which they blab-bered mindlessly, ostensibly on their assigned paper topics, which I would then "transcribe" by doing their research for them and actu-ally writing the papers. Only once did I get a B on some freshman lacrosse player's paper—I was sick with mono—and had to give the money back. It was such a slick deal that every writing center at each of the five colleges in the area trumpeted my business as if it were totally legitimate, and I'm sure they thought it was. Vi, however, would never have believed it. If she knew, it would be the bitterest disappointment of her life: *I may not be able to give you money, Sunshine*, she always said, *but I can give you brains and I can give you morals.* With my business, I used both badly, and I knew she wouldn't forgive me for it. She would look at me differently forever afterward. It would break both of our hearts.

"Clarissa," I said now. "Nasty, nasty. Blackmail?"

"Yup," she said. "I can't do it, Willie. You've got Vi to help you out. I've got Sully. I'll give you a call later. My soap's on right now," and she slammed down the phone.

I was ill, yes; sick at not being able to go to Clarissa. But the other feeling growing in my gut was a lightness, a brightness; perhaps (a little bit) of relief. I fell asleep again, and when I awoke at four o'clock that afternoon, I knew it was Vi's day off because she was vacuuming and kept knocking the machine against my door. The birds outside were trying to sing themselves over the racket, and when I awoke, it was to a thumping roar pricked with shrill little chirping, such terrific noise it made my stomach churn. When Vi shut off the vacuum to move it elsewhere, I heard her chuckling to herself.

"What?" I called out. "You think you're clever?"

My door opened and my mother put her head inside. "Yes," she said. And then she saw me, small and pale under my canopy and in my heap of pillows, and said, "Oh, heavens, you look horrible."

"Thanks," I said. Vi came over to my bed and sat beside me.

"Are you sick?" she began, but she must have caught the scent of residual alcohol on my skin because she froze, and her face fell. "Oh, Willie," she said. "You drank? What about. You know," and she looked away.

"The Lump?" I said.

"Yes," she said.

"I know," I said. "I don't know." I considered telling her that it was no use; there was no way I was ready to be a parent; that I had to forget about the Lump and worry about everything else. Then I considered the cross she wore on a thong so long it brushed my bedspread, and a little inner devil poked me into saying, maliciously,

"How was your little sleepover party last night, Vi? Did you have a good time?"

My mother cocked her eyebrow and made a tight little face. "Grand," she said, dryly. "Not as fun as yours, I guarantee."

I thought of Felcher and winced. "Mine wasn't fun at all." Then I thought of Clarissa, my half-sober conversation with Sully, and said, "Vi, I have to talk to you. I called Clarissa back." My mother's face lit up, and with her smile the flesh around her eyes rose, and she looked far younger than she normally did; she now looked like a woman of forty-six, her actual age.

"How is she?" she said, in her softest voice. "My little Clarissa."

As I thought of how to answer this, a knot of tourists passed on the street, and they were so loud I could hear their voices all the way in the back of the house, where my room was. At least four men seemed to be arguing; at least one child was crying; I thought I could hear the slow cataract of two women's voices as they complained. All the happy tourists are gone in August; in August, there are the angry tourists, the frustrated ones, the hot and sticky hopeless ones. Boston fans always came in August. I waited until they were gone and said, "She stopped doing her antibody therapy, Vi. The one I told you about."

The smile fell from my mother's face. "What?" she said.

I sat up in bed. "Clarissa is going homeopathic, and now she's in big trouble."

My mother frowned. After a while, she said, "What can that girl be thinking?"

"I don't know," I said. "Not too much, I think. Sully asked me to go back to San Francisco soon, to help him take care of her. I think he's so overwhelmed he's about to break. It's kind of scary."

"What are you waiting for?" she said, pulling the covers off me. "Go."

"I know," I said. "But there's a problem. I called Clarissa this morning, and she refused to let me come. She was furious. She said I'd be more of a strain on her than anything, and I should just stay here and let you fix me. That I was as much of a mess as she was."

My mother looked at me, and drew a hand over her worn face. In the light from the window, her skin looked mottled, pocked, and it sagged below her cheeks, as if weighted with beans. "Oh, Sunshine," she said, slowly. "You *should* be with her, and yet I don't think that she's wrong. I just don't think you should leave right now, I don't think you're healthy. Plus, if you left without knowing who your father was, just knowing that he was here, I think your brain would play its usual tricks on you. You'd have worse and worse thoughts about Templeton, about how every single man you ever met could have been your father. You'd start to hate it. You'd be scared off for good. And we wouldn't want that, would we?"

"I know," I said. "And I'm not sure I'd ever come back."

My mother kicked off her slippers and crawled up the bed. She settled in beside me on the headboard and took my hand. "I couldn't live with you never coming back," she said. "This is your town, Willie. And I know you can't give a whole town to your daughter, but your family has so much history here that you couldn't *not* come back. You have to. You are a Temple in the best way. And you've always known I want you to move back here someday. Whether that's when you retire at age seventy, or what, I don't know. I just know this town needs a Temple to live here. You can't hate Templeton. Now what should we do?"

For a while, we sat like this in the calm morning. I could feel my mother's pulse in the meat of her hand, and it was strong and warm. "You could tell me who my father is," I said. "Then I could go back to San Francisco and just deal with everything there. Break down Clarissa's door if she locks it. Set up camp in her hallway. If you told me who he is."

"I could," she said. "Do you want me to?"

"No," I said, surprising myself.

My mother seemed to have expected this, and I could feel her nodding beside me. "No," she repeated. "You can't just have it handed to you. I think you need to find out on your own. Otherwise, a little piece of you would never believe me."

"Plus," I said. "It keeps my mind off . . . things."

"All right," said Vi. "I'll talk to Clarissa, see if she can change her mind on one or both counts. So," she said, "where are you in the whole quest?"

I sighed and sat back against my pillows. "I just began looking into someone on the Hetty side called Cinnamon Averell Stokes Starkweather Sturgis Graves Peck."

My mother whistled. "Now, that's a name," she said.

"Big-time player," I said. "Five husbands. All dead. And I'm also looking on the legitimate side at Charlotte Franklin Temple. She's Jacob Franklin Temple's daughter. Novelist herself, I found out. Nom de plume of Silas Merrill. But I'm stalled out. No information on obscure Victorian ladies in the public record. Who knew?"

"Cinnamon," my mother mused. "Charlotte."

"Yes," I said. "I'm sure that if you keep just saying their names they'll magically appear and bestow all their secrets upon us."

"Charlotte and Cinnamon," said my mother. "They sound so familiar."

"Vi, now's not the time to have one of your little flashbacks, all right? I'm sure they were just folk singers in your heyday or something. Don't worry about it."

But my mother had turned her face to me, and she was blinking quickly. "My gosh," she said. "Wait here." Then she lifted herself off the bed and hurried away over the house, down the long hallway, down the staircase, over the shaky floorboards of the entryway and into the Victorian wing of the house. I heard her go into the little room where she kept all of her books and paperwork, and laughed as I heard her run back upstairs, her great, heavy footsteps quick as a giant's on the scent of an Englishman.

When she came back into the room, her face was flushed and she was almost pretty. She was waving a manila envelope so old that small flakes of it salted the ground around her. "Ta-da," she cried. "I'm not insane." She put the envelope in my lap and looked at me. "This is something my dad left when he died. I never opened it."

I picked the envelope up and read in the elegant spidery script of my grandfather, *September 14th, 1966. Correspondence of Cinnamon Averell Peck and Charlotte Franklin Temple. Do not open unless necessity forces you. Contents disturbing and painful.* That was my grandfather's voice from his little book, equally pompous and stern. I felt a wash of affection for that poor little man with his ingrown passions that he squeezed and squeezed and squeezed until they were sore.

Then I realized that this packet had never been read, that it had tempted my mother since Vi's parents died, nearly thirty years ago.

"Vi?" I said. "You never opened this? With all your love of our family? Never?"

She frowned then at the ground. "No," she said. "I knew my father, Sunshine. I just couldn't do it. Besides," she said. "I know all about Pandora."

"Hm," I said. "But in the myth in the Bible, it's Eve who lets evil into the world."

She gave me a little playful smack on the cheek. "Careful what you call a myth. And I don't know, I think we need a few more uppity women in the world. Which," she said, "brings me to my next point."

"That is?" I said.

"Clarissa," she said.

"God," I said.

"Don't blaspheme," she said. "And don't worry. I'm calling her."

I watched as my mother lifted the old telephone and dialed the rotary dial. Without even a hello, she said into the receiver, "Well, if it isn't Clarissa. I've got a great big bone to pick with you, darling, so you better listen up good now. I heard from a little birdy that you were just about to let yourself be a big, fat idiot, and go all alterna-nut on me, and not do your western medicine. I just have to say that since I want you around for a good while longer, I don't think you should be doing that."

She listened for a moment, then grinned and said, "Don't you dare turn all tough-girl on me. I was the original Tough Girl and your imitation is piss-poor. Listen," she said, and I watched my mother explain every issue to Clarissa, taking her arguments and turning them on their heads. I watched Vi as the sunshine crept across the ground, and spread up her thick legs, up her trunk, up her face until she was glowing, golden. She seemed to expand in a way that good people do when they're being great. I listened until I knew my mother had, at last, convinced her. When Vi turned around and showed me two fingers, I understood that Clarissa had agreed to let me come in two weeks if she wasn't better. I left the room with the envelope in my hands as Vi murmured and I stood in the hallway, feeling a vast and dark relief suck at me. I had time.

And then, before me, rose Vi's face as it was on the day when I was twelve and Philip Tzara called me a bastard. We were at the gym, and it was after swim practice, and since it was nearly the summer, the sunset was drifting deep gold over the cornfield around the gym. This is what I remember: Philip and me doing the strange tough-mouthed little dance that was flirtation back then, our wet hair, the stretching shadows of the stalks, the excitement in my belly, me calling him Retard, he smirking, saying Whatever, you bastard, then that tremendous black bubble rising up in me. I was bigger than all the boys in my class, and I decked him easily. He lay, stunned, on the ground, in the sudden silence of the kids around us. I'd split one of his teeth in two and cut my skin on it. I couldn't tell whose blood was whose.

By the time my mother walked into the gym manager's office that evening, Philip's mother had been threatening for an hour to sue the gym, and Philip was crying silently on the chair opposite me. I wanted to kick him for being such a wuss, for the way his mother looked at me, hot with hatred. The manager, normally a kind, round-faced man, had been worked into a purple fury by Mrs. Tzara, and so when Vi entered the room, he spun on her and s. And I saw Vi grow bigger in that office until she seemed larger than the rest of us put together.

She spoke so calmly and so quietly that we all leaned forward to hear what she was saying. "Nonsense," she said. "Willie is the smartest person I know. If she hit this boy, she had a good reason to. Right, little boy?" she said, turning to Philip.

And Philip, whose tears were dripping freely down his face, gave a little shuddery gasp and said, "I just called her a bastard . . ."

With this word, and with what everyone in town knew already about me, Philip punctured the adults' anger, and it went visibly hissing out of all of them. His mother's shoulders sagged and she wailed, "Oh, Philip," and the gym manager shook his head. "Oh," he said. "Well, in that case, I'm so sorry, Ms. Upton. I didn't really know."

"May I take my daughter home and make sure she hasn't broken her hand?" she said, coldly.

"Certainly, certainly," he said, and Mrs. Tzara hustled Philip out, and the manager, apologizing profusely, said I wasn't, actually, forbidden from going to the gym, of course, he was so very sorry for everything.

In the car ride home, I looked at my mother, wondering. So many nights I had held her head in my lap and comforted her after someone had slighted her in town, after her own delicate ego had been shattered yet again. The strong, huge woman driving our car across the dark town seemed foreign to me. Only years later did it strike me that however weak Vi could be about her own sorrows, when faced with others', she became spectacular. This is what allowed her to soothe the dying into calmer deaths, this largeness of Vi's, this softness.

In the hallway as Vi talked Clarissa off her ledge, I put a finger under the ancient envelope flap. I shook the little packets of letters in their dusty velvet ribbons out of the envelope and into my hands, and imagined Vivienne Upton filling all of Averell Cottage with her glory, until everything held the color and viscosity of honey in the sun. I held the old packet of letters in my hand and imagined Vi filling all of Lake Street with her goodness, then pouring and pouring out until she filled all of Templeton, entire.

WHAT WILLIE UPTON UNDERSTOOD ABOUT HER FAMILY, REVISED YET AGAIN AND ABRIDGED FOR SIMPLICITY'S SAKE

Hetty Averell *(slave)* ◂ **Marmaduke Temple** ▸ **Elizabeth Temple** *(wife)*

Guvnor Averell   Richard Franklin Temple   Jacob Franklin Temple
                              (no issue)

Flora	Marguerite	Rose	Jasmine	Lily	Lilas	Daisy	Charlotte
(all married and moved)					*(twins)*		*(Charlie)*
1812	1814	1819	1822	1824	1825		1827-1912

Ginger Averell   Cinnamon Averell
1832-1862   1834-1908
                      m. Stokes
                      m. Starkweather   Henry Franklin Temple
                      m. Sturgis   1862-1939
                      m. Graves   m. Hannah Clarke *(in 1909)*
                      m. Peck   1888-1979

Leah Averell Peck   Ruth Peck Starkweather
1867-1890 *(moved)*   1868-1910
                         m. Hiram Starkweather
                              1860-1908

Claudia Starkweather   Sarah Franklin Temple
1888-1923   1913-1933
m. Chuck Tipton   m. Asterisk "Sy" Upton
1887-1948   1895-1953

Phoebe Tipton ————————— m. 1951 ————————— George Franklin
1923-1973   Temple Upton
                                                1933-1973

                         Vivienne Upton
                             1955-
                    (Random Templeton Man) ——————————

                    Willie "Sunshine" Upton
                           1973-

Charlotte Franklin Temple
Watercolor from the mid-1850s.

Cinnamon Averell Stokes Starkweather Sturgis Graves Peck
A photograph taken in 1860, between her second and third husbands.

Cinnamon and Charlotte

TO WHOMEVER READS This Collection of Letters: Be warned. This is material that should not, by any means, be released to the general public, for fear of shaming two prominent Templeton families. These letters were discovered separately by me, over the span of two decades. I found Charlotte's packet from Cinnamon in a small trunk in the attic of the Franklin House as a young boy. Twenty years later, while searching for a missing stud-link, I found Cinnamon's packet in an old wardrobe of my wife's old Templeton family, the Averells. One can imagine my shock when I saw they went together. These are not, obviously, all the letters in the correspondence. Most were flippant and full of feminine nothings, which I donated to the New York State Historical Society. These few letters are selected from the many. Although they provide proof supporting my life's work, I have opted to keep them private. I have tried for many years to destroy them, but find I cannot destroy such history. I fear that these will fall into the wrong hands, but fear more terribly their destruction. I beg of you, whatever your affiliation with our family, to please be a good steward of these secrets.

George Temple Upton, 1966

From the Desk of Charlotte Temple, Franklin House, Blackbird
Bay, Templeton
The Thirteenth of November, 1861

    My dearest friend,

    *How my heart aches for you in your time of need! I could not
bear the depth of your sadness today, as you stood there in your
crepe, your beautiful small face composed so bravely as you
watched the bearers lower your fourth husband into the ground.
And I, who cannot imagine having, let alone losing, <u>one</u>
husband, I had to hurry away at the sight of your pain, after I
heard all those whispers from those terrible gossips. I wept in the
carriage all the way home to Franklin House, and am weeping
still for you. This is why I did not go to the gathering at Averell
Cottage this dark afternoon: I could not have borne seeing you
try to be strong under the false sympathy of those same gossips
who whispered so scandalously about you at your own husband's
funeral. They should be throttled! Shame on them! Shame on
me, for not being a true friend to you, for neglecting my duty to
stand beside you in your want. Should you forgive me? I wonder.
Please forgive, also, my hasty missive; my heart overflows and
I could not keep my pen from scratching through the paper with
my emotion.*
    Your loving friend,
    Charlotte Temple

Averell Cottage, Templeton
November 20, 1861

    My dear Charlotte—

    *I hope you will disregard the week that has passed since I've
received your note of sympathy—I had so much to do! I wanted
to save yours for last and to wallow in the writing of it, so as to
think of you, my dear friend, the whole time.*

*Other than being melancholy for my poor Godfrey, I am also
terribly bored. I must be in heavy mourning for a year and a
day—this decreed by the Graves family, a stipulation for receiving
my share of dear Godfrey's estate. After the year of heavy
mourning, we agreed on six months of full mourning, then six of
half-mourning. But it's the heavy mourning that bothers me so—
one full year of wool and crepe and jet jewelry, one full year
without music or dinners or balls, or any pretty laces or ribbons—
one year without visitors, without seeing your sweet face, my dear
Charlotte—and this is almost worse than Godfrey's death!*

*Ah! You know I didn't mean that—I said it to shock you. I do
love to shock you, how your face pales and you look at me sternly
and you sigh, "Oh, Cinnamon," as if I were hopeless! I am
laughing now at the thought of it and this, too, is unsuitable, it
seems—that French Canadian maid I've got, that Marie-Claude
is frowning at me under her heavy brows. Her ugly face is the
only one I suppose I shall see until next November, alas. At least
I have you to write to.*

*What am I to do while I am interred here, do you think?
I could paint, but the cottage only has a limited number of
windows, and I am afraid I shall exhaust them all before January.
I could read the* Freeman's Journal, *but all that talk of
meerschaum pipes and Vulcanized Rubber Teeth drives me quite
mad. I could maybe knit socks and bandages for our soldiers dying
in the South. What more? Perhaps I could find you a husband,
dear Charlotte—what do you think?*

*You with your devout heart will surely be appalled at my
carrying on, I imagine. I cannot help it—Charlotte, I am giddy,
and I am not entirely sure why. Perhaps it is the shock of losing
Mr. Graves. I fear I shall go mad here in this dark house. You
should move to Temple Manor on Second Street, as your nearness
alone would soothe me.*

*How my heart longs for fun—I just saw a gay little party go
walking down Front Street. Pretty girls on their way somewhere,
mincing past the soldiers, making the eaves of my old house ring
with their merriment. How it reminds me of us, Charlotte, when
we were so young. I think of how pretty and flushed and
sparkling you were at that party just before poor Godfrey passed,*

*when he was feeling poorly, that gay affair at Lydia Clarke's with
the sugared-violet petit-fours and the harpsichord music and that
new ugly old French teacher at Dr. Spotter's Academy, Le Quoi.
He was so very like a vulture, wasn't he, with his bald head and
beady eyes—how he stank of old flesh—he is a rogue, I am
utterly sure of it. He said he came from Nantes, where Henrietta
Bezier is from, my dear friend I know from Mrs. Beasley's
Finishing School in Albany. I have already written to her to
inquire as to whether he is what he says he is, or not. I suspect
not. We shall see, and delight in the drama.*

*Please write, Charlotte. Fill pages and pages with your words.
Tell me stories, of anything—write to me of that terrible
incendiary burning down all the mansions in Templeton. Speculate
on who it is—old Apothecary Mudge with his hideous face? Fat
Lacey Pomeroy with her affected little giggle and boiled walnut
hair (don't protest—I myself have seen the concoction she makes
to dye it)? The idiot son of Dirk Peck, that big lumpy boy who
touches himself shamelessly in the presence of ladies (I shock you
again!)?*

*You shall forgive my frivolity—this is a difficult time for me,
and it seems the only way I can manage. You understand me, if
no one else does.*

Your very affectionate,
Cinnamon Averell Stokes Starkweather Sturgis Graves

From the Desk of Charlotte Temple, Franklin House, Blackbird
Bay, Templeton
The twenty-third of November, 1861

Dearest Cinnamon,

*I admit that I have spent the last few days wondering at how
I was to respond to your letter of the twentieth. It is not like you
to seem so cruel to your husband's memory. At last I understood,
however, that yours is still a fresh grief, and you had been driven
to distraction by your sorrow. I do understand you, my dear friend;
but I pray that you only show your nerves to me; there are plenty
in this town who do not wish you well.*

I have sent, with this letter, some muslin as you have requested,

and a tincture from Aristabulus Mudge. He tells me that one drop
a day will calm you. He is a queer little fellow. I do not wish to
speak ill of a cripple, but he makes me shiver. And have you
noticed how he does not grow old? My father noticed this, bless his
heart; one day, we were working in his study, and he saw Mudge
out on the lake, fishing, and frowned his fine frown, and said,
"Charlie, beware of that man. You cannot trust a man who does
not age." I laughed then: I agree now.

Why do I tell you this? Perhaps because only you know how
terribly I have missed my father for these eleven years. No other
man could fill my heart as my father did, you know. I am destined
to die a virgin. No, Cinnamon, you must not exert yourself to
find me a husband.

I cannot write to you of the incendiary, for I know nothing of
it. We must be Christian and believe that it is someone who is
troubled and is in need of the Lord to help. I cannot move to
Temple Manor because I do not like it—it is cold and haunted—
and my father loved Franklin House, and I must stay in the place
my father loved.

Also, I am very sorry that I cannot write the hundreds of
pages you asked for today. I must be off in a moment: the George
Hydes have invited me to Hyde Hall for the week-end, and
I believe it is to pump me for more funds for Dr. Spotter's
Academy. I believe the Pomeroy girls and Solomon Falconer will
make up the party. I believe the Frenchman you were speaking
of will be there as well. I wish you wouldn't mock him. He does
not look so very like a vulture, and is said to have been of a
noble family that lost everything under Napoleon. He is the only
one in town with whom I can chatter along in my neglected
French.

Now, don't sigh for envy at my week-end; I am sure it is to
be dull, my dear, and you know my horrible shyness and how I
loathe such things. If only I had your vivacity and beauty! Alas,
what we love in others does not always suit ourselves. I shall get
through the weekend by wishing you in my place.

I hope this letter finds you more calm and easy of mind,
my dear.

Your faithful friend,
Charlotte Temple

Averell Cottage, Templeton
November 28, 1861

My darling—

*I am dying to know about your weekend at Hyde Hall! It is
already Wednesday and you have not written. I should think you
know my loneliness better. Write—I implore you.*
Your fondest friend,
Cinnamon Averell Graves

From the Desk of Charlotte Temple, Franklin House, Blackbird
Bay, Templeton
The Second of December, 1861

Dearest Cinnamon,

*I have not written you for I have spent this time wondering
what had happened at Hyde Hall. My head is all in a jumble; I
thought if I gave myself time, I could straighten it out; but I am
still as confused as I had been when I left the Hall so precipitously
on Sunday morning.*

*First, I forget that you have never been to Hyde Hall. It is a
tasty manor, indeed, a stone edifice on a natural swell on the
North part of the lake, an English mansion. In the Spring and
Summer, the gardens are lush and well-tended, though now, in the
Winter, rather sad. The outbuildings are simple and lovely. There
is a strange air to the place, however, almost of desolation, though
all is quite new and fresh.*

*Then there are the people: Susanna and George Clarke: she
beautiful, high-spirited, treacherous; he staid, stern, blindly in love.
Might I say that she had the gall to invite her impoverished
"friend," Nat Pomeroy, for the weekend, without inviting his
sisters? Alas, she did. And the air of discomfort this raised in our
breasts is important, I think, for understanding what happened
later. Also, to complete the women, there were Minnie Phinney
and the Foote girls, Bertha and Bettina, special friends of*

Susanna's. For the men, there were Nat Pomeroy, Solomon
Falconer, Peter Mahey, Dr. Spotter with his clammy hands and
blinking eyes, and his new French instructor, Monsieur Le Quoi.

On the first night, little happened. We arrived, settled, changed
for supper, played whist, listened to poor Minnie Phinney wrestle
with the piano, and went straight to bed.

After we arose the next morning and ate our breakfasts,
someone suggested we while away our time at taking a walking
tour of the grounds. We heartily agreed, and spent a nice two
hours in the air. Susanna, you see, loves the outdoors, and
although some of we ladies were rather frozen, she insisted on
pressing further. It <u>was</u> lovely. The early snow had melted and the
ground was firm and hard; the trees were filled with the whispers
of wind in the boughs, our feet made wonderful sounds in the dry
leaves. Somehow, we were paired off halfway through the walk:
George with Bettina, Susanna and Nat (scandalous!), Solomon
with Minnie, Doctor Spotter with Bertha, Peter Mahey with
Susanna's nippy little terriers. That left Monsieur Le Quoi to fall
back and offer his arm to me.

I must disabuse you; he does not smell like an old man; his
scent is fresh, like cucumbers, not like "old flesh," as you said.
His smile is kind and his manners sublime, much like my father's.
And, Cinnamon, we had a grand time talking together. He spoke
of his family in France (he is the son of a marquis; for once, the
rumors are well founded!), his lovely, smart students, his
adventuresome life—he has tried everything, and he even was a
Jesuit seminarian at one point. I spoke of my family's early travels
to France. It seems we know quite a number of people in
common.

I forgot my cold hands and feet, and was rather sorry when
we turned, and the men switched partners, and I found myself
babbling thoughtlessly to that handsome rake, Nat Pomeroy.
He looked at me, amused, and smoked all the way back to Hyde
Hall.

All afternoon, I and the other ladies sat in the drawing-room.
I tried to read, but Susanna talked to me so much, inserting the
Academy everywhere, that I was convinced I had been correct in
assuming it was a week-end to raise funds for the school. She
drove me mad, and I retired to my room for the hours before

supper. Imagine my surprise when I saw, on my bedstand, one blooming pink rose, a rose from the Hall's conservatory. There was a small card beside it that said, <u>From an Admirer</u>. My heart pounded, Cinnamon. I could not rest.

I needn't tell you how I could not speak at dinner, for terror of blurting out my surprise about the rose. How grateful was I that there was music and dancing all night, Bettina happily taking the piano from Minnie! As there were more men than women, I never sat one dance out. I had three dances with Solomon Falconer, who reminds me so of my father—physically only, of course, the man is morally a menace—two with Nat, two with George, one with Dr. Spotter, and one with Monsieur Le Quoi.

At last, I was able to take a rest when Dr. Spotter engaged Mr. Le Quoi in the corner for a conversation, and I slipped outside to cool down. I went wandering a little in the gardens, as they were astounding, silver and eerie in the moonlight, like the gardens of half-malign fairies. I was looking at the long slate of the lake when I heard a footstep behind me. I closed my eyes, drew my shoulders in, took a deep breath. A finger in a leather glove touched my chin very gently. And, when I opened my eyes, nearly swooning, I looked into the smiling face of Nat Pomeroy.

You, who know my heart so well, will understand what an extraordinary disappointment this was. Oh, Cinnamon. First, because I had expected another to follow me. And then, in the briefest of breaths, I was disappointed doubly, for I suddenly understood what the week-end was to be: Susanna was making a play to marry me to her impoverished lover, Nat. They would have chuckled over it, believing he could charm the ugly little spinster, give her enough attention so that she would be forever grateful. And then, when she had fallen under his spell, and they married, he would use her money in the pursuit of his beautiful Susanna.

Oh, wicked, wicked! I saw it all. I said nothing, turned, fled inside to my chamber. That night, a little outbuilding on the grounds burned down and all the men were needed to try to put it out—they returned at dawn, shivering in their wet clothing, clomping over the floors. And when they had fallen into their beds, and it was a decent hour, I left a note, explaining I had to return to Templeton for sudden business, and I rode back over the hills of East Lake Road in my little carriage, squeezing my handkerchief in my two hands.

Another confession: I am in despair. Perhaps I have been too precipitate by proclaiming that I do not ever wish to marry. I have been trying, perhaps, to flirt with Mr. Le Quoi, but I can't seem to. He is so charming, though not necessarily handsome, that all the women try to flirt with him, and I am stuck in the corner, burning when Bertha or Minnie giggle and chatter and make him say such gallant things. I think, perhaps, my heart is filling with him. Please say nothing about this to anyone. You probably laugh at me. Please don't. I am not like you, Cinnamon: I know I am plain and solemn and shy. Perhaps you could teach me how to flirt, how to make myself as appealing as possible. Please don't laugh. I do want to learn, quite desperately, and you are the perfect candidate to teach me. Do you think you could?

My face burns with embarrassment. I will end this letter and send it to you, in the hope that you do not laugh too much at me.

With great affection,
Charlotte Temple

Averell Cottage, Templeton
December 5, 1861

My dearest Charlotte—

You have given me so much joy! Here is a worthy project— I have often wanted to suggest to you a small improvement here or there, for if I am good at anything, it is at making myself agreeable to men—and I am certain that when we are finished with you, you shall be married. In fact, I guarantee it! But, first, I must scold you—take from your heart any silly affection for the bald old Frenchman—he is so below your station that you should barely notice him, even in the best society. Oh no—when I am finished, you will have wed a prince! We shall use your sisters' high places in society—you will make a brilliant match!

I have carefully considered and below is my advice. Follow it as best as you can.

Appearance:

1) Hair—*My darling, we must do something about your hair-style. Though you were charming at eighteen with your long masses of curls framing your face, you have a very young face, and the out-of-date style only now serves to make you look childish. Consider putting your hair up at your nape and cutting and curling small frizzes around your cheeks.*

2) Dress—*We* must *get you out of black, my dear. Although I understand you are in mourning for your father, no man dares to approach a woman whose whole heart is invested in a dead man. I should know. Your colors are purple or dark green. Zina Mix is Templeton's best dressmaker, but you must ask your sisters to send you the latest style-books from Europe. Also, please order slippers*—*one cannot wear the sturdy boots you wear and expect a man to marvel at your delicate feet.*

3) Jewelry—*My darling, at their very cores, men are all still the boys who built castles of sticks and gutted clocks to see how they worked. They are fascinated by whirling, clicking things. Earrings that dangle and tinkle like bells are your friends*—*bracelets that chime when you move and fill the air around you with music. This must be discreet, however*—*otherwise, you will sound like a one-woman band!*

Flirtation—*We shall work with, not against, your natural shyness, as if we were to work against it, you would only be full of artifice. And you know artifice, since you know Susanna Clarke, and how it is not attractive in the least.*

1) When a man comes into the room, allow yourself to blush. Now, I know you have little control over your blushing, but you usually hide your cheeks by ducking your head down so your hair covers them, or you ask hasty questions so attention is diverted to another. Instead, hold your head high, give a small, private smile, and try very hard not to look at the man of your choice. It will be apparent that this is what you intend to do— *good!*

2) When he speaks only to you, look at his lips or his eyes— *you tend to gaze at a man's collar when you speak in a tête-à-tête. Delicately bite your lip, smile up at him, through your lashes again, and mimic the way he is sitting on his chair or standing,*

*taking care to make it look ladylike—everyone loves a mirror,
even if one doesn't know one does.*

 *When you have mastered these points, you will be well on your
way. I shall teach you then how to write a love-note, how to
arrange for a secret rendezvous (don't be shocked—everyone does
it), how to convince your servant how to keep a secret, et cetera.*

 *I hope this is not overmuch. I am only interested in your
happiness! Please write to me as soon as you have mastered some of
these effects. Also, do not worry about stupid Susanna Clarke and
her paramour. They are not subtle, and so they are not dangerous.*

 Your loving,
Cinnamon Averell Graves

From the Desk of Charlotte Temple, Franklin House, Blackbird
Bay, Templeton
December the Ninth, 1861

 Dear Cinnamon,

 *Thank you for your kind advice. I admit that I am
overwhelmed by all the changes I must make to my person and
manners. I did not know I had so much to improve. I have ordered
the books and slippers from my sister Marguerite. I am not at all
sure of my eventual mastery of the art of flirtation, but I shall try.*

 *Also, I am afraid that I cannot dislodge Monsieur Le Quoi from
my heart. I have tried. But I saw him at Church on Sunday, and
his eyes are so kind that I wanted him near me again. Please say
you'll help me, even with him as my object. Please do.*

 Your friend,
Charlotte Temple

Averell Cottage, Templeton
December 11, 1861

 Dear Charlotte—

 *I have considered, and I will help you, even with the
Frenchman as your object. Sometimes the heart cannot listen to*

reason. I was like you with my first husband, dear Paul Stokes, and thought I'd die when he was thrown from his horse and broke his neck. I shall renounce all hope of a prince for you—for <u>this</u> husband, at least! I joke, but the Frenchman is quite a bit older than you, my dear, and you should be prepared for anything.

Remember, il faut souffrir pour être belle. I have been reading in French again, so that I can practice with you when I come out of heavy mourning in November.

I shall write more later,

Yours,

Cinnamon Averell Graves

Mon Cher Monsieur Le Quoi—

[rough draft, unblotted]

Please listen to the song of a small bird who would like to inform you that you have an admirer—the highest lady of the town. This little bird wishes for her happiness and would sing gladly to see you escort her on her walk home after Church on Sunday. She says she walks the miles to her mansion as a penance for her sins—but this little bird knows that she has no sins, and that you, monsieur, could turn her penance into a blessing.

A Friend

The eleventh of December

My dearest, kindest, most beautiful friend, Cinnamon,

Forgive the scribbled note. I am beside myself. Oh, Monsieur Le Quoi walked me all the way to Blackbird Bay from Church! Your advice works wonders, my dear. You are the most wonderful friend I could imagine. I must send this now with Joseph, who is going into town in a moment, and must go to my room and be by myself until my elation is gone.

Your loving (!)

Charlotte

Averell Cottage
19th Dec.
[rough draft in a wild hand]

Oh, Charlotte—

I don't know what to do—I am all in a muddle—I must write to you immediately—something terrible has happened—I had a letter, a long one, twenty pages, I was to send it to you in the morning, all flirtation advice, but it is useless now—I threw it in the fire. Now I fling this missive at you—you must help me!

You will get this as soon as I finish—I will send one of the stableboys with it immediately—I hope he can make it over the snowdrifts. I have not slept, I am all a-tremble. Oh, Charlotte, you remember the blizzard last night. The terrible wild wind and snow and the cracking branches—Marie-Claude went home early to care for their cows—I was eating my little supper, when there was a terrible knocking at my door, a pounding. And before I could stand, it was flung open, and there, a bear stood in the door, covered in snow!

No—not a bear, it advanced into the room, and grunted and took off the odd hat, with the long muffler, and shook itself, and suddenly, under the snow, I saw the face of my sister, Ginger. Ginger! Do you remember—so huge and bossy, Ginger who made you cry by forbidding you to play base-ball with her and the boys because you were a rich girl, Ginger, who ran away from my father when she was fourteen. Rawboned Ginger, grinning at me in the firelight, dressed in a man's clothes—she looked like a man, and if I hadn't known her face, I would have said she was one. She had not changed, just grew more massive. Ginger had come back to Templeton.

Before I could unfreeze from my place, to spring up, to close the door, to embrace my sister, she bellowed out, "Come in!" And suddenly there was a mess of people clomping in, all across the floor that Marie-Claude had just scrubbed that morning, there were only four, I counted later, but at that time, it seemed like a veritable army. All shook snow off, took off boots, jackets, all rushed in, a great babble of voices toward the fire. I had stopped breathing, and when I could start again, Ginger turned to me. "Cin!" she boomed, "I'm home!"

I gasped. "Welcome," I said, and one of the others with Ginger said, "Fine one, your sister, Papa Gin. Lady, in't she?" and it was a woman, I saw. And, I saw, they were all women— all in dresses so bright under their wrappings that my eyes were dazzled, and there was a strong smell, cologne and bodies, rolling up in the steam from their clothing by the fire. Ginger turned to the woman who spoke, and the woman ducked her head, like a cur. Ginger said, "Let me introduce you. Cinnamon, meet my girls. This here's Lolo—she's French from New Orleans. This two is twins from Indiana, Minerva and Medea. This last one is my best, Barbara, but his name's really Samuel." And then they were shaking my hands with their cold hands—the fat, indolent redhead with bright cheeks, the skinny ugly blondes, the beautiful boy I would never have known was a boy, for he wore skirts and had a long collar that covered his Adam's apple. I looked at them, dazzled, and looked at my sister, who was grinning at me.

"Oh," I breathed. "Ginger, what in the world are you doing in Templeton?"

"Been a long time," she said. "Lots of life happened. I done a lot of things, some I'm shamed of, some proud. Sit down," she said to me, and I obeyed her command, if only in shock. I was close to swooning—I had the queerest feeling then—as if I saw every characteristic of my parents isolated, boiled down, distilled, then pressed into the opposite molds of my sister and me. Ginger has my father's height and dark skin and flashing eyes—his strong jaw, his bad temper, his craftiness—though my mother's stout figure and straight chestnut hair, and—perhaps—a glimmer of her madness. I have my mother's petite height, rosy skin, her kindness and gentleness, but my father's thin build, coppery hair, his fluted voice, his cleverness with money. My sister and I—we are divided as people are who cannot be related.

Then Ginger at last broke the silence. "First," she said, "won't you offer the weary travelers refreshments?" and I, ashamed for some reason, though they were not invited, in fact this was scandalous—they should never have been there, I was in heavy mourning!—I stood and cut some ham and bread and cheese (the good cheese, from Starlin Yeoman's farm), and made some strong coffee. The girls in the bright dresses wolfed down this meal as if they hadn't eaten in days. At last, Ginger slid my bowl over to herself, the soup that had long since cooled, and drank it down without asking me. When she was finished, she sat back, patted her lips, smiled—it was a terrible smile, Charlotte.

"No children? I heard you had yourself four husbands already, Cin, and you don't got no children? You barren?"

"I don't know," I whispered. "And you?"

"Nah," said my sister. "Lost one early. Never could have no more after. Guess it makes the job easier." And my sister's girls all snorted into their teacups, hinnying dreadfully.

"What job?" I said in a panic. "Why are you here?"

"Why we here? Ah, Cin, you know why we're here. Always playing the innocent, ain't you. Ah, Cin, Cin," she said. Until that moment, I swear I did not understand their presence, but it all fell into place—the bright dresses, the perfume, the slatternly girls, the boy in a girl's dress. I fear your innocence, Charlotte—I must tell you—to be blunt, they were there to set up a bordello.

"Oh, Ginger," I gasped, "so it's blackmail?" I thought she wanted me to give her money so she would go away. But she laughed and her eyes bulged and she said, "A good idea, that. But, no, you couldn't never give me as much as we're going to get usselves. We're here to stay." I felt faint—I looked at the girls— I saw one pluck at a louse that was crawling across her cheek, crack it under her fingernails.

"To stay?" I said. "Oh, no, Ginger."

"Oh, yes," she said. "Gold opportunity. My girls, they don't like following no army around no more—too much competition— too many dead boys we seen. Diseases, too. No, we seen that Templeton's a transfer station for regiments from up here, and with all them rich boys at the Academy and what with the new hotel at the bottom of Front Street for the health-nuts, it's going to be a fashion town. With fashion people, come fashion money. Picked up a few tricks on the Mississippi, going to open up a billiards, cards

*place, too, someday. No, we're here to stay. Stay out of your way,
though. You won't need to worry about us. I call myself Papa Gin
Stone—nobody going to connect you to me."*

*And that unnatural boy in the girl's green dress fluttered his
eyelashes, said, "We be sure, Madam, to be quiet as church mice.
No one ever know we here."*

*Ginger just stroked the boy's cheek, said, "That's right,
darling. We'll stay the night here, only. We're gone in the
morning." Then the fat one who had been lolling her head on her
chest began to snore, and the others stood and unrolled their
blankets on the floor. And in the morning my sister was gone, as
was my entire set of family silver, and the housekeeping money for
the winter from that canister in the pantry.*

*I do not know what to do, Charlotte. It is morning—I am still
in my clothes from last night—Marie-Claude has come in and is
muttering French curses as she scrubs the floor again—I simply
don't know what to do. Please, please help me with your wisdom
and your discretion. Please don't tell a soul. Tell me what I should
do. Please forgive me for not writing a fresh copy—my hand
aches—I must send this to you, or else I feel I shall lose my
mind. I know this is hasty—I just beg of you to help.*

Your friend in need,
Cinnamon

Averell Cottage, Templeton
Christmas Day, 1861

My dearest Charlotte—

*You are an angel. What would I have done without you? You
have provided such comfort on these dark and terrible days, even
perhaps at the expense of your romance with your dear
Frenchman. You have not had time to walk with him as you
usually do. Oh, you did calm me, care for me. You are right—I
must be patient—I am not my sister's keeper—the Lord will
judge her, not I.*

*Charlotte, I do believe I would have harmed myself had you
not hurried across the frozen lake and up the lawn to come to my*

aid. *And returned, and returned, every day, until I was calm. I have taken the tincture you have sent again, and am drowsy, but before I sleep, I will send this present to you. I wrote Aristabulus Mudge and had him make it up for me—it is a love-potion—I have used it myself—believe me, it works well. You must put it into food that you make with your own hands, and have your beloved eat it.*

Have I told you that when I am drowsy like this, I begin to see my husbands? It is quite alarming. They are in the shadows. They do not smile. What am I writing? I can barely follow my own pen, I am so tired. Now, my dear, I must sleep. I am forever in your debt.

Your loving,
Cinnamon Averell Graves

Ginger "Papa Gin Stone" Averell
March 1862.
*Taken by Telfer's Studios in Templeton, this photo shows Ginger
in her woman's garb. She must have puzzled the poor photographer,
showing up out of nowhere one day, and disappearing the next. One
wonders why she chose to sit for her portrait as a woman: one suspects
she would have made a far more attractive man.*

An Interruption

I HAD BEGUN to read Cinnamon's and Charlotte's letters late the night before, after a dinner with my mother and an old black-and-white movie on television that I watched after she left for work at eleven. I was surprised, then, when I looked out my window with still half of the pack of letters left to read, only to see the sun beginning to slip from behind the hills and paint the lake a paler color. I yawned and stretched, then told the ghost in my room that I needed a little break. It was lilac colored, had seemed to be pulsing quickly all night, like a rabbit-heart bared, still beating. When I tried to look at it directly, it made itself invisible.

I went downstairs and made some coffee, then turned on the television, and laughed. Sitting primly before me on the screen, like boys at a spelling bee, the Running Buds were yukking it up with a pretty, petite woman, and she was giggling like a fool. It was a repeat of their interview on the *Daybreak!* show. But I only caught the end. The woman thanked the Buds for being on, and the camera cut away to a very handsome reporter who was striding purpose-fully forward.

"For the past week," he was saying, "professional divers have been trying to reach the bottom of this nine-mile glacial New York lake, in order to see if Glimmey, the 'monster' that was discovered last week, is the only one of its kind. Remarkably, not one single diver has been able to reach the bottom. This lake is so deep that the divers cannot swim any deeper than four hundred feet below the surface. Today, however, that will change. Today"—the camera slid off center to show a bright yellow machine beside the reporter—"a deep-sea pod will go under the fabled waters of Glimmerglass and will discover what, if anything, lives so far beneath the surface of this placid, lovely lake. And," he said with great solemnity, "exactly how deep the lake goes." Here, the camera shifted again, to show my lake, pink and golden in the sunrise, wreathed with wisps of fog.

I turned off the television and looked toward the lake, saw the yellow pod heading out like a bullet into it on an overlarge pon-toonlike contraption. I watched until it faded, and then I turned away so I didn't have to imagine it tunneling into the dark waters of the deepest parts of our lake.

AT PRECISELY SEVEN, the front doorbell rang. I was afraid for the moment that it was Ezekiel Felcher—I hadn't gone out the day be-fore, but I had seen his truck parked in front of our house for quite a few hours—and almost decided not to answer it, for fear of losing my temper and smacking him a good one across the face. But then I began to think of calamities that could have befallen my mother; a semi running over her as she walked home from the hospital, one meth-crazed loony shooting up the hospital, a peaceful aneurysm that came over her as she did the shift-ending paperwork, and I ran to the door, fast, tears already in my eyes.

When it opened, it was all I could do not to let those welled-up drops fall, as all six of the Running Buds were standing there, grin-ning at me, saying their gentle "heyyy."

"Willie Upton!" said Frank Phinney. "We *heard* you were in town. What are you doing, girl, not coming out to run with us? We are mortally offended, kid. I'm not sure we'll be able to forgive you."

"Don't listen to him. Nice hair," added Johann Neumann. "You look good, Vilhelmina."

Tiny Thom Peters, my pediatrician, held out a white paper bag glistening with arcs of grease. "We brought doughnuts," he said, smiling up at me. ".I promise not to tell Vi."

"Buds," I said, looking at these sweaty old men in their running gear, their legs almost indecently hairy in the soft morning. "It is wonderful to see you."

IT MUST HAVE been an hour that we sat at the table, but I began to feel a peace that I hadn't felt since I came home on the day the monster died. The Buds were their charming selves, spilling gossip and speculation. I learned that a baseball player who had just been inducted into the museum had had a little affair with a sixteen-year-old Templeton girl, and everyone was hopping mad. I learned that Laura Irving, Big Tom's daughter, had run away three weeks earlier, and nobody knew where she was. That's why he looked so fleshy, heavy. I learned that since I came home, I have been looking "pissed, pissed, pissed. Everyone told us so, so we came to see for ourselves."

This is what Doug Jones, my handsome high-school English teacher, said. He winked at me, then said, "But you don't look so angry to me. Just sad, I think."

For a moment, they just sat there watching and waiting for me to say something. To confess, I suppose, to what made me return home. I thought of telling them about Primus Dwyer and my arctic adventures, about the little nut of a Lump inside of me. But Tom Irving had sold me my car for fifty dollars; Doug Jones had cast me as Juliet and Desdemona; Sol Falconer had given me a college loan, and, as he was rich and childless, it was a loan that I was in no danger of ever having to pay back.

So I looked at them and remembered then the first time the Buds and I became aware of one another. It was June and I was four, and I had somehow learned that the Presbyterian Church was having an ice cream social on its broad lawn. I had only ever once had a bite of ice cream; one of my mother's male "friends" had slipped me some on a long silver spoon in Cartwright Café when my mother's back was turned, and I loved it. From what I knew of heaven, there it was, on my tongue: sweet and soft and cool and filled with surprising truffles of nut and fruit.

So the afternoon of the ice cream social I walked away from Averell Cottage, which was easy to do because my mother was painting the dining room walls, and the house was far too big to be able always to hear what a quiet four-year-old was doing in it. I went up the block and trudged past the Bold Dragoon and up the long hill toward the church. Though Frank Phinney was Jewish on his mother's side, Johann Neumann Lutheran, and Thom Peters Catholic, all of the Buds were there with their families, since the ice cream social was a Templeton institution, and no self-respecting gossip could possibly not attend.

By four years old, I had also somehow learned that if I spoke in a small, sad voice, and said that I had no father, I had a great mystical power over adults, and, mainly, over men. And so, when I leaned on tall Sol Falconer's knee, gazing hungrily at his rocky road cone, and he asked me what was wrong, and I whispered that I had no money and, softer, that I had no father to buy an ice cream for me, he leapt up and came back with a cup of vanilla.

"Here, sweetheart," he said, squeezing my little hand, and I stole off behind the bushes to eat the marvelous new food.

Tom Irving was my next target, because he was dozing in a lawn chair, and nobody else was around him. He smiled at me and bought me some mint chocolate chip, giving me a great fat kiss on the forehead. I was feeling wild and jittery by the time I approached Doug Jones, who was feeding his baby from a bottle. He looked at me a little skeptically—I had multicolored rings around my mouth by then—but handed me the remains of his bubblegum ice cream.

"Alas," said the English teacher. "I find I cannot eat with sad little waifs sighing nearby."

I think I stole, outright, Frank Phinney's death-by-chocolate, and he let me, laughing, and I was screeching around the church lawn like an airplane with the other children when Vi came charging up the hill. In the movie of my memory, she comes up the hill as grim and huge as a terrible troll, accompanied by organ music in a minor chord. But she was not quite twenty-two then, still had her baby fat, though her hair was always stringy and her face never quite lovely. She was much smaller than she became later, but to me, at four years old and guilty of unimaginable badness, she was immense. And when she collared me and saw the ice cream melted all over my body, her eyes bulged and she said, "Oh no, Sunshine. No, no, you're allergic to sugar!" and the men's faces paled and dropped. They, too, were frightened of her, I saw. And when, perhaps from suggestibility or too much of the rich food, I started retching everywhere, they rushed over in a six-man herd and apologized until my mother put the puking little me over her arm and walked back home.

From then on, the Buds looked out for me. And now, when they were asking me what was wrong, I just couldn't tell them the extent to which I had failed.

"Oh," I said, trying to smile. "The usual. Heartbreak. Blah blah blah."

They nodded, letting it go.

The door opened, and my mother walked in, then, in her nursing scrubs, seeming heavy, sad. She glanced up and gave a little startled yip, and then looked wildly from face to face. "What?" she said. "What is it?"

"Oh," I said, playing with her a little, "just my prayer group." The Buds chuckled uncertainly, then stood as one.

"We were just going," said Tom Irving. "Nice to see you, Vi." And then, with a great number of shouts about how I must come running with them, and they were glad to see me, and that we'll catch up more next time, the Buds filed out the door. I saw, at last, the source of their discomfort; Reverend Milky was standing there in the mudroom, and the Buds ducked their eyes and said "Morning, Reverend Melkovitch" as each one passed by.

"Well," said Vi, sitting in her chair at the farmhouse table, and rubbing the arch of her foot, "that was unexpected. Come in, John. I'll start breakfast soon."

Reverend Milky appeared sheepishly in the kitchen, and gave me a little nod. He was wearing what was almost a parody of hiking clothing, with a great fleece vest and too-short shorts showing his powdery thighs, replete with bluish veins. His red, hoary toes corkscrewed out of the kind of sandals that looked as if they were made from tires and old fan belts. And it was all, of course, topped with the great iron cross, his own personal millstone. "Willie," he said. "Nice to see you again."

"Yeah," I said. "All right, then. See you later."

"Wait," called my mother as I walked away. "I invited John over so that we could all have a nice breakfast together before I went to sleep for the day. What do you say, Willie? Feel like huevos rancheros?" Vi shoved a strand of greasy hair behind her ear, and tried to look eager, alert.

But I looked at Reverend Milky and said, "No, thanks, Vi. I think I'll skip. Not so hungry right now." But all the way upstairs, my mother's face as it had just looked, flat, disappointed, hovered before me, and I walked two or three circuits around the room before I came back downstairs again. "But I'll take some coffee," I said and sat at the table, opposite the Holy Milk. As she passed on her way to the kitchen, my mother gave me such a smile of relief that I was glad for a moment to look at the good reverend's pasty little face before me.

"So," I said as my mother rustled around the kitchen.

"So," he agreed.

"Going for a hike?" I said.

"Indeed," he said. "I hear you are quite the hiker, as well."

"I was," I said. "Then I moved to San Francisco. The mountains aren't that far, but you get so into your life in the city, all that excitement, all that movement, you find yourself lucky to go out into the hills once in a while and trot around. To be honest, I have so little time, I hardly ever go anymore."

He looked disappointed in me, and said, "But God's good earth is what he gave us to forget our worldly cares."

I just said, "Huh," for the sake of my tired mother moving in the kitchen beyond the doorframe, without pointing out that the earth *is* the world, and he was spouting nonsense. And that's all we could find to say to each other—the Bible-beater, the prodigal harlot daughter—until Vi returned with the platter in her hands, talking lightly about Glimmey. And after she prayed, as we ate our way through the spicy eggs—I found I was hungry after all—she talked of miracles and monsters, of paradoxical mashes of fish and mammal. I looked at her and saw the biggest paradox of my life, my great, proud mother holding the hand of a person she only would have scorned a year ago.

I will never, I vowed to the Lump, watching my mother, *be so lonely I date in desperation.* My mother might have seen the ghost of pity move on my face, because she narrowed her eyes and gazed at me sternly for a moment. "How are Cinnamon and Charlotte?" she said. "Making progress?" This meant, I knew: *if you're not going to be pleasant, you can scram, you brat,* so, with relief, I stood.

"Thanks for the food, Vivienne. So nice to see you again, Reverend. Hope you have a good hike. Don't get eaten by a bear," I said. Halfway through the dining room, I heard his worried voice saying, "Nobody ever told me there are bears here," and when I sat back down to my letters I was still chortling to myself. The ghost had reappeared as a small purple knot pulsing in the corner of the mirror. I said, "And we're off again," and turned over the next letter in the bunch, this one in Charlotte's hand.

18

Cinnamon and Charlotte,
Part Two

From the Desk of Charlotte Temple, Franklin House,
Blackbird Bay, Templeton
The Seventh of January, 1862

My darling Cinnamon,

*You must forgive my silence, for I was visiting with my eldest
sister in her country-house in Rye, and was working there on a
new book (as only you know). I have just returned, and even now,
my maid is still unpacking my things. I am glad you are feeling
better, and the tincture is calming you the way it should. You
alarmed me with the talk of your husbands, but I do believe you
were in a half-dream at that moment, and should not be taken
seriously.*

*Well, you have asked me to report to you anything I may have
heard about your sister: I do believe I heard something. I had
stopped in at the Reverend Belvedere on my way into town, to*

*deliver a letter from my sister. Over tea, the old gossip told me two
things. The first is that Schneider, at the bakery, in the early
morning of the day of the blizzard, reported seeing a vision when
he stepped outside to cool his head. It was, he said, a parade of
strange ghosts, decked all in white, ranged in order from massive
to tiny and wading up Second Street in the hip-deep snow.*

*The other bit I heard was that the Vanderhees bachelor brothers—
those two old Yorkers—had suddenly sold the Leatherstocking Hotel.
You do remember the Leatherstocking, I am sure: the brothers had
bought old Widow Croghan's hotel in the beginning of the century
and just recently updated it. Every room has a mural depicting a
scene from one of my father's Leatherstocking books: Natty Bumppo
leaping down a waterfall, Chingachgook scalping a Huron, Natty
weeping at the slaughter of Passenger Pigeons, et cetera. It was all
very beautiful. The two men came to see me, to bid adieu, though
even after so many years here, they can barely speak English. When
I asked them who had bought their hotel, they looked at one
another. "Large man," they said. "Smell like woman." This does fit
the description of your sister, I believe.*

*A secret before I must speak with my waiting housekeeper:
Monsieur Le Quoi has been very attentive since I took your good
advice, and gave him a little bonbon I made with my own hands.
We have walked together eleven times, and my French has gotten
so much better. He has taken to kissing my hand when we part,
and it burns my skin, Cinnamon, burns through my glove, burns
when I am away from him and burns anew when I see him again.*

*Oh, Cinnamon, my heart is full of gratitude to you, my
dearest friend, and your forced absence weighs heavily on me.*

With great affection,
Charlotte Temple

January 9th, 1862
[rough draft, unfinished]

Dearest Charlotte,

*I feel as if I'm breaking. There is something wrong with me.
I do not know what it is, only that you can help me, somehow.*

I need to tell you something terrible, you see. The world is dark and mean. I don't know what I . . .

January 14th, 1862
[rough draft, unfinished]

Dear Charlotte,

Why don't you write? Why don't you write? Are you too in love to write? Aren't you my friend, don't you know how sad I am, how lonely? Don't you know anything? You think you are in love—you are not—you are in love with your father, Charlotte, and what you see in Monsieur Le Quoi is only your . . .

Averell Cottage
January 17, 1862

Charlotte—

It is very late—I cannot sleep, have not been able to sleep for so long now, for a month, since Ginger returned—not without the tinctures, I can't sleep. I feel I am going mad. Charlotte, my husbands are in the shadows—I am so tired—they are around my bed when I try to sleep. I see them all there, looking down at me—they are in every reflection, in the dark spaces, husbands in the black window panes, husbands in the reflection of the moon on the lake, husbands swimming under the dark ice with the Glimmerglass Monster. Remember when we saw him, Charlotte—that day when we were walking along the shore, having just begun to know one another, and only twenty feet away, he emerged and looked at us, smiled his black teeth, then went down again—we were just girls, Charlotte, just twittering, and we had thought he was a myth, and there was something that day that cleaved me to you and you to me, despite all we pretend not to know about one another. My husbands are like that monster, hovering, and I have lit ten tapers here, the fire blazes, it is all as bright as noon, but in every reflection, every

dark space, husbands. I know they are not here. But they are.
They hide in the mercury of my mirror, they are not real, but
they are, there is no such thing as a ghost, but they are here. And
I am afraid—so afraid I cannot sleep—even Marie-Claude asks
me if I am not well.

I am deranged, I think. The nervousness I had since poor
Godfrey died has never gone away—I have just hidden it well—I
write to you because I can no longer read—the text wriggles like
worms. I feel feverish.

You are a writer (yes: only I know, and the whole town—you
think you have kept this a secret, but everyone knows). I will tell
you a story.

Here it goes: I was the princess, she the toad. This is how it
starts, always in those fairy stories—I was beautiful, delicate,
pretty, sweet—she dark, huge, hulking, defiant, no matter how
many switches my father broke on her back. He hated her, hated.
Took her out behind the tannery and beat her raw for the slightest
things. Since she was little, six five—for a broken mirror, for one
fresh word. You should have seen them—my huge, furious father,
my sister unmoving as a mule. She was always much larger than
I—I was the little bird—my father loved me, everyone loved me.
We slept, my sister and I, in the old haunted room in this house,
the room haunted by my slave Grandmother Hetty (oh, don't
pretend you haven't heard the rumors—yes, they're true, every
word—yes I came from slaves. One that your wonderful
grandfather brought to town, yes? The good Quaker, the great
Marmaduke. Hypocrite. That was one of the things they
whispered about me at Godfrey's funeral, yes, that I come from
slaves? That my father looked too like the old landlord
Marmaduke Temple for the town's comfort? That perhaps our
blood is not so dissimilar after all, my little plain friend? Oh, yes,
I heard it, I heard it all).

We slept in Grandma Hetty's haunted room. Ginger hurt me
badly. She would tie me to the bedpost and pull until just before
my arms popped from their sockets. She'd look up at me,
calculating, cruel, stick a needle under my nails, push until I
screamed.

Whenever my father caught her, he whipped her bloody.

Always. My mother never said a word. Didn't see, she was blind. Later, my father took Ginger behind the tannery to punish her, but there was no sign of whipping. At twelve, she was the size of a man, muscled like a man. She was good at work, Ginger, strong, could strip the skin from the fat in a bare second. At fourteen, she would slap me awake and force me from my bed. Down the stairs barefoot, out across the frosted lawn so cold it burnt my feet. Down to the tannery where she made me hold the lantern while the apprentices took their turns with her. One by one, in the stink of death and fat and hair, in that bloody place, one by one. She punished me—my punishment was to watch—her eyes gleaming, teeth bared, nightdress over her waist, her haunches, big, bare, muscled, gleaming in the light from the lantern I held—she'd snarl at me if I looked away. What the boys did to her, she did to me. She made me watch. But if one of them tried to touch me, she'd beat them hard. She made me watch.

Then came the night our father caught us. I, shaking, weeping, trying to look away, she not letting me, the lantern swinging light, one apprentice grunting like a pig behind her, the other two laughing, lolling on the pile of bark, then my father, big, quiet, in the doorway. His one eye gleaming.

"Cinnamon, to the house," he said. I flew, the lantern wild in my hand, the apprentices behind me, fleeing across the meadow. I watched from our bedroom window as my father came out, dragging Ginger by the hair. She'd fall, he'd tug her up by the hair to her feet. Dark blood on her face, on her legs. He slapped her against the side of the house so hard she fell down. He went in. I saw her lying there, in her white nightgown in the dark grass as he went inside. His footsteps on the stairs. I shuddered until he was shut in his room, reading the Bible aloud in his high voice. I went to bed. In the morning, she was gone.

Nobody ever said a word about her. Nobody—not my mother, not my father. It was as if she had never existed. And when she returned, that blizzard, I saw my first ghost—and she is real, here, and I feel her near me, dark and sickening, it is sickening us all, what I did not do to save her, what I couldn't do, what I can't do now. She sickens this town. She is infecting this town with her vice. She is calling my husbands up. I see the town sickening from my window—a pallor, a jaundice on it, men walking with venery on their minds. Sick, sick.

You will be shocked. Good. You will be made ill by this. Not nearly as ill as I. And you still think your Frenchman matters after this tale, do you? Pathetic, you little girl.

No, I won't send you this. It is too mad, even for your kind heart to bear. I can't send this. I will close it up, put it alongside your charming, banal letters. It will infect your letters. It will make them sick. This letter is too mad even for me, a woman you stare at, fascinated by the wildness in me—I know it—I feel it. Oh, Charlotte Temple, with your prissy little face, you wish you were wild as me. You have no secrets, you have no depth. Without your family, without your money, you are nothing, nothing. I could teach you a thing or two.

And as this will never go to you, I should say it—I hated, hated, the one novel I read of Silas Merrill, your alter ego, your pen-name. Stupid inanities. You call yourself a writer—you don't know a thing. Why sign this? It won't be sent. It would shock you to the very death, and I don't want you to die.

From the Desk of Charlotte Temple, Franklin House,
Blackbird Bay, Templeton
The twenty-eighth of January, 1862

My dearest Cinnamon,

Oh, my dear, I am so worried about you! It has been three weeks and you have not responded to my letter. At first, I was afraid you were angry because I did not write for so long. But then I remembered how distraught you were with your sister's return, and now I understand that you are simply sick with worry. I went to your house today, and purposefully waylaid Marie-Claude to press her about you. I don't know why you complain; she is a dear girl, actually quite pretty with her dark hair and pink cheeks. She babbled so excitedly to me about you, and I must say her French is so garbled and Canadian, that I had difficulty understanding her. Still, I understood that you were very ill, that you do not sleep, that you barely eat, that you have lost so much weight that your clothing hangs upon you and she can see your bones. She says that you have covered all the mirrors and windows and are burning twenty candles a night. She wept, Cinnamon; you have a good servant in her. She frightened me so that I almost ran into your house, in the broad daylight, propriety be damned!

I don't mean that, of course. I care about your reputation in this town, and will be as proper as I must be; but I must admit I care for your health more.

I will take this action: if you do not respond by the end of two days, I will steal over the ice the way I did when I comforted you about your sister's return. And I will nurse you back to health every day until you can stand again. We need you in town, Cinnamon; I heard Nat Pomeroy is looking for a rich wife. There! I am sure I made you laugh.

About your sister: I have not heard much. Of course, with all of the troops coming into town, there is little attention left over for strange women. What a terrible noise the young soldiers make. You wouldn't recognize Templeton; there is public drunkenness in the streets, and gambling, and the silly Templeton girls with their heads all in a whirl with the handsome officers paying them attention. Thousands of boys chopping through the ice to bathe in the cold lake; they find it funny, but it's a scandal, there is public nudity everywhere, in plain winter! Soon they will be gone, however, to the South, and some will never return to their homes again. I suppose we should have a little forbearance in the meantime.

Now I am going to tell you some news that will make you swoon, my dear. On our walks, Monsieur Le Quoi has begun to push me against a tree and kiss me until my knees bend despite myself. And should I shock you, for once? He has begun to press for more. Here is a note he has written me, in its entirety (I have translated it: I do not know how good your French is, after all these years):

My lovely violet,
I have returned to my shabby chambers at the Academy

*after having frozen my feet in a marshy bit of your lawn,
awaiting your signal in the window of your father's study. I
had urged you to adopt the plan so that bliss could be ours,
but, alas, I waited in vain. Why do you torment me so? There
are others in this town who have shown me some interest, but,
still, I await you, my chaste little chickadee. As I have assured
you, I do not need your money; when I come into my
inheritance, I will have more than enough for ten wives; I only
need you. Your pretty face! Your beautiful soul! Say the word
and we will be as husband and wife. I shall await your signal
every night until you can no longer resist me.*

    Fondly,
    Your admirer

    *Cinnamon, it took all the force in my body to keep my hands
from lighting that lamp in my father's study. Your little pupil is
learning so well! I shall have a husband shortly, it seems. Should I
give in before we have announced our betrothal? What do you
think? Oh, this is so indiscreet. But you will keep my secrets, won't
you? I cannot wait to hear from you. Please do write, my dear
heart. I am torn between my great elation and my worry for you.*

    My fondest regards,
    Charlotte Temple

Averell Cottage, Templeton
February 5, 1862

    My dearest Charlotte—

    *I am sorry to have been such a worry to you—I have been very
ill, indeed, as you saw when you visited. I frightened you—I
apologize. I do feel better after your ministrations. Perhaps you are
right—perhaps I could not sleep for the noise of the regiments in
the park below my house. Or, perhaps it was Mudge's tincture—
perhaps it wasn't strong enough. Nevertheless, I have slept for
three days entire, and feel as if in some part of me I am sleeping
still. I no longer see my husbands. Forgive me, though, my
superstition, as you called it, for I somehow know that they are*

still here. Knowing that they are near me, and not being able to see them—this is somewhat more frightening than seeing them everywhere.

I wonder, though, why you seemed to take fright when you entered my chamber. How was it that your eyes followed my Paul as he paced from corner to corner of the room? Or that you seemed oppressed when Abraham was leaning over the bed? I don't understand. Can you see them also?

Charlotte, I need a pledge from you. I have a terrible thing weighing on me, but before I tell you, I must extract, in return, a secret from you. You must tell me the deepest thing within you, the thing you never would tell a single soul.

Until you send me this proof of your affection, I shall tell you what I did just after your last visit. You will be shocked, I am sure. But, Charlotte, I dressed in my husbands' clothing— Godfrey's breeches, Sam's waistcoat, Abraham's boots, my darling Paul's cap tightly on my head. Thin as I am now, I pass as a boy quite nicely, and with Sam's false sideburns (he could never grow any himself) and the hat pulled low, I was quite convincing. And then—you shall be terribly surprised—and then I went out of my cold, lonely house, and into the nighttime street.

Charlotte—it felt so wonderful—I was set free. My soul felt unpacked, a dress unfolding from tissue. My darling, I walked in those busy, wintry streets (such teeming hordes of men! Oh, Charlotte, how the regiments and the Academy have quite filled this town up—men thronging the streets—handsome men, laughing men, drunken men, men in carriages, men on horse- back, men trying to ride the back of the poor Peck boy as if he were a horse—he laughing—drool shining on the idiot's chin!). I saw few faces I knew, none that knew me, boy that I was. I wandered, in my daze of humanity, drinking it in. I have been so lonely. And at last, I found myself before the Leatherstocking Hotel.

Let me describe it—the shadows moving behind the curtains, dark across light in the night, the line of men stretching out onto the walk and down to the greengrocer's, awaiting entry. I made my way, Charlotte, around the alleys, passed through the empty

*sheds behind the storefronts on Second Street, found the kitchen
door of my sister's establishment. There was no one there in the
kitchen—I went in. It was filthy, with caked plates, sweets, cakes
piled high, even flies, in the middle of winter!, dirt everywhere.
I slipped into the parlor. There was a man in a plaid jacket
playing the organ—it looked familiar—I do wonder if it weren't
the organ from the Temple Manor. I recall seeing one so very
similar in your family's house—so simple and unadorned and
strange-sounding. It wouldn't be put past my sister to steal from
your family's house. There was a large red parrot squawking at
the men who were drinking in the parlor and laughing. My
sister was there, in her men's garb, mountainous, severe, the
only concession to her femininity a peacock fan waving in her
face, collecting money from men who came downstairs and
went out.*

*I hid behind a plant that offered a full view of the room,
without allowing me to be watched. I waited.*

*And the men I saw, Charlotte—some, I dare to shock you—
those we know. Even Father Henrick, that German Catholic
priest, though he hid behind a screen in the kitchen. Solomon
Falconer. Nat Pomeroy. Even Dr. Spotter and his oily forehead.
More I could name, but won't. I cowered there for some time, and
nobody seemed to see me in the room. I was certain Ginger did
not see me—and yet, she stood at one point and said, in her deep
voice, "I feel a draft. Would anybody like a little cake while I'm
up?" And the men cheered—this must have been some sort of
code, and Ginger strode and rumbled by me, looking at me as she
passed and nodding, so I knew I was to follow her. I did, after a
minute.*

*Ginger was waiting for me behind the door as I came in. "So,"
she said, shutting it, leaning her bulk against it, laughing. "So,
Cin, you come to visit me at my place of business, I see. Breaking
your sacred contract to your dead husband. In this garb.
Sacrilege!" And she flicked at my collar.*

"I came," I said, "to see my sister. To see how she is doing."

"I'm fine," she said, surprised.

*For a moment, my sister and I gazed at one another. Then
the boy in the green dress came down the kitchen stairs, the*

priest behind him, and he gave the old man a little kiss at the
door as he went out. The boy turned to us, and his lovely face
lit up.

"Oh, Papa Gin," he said, softly, "your sister, she looks so like
a boy. I'm sure she'd hit it off good with the Academy boys."

Ginger laughed and kissed him on the lips, long, lovingly.
"Go," she said to him, "go back to work, my little love." And
when he curtseyed and went back into the parlor, my sister turned
to me again, her eyes still shining. "What you say, Cin? Here for
a job?" She stepped forward, as if to embrace me.

I backed toward the door. "I am a respectable woman," I
gasped.

Ginger pursed her lips and the smile died from her eyes. "Ain't
what I heard."

I was furious. "As if I care what you heard, Ginger," I said.
"You're going to hell."

She snorted. And then she said, so softly it could have been a
whisper, "Hell. Already there, aren't we. And your husbands, they
say hello."

I fled. At home, my heart pounded so loudly it drove me to
distraction and I dosed myself with too much of Mudge's draught.
I awoke today, three days later, Marie-Claude frowning down at
me in my bed, a bowl of soup in her hands. I ate it, and it gave
me the strength to write now to you.

Send me proof of your loyalty now, Charlotte, and help me
ease my trouble. Do it quickly, as soon as you get my letter.
Please, Charlotte—I am lost.

Your friend,
Cinnamon

From the Desk of Charlotte Temple, Franklin House,
Blackbird Bay, Templeton
The Seventh of February, 1862

My dear Cinnamon,

What a queer demand you make of me! I have had a fearful
two days, debating if I should tell you what you ask of me, but

I have decided that, yes, I shall. If anyone can help you ease your soul, I am the one who must try very hard to do so. Today I have not one, but two proofs of my love for you: two secrets, two confessions. I am sure you shall suspect the first. Last night, I lit the lantern in my father's study, and Monsieur Le Quoi responded. Presently, I believe I shall be a married woman, Cinnamon. Oh, it makes me laugh with joy!

The second I am sure you could never guess. Last night, do you remember the men shouting in the night, the fire brigades, the clang of bells? The courthouse burnt—perhaps Marie-Claude told you?

It was I, Cinnamon. I am the incendiary. How, you are asking, did I do so? How, when I was in my house on Blackbird Bay, more than one mile away, in the arms of the man who will be my husband? You will not believe me. Cinnamon, I do not rightly know how I do it. It has always been this way for me. In times of great emotion, I somehow set fires. That night at Hyde Hall, after Susanna Clarke's treachery, I set a fire in an outbuilding, though I did not leave my room: I set the fires in Phinney's printing press on a night when Monsieur Le Quoi said he loved me: I set the fires before I met Monsieur Le Quoi on nights when I was so sad because I was old and lonely and would never be a spouse or a mother! I, the one you would never guess!

It has always been like this; my first fire was in a field in France when I was just a little girl, and I was sure my father was about to leave my family. I stared at the field so fiercely, three bearded grasses caught fire and the flame spread but then the wind killed it when it was just born. And then in a hotel in London, when my sister Daisy slapped me for having cut her little dolly's dress: I set a fire in the parlor there, though we were playing in the gardens in the back. And then, on our first night in Templeton, I set a fire to a barn, and on and on: I was slighted by Mr. Woodside, who was building the mansion on the hill; I set the foundations aflame; all of the recent fires in town, all I, under my emotion!

Last night, I was so happy, the courthouse went up in flames. We are lucky the Phinney Brigade is so good, or else the poor

*prisoners would be only cracklings today. When I can control my
emotions, I can control the fires, also. When I cannot, things alight,
and the poor courthouse that my beloved grandfather built is now
charred and gutted. I would like to feel sorry for this: I am too
happy.*

*I don't expect you to believe this. Who could have such powers?
But, Cinnamon, this is the truth. I shall show you. Build a fire in
your grate tonight at eight o'clock, but don't set it alight. At precisely
the hour, I will set it, and it will flame up first green, then gold.*

*You have them, my two dearest confessions. Now you know
everything—now you can see inside my soul. Please tell me yours,
for I am so eager to help you bear your burdens, my darling. I
almost ripped this to shreds again—I have made this confession in
other letters, but I could never before reach the end. No, I shall
send it. I trust you completely.*

Your greatest friend,
Charlotte Temple

February 9

Charlotte—

*Forgive my scribble—I do believe you—I saw the flames in
my grate with my own eye. I am glad of your confession—here is
mine. Oh, I pray you will not hate me—but I will die if I do
not confess this to a kind soul! Here it is—I poisoned my
husbands, but only three of them, Paul died naturally, thrown
from a horse. Godfrey and Sam, strychnine, Abraham, arsenic.
All purchased from Mudge. He hissed, "Big rats, you have
there." I was simply tired, of the husbands, of their hands, always
wanting, always wanting me, always coming into my room, never
leaving me alone. I am a terrible person—I will go to hell. But
now that I have told, they are leaving, I feel them drawing
away—what relief. They are leaving! Yet I fear I shall harm
Ginger, too—I am as worked up as I have always been when I
decided to poison before—she is poisoning the town, I should
poison her. We will be so peaceful when she is gone, Templeton
will grow healthy again.*

*There. I have done it. Now you know everything, everything.
You shall forgive me—I know your secrets, also—and now you
know mine. It is as if the burden of the world were lifted from my
shoulders, Charlotte. I can breathe, at last!*

    Cinnamon

Averell Cottage
10 March, 1862

    My darling Charlotte—

    *You have cured me! Thank you for allowing me my
confession. I was all in a fever for three weeks after I sent you my
note, but over the last week, I have been better. You have not
written—you are perhaps busy with the follies of love? I would
be careful of the Frenchman, however—I did not have the chance
to tell you this, but it is quite likely he has secrets. You have
already given yourself to him, and that is regrettable, but I warn
you very gravely—do not give your hand. I know this is not a
sweet thing to hear in the midst of love, but I thought you should
know from a friend of your heart. If you do not believe me, or if
you request proof, I can provide it—I simply wish I should not
have to.*

    *Please do write to me. The spring breeze is warm across the
melting snowdrifts—I do feel so alive, so much more vibrant than
I had been in this terribly dark winter.*

    Your loving,

    Cinnamon Averell Graves

Averell Cottage
15 March, 1862

    Dearest Charlotte—

    *You alarm me! It has been nearly five weeks since I wrote and
you have not responded. I have waited, so anxiously. I have sent
you other notes. Do you hate me? I think you do. I am sane
now—I sleep now—I have regained my old beauty—even Marie-*

Claude says so. I am not sure exactly what I wrote, just that I confessed my darkest secrets. Can you find it in your heart to forgive me?
　　Your friend,
　　Cinnamon Averell Graves

Averell Cottage
20 March, 1862

　　Charlotte—

　　Still you do not write? I am afraid of you. Please write.
　　Yours,
　　Cinnamon

22 March

　　C—Please write. I fear if you don't I will do something rash.
　　—Cinnamon

24 March

　　Very well. It seems I am reprehensible to you. I cannot believe you know me as well as you do and yet you have chosen to cast me aside. I know you know of what I am capable. Poor, poor Charlotte. This is the last time I will ever have any pity for you.
　　—Cinnamon

Averell Cottage
March 25th, 1862

　　Mon cher Monsieur Le Quoi—

　　Or should I say Monsieur Charles de la Vallée? We met, I believe, at a party in October—I have been in heavy mourning *for your entire courtship of Mlle. Temple, but I have seen it all. I would say that you should consider leaving your chase of the dear girl and returning to Nantes, where, it appears, you had been a Prefect of Police, sent to jail on allegations of graft? Is this possible? And to take your valet's name—you should be ashamed. My friend who lives in Nantes sends me a poster of you during your—how do you say it—your <u>fuite</u>? The drawing is not flattering, of course. Then again, it is a good likeness of you.*

With goodwill,
Cinnamon Averell Stokes Starkweather Sturgis Graves

Spotter's Academy, Templeton
le 27 mars

Chère Mme. Graves,

Malheureusement, your letter does not frighten me a whit. Quite the inverse, rather. It makes me to a decision I was hoping I would not force to make. I have asked Miss Charlotte Temple to marry me and she has delightfully given her accord. I have come clean with my past, most of it, at least. How do you say it? Made a clean breast? It seems she has also had some rakes in the family. Her very noble grandfather, even, was of strange circumstances, she tells me, with a slave, perhaps. Although perhaps you know this. Though there were tears, quite copious when I told her of my circumstances, I was on hand to kiss them away. One's past is quite lost in such a bright future, is it not? This, we have agreed together. We shall wed in April 20th, at Christ Church, where her family lies dead. I should invite you, but you are in mourning, and one cannot see <u>la belle veuve</u> before it is her time, I hear.

As I value my freedom at least as many as I do the money, there is a piece of me that regrets this step I find so necessary now. But there is consolement. Miss Temple is pretty enough, and her great money will allow me to do anything I wish. Do you not agree?

With great respect and good wishes,
Charles "de la Vallée" Le Quoi

Averell Cottage, Templeton
March 29th

Monsieur "Le Quoi"—

*I do find your name so appropriate, you know—The What.
Precisely!*

*Perhaps your future wife would be interested in hearing that
you frequent—three to four nights a week—a certain house of
ill-repute in Templeton. She would assuredly call off your marriage,
and you would be left with nothing in the world, including
your little fiancée and all her money. You probably would no longer
be deemed fit to maintain your current position at Spotter's
Academy once the news got out. What a shame that would be.*

Your friend,
Cinnamon Averell Graves

Spotter's Academy, Templeton
le 1 avril

Mme. Graves,

*Forgive me, this is the day in France which we call <u>le poisson
d'avril</u>, and people make jokes upon one another. I believe this,
your threat, is such a joke? It is sad you are to have no proof. The
most delicious mouths can be stuffed with money, and never would
tell a thing. As well, I doubt my dear fiancée would believe you, as
apparently you are no friends much longer. You once were, but now
she will not speak of you. Why such coldness, I wonder, when
before she could only speak warmly of you? I have not succeeded
in understanding. But I shall. I must wonder why you are eager
to so pursue me? Is it perhaps that you fear for your "friend's"
happiness? Or is it perhaps that you do not wish her any such
happiness? I wonder. Of course, I am here for to assist you. Perhaps
one offer will be made such that piques my little interest, still.*

Your servant,
C. Le Quoi

April Fifth.
[rough draft, unblotted]

Madam Ginger; forgive this anonymous note. A person you know wishes you ill. I have prayed for many nights upon this matter. In the end, I knew that though you are fallen, and will be judged for your sins, it is my Christian duty to warn you. Please leave a note, if you wish to respond, under the stone under the statue of Chingachgook and his dog by the Susquehanna.

One Who Does Not Wish You Ill

April sisth.

One Who Does Not Wish Me Ill But Not Well Neither; I don't need no warning from you, whoever you are, your a woman, thats for sure. Backhanded slut. Nobody in my life never wished me more than harm. I can take care myself. You think your Christian. Pray for your own sole, youl burn in hell.

"Madam Ginger" as you say

Averell Cottage
April 16, 1862

It has taken me weeks, but I have spoken to my attorney and I can give you $20,000, legal tender, all my father left when he died. If you come to my house at 8:00 pm on the night of April 17th, I will provide you with a fast horse and the money in a strongbox. You shall sign an agreement that states you cannot return to Templeton, and will stay away forever. If you agree, you will send me a letter today.

—C. A. G.

Spotter's Academy
The 17th, April

*Ah! Enfin, you speak my language, Madame Graves.
$20,000, not a fraction of the fortune of Miss Temple, but I won't
have to spend thirty years to listen to her babble, either. Alors, I
agree. I shall see you tonight. You have lifted quite a burden from
my shoulders, Madame.*
    —*Le Quoi*

Averell Cottage, Templeton
The eighteenth of April
[rough draft]

Dear "Papa Gin Stone,"

*Well, my dear, here we are at last. Today I have sent away one
of your best customers, Monsieur Le Quoi, and in recompense, I
am sending you my servant, Marie-Claude. She is perhaps
crying—I have dismissed her for good, and she feeds her family
on the wages I pay her. Perhaps you will have a use for her. She
is a good worker, and would be diligent even in a place such as
yours. If you want her for other purposes, I suppose she's pretty
enough. I'd recommend $50 a month—the poor fool will think
that a fortune. Also, take these nutcakes I am sending you. I was
in one of my frenzies this morning, and baked too many for the
Ladies' Auxiliary. Perhaps we can become friends, Ginger. I am
lonely.*

Averell Cottage, Templeton
April 18th, 1862

Charlotte—

*You scorn me—you judge me—fine. Perhaps you missed
your French friend today, have you not? He told me you were*

*visiting with the minister this afternoon, for your wedding in two
days. Alas, the Frenchman didn't appear. And when you sent to
the Academy to see what was the matter, he was gone. And
greasy old Dr. Spotter so embarrassed: all of the Frenchman's
things gone, snuck away, that rat, didn't he? Oh, you poor
thing. I have had my claws in him, of course. No—he is
alive—simply riding to Albany, where he will catch a post-chaise
to Boston, there to start a life anew. He left you the note I have
enclosed.*

*Charlotte, mon chou, I could no longer dissemble. In the
end, I loved more my freedom than I did you. If it is a
consolement, I did love you a good bit, at some point, in some
way. I wish you happiness. Charles.*

*You see, darling? He did love you a good bit. It is quite all right.
And it is best, anyway, that he has fled this den of thieves, the nest
of vipers, the horrid little town that is Templeton. The Sodom, the
Gomorrah! Oh, isn't it? I have done you a favor, you see.*
Your friend,
Cinnamon

Averell Cottage, Templeton
November the twentieth, 1862

Dear Miss Temple—

*I daresay you remember me, though you have not written in so
very long—since April, has it been? I heard today that you were
to return to Templeton, and were bringing your "nephew" with
you. I do hope you have been well at your sister Daisy's in
Manhattan—such a pity about her death so shortly after her dear
husband's. Especially with her baby that was born a month after
she was laid in the ground! It must have been terribly painful to
the poor corpse. A miracle, truly. Don't worry—nobody here
knows the true date of her death, only I, for I have been
corresponding with your sister, Marguerite, and she let it slip. I
won't tell anyone your secret.*

My, we do have so many secrets between us, don't we? For

*instance, nearly the whole of Templeton burning on that fateful
night in April. Do you remember? Of course you do. The blazing
bells, the four fire brigades, the bucket brigades of all of the
Academicians and the regiments in town—and still, almost all of
Second Street, devoured! All the way from the Eagle Hotel to the
greengrocer's and past Schneider's Bakery! That whole stretch,
burned up, all of the little buildings there from the very days of
your own grandfather's first founding of the town! It even took
with it the lovely little Leatherstocking Hotel, of all strange places.
Can you imagine—they pulled the skeletons of four unknown
women and one boy from there—nobody has confessed to
knowing any of them, save the huge woman, who had apparently
bought the place from the little Yorker bachelor brothers. It does
make you wonder why they didn't have the presence of mind to
escape. Why they couldn't rouse themselves to run out of the
building—one does wonder.*

*The town is rebuilding nicely, though there have been many
shamed faces in town since the great fire, you know. It was
horrible. Old Mother Gooding died in the apartment above the
harness shop where she'd lived for so many years. And, of
course, so did that poor idiot son of Dirk Peck, the lawyer, that
filthy boy who touched himself at the sight of a woman. They
say he was in the very outbuilding where the fire started—some
blame it all on him—that is a piece of news you may be glad to
know.*

*Speaking of Dirk Peck, I have been comforting the poor,
hideously wealthy lawyer quite a bit. A handsome man, I must
say—he has secretly asked for my hand, and I have secretly said
yes, though we will wed when I am fully out of mourning. I like
him. Perhaps I will keep him.*

*You did hear of your fiancé's capture in Boston didn't you?
Shameful, really—he was trying to sneak onto a boat headed for
Martinique, and the French Lieutenant who caught him
recognized him from the scandal in Nantes—they say he was the
son of Monsieur de la Vallée, and took his valet's name of Le
Quoi. An ironic end for such a man.*

*One last thing. I believe I have a packet of letters you might
want. You do have a packet of letters I want. Could we, perhaps,*

engineer an exchange? We shall perhaps talk about this when you have returned to our fair town. I am eager to kiss the cheeks of your nephew. I do suppose he is bald at this young age, is he not? I do, however, hope he grows your abundant red-brown hair.

My warmest regards,
Cinnamon Averell, et cetera, soon to be Peck

Post-Script—I forgot to mention the most important event of the terrible night of the fire—apparently, I am sure you know, that the Temple Manor also burned. The portraits of your grandfather, grandmother, and father are being kept safe for you by the Pomeroys. Unfortunately, all of the furniture that had remained there is gone. It is a terrible feeling, you know, to walk through what remains. The charred beams like the ribs of some dead whale, the mirrors' mercury pooled on the ground. Such history that burnt down that night! I do pity you for your loss.

The Capstan Building, Park Street, Manhattan, New York
December the First, 1862

Cinnamon,

No double-talk. No mendacity. You are a dangerous woman, true, though I am also dangerous. I will not return your letters. This bundle is my only protection against you, and perhaps a fire I could summon, even from here, if need be. I am sure you wouldn't want to lose Averell House.

Your gossips are correct. I am returning to Templeton. My nephew will benefit from my family's town. But, no, you will never kiss his cheeks, or wonder at his fine head of red hair. You will never address him. If I hear that he has spoken with you, I will probably lose my temper, and you understand what happens then.

In Templeton, we will be acquaintances, civil and cold. In Templeton, we will not mix, as we are truly not of the same social class, not at all. People always wondered openly why I forced doors open for you. They called you a manipulator and a black widow, after the spider that eats its own husbands. I always laughed. I always told them that I helped you in society because you were such a good person. So kind, I said, and such an excellent friend.

I will not salute you, for this is our last missive.

Charlotte Temple

WHAT THE LETTERS OF CINNAMON AND CHARLOTTE REVISED IN WILLIE'S IDEA OF HER FAMILY

Charlotte *(Charlie)* Franklin Temple
1827-1912

Philippe de la Vallée *(aka Monsieur Le Quoi)*
1798-1869 *(died in jail)*
(Henry was Charlotte's natural son with Monsieur Le Quoi)

·
·

Henry Franklin Temple *(illeg.)*
1862-1939
m. Hannah Clarke *(in 1909)*
1888-1979

·
·

Sarah Franklin Temple
1913-1933
m. Asterisk "Sy" Upton
1895-1953

·
·

George Franklin Temple Upton
1933-1973
m. Phoebe Tipton
1923-1973

·
·

Vivienne Upton
1955-
(Random Templeton Man)

·
·

Willie "Sunshine" Upton *(illeg.)*
1973-

19

One Sees by the Light There Is

I LOOKED UP from Cinnamon's and Charlotte's letters to find myself shaking.

After I had read Sarah Franklin Temple's journal, I saw a previous Templeton overlaid on the one I knew; after I read Cinnamon's and Charlotte's letters I saw, at first, only a deep, dark midnight falling over my town. I didn't know what to think. All day, then all night, I read, then reread the letters. They could have been a hoax, I imagined, the fruit of some fevered novelist's mind, a novel abandoned somewhere, half-finished. But the letters themselves smelled of antique rose water and age-crisped lace, and were brittle with the years. The women's script was wildly different and the papers were different, too. Charlotte's writing was elegant but small, controlled, perfectly blotted, her paper thin and feminine. Cinnamon's paper was so thick and good it felt like cloth, and from afar, her script was gorgeous. Up close, however, her writing was a little wild, and there were odd breaks in more troublesome words, as if the writer had paused after four or five letters and checked a dictionary to ascertain her spelling.

"Are these letters real?" I asked the Lump.

Hours later, as the moon had shifted itself to the other side of the lake, I answered myself. "I think they're real," I said. I had remembered a fifth-grade walking tour of the village led by our portly little mayor with his brass cane and his short-shorts, when we heard about how Templeton had once almost burnt to the ground. *All of Main Street*, the mayor had been proclaiming in his basso profundo voice, gesturing widely with his arms, *from the Temple Manor to where Schneider's Bakery is today, all the way up Church Street was a blackened, charred ruin. And yet, children,* he'd said, voice trembling with emotion, *we rebuilt. We Templetonians always rebuild.* On and on he talked while I imagined my hometown a smoldering ruin and longed for a ten-cent fudge pop from the bakery. His mention of Templeton's great fire hadn't surprised me, and I realized then that it was one of the strange, floating bits of knowledge that natives of a small town sometimes know without ever being told.

By the time I looked up, dazed, from the letters, and out the window into the dark and sleeping town, I saw another change. I felt as if I were rising out of my body, then through the roof, and when I looked down, it was on a different Templeton, busy even in the earliest parts of dawn. I could hear the sleeping regiments in the fields out by the river, the night watch's boots on the frozen ground. I could see Main Street still moving with half-drunken men, like hard-shelled insects silvered by moonlight. It was a different Main Street from the one I knew, before the great conflagration that Charlotte had somehow started; the buildings were all different, and one hotel hung plumb out into the middle of Pioneer and Main. A line of men snaked from behind a large building, the Leatherstocking Hotel, and even from above, I could hear their muted talking. Up on the hill, opposite the Presbyterian Church, was a huge building with rows and rows of sleeping boys on the top floor, the dormitory of the Academy. Consumptives sat on the porch at the Otesaga Hotel, to get the early air. Lanterns burned at the backs of the huge mansions in town, servants up already baking the bread for the day. The town was cold, and it must have been winter, but it was still pulsing with life. It smelled of burning wood and melting ice, the thick garlicky stink of many bodies in one space, mingled breath. This was Cinnamon's and Charlotte's Templeton, exciting in that time of war. Had I lived then in this bustling town, I would have said that Templeton would certainly be a bustling, important city 150 years later, not the insular village it is now.

My mother, after her night shift the day before, had silently delivered my dinner to me on a tray when she saw I wasn't coming down. I was distracted, hadn't even seen that I'd eaten an entire wedge of quiche—a food I despise—until she came back to pick up the tray, and chuckled with surprise to find it gone. I heard her go to bed at nine, then the house creaked and moaned with 300 years of rheumatic pains in its joists and beams. I was sorry when I awoke to my modern tourist's village, even though that morning the fog was lit by the sunrise like a lamp under batting.

WHILE MY MOTHER slept her weariness away, I worked in the garden. I still had to digest Cinnamon and Charlotte, and didn't want to move on without talking to Vi first. There was still so much to fathom: that Henry was Charlotte's son and not adopted from one of her sisters, that she was an arsonist; that Cinnamon had murdered her many husbands. I could say with some certainty that the two ladies weren't the sources of my father, but I would only know for sure if Vi told me.

So, I plucked green beans and tomatoes lusty with juices. I pulled weeds from the rows of lettuces and found tender baby squash under the broad leaves. I filled a little container with raspberries and squashed copper-coated Japanese beetles between two gory rocks. When I came up to the house, my mother was up, warbling along in her shower. When I passed through the dining room on my way to wash up and dress, though, I saw a letter in the mouth of the little toy horse on the dining room table, which Vi had put there in a bizarre attempt at levity. The letter was addressed to me.

Willie Upton, Templeton, NY, was all it said.

And it was written in Primus Dwyer's handwriting.

And it was postmarked from Alaska.

This was as far as I got by the time my mother appeared in the doorway, rubbing her hair with a towel. "Whoa," she said, "Willie," because by that time, I was halfway to the floor, woozy, the letter still clutched in my hand.

WHEN I COULD focus again, I was propped up in a dining room chair and my mother was across the table, frowning at me. The envelope was torn and she was skimming the letter.

"Vi?" I said. "That's mine."

She folded the note up again and raised an eyebrow. "Maybe," she said. "But I'm not sure you want to see it."

"Oh," I said in a very small voice. "Uh-oh."

"Should I read it to you?" she said, and I could now see that she was angry. Very, very angry, and it wasn't, for once, at me.

"Okay," I said, but she had already started.

"*Wilhelmina,*" she read, in a staccato voice. "*I can't believe what happened. Hope you know how sorry I am. Poor Jan still wants to press charges but she's being calmed. One week, I warrant, and it'll be fine. Going into Fairbanks next week, will try to call. There was a huge development—well, you know what it is! Don't worry—you will be an author. You seem mediagenic— maybe you can go on the* Daybreak! *show for us, pretty girl like you. Better than fat old professors and gormless PhD blokes. Ha-ha! Oh, Willie, what a muddle we made of things! Hope you don't hate me. I have forgiven you, I know you were only in the throes of what was between us when you tried to hunt down poor Jan. I've got to run (nobody knows I am writing this, of course), but I think of you often—Yours, affectionately, Primus.*"

I stared at my mother, and she stared right back. The Lump twisted and twisted in me, hard as a cramp. I grabbed the paper from Vi and reread it three times, only feeling its proper sting on the third. And then I stood, ran to the bathroom, and threw up my impromptu lunch of garden vegetables. When I came back, my mother didn't speak. She just held out her soft arms, and I put my head on her shoulder and buried my face in her clean smell. I pressed my face to her neck and my body to her body, and for that long while we stood there together in the mudroom, her cross pushing into the skin of our stomachs, until I moved it aside.

"Assholes like that," she said then, and her voice washed warmly over the knockings of her heart, "are why, no matter what John says, I think it's natural that some women are. Well. You know."

"Lesbians," I said, into her skin.

"Exactly," she said. "Because of insensitive boors like this Primus one you've got here."

"Yeah," I said, and pulled away, feeling tiny and very, very frail. "To be honest, I'm tempted to give up the whole Y chromosome for good."

My mother put her hands on my face and looked up into my eyes. "If you want," she said, in a horrific thug-Italian accent, "I still have some connections in San Francisco. I could arrange a little sumpin-sumpin. Take him out, quietlike."

"Sounds good to me," I said, and we both laughed a little. A motorcoach carrying baseball fans sighed as it passed our house. A mockingbird gave a tentative rill on the windowsill beside us. When she moved, Vi's crucifix swayed and swayed on the bulge of her stomach, like a pendulum counting the seconds.

THAT EVENING, MY mother and I took a long walk around Templeton. The twilight had dimmed into dusk and the windows in all of the mansions began to twinkle. The heat of the day had cooled into a gentle warmth, and the families, sitting on their porches or on the benches of Main Street, all seemed to be murmuring, eating ice cream, watching the sleepy flickers of late lightning bugs in the hills. Those who were only here for the museums had gone home. The town was safe again for the natives, and we had emerged, shyly, like big-eyed ungulates of the fields.

Vi walked beside me, her jowls shivering with each step. I noticed this, and that she had crow's-feet etched deeper beside her eyes than I had ever seen before. She, too, stole small glances at me as we went up and down the streets, as familiar to us as the whorls in our own fingertips. My town had begun to insert itself subtly under my skin again. I could feel it there, moving shards, painfully alive.

"So," I said to keep from thinking, "it was nice to officially meet your beau yesterday."

She seemed peeved at me, and just said, "Great."

"He seemed like a good person."

"He is," she said, and a small smile now alit, mothlike, on her lips. "He is a great person."

"He should be. With the whole ministering thing and all. Did the religion come first, or did you date before you were a convert?"

"I sat in the back of the church for about a year," Vi said. "The whole time just saying to myself, good grief, this is all such nonsense. I thought it was a crock, but I just kept coming back. And then I just fell into it all at once. Belief. Love. Just looked up one day and saw both just sort of shining in his face."

"Love?" I said. I tried not to grimace. "Shining in his face?"

"Yes," she said.

"Well," I said. "That's grand. Just grand."

"Don't make it sound cheesy, Sunshine."

"Oh, I'm not. *I'm* not," I said. "Now, tell me, Vivienne Upton, why is it that you all wear those crosses everywhere? Makes you all look like a cult."

"These?" Vi said, poking at her crucifix. "Oh. Well, some of us just like them. I mean, the weight of it around our necks is like the weight of being good. It's a reminder. But John first thought of it as a way to make enough money for our sister town in Kenya where we're trying to build a clinic. He calls it a visual reminder, but I think it's sort of a passive-aggressive technique to shame the town into giving. People who aren't part of the flock give so that they don't have to feel guilty every time they see these crosses. People in the congregation give because they're reminded every day. Me?" she said. "It's the weight I like. The reminder."

"Well," I said. "I have to admit that the passive-aggressive thing is pretty ingenious."

"Well," she said. "I hate to brag, but that's John."

We were nearing Averell Cottage, but something in both of us made us slow our steps so we wouldn't have to go in immediately. "Tell me one thing. Do you sleep with him?" I said. "On your sleepovers?"

She looked at me, startled, then stopped walking. We were in the garage by then, and I blushed a little, remembering Felcher in this place, only a few nights earlier. "No," she said. "John doesn't believe in sex before marriage. I'm not so sure about marriage. So, it's a standoff."

"What do you do, then, when you stay over?" I asked.

Her face folded into a little wince, and then she said, "You ready for this? We pray a lot. We pray over dinner, then before bed. Then we both get into our pajamas, and I crawl under the covers and he crawls above them beside me. And then he holds me all night long."

I couldn't keep the disgust at bay this time, and Vi saw it, and belted out a laugh. "I know," she crowed. "It's so pathetic. I *know*. But sometimes when I wake up and feel his arms on me, it's just nice. Just, I don't know. Really nice." She gave me a little tap on the cheek and said, "It's not that bad, Willie. Get that look off your face. I just hope you'll know how it feels someday."

"I do know how it feels," I said, but it came out weakly. "I think I do," I said, remembering certain moments, men sleeping beside me over my long and illustrious life as a bachelorette, the rhythm of their breath, the delicate swoop of their eyelashes on their cheeks, their manly smell. Vi shook her head, giving me an affectionate moue of disbelief. I thought of Primus Dwyer. "I really do," I said as I went in.

IT WAS BECAUSE I was thinking about Clarissa, and because when I thought about Clarissa I necessarily thought she was thinking about me, that I answered the telephone that night already talking.

"My God," I said, "am I glad to talk to you. Have you ever had those days where so much has gone wrong in your life that you just sort of find yourself in the calm epicenter of the storm while everything else rages around you? That's the sort of day I had. I'm not feeling horrible at all until I start to think about how horrible I feel. But don't listen to me. I am a total jerk to not ask you about how you are. So. How are you?"

"Great. And, yes, I have one of those epicenter days every day. Man, I'm really, really relieved to talk to you. I thought you were so pissed at me we'd never talk again, Queenie."

It took me to the end of the second sentence to understand that the voice I was hearing was a man's; it took me ten seconds more to understand it was Ezekiel Felcher's. But as I was trying to place it, time seemed to slow down, then stretch interminably, and he, at last, said, "And you weren't really talking to me, were you. You thought I was someone else."

I debated just hanging up then, so suddenly furious with this chunky old boy on the phone that I went numb and clammy in the extremities. But before I did, he said, "Okay, just hold on. I was

prepared for this," and there was a distant twanging and some guitar playing and then, voices beginning to sing.

"Ooooh-ooh, so sorry I feel. Oooh-ooh-ooh, I'm sorry, for real."

The lyrics were embarrassing, but the guitar chords were complicated, embroidered, and I finally placed the harmonizing voice.
Peter Lieder. Though he had lost all that weight, he still had the
rich voice of a fat boy.

When the song was over, I was laughing so hard I could barely
speak. When I was only hooting, wiping my eyes, I said, "Put Peter
Lieder on."

There was a shuffle of the phone, and Peter Lieder's normal, thin
man's voice was saying, "Hello? Willie? Hello?"

"Peter-Lieder-Pudding-and-Pie," I said. *"Don't* kiss the girls and
make them cry. Tell your friend." And then I hung up.

Noname

THERE WAS THE before, then the after.

The before was large. I ran through the grasses and trees. Twigs bit my winter-soft feet. My people moved in the night in silence, chased by something dark and bad. My mother's head bent with mine over the King James, pages like flakes of skin and her finger bright in the sunlight, tracing the words, saying them soft in my ear. *And the earth was without form, and void; and darkness was upon the face of the deep. And the Spirit of God moved upon the face of the waters.* The strange language slipping from her mouth, sounds glistening like fish. My mother's hand against my cheek, her arm strong around me. My father's face, growing sadder and sadder.

The after was seven strides in each direction, a dirt-packed floor, the color brown, a hut smelling of meat and men. One small room of wood and mud, a place where nobody touched me, my skin hungry for human warmth. Darkness and the sweet smoke of Davey's pipe, Davey's curious inward laugh, my grandfather's herbs drying on the ceiling. Alone in the hut during the day, the sound of the town below us a dream, the humming of a living thing that I could not see, but craved. The after was one new doeskin shift a year, my grandfather moving the awl in and out by firelight as the hounds snored at the hearth. His hands fleet as birds, weaving, sewing, stirring. The moon a buckle slipping over the lake. Longing the color of sky. A hut I couldn't leave. My silence.

The lake, slippery and speaking, infinite bright glimmers in my eye.

What was between the before and the after was a story my grandfather wove, strand by strand. He would tell it in the long night, in the fire-smoke, softly, beginning with these words: Your father, my lark, was Chief Uncas, your mother was Cora Munro. For years, your tribe had been threatened by the settlers in the lake land in the west. The settlers with their guns closed in, and your tribe moved often to keep from being found.

One day, my grandfather always said, you were found.

It was the autumn when Davey and my grandfather left the lake to go west, to search for my family and spend their last days with the tribe. But in each place they found the ashes still warm, the scent of bodies in the air. The last place they came upon, they were hours too late, and everything was smoldering, dusted with snow. There were babies on bayonets like spitted pheasants. Squaws' heads gazing upon their bodies from three strides away. My father and mother both naked, charred, holding each other. They knew Uncas only from the tomahawk buried between his shoulderblades. Cora only from her father's signet ring clutched in her hand.

My grandfather felt the life leaving him, looking at them. He wept, as did Davey. They dug into the hard frozen ground and buried everyone.

Later, in the dark, my grandfather chanting for the souls of the dead, there was a small movement by the edge of the firelight. Me, naked and blue, blood across my face, down my legs, darting toward the warmth. My grandfather saw my father in my eyes, my mother in my form. He was struck to stone, yet felt life flaming up inside of him again. I reached my frozen fingers toward the muskrat roasting over the fire, and put a handful of raw meat in my mouth. When my grandfather dug it out, he couldn't tell what was meat and what was tongue. Both were raw and bloody. I was missing half a tongue. I was four years old.

They returned to Templeton and, not knowing my name, called me Noname until they could find my real one. Speechless, I couldn't tell them. They never found another. They kept me indoors because women were scarce in those parts and a native was hardly deemed human. No telling what the woman-hungry settlers would do to me if they found me alone, even a girl as small as I, they said. What they meant by this, I wondered at, for hours, until one day I simply knew.

I did remember that night, though. But while my grandfather's story was whole cloth, my own was only in flashes, like the dark world turned strange in dry streaks of summer lightning. Of the last night with my mother and father, I remember the cold, the silence as we found our campsite and began to set up camp. I, stealing my mother's book to look at while she spoke with the other squaws. My father looking out, giving a cry, leaping up. Then, the roil, horses and men, loud reports, blood; one settler upon me, and the cold ground on my back and pain, and then a spray of blood where his head was, and my father with blood dripping from his tomahawk, carrying me by the arm, throwing me up into a tree. My mother screaming, and my father turning back; the King James still warm in my hand; the great fire. Then, silence for a very long time. For whole lifetimes, I sat in the tree.

When I climbed down, my grandfather's fire spun before me as I walked toward it. The muskrat smell made me shudder, and before I ran into the circle of light, I spat out the meat I had found in my mouth, my tongue, which I had bitten through.

It was thus that I came from a large life into a life so small that the smallest things became large. Two meals a day each became feasts. My grandfather telling a story became thrilling as the dances that I remembered vaguely, night and thrumming and voices and red-gold firelight with legs flashing black through it. I made pets of flies and brothers of the hounds and looked for hours out the window, watching the small changes of clouds, the shadows they pressed on the trees. All those years, there was an egg-shaped emptiness inside me, aching; all those years, time stretched long as late shadows. I dreamt and wove tiny baskets and looked at my

book, brown-spotted with blood, until Davey showed me some letters, and then I learned to read, slowly, painfully, things I could not
fully understand.

Queer old Davey, my intended; I always knew, I heard them talking. But he was good to me. So careful around me, not to look, not
to touch, especially as I grew. But his heart was in the stews he
made, in the first pale bud from wintry tree, trembling as he put it
in my hand. A good uncle he was, until I reached twelve, and then I
began wondering what *husband* meant. Once, alone in the hut with
my grandfather while Davey was still out in the forest hunting, I
asked about it, signing the way my grandfather had taught me, but
he only smoked his pipe and watched me until I sulked away. I
wanted to throw his pipe embers in his eyes; I played with the soft
ears of a pup instead.

Times like those, I only pretended to be good. But I was never
truly good, at all.

For, every day from the time I first came into the hut, I, bad,
moved closer to the door. Outside was forbidden; I would have
been punished if caught. After the second year, when I was six, I
dared put a toe outside. For a year, when my grandfather went into
the town to sell his baskets and Davey went into the woods to hunt
our meat, I warmed my toe in the good touch of the sun. At night,
I would feel my foot, warm from the day, and a wildness would rise
in me like a sudden winter blizzard. My grandfather would look at
me, and I would look away and Davey sat and talked and smoked,
comfortable and warm, seeing nothing.

In another year, I dared putting my shoulder and whole leg out,
looking out, feeling the wind. In another year or two, I stood in the
shadows under the pines, listening like a doe to hear any footstep,
darting in when Davey was still half a mile away. When a question
was put to me, if I wanted an extra potato or some maple sugar, I
sometimes spoke the opposite of my desires, and held my lie in me,
like a warm stone. It made me laugh late at night when I was sleepless. I was shameless, and for weeks afterward, I would act nicely,
cleaning the hut well, making beautiful baskets. And then it would
slip again; I'd lie; my grandfather would look at me, and I would feel
goodness curdle in me, sour.

During my tenth year, I dared walk twenty paces toward the lake that waved and sang to me. The wind held and released me. I was hungry for its skin on my skin. In the woods, I saw the drunken insects stuck together, and I wondered at this. Outside, the world felt rich with possibility. Inside, I felt some strange heaviness keeping air from my lungs.

During my eleventh year, I went all the way to the lake itself and felt the warm shallows move over my feet, felt the tiny nibbles of the minnows on the hairs of my ankles, and almost wept with the touch. That day, I waded in to my knees and, so frightened by my daring, didn't do it again until my twelfth year, when my shift began fitting differently, when my skin turned hot in places and Davey stopped looking at me at all. The wildness rose in me; I chased his eye, imagining during the long winter what would happen if I slipped inside his blanket. Then I would look at my grandfather, and, in shame, think of other things.

That badness in me grew, hardened. When my grandfather brought home his coins from his baskets, I once took a shining one and buried it under a pine. I made one of Davey's knives dull, because I could. I took off my shift and slept the long afternoons, skin to fur, until a step nearing woke me, and then I dressed in haste.

When it at last became unbearable, I went into the world, and that day I felt everything, the sun, the rocks, the small animals in the trees, watching me. I went to the lake and walked in over my head, and watched my hair float up to the surface, watched it weave and spin in the greenish light down there, the nits bubble up.

That day, when I came out I watched from afar as small figures of people moved on the streets of the town. I squeezed myself between the boulders beside the road and, hidden, watched the people pass, the ladies with their squeezed waists sitting on one side of their horses, the men galloping up feathers of dust. I saw a mother holding her son in her arms, lovers arm in arm, the squeezing of hands when they met; I felt it in my own body each time the people touched. I loved them all, the people, I loved watching them, imagining their words, soft and formless in my ears, but I mostly loved the men. The one with the hunched back and kind face, the fat and very hairy one, the lonely little boy one with the nose like a needle who spoke to himself, the very large one who had red strips in his white powder where his hat pressed in.

I slipped home, feeling the badness grow in me. I saw my grand-father in my mind, his sad face, but it did not stop me from laughing as I ran. The hounds greeted me, their cold noses sweet on my legs. The hut seemed like less than nothing.

All afternoon, I sat with the King James, letting the pulse of the words pull me through the hours. Like a window the words were to me, like light itself, and I could see my mother through them. Even as I sat there, with the book in my hands, wind through the window ruffling the thin leaves quietly, I knew I would go out to the lake again. I would steal to the shore again, go in again naked. I would banish my grandfather's face from my thoughts. The fishes would slide their smooth slide around me, the eels would nibble my hair. The lake weeds would part at my feet; the light would quiver as it passed through the deep. I would go in farther and farther until I walked my way along the rocky bottom to the town. And then I would come out of the water and join the others. I would move into their streets, walk into their lives, and they would turn to me. And the ladies would clap their hands with wonder and the men would embrace me with their strong arms and the children would run around me in circles and everyone would stop and smile. They would reach out their hands; they would touch me. I would pass like a babe from person to person, touching all the people of Templeton. At last, at last, everyone would welcome me in.

Fame in Failure

I HAD A hard time, for some reason, returning to the New York State Historical Association library. All that week, whenever I thought of seeing Peter Lieder or Zeke Felcher, a strange shyness washed over me, and I found myself reluctant to do anything that involved leaving the house. Instead of doing the research I needed to do, I called Clarissa for hours. She told me about Sully's growing silences around her, the lupus slowly being beaten back with her experimental therapy, an assignment she felt strong enough to take. I talked to her about Primus, the Lump growing in me, my father hidden somewhere in Templeton like one of those books where you searched through crowded scenes until you found the little man in the red-striped shirt waving at you. We talked until she fell asleep or until she gave a little impatient laugh and said, "Willie, honey, you don't have to talk to me all day, you know. I mean, I'm not alone. I read, I sleep, I've got my soap operas."

And I also read and reread Cinnamon's and Charlotte's letters until I couldn't ignore the solid reality: those two women, though strange, were not the source of my father. When I asked my mother at last one day, she was painting her toenails a suitably Baptist white, sitting in her antique wicker chair. She didn't look up when she said, "Took you long enough, Williekins. Up up and away. Time to try the next step."

"Guvnor Averell?" I said, making a face. Whether or not Cinnamon had made everything up about her father, he was still a frightening man, very cold and stern-looking in the portrait of him on the hallway wall, his one wonky eye glaring in the picture. "Jacob Franklin Temple?"

"Good job," she said. "Get to it. Try both of them. You need to be back with Clarissa asap. And school," she said, putting the brush back in and shaking the bottle, "begins in only two weeks. I saw online that you're teaching a survey course. Congrats. You're going back."

I stood in the doorway with my arms folded across me, staring at her. "Vi," I said. "That'd be true if I didn't have a slight problem. A small child to feed and raise. Right?"

Now Vi looked up for good and frowned at me. "At last," she said. "You asked my opinion. Well, Willie, I'll tell you. I am sorry. You just can't have the baby," she said.

The sunshine on my mother's head made her graying hairs seem flinty, like wires. She held her face up, watching me as I caught my breath. I took a step into the room and said, "You're kidding. You're a religious freak. Don't tell me you're advocating abortion?"

"What I'm advocating," said Vi, "is responsible parenthood. You are nowhere near ready for a child. And this world does not need one more semi-unwanted child. I'm religious, yes," she said, and she stood to face me. "But I'm also rational, honey, and a medical professional. In the first trimester, there is nothing wrong with it. The fetus is not viable on its own. I would recommend that you get it out quick, and have one later, when you're ready. I'm sorry if this hurts your feelings, or is not what you expected me to say," she said. "But I love you and any future child you are going to have. And this is best for all of us."

"Whoa," I said. "Whoa, Nellie."

My mother held my eye for a beat until she frowned and said, "Don't think this has anything to do with you and my situation when you were born, Sunshine. In that case, I had nothing, and you were the best thing that happened to me. I was doing lots of drugs, engaging in unprotected sex, living a terrible, unhealthy life. In your case, you have everything. I have worked all my life to give you everything, and so have you. Having a baby right now would be the worst thing to happen to you."

"I'll be the judge of that," I said, but even to myself I sounded unsure. "It's nobody's decision but my own."

"That's right. I can make an appointment for you," she said, patting me on the arm. "I can urge you to do what's best. But I can't make the decision for you, sweetheart. You have to do that yourself. Tell me what I can do to help."

My mother left the room, then, and it felt as if a subtle, intense pressure left with her. All the time I had been home I had been afraid of this confrontation; I had been afraid of my own resolve to do what I knew was best. It's true that somewhere in me I wanted to keep the Lump, to hold its wailing newbornness, to watch it develop into a real person. Just as intensely, I wanted it out of me. One step was irresponsible, illogical, totally wrong; the other was so right it screamed its rightness until I clapped my hands over my ears. When I left the room, I caught a glimpse of my face in the mirror and I saw how drawn and ill I looked.

SO I STEELED myself. I swung out into the glorious Templeton August with my notebook and pen. I would just get on with my real work. And then, when I came home, I would call my doctor and ask for an appointment. It would be easy, in and out. Surgical. Clean. I would find my father. I would rid myself of Lumpishness. I would only have my broken heart and that cad of a Primus Dwyer left to handle.

But things do not always happen as we expect them to, and like the heroine of a fairy tale, on the mile walk up to Franklin House, I was stopped three times.

The first was when a red convertible came slowly down West Lake Road. In it rode three divas from the Opera, in the middle of an improvised aria competition, to see who could out-sing the others.

"*Il destin così defrauda, le speranze de' mortali,*" they sang, louder and louder. "*Ah chi mai fra tanti mali, chi mai può la vita amar?*"

The sound was so overwhelming on that sunny country road that I stopped and felt my heart shatter like crystal, but it only skipped a beat. The sheer perfection, the sheer gorgeousness. I felt tears in my eyes, and then the women stopped singing and laughed at one another, and drove on. One pretty Jersey cow and I were left alone in the buzzing morning, gazing at each other, dreamy-faced.

I was still holding the moment in the pit of my stomach when I crossed up past the country club's stone gates and saw that standing there, beside the big yellow deep-sea pod, were people sleek as seals in wet suits, gazing at a map on the ground. They looked like crows over carrion. I thought of my hand pressing into the freezing, peach-fuzzed hide of the monster, and felt a wild grief come over me.

And the last stop came because I was not yet ready to go into the library, and so I fled into the dusty safety of the Franklin House Museum. I was alone; nobody was there to force a ticket on me, and so I ducked into a pretty little room off to the side, and looked down at the lake over the green grass. It was a dim room, walnut-paneled, high-ceilinged. When I turned around, I found that I was caught in the middle of a Mexican standoff.

There was Marmaduke Temple in his jowly, stern portrait over the mantel; it seemed as if his eyes were resting on me. Then they seemed to swivel across the room and up the wall, to rest on the other side, where the original Jacob Franklin Temple portrait hung, the novelist smirking, the nimbus bright and angry around his head.

I felt stretched taut between them, the father and his son. I stood in the middle of my ancestors, the landlord, the great novelist, and felt like the rope in a tug-of-war of wills.

"Cool it, boys," I said, at last. "Just leave me alone," and I fled.

I FOUND MYSELF driven into the library, trying to find sanctuary in a familiar place. But when I came into the dim little place, heartsore and shaken, the little old lady behind the desk looked at me and frowned and said, "Your friend. Peter. He's out. Don't ask me. I don't know why."

"Oh," I said, and though I was relieved, I was also now at a loss. I was counting on Peter's help. I did a circle in the library, and then came back to the lady's desk. It was perhaps because of the surrealness of the morning—the singers, the divers, the portraits—that I felt tears in my voice when I said, "Do you have any idea where I could get some information on Jacob Franklin Temple?"

The woman blinked at me like a toad.

I waited, figuring no, figuring that she was so old she could barely boil herself a cup of tea.

And then the goat-woman broke into one of the loveliest, beamiest smiles I had ever seen. She said, "Well, isn't today your lucky day. You've just met one of the goldarn world experts on Jacob Franklin Temple, honey."

WE MADE OUR slow way to her little room in the back, where I waited as the old lady dawdled over her hot pot. At last, she sat. "I'm Hazel Pomeroy. I've been here for, gosh, ever. And who the heck are you?" she said. She sipped the green tea she had made; I was wrong even there; she did know how to boil tea.

"Wilhelmina Upton," I said, sighing a little. "I'm trying to find out if Jacob could have slept around, had a little, well, bastard somewhere."

Hazel's eyes bulged, and for a moment, she looked as if she had so much to say it clogged her up, like a dam choked by windfall branches. At last, she said, "Oh, my. So you're Wilhelmina Upton? Let me take a look at you."

I was used to this: all my history teachers, even in college, were so thrilled to see me, a living fossil from a notorious family, that I was often examined for likeness. She narrowed her eyes and looked me over, and at last shook her head, smiling.

"You're much like Marmaduke, you know," she said. "That reddish glint in the hair, the height, the firm jaw. The pink cheeks. Such a stunner."

"Thanks, Hazel," I said, but she wasn't finished.

"Nothing like your old granddaddy George. That *there* was a piece of work. What a coot," she said. "He was my fiancé, you know."

The world went still then, the motes hung in the beams of light as if they, too, were startled static. Perhaps, I thought, Hazel Pomeroy was the source of my father. Perhaps I was wrong about George, perhaps he fooled around. Perhaps I was looking at a grandmother right here.

But then Hazel squawked to see the look on my face, and said, "No, not really, honey. I was only sixteen when he married your grandmother. I was just a silly girl. He came home from Yale one summer and was the catch of the year. PhD, a Temple, son of Sy Upton, not ugly, and what have you. He took me for a sundae at Druper's Five-and-Dime, and I believed that meant we were engaged. I told everyone. Such a mess when I come to find out that only a week later, he's proposed to your grandmother. Blindsided, all we girls were. Because she was an old lady at the time. Twenty-eight years old, and no looker. No offense, I know she's your family, but she was ugly as sin, and he was ten years younger than her. I still can't figure how she got her nippers in him. Later I figured out that he didn't marry her for *her*. He married her for being related to that lusty old slave Hetty Averell, for her family. Which is to say, in a queer, twisted way, that he married for his own family, to join the Averells to the Temples. I was heartbroken for all of, oh, a month. Strange how when we're young, we think we'll die over things we chuckle about when we're old."

I would have thought that Hazel had said this innocently, in the wandering, sweet way of old people feeling the urge to give the gift of their nostalgia, save for the sly look in her eyes. I wondered how much she guessed about why I was home. I looked away.

"Anyway," she said, "didn't bother me much. All respects to the deceased, but your granddaddy was cold as a toad. I know what they say, but there was no way it was a murder–suicide, either, the way he and Phoebe died. Accident, pure and simple. That man had the worst eyes of any man born to hold a driver's license. I can't count the times he ran off the road just driving from Averell Cottage to here. One mile. Drove me nuts all the times I had to pull him out with my old Ram. No, I never missed having him. Had a much better life as a bachelorette, you know," and she winked at me.

"Good for you," I said. "Was George as tedious as I imagine?"

She blinked and said, "No, he was very nice."

"Oh," I said.

And then she began to smile and said, "And I just lied. You startled me with your 'tedious' talk. He was my boss, you know, here at this library. A disaster. I did all the work for this place, you know."

"I can imagine," I said. I noticed my tea had gone cold in my hands and I set it down. "Now, Ms. Pomeroy, what can you tell me about Jacob Franklin Temple?"

Hazel Pomeroy leaned back in her chair and looked at me with the same sly smile. "You have a few hours, Wilhelmina?"

"Call me Willie," I said. "I have a few days."

"Good," she said. "Let me tell you a story."

THIS IS WHAT Hazel Pomeroy told me, over endless cups of tea that day:

Jacob Franklin Temple was the youngest child of seven, all of whom died, save for him and his much older brother, Richard. By the time he was born, Marmaduke was already wealthy. Richard was already a man, so thickly pelted with hair that his eyes were barely discernable in his face, and he had a soft padding between his clothing and his skin. Their mother, Elizabeth, was an invalid, and delicate.

The myth went that Jacob was born the day his mother at last came to Templeton from Burlington to stay in her husband's famous settlement. She just made it into the Manor House before he leapt from her, squalling. There was nothing to substantiate that myth, save for the fact that he was a screaming meemie for the rest of his life.

From the first, Jacob was Marmaduke's pet project, as Marmaduke came from nowhere and educated himself, Elizabeth could read but not write, and Richard's education was spotty, at best. Marmaduke was determined that Jacob would be a gentleman, with a gentleman's education, and so, by the time the boy was two, Jacob could read and write his name. By four, he could speak French like a Frenchman, declaim poetry by heart, do simple arithmetic, already had a good writing hand, and had begun Latin. By the time he was fourteen, his father had been dead for five years and Elizabeth sent the boy to Yale, as per Marmaduke's wishes.

It stood to reason that a boy so young and rich would have had a hard time. He drank, gambled, fell in with a bad crowd. By the time he turned sixteen, he was sent down. He'd exploded a classmate's door with a bucket of gunpowder, some drunken prank, and though all his friends fled, he was so drunk he couldn't. He collapsed at the feet of the dean, giggling. This was his first failure.

He came back to Templeton, then, and his brother helped him find a place in the merchant marines, as he had always dreamt of foreign places, geishas and giraffes and other wondrous things he'd learned of from his readings. He mostly sailed around Lake Erie, though, and left the navy's life when he was twenty-one. That was his second failure. Then he went to Manhattan and, without a university degree but with the help of his father's powerful friends, tried to become an attorney. He was no good at law, had no grasp of it. Third failure.

In Manhattan, he fell in love with a pretty, flighty girl named Sophie De Lancey. She had a very well-connected family and normally wouldn't give him the time of day, as she had plenty of suitors as rich as Jacob, and most were from much more reputable families than the Temples, who, only a generation before, had sprung up from the mud. But something happened, and Sophie agreed to marry him. Nobody knew exactly what caused the rapid change of heart, but the couple had their first daughter about eight months after the wedding, so people drew some conclusions.

They were given land on the Hudson by Sophie's parents, and Jacob tried to make a go at it as a gentleman farmer, but he was horrible at this, too. Hemorrhaging money, as the land didn't give much and Sophie was an expensive wife to have.

Then, in the midst of this, his fourth failure, one night after a long day when some of the cows had to be put down for anthrax, he was reading a book by Susanna Rowson and just up and hucked it across the room. *Such tripe!* he shouted. *I could write better in a fortnight.* And Sophie put down her sewing and snapped, *Well, then, do it,* and he said, *By Jove, I shall,* and he did. In a fortnight he came back and assembled his family—he only had the first four daughters at that time—and began to read from a sheaf of papers in his hand. They sat, spellbound, as he read every night for a week, and when he was done, Sophie threw her needlework down and ran to her husband and said, *Oh, I knew you weren't a failure, I knew it!* and he printed the book himself under a nom de plume. It was a great success, though nowadays looks like a pale imitation of the kind of parlor novel so popular in England then. Pale heroines with roses in their cheeks. Stern lords with hearts of gold. Minuets and needlepoint, compromised younger sisters, forgiveness, lovemaking.

Jacob was inspired enough to keep writing, and within a few months he had another manuscript, which he published under his own name. It was patriotic to buy his book, as all the novels consumed in the new country until then were written and published in England, and now there was this American writing as well as the Brits. He was a round success. He began to write and write, with a promiscuity that's surprising when one considers that they had no computers or typewriters, only paper and ink and cut quills, and, later, those newfangled fountain pens.

So the family went off to Europe for ten years, spending all of the money Jacob made from his books, plus whatever was left of Sophie's fortune, and his, too. They lived in luxury among all of Sophie's male admirers, and all those female necessities—the fans, the laces, the ribbon—it all added up. By the time hairy old Richard wrote to say that he was cutting Jacob off the family teat, and that he should come home to Templeton to sort out his finances, the Franklin Temples were impoverished. They had eight daughters by then, all named after flowers, save for the youngest, Charlotte, or Charlie, her father's pet.

HAZEL POMEROY LEANED toward me then, misty blue eyes open wide. "Here's the secret spice," she said. "Here's something you won't learn from anybody else. Take a look at this," and she flipped open a book to a vivid print. "This is a picture they had done of their girls at some painter's in Paris. Just take a look and tell me what you see."

I leaned forward and peered at the print. There were eight pretty girls in a row, all in nineteenth-century dress. I looked and looked in vain for whatever it was Hazel was trying to tell me until, at last, it clicked. There was a wide range of hair colors, from the baby Charlotte's dark reddish curls to the bright fairy blondness of her sisters who were twins. There were varied skin tones, from Charlotte's pale to another's dark olive, and such a range of noses, lips, cheeks, eyes that they could have been an assortment of orphan girls. Only Charlotte had her father's dark eyes; only Charlotte had Marmaduke's—and my—broad chin.

"They don't look like sisters," I said.

Hazel Pomeroy nodded. "Nobody would say it outright. But

some think that Sophie didn't pay much attention to her wifely duties. If you know what I mean. Charlie was maybe a fluke. In one of her first letters as a married woman, Sophie De Lancey Temple says to her sister, and I quote, '*How strange, Dorothée, but my new husband, though he sings and is glib and cheerful, seems at the least convenient times to have ice in his veins.*' This seems to be code that the man was disappointing her in the boudoir, I think, because in the return letter, Dorothée says that her sister should give her husband a tisane of summer savory and ginseng and mandrake root—all aphrodisiacs, mind you—and use '*the highest of the charms our mother has taught us,*' I quote. Here's another secret—their mother was a beautiful Frenchwoman who had mysterious roots. Some whispered in society that she may have been a courtesan before Hiram De Lancey brought her to Manhattan from Paris."

I whistled and said, "Okay. So Sophie's a nymphomaniac. And Jacob is impotent. Christ, Hazel. You couldn't make this up."

Hazel Pomeroy gave her raspy chuckle. "Well," she said. "I have no actual tangible proof, and wouldn't go so far as to publish it until I do, but it seems as if there was only one legitimate Temple in Jacob's whole bouquet. Charlotte. And that," she said, stretching her matchstick arms above her head, "is what I think about your whole idea that Jacob Franklin Temple would have a bastard, as you so nicely put it. If you ask me, he's more like your cold-fish granddaddy than anyone else in the family."

I looked at Hazel and narrowed my eyes. I think I intended to test her when I said, "Well, then, you're saying I'm not directly related to Marmaduke, if you don't count Hetty. Because if Charlotte only adopted her *sister*'s son, and none of her sisters was related to Jacob, then there's no legitimate Marmaduke blood in me."

Hazel blinked and then she grinned. "That's where you're wrong," she crowed. "We have a letter by one Manhattan doctor who claims he assisted at the birth of Charlotte's son. And it was a few months after the death of Charlie's sister, the one whom everybody thought was Henry's mother—obviously Daisy couldn't possibly have had a child from beyond the grave—so it's almost certain that Henry was truly Charlotte's, after all. As you know, if Henry was Charlotte's, and Charlotte was the only one of Jacob's daughters who was actually related to him, Henry would definitely have

Marmaduke's blood. Ha! In any case, it has been my research of the entire last decade to try to find more substantive proof that Charlotte had birth out of wedlock. I'm writing a book. It's called *Secrets and Slander: The Amazing Story of the Temple Family*. You'll be in it," she said, her candid eyes glowing. "And your mother Vivienne's story about her free-love commune. I keep asking her if I can dig around in the attic, but she keeps saying no. I tell her she's hindering American scholarship, but you know your mother. She's a sparkplug."

I could very easily have pulled Cinnamon's and Charlotte's correspondence from my bag then, given it to this ancient lady, in one moment making her career, making her life. But some mean sprite in me kept silent, fearing, perhaps, that she would have heart failure when it was in her hands; or maybe I was just furious that this stranger woman would want to spill my family secrets to the world at large. At the moment I was about to open my mouth and let her have it, I felt a terrible cramping in my gut.

I gasped, and Hazel looked at me, worried. "Are you all right, honey?" she said.

"Fine," I said. "Fine, fine. Thank you."

We sat like this in the dust-thick afternoon sunlight in the little back kitchen of the library. As the pain clutched me, I imagined the sardine-head of the Lump swiveling about in confusion as its world rocked like an earthquake, thinking *What the hell is that?* Then the cramp relaxed, and when I looked up, Hazel was looking at me, a shrewd expression on her face. "You never," she said, "told me why, exactly, you're looking for an illegitimate ancestor. What are you looking for?"

I just smiled at her and said, as lightly as I could, "Oh, you know. Curiosity."

"Huh," she said.

"Still," I said, "you have no actual proof that Jacob was cold, do you? Just a hunch, right. You have no tangible proof?"

"No," she said, "I don't. But I've read every single journal by him and book about him. I've read every single letter to or from him, honey. I've read everything in the goldarn world, but can't find anything. No, there's no proof. But he seemed as obsessive about his writing as your grandfather was about his history, and

George was the coldest man on earth. Wouldn't surprise me if it were a family trait." She made a bitter little face, then gave me her sly smile again.

"Okay," I said. "But say *I* want to find out if he had an affair. What should I do?"

Hazel Pomeroy sighed very deeply then, and closed her eyes. I felt sheepish for having asked such a rude question of the frail little woman. The sun clicked down over the west hills and the sky darkened to navy. And then she opened her eyes and said, "Only thing left to do. Read his fiction."

"What?" I said.

"Read his fiction. Lord knows, honey, it isn't proof in the normal sense of the word, but you find out obliquely if he's hiding something. Amazing thing, fiction. Tells you more, sometimes, about the writer than the writer can tell you about himself in any memoir."

"All right," I said. "That I can do. How many books did he write?"

And the tuft on Hazel Pomeroy's chin waggled as she said, "Only fifty-five." Then she gave her bleaty cackle as my heart sank, and her laugh filled up the old library and seemed to echo back. Fifty-five books! the echo seemed to say. In ten days! Ahaha! Then she stood and tottered away. She came back pushing the cart a few minutes later. She handed me, one by one, the ten books on it. "Here you go, honey," she said, cheerfully. "Start with these and press on."

"Thanks, Hazel," I said, standing up, the crinkle of my grandfather's manila envelope the very sound of my guilt. "And thanks for the tea."

"Don't mention it, kid," she said. "Keep on the lookout for any letters or such in your house for me, will you?"

"I'll see what I can do," I said. I packed the books away, trying to stifle my dismay. As I did, though, a marvelous thought crackled into my head. "Hazel?" I said. "You mind if I use your phone? Long-distance," I said. "I can pay you back."

"No need. We're state-funded," she said. "And then skedaddle. It's time for me to close up shop."

As Hazel shuffled around in the background, I dialed Clarissa's number, holding my breath. "What?" she said when she answered, sounding half-asleep.

"Clarissa," I said. "You know how you're just kind of sitting around, doing nothing?"

"Doing nothing?" she said. "You're joking, right? Without me, the World wouldn't Turn. The great Guiding Light would flicker out and plunge All My Children into darkness. General Hospital would become remarkably specif—"

". . . Yes, yes, hilarious," I said. "Listen. Remember how you used to speed-read books in college?"

Her voice sounded dreamy when she said, "I made it through *Père Goriot* in an hour. *The Poetics of Space* in three."

"Right," I said, hefting my bag, all those heavy words of Jacob Franklin Temple onto my shoulder. "You up for a challenge?"

"Oh, boy," said Clarissa, giving a little hoot. "Always."

By the time I had explained to Clarissa what I wanted her to do, and worked out that I would overnight the books in the morning, Hazel had finished her cleanup and the lights were off in the library. She stood at the door, jingling her keys. "Need a ride?" she said.

"Nah," I said, smiling at her. "Thanks. It's a nice night. I'll walk."

Hazel patted my cheek. "You should smile more," she said. "It suits you," and then she doddered to her yacht of a car and pulled off down the drive with a great rumble of the engine and puff of diesel smoke.

IT WAS LATE enough and dark enough so that I could risk the golf course without being beaned by a hurtling ball, so I walked down the lawn of the Franklin House and picked my way across the shore and up over the smooth green grass of the course. I cut through the country club parking lot and down behind the restaurant, where Hawaiian music was playing and the unmistakable fatty smoke of a roasting pig perfumed the air. Up on the porch, the adults were milling about, laughing, and I went down the hill and through the game of tag that the little kids were playing on the beach, their chubby little bodies hurtling by. Two old men were still battling on the tennis courts, though the ball was a bare green shadow shuttling between them. The golf course was smooth and fine.

I discovered I was talking to the Lump aloud when I heard my own voice. "I am not the kind of person who does existential

crises," I said. "But I don't know what I'm going to do when I have
to get rid of you."

And then I thought about just giving up. Letting the Lump grow
bigger and bigger until my belly imposed itself on the world. Letting Ezekiel Felcher woo me over and awakening one day in a small
colonial house in the cheaper section of Templeton with three babies and a de facto husband who was an excellent barbecuer, who
invited our friends over for beery parties every other week, who
convinced me to join the bowling team. I would open up a non-
baseball-related store on Main Street, and it would be filled with
such beautiful things that our family would do fine in a comfortable middle-class way. When my mother passed, we would move
into Averell Cottage, and replace the broken pool with a nicer tiled
model. My children would go to good, medium-range colleges—
Bates, Skidmore, Boston College—and find jobs with good compa-
nies. When I was old and Zeke retired, I would be so harassed that
I would begin again to read as voraciously as I had before I returned
to Templeton. I would go into my dotage a scholar again, with no
hope of making any more of a mark on the world than my three
relatively successful children.

Though there was a little bit of comfort in this projection, the
very idea made my skin feel as if a horde of ants were slowly chewing their way out of it.

I cut across the Otesaga grounds and down over the neighbors'
vast lakefront lawns. My head was down as I reached our yard, with
its calf-high grass, and started up the hill, past my mother's exploding vegetable garden. Past the raspberry patch. Past my ancient
flaking wooden swing set, thinking about nothing in particular. It
was only when I reached my grandmother's perennial beds, now
overgrown with Vi's lush sensibility, that I looked up.

And then I stopped short. I saw first the tealights sputtering
around the pool-cum-frog pond, the three kickboards filled with
guttering candles on the scummy surface like small islands afire.
Only after that did I see the table under the linden, a circle of white
where the candle's light illuminated the tablecloth. Then three
shadows sitting at the table. There was a discordant plucking sound,
and I stopped and watched under the old lilac tree, wondering what
I had stumbled upon. Reverend Milky turning romantic, a little

nighttime nookie? The return of one of Vi's Gaia ceremonies from that time in my youth?

Then I heard Vi's voice clearly among the murmur of voices. The wind rose and flicked the candlelight over the other two faces, and I saw Peter Lieder strumming a violin with his thumb, and Ezekiel Felcher staring straight up at the night sky through the linden branches.

"Where the heck is she, Ms. Upton?" said Peter, and he gave an impatient little twang on the strings of his instrument.

"Knowing Willie, she could be anywhere," said my mother. "She's a nut."

They laughed a little at this, all of them, together. I grew a little angry, then, and stepping out of the lilacs, I said, "I'm here." They spun around toward me, clearly having thought I would have come in by the plate glass door of the seventies wing, and Peter Lieder leapt up so quickly that his chair tipped over backward. Vi stood, and the candlelight made her fallen face look somehow tight in the shadows, lovely. Felcher came over to me as Peter began to play his violin and he took me by the hand and led me to the table. It was laden with cheeses and salads, breads and wine, and I sat with my back to the house, looking out at the tarry sweep of the lake, and Felcher pulled from beneath his chair a great bouquet of my mother's lavender. I sat, struck dumb, as the violin stopped, and in the new silence, the frogs twirped and the Hawaiian music back at the country club floated gently across the water.

"Now someone tell me what's going on," I said.

Felcher leaned forward and said, "We felt bad for the other night, Willie, 'cause you've been having a hard time and somehow we just made it harder. We just felt bad for you, me and Pete. So when I called today to try to say sorry again and your mother picked up, I had a little chat with her and she suggested we do something like this for you. Pete here and your mom made a nice dinner and Pete's going to play some music after we eat, and we're going to all just have a nice, quiet night, and maybe, if we have enough wine, do a little swimming in the lake."

"This is so romantic," said Vi, her voice already rich with wine.

"This is so *not* romantic," Felcher said. "We're just being friendly."

"I'm speechless," I said.

"That's what we were gunning for," said Peter warmly.

"No," I said. "You did this out of pity for me? Out of pity, for God's sakes?"

"Uh-oh," said Vi. "You've touched her pride. Dangerous thing to do."

"Vivienne," I said. "Shut up."

There was a long silence then, and my mother began sawing into the baguette. Then Felcher said, dropping the hick accent, his voice tight with anger, "You know what? We just wanted to do something nice for you, Willie, but if you're going to be like that, fuck it. I mean, obviously you're having a hard time. You come back to Templeton all skinny and exhausted-looking, with this trucked-up story about finishing your PhD, when you're an archaeologist, for Christ's sakes. You don't come to Templeton to spend every single day in the Historical Library when your PhD is in archaeology. It just doesn't add up. And I haven't seen you in the however many years we graduated from high school, and all you got is abuse for me. 'I don't want to be seen leaving the Bold with you, Ezekiel.' 'I'm surprised you can string together a coherent sentence, Ezekiel.' 'You're not good enough for me, Ezekiel.' Well, fuck you, Willie Upton. I am too."

He stood then but sat back down, heavily in his chair. And there was another long silence, and Vi began pouring wine into the glasses, and Felcher screwed up his mouth like a little boy and I perversely wanted to reach over and touch his twisted pretty lips, but before I did, Peter gave a sigh and said, "We just did this because we like you, Willie, and because you're not happy, and we want you to be happy."

Somehow, this chipped away at the rest of the ice. In the dim light, Vi's face gleamed, pleased. Everyone save me began eating. I felt smaller and smaller as my mother complimented Peter on his foie gras blinis with fig compote, and Peter complimented her back on the crab-stuffed artichokes and Felcher talked about the superiority of Chilean zinfandels in comparison to their cabernets, and found tobacco and black currant in the one we were drinking and Peter said that one of the frogs in the chirruping pool had a devastatingly pitch-perfect A-flat.

And then Clarissa's favorite pun rose up: *Show me a piano falling down a mine shaft and I'll show you a flat miner*, and, with the mere thought of Clarissa, I couldn't bear myself anymore. I said, in a very small voice, "I'm sorry."

"What's that, Queenie?" said Felcher. "Couldn't hear you."

"I'm sorry," I said. "I have a very bad temper. Thank you for tonight. I'm a jerk."

"Good," said Felcher, smiling at me now, and I saw him as a whole for the first time since the Bold, and saw that he looked good. He was thinner already and well shaven, and in a nice button-down shirt with cuff links. He was letting his hair grow longer, and it hid some of his overlong forehead, especially in the half-dark of the table. He held up his glass, and said, "Then, to Willie."

"To Willie," said Peter, a nervous finger smoothing down his mustache.

"To Willie," said my mother. "May she find what she needs." She sent me a kiss through the candle flame so, for a long moment, the light flickered and wobbled and danced.

ONE BY ONE, the tealights dipped themselves out, and a frog must have been curious about the blazing kickboard because he leapt on it and tipped it and the candles hissed out in the murky water. By the time my mother fetched the little pots of crème brûlée from the kitchen and began to torch them at the table, the only light was the blue flame in her hand and the citronella that threw rings on the tablecloth. Our eyes had gotten used to the dark.

While Vi torched away, I at last explained my quest for my father to Peter and Felcher. "And so I've backed all the way to Jacob Franklin Temple, looking at his books to see if he has any mistresses or anything. Hazel Pomeroy says there's nothing else available, so I have to try to pick stuff out of his fiction. It's all pretty far-fetched."

Peter, wine-silly, was giggling the whole way through the explanation because he found Vi's commune alibi to be "sheer genius." Felcher was leaning back in his chair, looking at me inscrutably.

Then, out of the thick shadows under the linden, a figure stepped, briefly illuminated by the moon. And then Felcher's chair had flipped over and he was on the ground, and the figure was standing akimbo over him.

"So this is where you're at," a brassy voice said, and I realized with a terrible sinking feeling that this was Melanie, Felcher's not-really-significant other. Huge, now. Platinum hair down to her tail-bone. Fists as huge as hams. "I seen your truck out front. Figures you'd be here," she hissed.

"Mel," said Felcher calmly from the ground. "What's up? How're the boys?"

"Don't you 'what's up' me," she said. "That's bullshit. They're at my mom's."

"Nice to see you, Melanie," said Peter. "Come and have some dessert with us. We made plenty of them."

"Shut up, you," she said, but there was a wobble to her voice now. She had yet to look at me. "All the girls said that this bitch was back and you was with her at the Bold Dragoon, but I said, nah, he always thought she's a total fucking snobby asshole, and he'd never even talk to her. Remember what you called her in high school? Miss-Stick-Up-Her-Ass? Cuntface. You definitely called her Cuntface, like the time she wouldn't dance with you at the home-coming dance. Queenie Cuntface, you said then."

My mother, I noticed, had stopped torching the desserts and the blue flame now licked out in Melanie's direction.

"Mel," I began, but didn't finish. Because what, really, could I have said? I have no attraction to your nonsignificant other? I couldn't, because though I wanted that to be true, it wasn't. That there's no way Felcher and I would ever get together? That was true, but hurtful. That in high school *my* friends always called *you* Hoochtastic-5000 and Slutty Slutkins? This was true, and I consid-ered it briefly before my kinder side kicked in, and I said nothing.

"You," she said to me and for the first time turned to glare at me, her little eyes bright in her marshmallow face. "Don't you fucking talk or you'll get a fist in your pretty face."

"Mel," said Felcher, still on the ground. "I haven't seen you in, what, a year? So, how are things? I know you've been getting my child support. Cashing the checks and all that jazz. Found a job yet?"

"It's only been ten months since we seen each other. But what-ever. Get up. Let's go." She stepped back so Felcher could stand. He did but righted his chair and sat down again.

"Get up," she shouted at him, and kicked the chair leg. Although he jerked sideways as the chair did, he didn't move.

Then Peter's hand was on my shoulder and he had taken the other and was petting it. "Mel," he said, very softly, "I think you might be mistaken. Willie and I are"—here he gave me a sweet smile—"together. Zeke's just here as a friend."

"Right," said Melanie. "As if." But her voice had become uncertain again, and when I dared to look up, little trails were running down her cheeks, gleaming in the moonlight. Her eyes were darting among all of us, Vi to Felcher, Felcher to me, me to Peter. She pushed a hand across her face and took a step back.

"Melanie," said Felcher. "I am going to have some dessert now with my friends. You've been invited to eat some with us, if you like. If not, I'll call you and we can talk about this later."

"You," said Melanie, gasping a little, "are the *father* of my *children.*"

"Yes," said Felcher, "I know, honey. And the courts have established that I belong to them and not you."

"You have responsibilities," she said.

"To Joey and Nicky," he said. "Not to you. Mel, please don't make me get another restraining order."

At this, Melanie turned around, and her large back seemed to quake. She turned back, staring especially hard at me, and when she walked away, I felt withered and tired, even more than I had been before dinner. My mother continued torching. Peter gave me a kiss on the cheek and his thin mustache tickled. And, as our spoons crunched through the burnt candy on the custard, Felcher said, "I'm so sorry about that."

"Ah," said Vi, and her voice also sounded shaky. "It's life. Children can make you go a little nuts." She patted Felcher's shoulder and said, "I know how it feels to be that poor girl. Felt it myself. But I also know you can't force someone to love you. She'll learn, with time."

We ate the rest of our desserts in a silence punctured by the pool-singing frogs. I looked up at Felcher from time to time, and when the dark look on his face softened and lightened when he caught my eye, something turned over in me, and I knew I couldn't call him Felcher anymore.

"Ezekiel," I said.

"Yes?" he said, smiling.

"Nothing," I said, and laughed a little. But then I thought of Primus, when we hiked together in the bright night over the tundra, his warm hand holding my own, and felt a great flip of sadness that we would never be there together again, marveling at the millions of subtle colors in the lichen. When I looked up, Felcher was still smiling at me, expectant. But I had stopped laughing, and looked away.

IT WAS MIDNIGHT when the boys left and Vi and I washed and dried the dishes, Peter's violin still wailing in our heads. After she rinsed the last bowl and handed it to me, Vi yawned.

"That was nice. I can't remember when I had a night as nice as that," she said.

"You mean other than the fisticuffs," I said.

"Can't blame the poor girl," said Vi and took the dry bowl from my hands and stacked it in the cupboard. "It's clear Zeke's in deep smit. Hopelessly smitten. Smited, in fact."

"Hm. He's not really my type, Vi."

"True, but a little physical something with someone like Zeke could help you get over that Primus asshole. And who knows. He's a nice guy, seems smart. He's still drop-dead gorgeous. Maybe he'd grow on you."

"Ezekiel Felcher is *not* gorgeous, Vi. He stopped being gorgeous in 1995."

"Your problem, Sunshine," she said, thumping the next bowl down, "is that you can't see straight through your snobby little worldview. Nobody in Templeton would ever be good enough for you. If they're in Templeton, it means they're second rate in your little head."

"That is so not true," I said.

"It is," she said, "so true. But I raised you to believe that. It's my fault. I pushed you and pushed you. Made you so ambitious you're ashamed of where you're from. No wonder you snapped. But I have no worries, Willie. You'll rebound. Go back, live your life in San Francisco and someday come back to Templeton."

I wanted to tell her that if I left there was little chance of me ever coming back to Templeton to live. But I stopped; I couldn't break her heart. I sighed and said, "Maybe. If I ever resolve any of this father shit."

"How much time do you have?" she asked.

"Six days," I said. "Then I have to go relieve Sully. He's not sleeping anymore. Clarissa says he's a zombie. She says it's not fair—he's stealing her role as the family undead." Vi blinked at me, startled.

I said, "It was funnier when she said it."

"Six days. Well. You'll make it," Vi said, and flipped off the kitchen lights. She moved in the dark to the back stairwell, and I heard her heavy step as she crossed the house and closed the door of her room.

FOR A LONG while, I stared out into the darkness at the nickel-plated lake, the heap of hills. I imagined that huge monster still alive, in the deep, swimming gently up through the water, and breaching for a breath, resting on the surface before diving deep again. I was about to head up to my little-girl room when the telephone rang. I thought of Clarissa taken unexpectedly ill, ugly visions of catheters and ambulances dancing through my head. I picked the phone up before the second ring and said "Hello" so fast it came out as a whisper.

"Willie, girl," a voice said, smooth and mellow, in my ear. "It's bloody great to hear your voice."

It was Primus Dwyer.

Primus Dwyer: Or, The Great Buffoon

I GASPED AND sat on the cold hardwood floor. In the darkness, the VCR light at the end of the room blinked a syncopated rhythm.

"Willie?" said Primus. "You quite all right?"

"Yes," I whispered. "No. It's been a month and you haven't called."

"You dear, silly girl," he said. "I can't very well pick and choose when I'm going to call, you know. Mobiles don't work on the tundra, dear."

"Well," I said. "I knew that."

There was a long silence, and I could hear the terns and gulls in the background shrieking. There was the familiar roar of a truck going by; voices; Primus was in an inhabited place, a city, perhaps. Then I heard the noise of waves, and from this I surmised that he must have found a pay phone somewhere outside, near the ocean.

"Where are you?" I said, barely hearing my voice over the thrumming of my heart.

"Ah, yes," he said. "Well, I'm at supper. Rather, I was. They think I'm using the loo right now. Jan's been watching me nonstop since we left the site, you know, save for supper tonight, and so I took the opportunity to phone you. We're all a bit soused, you see. Celebrating. We finished the article, Willie, we did," he said. "We've submitted the paper to *Nature* today, and it will be reviewed before the next issue, and, with luck, appear in short order. Hooray! You're an author, of course. I had to fight, but I did. Fight. For you."

"Oh. Hooray," I said.

"Listen, darling. I can't be much longer, or else they will miss me. I just wanted to call to ensure you weren't furious with me still. You can't be. You're too brilliant a student, and a lovely girl, you know, just lovely. I'm very much looking forward to seeing you back at school again, eh? We can maybe pick up where we left off?" His voice had dropped, become honeyed the way it did in Alaska before he laid a hand on my thigh or the small of my back. On the cold hard floor of Averell Cottage that night, I longed for the weight of that hand, the warmth of it on my skin.

"Wait," I said, beginning to breathe a little jaggedly. "I think my head's exploding."

He gave his little bark of a laugh and said, "Why, darling?"

I said, "I thought I was going to be kicked out of school. For trying to kill, you know. Your wife."

He gave his low chuckle and said, "Oh, yes, that. No, no. She's rather jealous, that's true, but we have calmed her and we certainly don't have to tell her about your being around. Besides, you only have one chapter left to write for your dissertation, and then you may defend it before December, early, of course, and then you're off to a brilliant career. With this publication, you could find a position, well, anywhere. Rather, I could find a position for you. I will, too. I heard there may be a position at Princeton. I shall make some enquiries."

"Princeton?" I said. "But that's so far from California." I took a breath. "From you."

"Oh, darling," he said, and was quiet for some time. I was content, for the moment, to hear his breathing in my ear; I pictured his summer-ruddy cheek dimpling prettily. But when he spoke again, he spoke more slowly and his tenor had turned to bass. "Darling, I am so very sorry, you know. I didn't realize. I thought you were, well, more hard-boiled than that. The stories they told of you, well. Not that you were promiscuous, but, you know. You never find yourself attached. To any one man. You're unattached."

"I'm not," I said. "Unattached. I get very attached. Who told you that?"

"Your fellow student, John, you know. After you left. The stories I've heard of your debauchery. What a naughty girl you are!"

"I'm not naughty. I'm not a naughty girl at all," I said. "I just fall easily."

There was more silence, and then his voice came back, a little more sternly. "Oh, Willie. Had I realized. Well, I wouldn't have even. I just didn't realize you would have formed an attachment. Willie, I am so sorry, but we can't, you know. Be together. Well, we *can* until you're finished with your dissertation, but that's pushing it, and then we will meet at conferences every few months. But you can't be around me, or else my wife would grow entirely suspicious, and that cannot happen."

"Oh. Right," I said.

"I really do like you, of course, quite a bit."

"Sure. Of course," I said.

"You're gorgeous, and, if I do say so"—here his voice lowered, became intimate—"quite a good fuck. And brilliant, of course. I have no worries for your future. None whatsoever. You can do whatever you wish to do."

"Hm," I said. "Thanks."

"A darling girl, darling. You know it well. Listen, I have to go back before they think I've flushed myself down the toilet and come investigate. Ha-ha! Ta. Take care of yourself."

"Wait," I said, and my voice rose in the darkness and seemed to ring against the old beams of Averell Cottage. "I have something to tell you."

And, like that, I found I had shoved the lever and this, right now, was the split second before the floor fell away and left me dangling by the neck.

"Sure, darling. Anything," he said, but I could feel his anxiety growing with every second, I could feel how much he longed to be back in the restaurant beside his wife. I imagined him there, in the sunny Alaskan night, the gulls circling his head, the streets bare and trash-blown, kicking the ground with the heels of his hiking boots.

"Dr. Dwyer," I said, slowly. "I am pregnant."

There was a very long pause, and then he said, "Oh, my. So you're not coming back to Stanford, then, eh? Is that it? Is that what you're telling me, that you're going to keep it, Willie?"

"I don't know," I said. "It all depends on you."

"Me?" he said. There was a longer pause, and then I heard the smile in his voice. "You're not saying," he said, "that *I'm* the father?"

"Yes, I am saying exactly that," I said.

"No, no. I cannot be."

"There is no one else. It's impossible. Nobody else."

"But you're entirely sure?"

"I've only slept with you since December," I said. "Yes, I'm fucking sure. There's no one else."

"Oh, Willie," said Primus Dwyer heaving out a sigh. "But, you see, it cannot be me. I had a vasectomy many, many years ago, my poor darling. My wife, she never wanted children. I have a sperm count of zero, darling. It cannot be me. It must be someone else."

"There is no one else," I said, in a whisper.

"There must be," he said.

"No," I said.

"I'm sure if you thought of it, you'd come up with someone. At a party or something, you know. Might have slipped your mind. Now, Willie, I really must go. I shall try to call again. In the meantime, I expect to see you in my office on the first day of school. Will you be fine, darling? Oh, I am sure you will. You're a tough cookie, as they say. A biscotti! Ha. All right, then. Good-bye, darling."

"Slipped my mind?" I said, but there was already the click, and he was gone. I took a deep breath. "Slipped my mind?" I said again into the long silence, into the nothing, into the great, terrible, dark nothing buzzing in my ear.

FOR A LONG time, I sat there, tempted to call Clarissa. But every time I lifted the phone off the hook, I had an image of her little body, in bed, exhausted. I couldn't do it. I climbed the dark stairs and went to my room.

And even though I felt emptied, even though I wanted to weep into my pillow until it was soaked through and gnash my teeth, even though the old ghost was there, in a sweet and tender lilac, I crawled into bed, and opened a book I had brought with me and began to read Jacob's purplish prose. The writing seemed like the books that held it; crumbly and antique and bearing the stink of centuries. Still, it was compelling. His voice was smooth and kind, and once in a while an observation would ring so true it vibrated like flicked crystal.

That night, Jacob Franklin Temple sang me a lullabye in his queer and convoluted syntax. The ghost ringed around me tighter, squeezing the air in me closer, throbbing me calm. Thus comforted, thus spun back centuries before my wounded heart, I fell asleep sometime before dawn.

THE DINING ROOM was lit like a lantern by the midmorning light when I heard the voices, the urgency in them. I awoke with a start and was out of my bed before I knew what I was doing, and had already started down the stairs when I heard my mother and Reverend Milky arguing. I stopped at the edge of the ancient Persian rug in the dining room to eavesdrop. My mother's coffee cake was sending out warm feelers into the air, but there was no happiness in the house, not then. When my mother's voice rose, I moved crabwise toward the corner cabinet.

As I listened, I picked up the little horse toy from the dining table and held it absently in my hands. My gut had started to cramp again, and I studied the horse to take my mind off the jabs of pain.

My mother's voice was touched with acid as she said, "John, I notice you don't have any children. So, really, you don't know what you're talking about. So, really, we should change the subject, shouldn't we."

"Oh, Vivienne," said Reverend Milky. "Nothing is gained by running away from this subject. It is dire that we try to save your daught . . ."

". . . right," said my mother, "but a whole lot is gained by running away from other subjects, like the one I keep bringing up with you but you don't want to hear. Like, for example, why you can't seem to muster up the slightest interest in . . ."

". . . Vivienne," came Milky's voice, and the oleaginous outline to his voice was gone now. "Don't begin this again. I am a man of

the Word, and my own word, and I cannot until we're married. I've
offered a million times. If you'd only agree to . . ."

". . . as you know, John, I don't believe in . . ."

". . . I understand, though I have to say it's a real slap in the face.
I don't understand what's so terribly wrong with me that you don't
want to marr . . ."

". . . and I don't see what the problem is, John—it's just a little
skin and a few fluids, and . . ."

". . . well, I don't see how, then, we're going to solve this little
impasse, Vivienne. Sex before marriage is a sin, and as a Christian,
you should know this. I love you, but not enough to damn my
everlasting soul. Besides, how would I be able to lead my flock if I
were not to adhere to the rules I preach?"

My mother sucked in her breath sharply, and let it out with a hiss.
"Then I," said Vi, "don't see why we are in a relationship at all, John."

There was a very long silence, and the beam of light dug into the
cabinet, catching a bowl of ruby glass and igniting it so it seemed to
explode. The silence lasted until the beam moved into an indigo
vase and blasted petals of color onto the far wall.

At last, Reverend Milky said in a voice so sad that even I felt a
little sorry for him, "Well, Vivienne. If that is what you want, then
I find I can't protest."

"Okay, then," said my mother.

"Okay," said Reverend Milky. "Well, then. Please make sure
your daughter reads those pamphlets I brought over."

"Right," said Vi. There was a sound of fabric shifting, feet shuffling. I heard the tread across the kitchen and into the mudroom,
where Milky was sliding his shoes onto his feet. Then the door to
the garage opened and closed and I heard my mother heave one
sob, then catch herself, fiercely, before another happened.

I stood there in the dining room, listening to her move around
the kitchen for some time, the *thwick* of her slippers on the tile. I
was watching the little horse, glorious now in the moving sun,
when my mother shuffled into the dining room and over to me.
Her face was red, and her hands bulged.

"Reverend Milky said to give you these pamphlets," she said.
Then she threw the shreds into the air and they spun and fell
around me like so much godly confetti.

Jesu, said an orange snippet that fell on my sleeve.
oad to salvatio said a pink one that fell on my lip.
oves you said a sky blue piece that settled in my hand.

I kissed my mother on the cheek, and she ran her hand over the horse's little mane. "I've always loved that old horsey," she said, the thin string of her mouth beginning to quiver. She put her head on my shoulder. When she pulled her hand away from the toy, her fingerprint remained on its tiny glass eye, thin as a membrane, round as a spore.

THAT DAY, MY mother's sadness took a heavy form, as if her hands and feet and head were stuffed with lead shot, and were too weighty for her to lift. I found her staring at nothing in particular, or stroking the iron cross around her neck. She didn't go to church the next morning, which was Sunday, but I saw her praying everywhere.

I heard her say in a whisper as she went past my room at night, "Save us, Lord . . ." and she trailed off as she passed. I heard her pray for herself, for me, for the monster. For Glimmey was the Earth's only good soul, we were told by a smelly, apocalyptic shaman who had begun to camp out in Lakefront Park a week earlier, drawn like a fly by the news of the beast. When I walked by and gave him a dollar on Main Street one day, he snatched my hand, and his fingers were tanned and gnarled as oak twigs. He and Piddle Smalley, the town loco, sat across from each other all day, engaged in a furious battle of glares, Piddle driven even madder by the shaman on his turf; and when the shaman grabbed my hand, Piddle gave a low yowl.

So my mother prayed for Glimmey, and she prayed for the shaman, and she prayed for poor, soaked Piddle Smalley. She prayed for my invisible father, for him to have the strength to understand when I came to him and told him I was his daughter. She prayed for the Lump, that I would be able to have the courage to do what needed to be done. She prayed a great deal for me. The night of their blowup, she even prayed for Reverend Milky, that he would unbend a little and learn to freaking relax. She caught me listening to that particular prayer and turned away with the trace of a guilty smile on her face.

My own sorrow was light, ghostly. It kept me reading through the Jacob Franklin Temple canon, through the popular books and onto the obscure ones, trying to escape its damp grasp. When I called

Clarissa, she was knee-deep in her own set of books, and her voice had taken on that abstracted, cottony tone she used when she was heavily into something. "Willie," she said. "Some of this is amazing stuff. Haven't found anything yet, but I'm kind of digging old JFT. Maybe I'll do an article on him, or something." I was glad for her, but after I hung up I punched my pillow when I thought of Primus. Even though had I tried to work up my fury against him on the predawn runs I began taking again, I started to see him everywhere. He was in the fog gently scooping up from the morning lake, in a cup of daisy ribbed with shadow, in the bearlike forms of old-men baseball fans as they walked up and down Main Street, in the vast purple rain clouds that descended on the town, drenching the Running Buds so their shirts were opaque, and their nipples were visible, tender as the snouts of mice. I saw him as my mother and I sat in silence on the back porch, looking at the glimmer of moon on the lake, and eating mint chocolate chip ice cream. His face, imprinted on the far hills. I blinked him away, and said, "Remember when I was little, Vi. All those times when we sat here and ate our sugar-free soy mint chocolate chip. Remember our little mantra?"

And my mother gave a sigh and smiled for the first time since her fight with Reverend Milky. "I remember," she said, "when we were done, you used to wait for me to put my bowl down and say 'Ah, now that's the taste of summer.' Then you'd laugh hysterically for no reason. I never understood why."

"Well?" I said.

"Well, what?" she said.

"Say it," I said.

"No, Willie," my mother said, standing and lifting my bowl into hers. "It doesn't make sense. No matter how you act when you're home, you're not a little kid anymore." Then she disappeared inside, and slid the great glass door behind herself.

I used to laugh, I remembered as I sat there alone in the overcast night, because no matter how many tiny changes happened to my body, no matter how many small shifts happened in Templeton, my mother always said the same thing at the same moment, in the same way, with the same great gusto. I found my glee in the fact that she was constant; that, alone in the world, Vi would never, ever change.

Richard Temple

MY PARENTS MET General Washington once, when I was a child in arms. My dear mother was young then, happy; my father was at work on his first Templeton, the one in New Jersey. As the noise of the revolution grew near, all the townspeople fled, save my parents, who owned the village and ran the inn.

One day, there came a knock on the door. When my father opened it, General Washington stood on the step. He bowed. My father bowed. The general entered, and he was such a gentleman he did not act surprised when he saw me, though I was hairy as a little monkey, even then. He sang me a lullabye and dandled me on his lap before he retired for the evening. Many years later, in the second Templeton in New York, my father told all who would listen about Washington in a hushed and wondering voice, made more quiet because he was normally so extremely loud. A man who radiated goodness, he said; a great, good man.

But to me the story is only complete when a second tale is told afterward, that of the Hessian Colonel Van Dunop, fighting for England. Like Washington, this colonel knocked, came into the inn. I remember his weasel's face and his long yellowed nails. Unlike Washington, this fine gentleman did, in fact, startle when he looked upon me. He made a distasteful face, asked my mother to take me away. I was harassing his appetite, he said, waggling his nails in my direction. My father, in his wrath, slipped a little tart emetic in his hare pie. The colonel was so ill that the American rebels easily won the battle the next day.

Years later, after my father's death, I told my wife, Anna, these two stories, intending to make her laugh. She was brushing her hair before bed, and I was muddling my hand in the blond cascade the way a child dabbles his hand in a pond. She was very large with child then, and even more beautiful to me than she seemed the first time that I, shy as a mole, understood she was angling for me to be her husband. For months, this large, ruddy farmer's daughter had walked beside me home from church, chattering so gaily I had no need to say a word myself. One day, she laid her hand on my arm, and, with a shock, I understood her intentions. I glanced at her, and she looked flushed and sweet as a poppy. I am not prone to rash action, but I understood my luck, and asked for her hand at that very moment.

That night, a year into our marriage, after I told her the two stories, she turned to me. I could see in the candlelight that there were tears in her eyes, and I started up, fearing she was somehow in pain. But she only put down her hairbrush and took my hand in hers. Oh, Richard, she said. You *do* know why you tell those stories together, don't you?

Oh, well, I don't know, Anna, I said, a little crossly. I had wanted to cause her to laugh; instead, I caused her to cry. Unlike my brother, I was never adept at making others merry. I am sorry I pained you, I said. I imagined the stories were more humorous that way.

She squeezed my hand and smiled at me, dabbing at her eyes. You didn't pain me, she said. But I know why you tell them so.

Oh, do you? I said to the dear girl, brushing her pretty cheek with my thumb.

Yes, she said. I do. Together, they prove your father did love you.

You fear that he did not, Richard, but somewhere deep within you, you know that he did. And someday you will forgive him, you know.

I was struck to the quick. I had never told her that I could not forgive my father; I had never told anyone. I had only ever written it in my journal, and my Anna was far too honorable to have read anything so private. My dear one had somehow divined this fact from my character.

I don't recall what I next said to Anna, and this is to my great sadness, for that night was one of my last memories of her. In one week's time, she died in childbirth, and our son passed away only moments after his mother, so small and silent, so blue.

In a quiet moment, when I am perhaps riding between farms for the rent, sometimes the words of Publilius Syrus come to me: *Amor animi arbitrio sumitur, non ponitur;* we choose to love; we do not choose to cease loving. One of the few bits of knowledge my drunken tutor taught me during my Burlington childhood. It applies, I think, to both Anna and my father, although perhaps in opposite ways. I could never choose to cease loving Anna; she is as deep engraved in my heart as a vein in the rock below the earth. Though I would have chosen to keep my love for my father, I could not.

And I had adored him, deeply. All those years when my father was gone to create Templeton, it was only my mother and me in the house—and the servants, and my gouty, furious grandfather Richard. When my father arrived home as he did once or twice a year, my mother's gentle, pious world would explode, and it was as if I was now seeing all the colors of a garden when I had only before seen gray.

Richard! he'd shout, handing the reins to the stableboy, Where's my little baboon? And I, the size of a man at ten years old, would barrel out of the house. He'd throw me up into the air, as if I were nothing, a puppy, and he'd catch me as I fell. When he was home, I hid in the clothespress in my parents' bedroom and memorized the lineaments of his face as he slept. I followed him like a smaller, hairier shadow of himself.

Those times when he was away, my mother had me sit next to her by the fires at night, and, in great contentment, she spoke of my father. She knitted, I whittled boats and houses from the kindling, and my tutor either snored into his chest or worked endlessly on his epic poem, which took the place of my education. Although sometimes I longed to run outside on the streets of the town, my mother was a simple soul, not stupid, but plain in her thoughts and manners, and I was happy enough beside her.

I longed to go up to Templeton, to see the lake my father spoke of with such poetry, to know the natives, to meet old Natty Bumppo, the funny sharpshooting hunter he told so many stories about. I wanted to see the vast beast in the lake, Old Sad Spirit in the tongue of the natives, even though my father scoffed at the myth, saying only women and fools ever saw it. I wanted to sit at my father's shoulder and learn what he had to teach me. When he was gone, the world seemed grayer, and my quiet mother, with her books and her flowers, with her pregnancies lost or babies too weak for this world, regained her rightful place in my heart. Still, I dreamt of Templeton, at night, the broad, glassy lake, the hills; I wished Templeton into a golden Arcadia, the streets shining with polished stones, the wind singing in the trees, the people plump and fair, like him.

And then one day my father arrived home from Templeton to find my mother incoherent with laudanum, for she had just lost another child, and the doctor wanted to keep her peaceful. My father roared and shook the house, stomping about. He threw the doctor's hat in his face, and dispatched the servants to pack. For an entire night, I quivered with joy. We were off, then, to Templeton! When it came time to leave, all our goods were packed, and the house was bare, save for my mother's room. Drugged, hardly able to speak, my mother held her ground, sat in her chair, refused to stand and convey herself to the carriage. At last, in a fury, my father picked her up, chair and all, and hefted her above his head like a queen. All down the staircase, I followed, arms open to catch her if my poor, plain, terrified mother fell. Outside, a crowd had gathered around the train of our goods and people, and there was such hilarity at this sight that my mother buried her head in her apron and sobbed out her shame when my father placed her in her chair, firmly, in the back of the last wagon.

When he did so, he turned to me. Richard, my boy, he said:

come. He leapt onto his charger and held out the reins of the mare for me. But I could not leave my mother like that, alone, trembling in humiliation, and so I averted my eyes. I burnt. My father gave a grunt, put his spurs to his mount, and rode off, and for a long time afterward I believed I did hear a crack when my heart broke. Still, I rode beside my mother through Burlington, timidly touching her wrist. When we passed my grandfather's house, she leapt lithe as a cat from the wagon and took shelter in her father's garden. I had no choice. I accompanied her, watched as my father disappeared down the road, feeling as if that was the last I would see of him, utterly bereft.

Thus, when, at last, my mother and I rode through the hard wilderness all the way to Templeton, my soul nearly burst of joy. Although it was still but a small settlement, still rude, that day we arrived, it seemed perfect to me. Jacob was born nearly as soon as my mother entered the Manor, screaming for attention as he always would. After his birth, my mother had no eyes for me anymore. Jacob was a beautiful child, so spirited it took Remarkable and my mother both to care for him, so wild that sometimes they would fall asleep together in their chairs and poor Mingo would have to follow the boy as he climbed over all the furniture in the parlor. The pet of everybody, not only in the Manor, but also in the town, and it was no wonder he turned out the way he did. There were times I thought that since nobody else was being strict with him, I, as the elder brother, should try. I would scold him for some minor infraction or another. But he would stare at me with his sparking black eyes and either kick me in the shins or go screaming off to our mother, who would look at me and wonder aloud why I must torment my brother when I was a man and he was but a baby. He'd watch me with those laughing eyes, sucking a finger, this child who, at two years old, said things about me to his tutor that made the old Frenchman giggle into his beard. When he was five, I ceased trying. The result, I must say, was uneven, at best.

But in the first months after my mother and I had reached Templeton, I was young, and, since I had failed my entrance exams for university (my tutor, the poor, blighted soul, having neglected to teach me anything), I clung close to my idol, my father. He was busy, seemed even larger in his own town. Neck-deep in papers, the little Indian amanuensis Cuff took one look at me, so eager, and saw a replacement. In a fortnight, he had fled, and I became my father's secretary.

The years clicked by, and my admiration for my father only grew. He was the one the settlers ran to when they wanted a road leading to their parcel, when they wanted to marry, when they had a squabble. He was the strong man, the one nobody could wrestle to the ground. I became my father's sergeant, taking over more and more as he began meddling in politics. I rode to the distant farms and accepted the rents; I kept the books. All for a slap on the back. All that effort, that work, hard, dirty, cold, so that my beloved father would reach his arm to me and ruffle the hair on my head late at night, as I wrote a letter from his dictation, cramping my hand for hours.

When I was only a boy, I sometimes longed to be like all those rosy young people I saw laughing in their sleighs and playing games in the park. But at fourteen, I didn't know how to speak to young men, young women; I didn't know I even had the right to look at a girl in admiration. During the long months after poor Anna passed away, I sometimes looked at the taxidermied catamount in the Men's Club, feeling an uncomfortable likeness to it. Like the wire and cloth within the beast, my father had stuffed me into his own form.

Late, my father became a Tory. If I had doubts at the time, I kept them to myself. I believe, though, that I was still too enamored of my father to have had real doubts. I barely noticed when Elihu Phinney turned away from us. I never heard the gossip about my father, all that talk of the serving girls, the bribes. I barely noticed that my father, who had once been a poor, uneducated soul, began to scorn poor, uneducated souls.

And then came that trip to Albany, two months before the election. My father, a senator, went to sit in session, and his infernal lawyer Kent Peck and I came along. From the day he arrived in Templeton, I hated Kent Peck, that carved face, that rancid stink coming from his clothing. The way he called himself a third son of my father. On their trips, my father and Peck had long been in the habit of taking a cup of whiskey from every roadside inn and tavern along the way, and so by the time we reached our boarding-house in Albany, they were falling off their mounts. I never drank, and so I was tending to the baggage and then the horses when my father and Peck stumbled out of the door of the boardinghouse, a hunk of cheese and bread in each hand, ready for their rounds of the town. My father saw me, in the stables, in the light of the lamp.

He stopped, and roared at me, Richard, my boy! Come with us, come, come. Let us see if thou hast what it takes to be a man.

I would have declined—I always did on our trips, liking more my journal and a bit of supper and a fire before I slept, disliking what spirits did to my brain—if Kent Peck hadn't spoken. Who, Richard? he sneered, then gave a little hiccough of a laugh, almost falling into the rain barrel under the eaves.

That did it; I threw the currycomb to the yawning stableboy, and followed my father and Peck out into the night. For hours, I trailed them, grimly. First to the gentleman's club, where all sorts of granite-faced men shook my father's hand vigorously. A stop to sup on some pickled herring and roast pork. A tavern at which Peck spat toward the spittoon, never quite achieving it.

At last, we went into the dark night, my father and Peck with their arms around each other, singing *And I'll drink out of the quart pot, here's a health to the barley mow,* and as we neared the river, the buildings became seedier and seedier, rats scuttling freely in the street. At last, we knocked on the door of a squat, stone building and my father hissed something into the door, and we entered.

It was a dim place, smelling oddly, I thought. There were men sitting in any number of chairs around the fireplace, some of whom we had already seen on our trip through Albany that night. There seemed to me to be too many serving girls carrying mugs of punch, all of whom were extremely poorly clad. I felt a fire in my cheeks, and looked at my feet, glancing up from time to time.

One by one, the men disappeared, although I never saw any go out the front door. The girls did, too. At last, I watched the back of Peck's head, disappearing behind a curtain. I saw my father whisper in the ear of a fat red-head, who was sitting on his lap. She smiled, looked at me, came wobbling over. She sat beside me, began stroking my knee.

Such blind ignorance. It wasn't until the red-head began breathing her salty breath into my ear, and I saw my father take the hand of a tiny brunette, that I knew where I was.

I watched my father stand, head bowed for the low ceiling. Then I pushed the girl away, stumbled out into the night. I wept as I ran; me, a great man of twenty-four.

At last, I found my way to the inn, took my things, saddled the horse, and rode through the long morning. All that time, I thought of my poor mother. So small, so devout. I must tell her everything, I thought. She should know, though her spirit would certainly break with the news.

Through the long ride, though, my resolution faded. At last, as I rode through the gates of Templeton Manor, my heart heavy, I knew I had to protect her from what I knew. Though it left a terrible, bitter taste in my mouth, I would have to swallow my disgust with my father, act as if nothing had happened.

Inside, my mother embraced me, and I had to explain what I was doing home so early. I hid what I knew in short answers, in my usual silences.

When my father and Peck returned, my father pulled me aside. Richard, my son, he said. I have no excuse. I would ask of thee only thy discretion. Out of love for me, he said. Please. I bit my tongue and nodded. I pretended little had changed. Though in the end I had to pretend for only a few months, my acting took a terrible strain on me.

The night my father died, when Mingo first began his howling, I knew what had happened. And as I sat for a moment in the Eagle, before I stood and rushed to the street, the feeling that first rose in me was not that of anguish. The black spot on my soul is this: it was relief.

All those years, all those years. My hatred buried in my journal, for my mother's sake. My fury at Jacob, as he sapped our fortunes slowly, with his merchant marines, with his gallivanting in Europe with silly Sophie and his too-many daughters, into the journal. My journal accepted what I felt when I watched my mother mourn for the absence of her favorite, my younger brother. My jealousy went in that book when Jacob came home. When Anna died, my grief. Without her, I became a skeleton of a man. Without her, my goodness in me flew away. I stopped finding words on my lips for kind people, laughter at jokes. The gentleness of certain people of Templeton—Davey, Hetty, Mudge—would bring tears stinging to my eyes.

In time, I tried my hand at a story. Nothing too large. Nothing in great long sentences the way my brother wrote, nothing in words I was uncertain how to spell. I tried to tell a truth about our father, Marmaduke Temple, and it was not a pretty truth, but it was what I knew. I liked it and called it *The Pilgrims of Templeton*. I wrote the fair copy into my journal.

But one day I returned late to the office and found my journal disappeared from the safe where I kept it. I remembered, then, how that afternoon, as I sat at my father's desk in the Manor, I heard, like an undercurrent or a fly's buzz in the room, my brother talking downstairs to our mother, telling of a great story he was going to write, the greatest. That night in the office, I stared at the empty safe, and for a long hour I felt red fall over my eyes. Had he been before me, I would have crushed my brother's thin neck under my thumbs, to feel the life drain from him, pulse by weakened pulse. I would leave his girls fatherless. I would bloody my hands. For I understood what had happened: my brother, who worshiped our father, had read my words, and was shocked at what I had written. He knew his version of the story was the one to last the ages. He rid himself of alternate versions of our father. He drowned my story like an unwanted kitten.

In the end, though, I could not harm him. He was my brother, blood thicker than anger. I sat at the supper table beside my mother that evening, and listened to the din of my brother's daughters and heard my brother boast to his guest of the day—they were always having guests—about his new story. A masterpiece, he proclaimed. About our father, the great man, Marmaduke. My mother twittered in joy, Sophie dreamed aloud about the carriage they'd buy when he sold the book. Jacob's eyes darted at me; we were children again; he was daring me to tell. I said nothing. Silently, I blessed my brother. I hoped that he would prosper and be happy. I ate my lake bass and parsnips. Then I went home to Edgewater, my brick house on the lake, my house I had built for Anna and our brood of children we had dreamt of. The servants were away at a dance and the empty house echoed.

For hours, as night spooled long, I sat in the silence, weak, eaten by grief. Without pages to put my anger into, I could feel it grow black and thick within me. In time, days or years, it would eat me, I knew. Already, I sensed, it was halfway finished with its meal; soon, I knew, too soon, it would begin on what was left.

Richard Temple

*In an etching, circa 1833. He is standing on the porch of
Edgewater, which he built for his bride and finished shortly before
she died in childbirth. Note how the illustrator, though he has
tried to make Richard as smooth-skinned as possible, cannot keep
himself from drawing masses of fur all over the poor man's
jawline. He was extraordinarily hirsute.*

What Happens When the String Is Pulled

IN THE LIBRARY, a few days after my mother's breakup with Reverend Milky, I realized that Jacob Franklin Temple almost never wrote about women. Or, rather, he wrote about a few cardboardy women who were necessary to offset the inherent nobility of his men. His Native American scouts were noble and mostly silent; his sailors were noble and mostly singing; his lords were noble and mostly refined; his best character, Natty Bumppo, was just plain noble. Even Natty Bumppo's gun was an extremely long-barreled and noble rifle. *La longue carabine,* it was called.

I hadn't read my ancestor since my one summer of Jacob Franklin Temple-mania when I was in my early teens and infused with a boiling pride in our hometown novelist, my kin. I would take the book I was reading down over the long sweep of the lawn almost to the lake's edge. There, the ancient willow tree in our backyard that had been struck flat by lightning a very long time ago would make a natural fort twelve feet in diameter, and I'd sit until lunchtime, engrossed. I was reading for plot then, and finished four of his books quickly, because if there's one thing Temple could do as a writer, it was to spin a ravishing yarn.

But now, with my speed-reading through his canon on that miserable day of mid-August heat, I was looking for ideas about the man himself. Hazel Pomeroy snoozed and muttered to herself, while digging up increasingly esoteric volumes for me. Peter Lieder rubbed my shoulders, which only made them tense higher toward my ears.

I learned:

That, like me, JFT was a cynic. He said, in *Notes from an American Waistcoat*, that "Equality, in a social sense, may be divided into that of condition and that of rights. Equality of condition is incompatible with civilization and is found only to exist in those communities that are but slightly removed from the savage state. In practice, it can only mean a common misery."

That, unlike me, he was a bit of a prude. In *At Home, At Last* he said that on his travels abroad, "The women had the abominable custom of dropping belladonna in their eyes to make them sparkle like the diamonds that crusted their hands; painting rouge in pink spots on their cheeks and lips to simulate lascivious thought; and baring the great white expanses of their bosoms, all their voluptuousness on display for the consummation of Society."

That he, in a vastly different manner than me, had a major daddy-problem. In *Luciferslips,* his protagonist, Cornelius (Corny) Legge, is the son of the patroon of Albany, a young gent who cannot do anything right, and his father disowns him in favor of his brother. Corny goes to the town of Luciferslips in the gloomy wilderness, so named because there are two lakes there in the shape of a pair of lips, reputedly from when Lucifer was cast from heaven and did a mighty face-plant on the ground. There, Corny learns how to be a great man and slowly becomes rich and mighty. He returns home to Albany to show his father who he is, when the great man recognizes the prodigal son and chokes to death on a piece of mutton.

But I found nothing at all about women. No adulterer appeared in any of the books. No mistress is mentioned at all. Women are pristine and innocent in the world of Jacob Franklin Temple, the best of them both chaste and courageous.

Still, I was not without hope. When I called Clarissa the day before, her voice had been rich with excitement. "I just put something in the mail," she said. "I don't know what you're looking for, but it was pretty fascinating to me." And, though I pried and coerced and threatened her, she just chuckled and refused to tell me what it was. "You'll see," she kept laughing. "Wilhelmina Upton, just you wait and see. It's good. Oh, boy, is it weird."

In the meantime, waiting for her package, I sat in the library, searching, searching. That afternoon stretched long before me, and when at last Hazel's goaty bleats turned loud enough to chase me out of the library, I yawned and stretched and ran my fingers through my hair. All day, my stomach had cramped, but I was fixated enough on the books not to pay attention. Now, though, I had nothing else to think of, and so when I put my arms down, I felt the insistent cramps now like dagger-jabs in my stomach. I pressed my hands to them and closed my eyes.

When I opened them, it was to Zeke Felcher, bright golden in a beam of light on the far end of the library, in a chair, watching me. He had a Jacob Franklin Temple book in his lap. He saw me watching and gave a smile and the far cheek seemed to dimple. Like that, I didn't notice the Carhartt jumpsuit; like that, I didn't notice his thinning hair.

But he said nothing until I began to smile, too, and I said, "Ezekiel."

"Wilhelmina," he said.

There was a very long silence between us. Outside the lake glittered. A flock of white seagulls fell like scraps of paper onto the lawn. Hazel wheeled the squeaky cart into the back room and, still, we looked at each other, beginning to smile like fools, and that is when another spasm came.

I winced and pressed my hands to my gut again.

"Willie?" said Ezekiel Felcher now by my side. "You okay?"

I groaned and said, "No."

"I'll take you home," he said, and his arm was around my shoulder, and I had a moment to sweep a pile of books into my bag, and then we were out of the musty library and into the day, and he was helping me up into the messy truck with its bobble-headed Pirates player on the dash. The cramp passed. We were out on West Lake

Road already when I opened my eyes to see the Farmers' Museum passing on my right.

"Ugh," I said.

"You okay?" he said. "You'll be back soon."

"I'm okay for now," I said. "I must have just had a bad lunch."

"Gross," he said, and gave me a tiny smile of concern.

Out the window, the Otesaga Hotel slid by, all red-gold in that light. We went up Lake Street, past the mansions, and into the driveway of the Averell Cottage.

Then Ezekiel Felcher very deliberately turned off his truck and turned to me and seemed to want to say something but didn't, but then leaned close, then closer, and I could smell the metal of his breath before his lips touched mine. I was still staring straight ahead, surprised, when I saw my mother run out of the house only in the top part of her nursing scrubs, her vast white underwear like a button-top mushroom above her fleshy thighs.

She knocked on the window, and Ezekiel pulled away, flushing red. I hopped out of the truck, and my mother said, breathless, "Sunshine, Clarissa's on the phone, and she sounds bad. She didn't say why."

"Shit," I said and ran inside, leaving Ezekiel in his great tow truck, and Vi, semiobscene in her seminudity, staring at each other, one full beat behind me.

I GRABBED UP the telephone in a moment, and could hear nothing on the other end. "Honey?" I said. "Clarissa?"

"I think, Willie," Clarissa said, in the almost clinical voice she used when she was deeply upset, "that Sully maybe just left me."

"Wait," I said. "What?"

"Sully," she said. "Just definitely left me. For a yoga instructor who works in Arizona. Ten minutes ago. She carried all his shit down to the car for him as he broke up with me."

I took a deep breath. "Holy shit," I said.

"I don't know what to do," she said.

"Holy shit," I said again.

"She's really tall. Like six-four. And has wonky teeth. And is not even all that pretty, not at all. But," my best friend said, "she's got one thing going for her. She's healthy. Just bursting with health. Not a lupus-addled pain in the ass, apparently. They met in the hospital café while I was getting my treatment. She had an infected splinter," she said, giving one terrible lick of laughter. "In her pinky toe."

The house suddenly became still and quiet, and had I been listening, I would have heard my mother's bare feet stepping up the stairs, the floorboards squeaking, stealing to her own room. "Oh, Clarissa," I said.

"Don't," Clarissa said. "I don't want to start to cry. It's all over if I start to cry."

"I'm coming," I said. "Tonight, I'm coming. I'll be there."

"No," said Clarissa. "I *hate* this apartment. I *hate* this city. I can't be here. Reminds me of Sully."

"I *hate* Sully," I said.

"I love him," she said, and grew wild. "I don't know what to do. I don't know where to go. I don't know what to do. I swear to God I'll kill him if I see him."

This kind of talk was a precursor, I knew from long experience, to everything falling apart for Clarissa. And when someone as strong as Clarissa falls apart, it is Samson all over again, bringing the pillars of the temple upon himself, a mighty, ugly mess. I sucked in my breath and began to think, which was hard going, because I was about to fall apart, myself.

It was then that my mother, who had been shamelessly eavesdropping from the telephone in her room, spoke up. "Kill Sully?" she said. "Nonsense. You're coming here to Templeton, Clarissa Evans. I'm a nurse, and though I don't work in rheumatology, I can tell you that our facilities here in Templeton are primo, top-notch, first-rate. Plus, I get to take care of you from up close. Not far away, where I can't feed you or take care of you or anything. Your room is waiting for you."

"Oh, Vi," Clarissa said, helpless, over the line. "You're a *critical care* nurse."

"Oh, Vi," I said, softly. "What the hell are you saying?"

"Stop it, you two," she said. "Big dummies. Of course Clarissa won't be in critical care; she's going to get better here, in Templeton. I'll make the reservations and get an old friend of mine to take you to the airport, Clarissa, honey. He lives in Noe Valley. Give me fifteen minutes," she said.

"I have to go," Clarissa said abruptly. "I just have to." Then there was a click, and my mother and I both said "Clarissa?" into the phone.

I hung on to the line, listening to my mother's breath. "She'll be a-ok," she said. "I'll call back as soon as I've made the arrangements."

"Thank you," I said. "Thank you so much, Vi."

"It's not for you I'm doing this," she said. "So you don't have to thank me."

It was then that I felt the burst and looked down at my bare legs. I felt my heart rise in my throat. "Vi?" I said.

"Willie, what? I have to call the airline."

"Vi," I said. "I need you. Right now. *Right* now."

I dropped the phone back on the cradle and heard my mother's footsteps as she ran to the stairwell and down. I stood still as she rumbled through the hallway, the formal living room, the dining room, then into the 1970s wing. She burst through the door like a wild woman.

My mother's eyes took in my legs, and her hands rose to her mouth. For the length of one sonorous chime of the grandfather clock, we stood there, in the doorway, both of us staring at my legs, where there were brown streaks of blood to my knees, a bright bloom already drenching the crotch of my shorts.

Storm

I SAW IT all clearly, but somehow I wasn't involved; somehow, my brain clicked off and my body moved into action, sliding off the shorts and swabbing myself with the washcloth my mother handed me, taking new underwear and jeans and a maxi pad and putting it all on; and somehow, amid all this, I thought to grab the thick envelope that I'd gotten in the mail that day so I'd have something to read during my hospital wait. I followed my mother outside, meek as a dog, into the car that she threw into reverse and sped with reckless endangerment of the tourists' drosophila lives, squealing by so fast that their ball caps blew off their heads and their cotton candy smeared pink across their chins and the baseball bats that they jauntily carried over their shoulders fell clanging to the ground. We swerved up River Street, and the Susquehanna River roiled on our left, fat from the previous day's storms, and my mother pulled under the carport of the Emergency Room wing. She put me into a wheelchair, and rolled us past the intake desk and under the eye of the attending, who was snapping some small boy's shoulder back into joint, where my mother described what was happening to me in no uncertain terms, and the small boy's eyes grew so wide they almost burst, and I imagined the great fluidy pop that bursting eyeballs would make, like a grape pinched and splitting its skin in a goopy shower of vitreous humor. The attending, wordless, left the dislocated boy to the resident, followed my mother into the examination room and helped her undress me, and then, because my mother's voice had begun to rise in pitch and grow loud then louder, he banished her to the waiting room where one of her thick-ankled friends seized her in a bear hug. As the curtain closed, the doctor with his weary eyes behind the hipster glasses patted me into the paper-coated bed, and with a voice calm and flat as a plate, he told me to lie back and relax, and we'll see what we can do, and relax, darling, let me look and relax and relax and relax, honey, relax . . .

26

Après Storm

AFTER THE ULTRASOUND, which left a slug trail of goop across my belly, after the strange, crumpled psychiatrist who smelled of popcorn and sleep, I waited, shivering in my paper pinny, to know whether I had lost the Lump. I thought of Clarissa, of Vi, of the ghost in my room drawing thick and warm around me, to keep from imagining the Lump still in there, bleeding from its little wrists because it couldn't bear to be born into the world with such a fool for a mother. I imagined it tying a little noose in the umbilical cord and sliding its mole-star head inside.

Time ticked on in the hospital. On the floor above, I heard a slow pacing, the shuffle-drag-shuffle-drag of a sleepless someone with an IV tower. There were the groans of the nurses' shoes, a low murmur of conversation, once in a while a whiff of coffee from the cafeteria down the labyrinthine hall.

And under the weight of all that time alone, I thought of our lake monster, those centuries under the dark water, its immense solitude, and wanted to weep for the poor, sweet beast. Such a long sweep of time, such cold. Glimmey, looking longingly up at the boats zipping atop the water in the same way we watch movie screens, to see reflections of ourselves.

At last, my mother came in, her head down so I could see the zigzag of her part. I watched her, holding my breath as she took a chair and pulled it to the side of my bed, and sat. She took my hand and kissed it.

"So I lost it," I said. "Okay." I only felt numb, not dismayed, not relieved, either.

But my mother said nothing for a long time, just rocking a little in her chair, her eyes closed, giving, I presumed, a little prayer in her head.

She opened her eyes. She cleared her throat. Then she said, wincing, "When you found out you were pregnant, did you take a test, Sunshine?"

"Oh. No," I said. "No test."

"Why not, honey?" she said.

"My period stopped," I said. "I was nauseated all the time. It was clear."

"Ah," she said, and closed her eyes again.

Again, there rose between us the noises of the hospital and the sound of her foot in its clog tap-tapping on the ground.

Like this, she said, "We don't think, Sunshine. Well, that you ever really were pregnant."

I blinked. "What?" I said.

"Have you ever heard of an hysterical pregnancy? Pseudocyesis, we call it. *Grossesse Nerveuse.* You can manifest all the symptoms of pregnancy, without actually being pregnant."

"What?" I said. "That's not what happened."

"Unfortunately," my mother said, "it appears to be."

"No," I said. "I'm not crazy, Vi. I missed three periods. I was sick all the time. My belly was growing. No, that's not what happened. I was *bleeding.* There was a Lump."

"Willie," said my mother. "The blood was excessive menstruation. The rest, well."

"Well?" I said, hearing the panic sharpen my voice.

"Well, the brain is sometimes much, much stronger than the

body, and can sometimes trick the body into believing it is wrong. Or, sometimes, it's the fear of pregnancy itself that tricks the endocrine system into believing the wrong thing. The psychiatrist said you had a normal profile. Just that you seemed to be under a tremendous amount of stress."

There was a giant pause and I could hear a nattering television, a cart going by, a small child wailing somewhere that he just wanted to go home.

"Oh my God," I said. "I can't believe this."

She smiled wearily at me and said, "You're not the only one in the world this has happened to, Wilhelmina. It's even happened to men, if you can imagine. It won't get past this hospital."

"Right. Name me one other person, Vi. This is so fucked."

My mother thought, then said, "Mary Tudor, Queen of England. She thought she was pregnant for a really long time. She wasn't, of course. Sterile."

I gaped at her. "You mean Bloody Mary?" I said. "You mean, the woman responsible for the deaths of thousands of her own subjects?"

"I didn't say," said my mother, biting back her grin, "this necessarily happened to sane people."

"You said I had a normal profile," I said.

"You do," said Vi. "To the best of our knowledge."

"I'm going to throw up," I said.

"At least we know it's not morning sickness," said Vi.

I watched as the silvery fillings in her teeth flashed in the fluorescents, her mouth opening wide as she smiled. I said, "I love you, Vi, but sometimes I think I hate you a little, too."

"Yes, yes," she said, standing and kissing my forehead. "I love you, too. I'm sorry about that. It was uncalled for. And I'm sorry for your loss, truly."

"I did," I said. "I did lose something. I feel as if I did lose something, Vi."

She pushed my hair off my cheeks and looked at me in a long and strange way. "I know you did, Willie," she said. "I really am sorry for you."

As Vi left to fill out the paperwork, I passed my hands over my navel again and again. Where I had once felt another heartbeat, I now felt nothing. Air and stomach, fluids and blood. Nary a little growing thing in me; nary even the weeniest little Lump in the world.

AND SO I waited in the hospital, under the wan humming lights, in the hushed din of so many bodies exhaling sickness and sadness into the cycled air. And when I realized my mother must have gone off to give me a moment, I picked up the envelope I'd brought with me, Clarissa's wild scrawl on the outside. I couldn't stand being alone, just then. As the night thickened in my high window, I tore the flap open and pulled out the photocopied pages and read it all once, then twice. Still, Vi didn't return. That night I read the pages over again and again, because reading made me forget about Vi and the Non-Lump and Clarissa, and the ill puce light around me entirely; it was a blessing, it was a reprieve.

Jacob Franklin Temple
  CIRCA 1822, *painted by Jarvis. Note both his smirk and the apparent nimbus around his head.*

27

Shadows and Fragments

THIS IS WHAT I saw when I opened the envelope:

1. *A note in Clarissa's loopy handwriting:*
   W—check this out—I found it in this sort of a miscel-
   lany of JFT's leftovers: *Shadows and Fragments: A Posthu-
   mous Collection of Jacob Franklin Temple's Words, arranged
   and edited by his Daughter, Charlotte Franklin Temple.*
   Printed in 1853; One of a series of a thousand by E.
   Phinney and Son Publishers, Templeton, New York. Also,
   get a load of Charlotte's note at the end. Maybe it's a
   clue? Love, C.

2. *An excerpt, page 334:*
   . . . how it holds great puzzles! For instance, only one year
   previous, a mightily strange story circled in the village, as
   follows. One day, three maidens venturing out into the
   greater forest on a strawberry-hunt wandered far from

their path, and soon discovered themselves lost. Upon erring aimlessly in the dark and frightening woods, the girls, in their distress, began to quarrel, and at last, one of their party ran away from her friends, piqued. Because night was falling, and there had been rumors of a great bear in the woods, the other two began to run until they found their path. On their way home, however, a scream arose from the woods that nearly curdled their blood, and they arrived at their houses scraped by thorns and barely speaking in the clutch of fear. When the third girl failed to arrive at her house by the next morning, the men of the town gathered and gravely went looking for her, but only found one tattered fragment of her hem. All assumed that she was lost.

That is not the depth of the mystery, however, for, by the next spring, the missing girl was discovered living in her house as if nothing had happened at all. Though her family's mouths were sealed tight against questions, soon a number of evidence rose up, some of it contradicting the rest: that there were three terrible cicatrices like claw-marks raked across the girl's visage; that a white shock had sprouted in her raven hair; that her mother, after only one month of confinement and her figure as thin as a rake, gave birth to a strapping, rather hairy baby boy; that during the time she'd been away the post-man had seen her in Oneonta, washing clothing, and certainly not pregnant in any way. Most puzzlingly, however, was the observation that whenever the girl saw one gentleman from the village, she would quake and run to hide; and what was strange about it was that this gentleman, though admittedly ursine, was of a great village family and was universally considered almost womanly in his gentleness, and would never have . . .

3. *Charlotte's note:*
This is an especially puzzling fragment, for I know not from what larger piece my father banished this story, or why he kept it amongst his most important papers. Yet it

is fascinating, for it was founded on a piece of actual gossip that I recall from when I was just a girl. In the true version, there were not three, but four young women between the ages of eighteen and twenty-two who went into the woods that day. Only two returned that night; one never did, and one returned as was related above. The girl who did not return was young Lucille Smalley. Poor Adah Phinney appeared as described above, and it was perhaps a mercy that she died of measles not long after her sudden reappearance, for the oft-repeated rumors that her brother was actually her son would have shamed her deeply (another untruth here is about the hairiness of Simon Phinney, who has had a bald pate since the age of fifteen). The other two girls, the ones who returned unharmed, developed into beacons of our town: Euphonia Falconer, née Shipman, became a devout member of the Methodist choir, and Bette Rhys, née Cox, married our beloved mayor and had a brood of ten children.

Chingachgook, or Sagamore, with dog
*The bronze statue called "Indian Hunter" in Lakefront Park.
Templetonians are frequently confused about who this statue represents—
Natty Bumppo, or his Native American companion—though Willie has
always believed it to be Chief Chingachgook.*

28

Sagamore (Chingachgook, Big Snake)

FIRST SENSED THE girl was a wild creature one night. Eight years, nine years old. Woke to hear her moving across the hut. Saw her lift the oilskin, lean out into the brighter night, the fistful of stars. Broke an icicle and put it in her mouth. I shut my eyes. She wanted to eat the world.

Seven years. Seven years we kept Noname in the hut. My granddaughter. Such terrible things done to her, the child, she lost her tongue at four, five years old. Nine years, she grew beautiful. Mushroom skin, no sunlight, tender as a mouse's belly. Cora's face, my son's face, Uncas's eyes, Cora's fine shape. A body that came early under the fawn-skin shift I made for her, soft on her body. Twelve, she was ready for a husband.

Hawkeye spent his time hunting, fevered with her nearby. No heart to give her to him yet. She was too young. Instead, we ate well, his bounty. She slept on furs.

In the night I sang to her the old songs. Taught her the crafts.

She made baskets with weave so small the ladies thought they were of thread. But she spent her days looking down at the world, Templeton, the granite-colored lake.

All day, I sold my baskets, saving for her when I was not here. A very old man, I felt my joints turning to stone. My bones ached. Wanted to drink the potion and leave this earth for better grounds. Instead, coin after coin leaping into my small pouch like fish up a stream. For Noname.

One day, I returned and her long hair was wet. She was panting. Her face looked bright as the sun. She had stolen out to the lake to swim. This was bad, bad. The men in Templeton rough settlers, a young Indian girl not human to them. Prey. But I had no heart to scold her. Should have stopped her. But I did not. Felt so old in the face of such joy.

All spring, she came back, wet-haired. One day, something happened. She was wilder than ever, shudders through her body in the bed, her teeth bared in a smile. Could feel it coming off of her, the joy. Asked and asked her what happened. She didn't sign to me. She turned her back and laughed her silent laugh, strangely so like Davey's.

And I watched her. Ten days passed before I saw it in her body. Twelve years old, unmarried, kept for seven years in a hut, and she was with child.

Who was it? Suspicion hatched in me. But I did not tell. She had to be married and I married her to Hawkeye. On their marriage night I spent the night on the cliff over Lake Otsego, thinking of my poor girl. Stared at the water until the old white monster came to the surface. Watched it turn its belly to the night sky, I saw it become a great moon on top of the lake, watched until it went down again.

The first time Noname came into town, a married girl, a woman with child, she struck everything still. So beautiful. More beautiful even than that Rosamond Phinney, with all her roses in her cheeks. The horses stopped walking, feet still in the air. The boys stopped playing ball. Widow Crogan stopped sweeping, and the dust swirled about her like a dustdevil. A sparrow, struck by my granddaughter's beauty, stopped moving its wings and dropped to the ground. Noname moved through the town, gentle and innocent. Everyone watched her, thinking of miracles.

Noname grew heavy, she grew fat. The summer deepened, became filled with gold. The fall came, and the gold weaned itself away. The cool set into the air. The snow fell. Noname's time had come. Hawkeye believed it was his, still. He awoke that day, singing.

But not I, I suspected. A horrible suspicion. As I sat outside the cabin, Midwife Bledsoe moving inside, whiskey-palsied, it was like a sickness, my suspicion. Davey pacing the lake path, scared of what he thought he's done. He was afraid he killed the girl with his seed. Drunk as a crow in the winter berries. A servant from the Manor came up and set everything neat and clean inside. Orders of the mistress, the girl said. Charity for the poor.

No screams arose from that poor, tongueless throat. My poor Noname, poor wild girl. And every time Midwife Bledsoe smoothed the hair from that little face, I felt for the tomahawk by my side. If the baby came and it was what I think it would be, I did not know if I could stop my hand from dashing its brains on the hearth. Or running down to Templeton on my old bones. Finding the terrible man who did this to her. Killing him with one sweet blow, which I should have done the first time he came to this lake. Should have done it the first time he stood over the lake alone that day on the cliffside. As he sunk to his knees and saw a vision. Before he claimed it all, all of it, too much of it, as his own.

Camp We-no-kow-to-hawk-naw

I HAD FALLEN asleep and my room was dark when I awoke again. Vi was sleeping in the chair next to me, her face planted on her chest. "Vi," I said, and like that, so smoothly, she slid out of sleep and stood and helped me dress again. She even acted as a lookout so I wouldn't have to see a soul on my way out of the hospital. I burned hot and cold again, so grateful it was late at night. As we slid through the dark town in the old car, I watched my mother's pale profile.

"I'm so tired of it, Vi," I said as we wended down Lake Street.

"Of what?" she said. "What are you tired of?"

"Humble pie. I've eaten enough of it for a lifetime, I think."

Vi turned off the car in the driveway, and stared straight at the garage. Averell Cottage's lights were bright before us, Reverend Milky's manatee silhouette outlined against a window in the mud-room. "Things happen for a reason, Willie," she said. "I think maybe you needed a little humility."

I did not have the strength to lash back. I just nodded, climbed out of the car, and went inside behind my mother. She embraced Reverend Milky, putting her head against his fleshy, warm chest. I heard him murmur into her hair, "Clarissa will be on the plane tomorrow afternoon," and heard her grunt back, tired. He gave me a smile filled with such a depth of pity that I dropped my head in confusion. And, when I stepped around them to climb the old stairs, saw how they were enlaced, two unlovely aging bodies, I felt, for a moment, the darkest envy I have ever felt in my life.

I awoke to a day gray-felted with raindrops, the smell of the August dirt softening into mud. Though I normally rose at dawn, I lay in bed long past eight, listening to the rain thump and trickle off the roof. If I kept my eyes closed, I knew, I would eventually go back to sleep. If I slept enough, I would forget all about the Faux Lump and how it infected my brain and my body; I'd forget about Primus Dwyer and that unsettling Ezekiel Felcher; I'd forget that Reverend Milky was always hanging about; I'd forget everything to do with my sperm-donor father and the many messy centuries of my messy, messy family.

I was about to say all this to the Lump, the way I'd grown accustomed to our private little asides, and then I remembered that there was no such thing as the Lump, and that there never had been.

And so I concentrated on putting myself into a five-day coma; long enough, I imagined, to take the edge off the sting from the hospital visit, long enough to let the first day of school arrive with me still on the wrong side of the country. But before I could achieve even a fragment of a coma, my mother knocked and came into my room. She stood over the bed, fiddling with the pearl buttons on the strange, flabby orange cardigan she was wearing.

At last I sighed and stopped pretending to sleep. "What are you wearing?" I said.

She looked down at herself, and flicked off a few pieces of lint. "This?" she said. "John made it for me for Christmas. It's very warm."

"He *knits*?" I said.

"Idle hands," she said, "are the devil's playthings. Speaking of which," and she shook my foot underneath my coverlet. "You devil. Up and at 'em. Four days left until you go back to Palo Alto. Only four days to finish your little quest."

"Nope. I can't go back to California," I said. "I just can't, Vi."

My mother sat on the bed, and it creaked and dipped under her weight. "Wilhelmina Sunshine Upton," she said. "You have to go back. Finish your dissertation, get the heck out of Dodge. I didn't send you to school for more than half my life to have you wimp out just before the end. No way."

"But, Vi," I said. "*Primus* is there."

"You're stronger than he is," she said. "And I frankly don't care. I can't believe I'm trying to convince you to *leave* Templeton after all this time that I was afraid you'd never come back, but you have to go back to Stanford, Willie. You're not a quitter. You'd be devastated if you let yourself quit. You'd never recover."

"But what about Clarissa?" I said. "Now that she's coming, she needs me here."

My mother made a flatulent noise with her lips. "Come on," she said. "She needs anything *but* you here. She needs quiet and calm and someone paying attention only to her. I can take care of her well enough. Trust me."

I thought about this for a moment, wondering at the wash of relief that came over me. I looked at Vi, but her face, somehow, seemed less tired than it was even a month ago, when I returned in all my shame to Templeton, as if my many troubles had rejuvenated her.

"You love a challenge," I said. "Don't you."

She gave me a wry little moue. "I am happiest when I'm fighting for something," she said. "And you get that from me."

"And you don't mind taking care of Clarissa?"

"I love Clarissa," she said.

"Ah. Now I see what this is," I said, sitting up at last. "Your favorite daughter's coming back, so you can get rid of the rogue one. I see how it goes. You're replacing me with a better candidate."

Vi snorted. "I didn't look at it like that until now," she said. "But now that you say it, I guess that's what I *am* doing. I can't wait. A kid who will give me all the respect I deserve. It's a dream come true." She pulled the comforter from the bed, and waited until I stood, grumbling, and pulled some sweatpants on.

My mother watched me, twisting the comforter in her hands, until I turned around and frowned at her. "What?" I said.

"Nothing," she said. "Just that I have to go to work soon, and I want to make sure you'll be okay."

"I'll be okay," I said.

"You sure?" she said. "Anything I can do to help?"

"No, Vi," I said. "It'll help me to get to work again. Take my mind off. Things."

"That was exactly what I was about to say," Vi said, turning to leave. "You're getting smarter in your old age. I made you cinnamon buns. They're still warm."

"And you're getting nicer in your old age," I called out, and listened to her footsteps on the squeaking stairs. I ran out to the top of the stairs when she reached the bottom and called down. "Vi?" I said. She looked up at me, her jowls disappearing as she craned upward.

"I'm sorry if I didn't say this before," I said. "I am very happy that you are happy. That you've finally let yourself be happy."

My mother bent her head, and I watched from above as her loafy braid moved up and seemed to clad her neck in armor. "Thank you," she said quietly. And when she looked up, she beamed at me such a sunny smile that I, too, felt my heart take wing, a little.

IT WAS A Saturday, still early when I called Hazel Pomeroy at her house. I imagined her shuffling to the telephone in her little cottage beside the lake, in a threadbare paisley wrapper, grumbling. She didn't answer the phone with any standard hello, but, rather, a honk of a "What?"

"Ms. Hazel Pomeroy," I said. "It's Willie Upton. Sorry to bother you, but I have something to read to you, if I can."

Hazel heaved a great sigh and said, "Let me fetch my tea." There was a clunk of the phone on the counter, and a very long expanse of time before Hazel came back.

"Had I known you had to boil the water, Hazel, I would have called back," I said when I heard her breath again in the receiver.

"Nah," she said. "I'm an old lady and forgot about you. Pure luck I came out when I did and saw the phone off the hook. Now, read to me. Go on."

I read her the story aloud, and at the end, she said, "*Shadows and Fragments*, huh. I know it well. Well, what do you want me to say about it?"

"Nothing. It's just. Well, you told me to read between the lines, and it seems there's a lot going on between these particular lines. Do you think maybe Richard's the ursine guy JFT's talking about?

Do you think it's possible?" My heart raced; I felt extraordinarily close to the end of the puzzle.

She sighed. "Oh, Willie," she said, "I could have told you all this long ago. I truly don't think anything like that happened. I think that story's all a fabrication, wish fulfillment, in a way. All his life, Jacob was very, very angry with his brother, you see. For being the firstborn, for being his father's favorite. And then, after Jacob spent the family fortune, Richard called Jacob home from Europe and treated him almost as if he were this naughty little boy, and Jacob just plumb resented it. I think he wrote that little vignette as if to imply his brother had done something bad, but Jacob could never really see it through to the end. Too ludicrous. That's why it ended up in *Shadows and Fragments*, and not some novel."

"Fine," I said. "But the story has to come from somewhere, right? Just because it isn't *literally* true doesn't mean that Richard didn't have some illegitimate offspring or anything. I mean, even if it didn't happen, something like this *could've* happened, right? Or he really did have an affair with Adah Phinney or something."

"Well," said Hazel, "if you know as much as I do about that family, I think it's pretty dang unlikely. Richard was, I think, almost a pure soul; Marmaduke always said that his eldest boy had the best heart of any man alive. From all accounts back then, he was chaste, to the point that he barely even talked to a woman who wasn't his mother, and he was so afraid of them, they say, that his wife, Anna, had to hound him for months before he ever looked her full in the face. Plus, Adah Phinney, it turns out, had an Oneonta marriage license from that autumn she ran away. I wondered about that, too, and dug it up a few decades back—appears she took off with a man named Gar Wilson. Some young rake, I suppose."

"But maybe some part of it is true. Maybe he was right and Richard just snapped, absconded with some girl," I persisted, though I felt all my careful theories beginning to crumble into dust. "That Lucille Smalley, the one who never came back."

"No," said Hazel. "Learn to listen better. It is impossible."

"But why?" I said.

"Because, Wilhelmina Upton, I also happen to know that by the time that episode happened in Templeton, the strawberry-picking party, Richard was already dead. So there," said Hazel. There was a very long silence, then, and I could hear Hazel's quick breath in the receiver. "Oh, crap," I said, sadly. "Back to square one."

"Well, Willie," said Hazel. "That's life. Now, it *is* odd that you call me up with this story because I've been thinking, and though your idea about Richard is obviously wrong, I have my hunches that you're in the right area."

"Right area for what?" I said, suspicious.

"The Temple link to whoever your father is, of course," she snapped.

I blinked at my window, brazen with light, until I heard Hazel realize what she'd just given away. She clucked to herself, "Drats, Hazel Pomeroy," she scolded herself. "Loose lips, sinking ships, as usual."

"Who told you I was looking for my father?"

"Your pal Peter Lieder," she said. "He knows about my research into your family. It slipped out one day."

"Damn him," I said.

"Listen, honey," she said. "I've always had my suspicions that your mother was hiding something. I just never knew the extent of it. Now, do you or do you not want to hear about who I think is your 'randy' ancestor, as you put it?"

I groaned. "Of course I do," I said. "Who is it? Guvnor Averell?"

"Maybe," she said. "Who knows how much you'd be able to dig up on him, though. He wasn't literate, I suspect. I was thinking more along the lines of Marmaduke."

I actually lost my breath for a moment. "You're kidding," I said. "Really? Marmaduke?" I thought of Hetty, and how Guvnor had red hair and freckles and Marmaduke's fierce glare; if it had happened once, it could possibly have happened again. I couldn't believe I didn't think of this sooner. But then, upon reflection, I wasn't completely sold. Hetty could have been his one mistake in his whole life, the warm bed in a cold winter after Elizabeth had refused Templeton for the *n*th year in a row. I said, "But wasn't he a Quaker?"

"Yes, but"—Hazel's voice fell into a whisper, as if there were eavesdroppers on the line—"but here's something nobody knows, kid. Here's something that you won't hear from anyone but me. This is a doozie. Marmaduke didn't die of pneumonia, as all the books have it. Marmaduke was murdered, Willie."

My breath caught in the back of my throat, and I couldn't say anything at all. At last, I found my voice and said, "Murdered?"

"Wilhelmina," said Hazel. "Come to my house whenever you can. I have something to show you."

OUTSIDE, TEMPLETON WAS still a pigeon gray, but over the far hills a sunburst split the seams of the clouds and blazed one stamp of trees a strange green-gold. I had dressed in a short yellow sundress from high school because I felt so sad and only that dress seemed to hold an element of light in it. As I walked in the damp mist, I thought of Marmaduke Temple. I knew no more than when I started but couldn't stop now, with all my many ancestors mounted in the hall of infamy in Averell Cottage, waiting with their silverfish eyes for me to discover the deepest family secret of them all.

Hazel's cottage was a tiny green-black hut on the east side of the lake near Pomeroy Hall, a former summer camp with a sign made of nailed sticks above the door that proclaimed it Camp We-no-kow-to-hawk-naw.

I knocked on the door, and inside could hear Hazel cuss under her breath and shuffle endlessly toward the door. At last, she fumbled with three distinctly different locks, and when she thrust open the door, she was wearing a wispy white nightgown buttoned to her chin and slippers in the shape of frogs. She squinted at me. "You all right?" she said. "You look pale."

"I'm fine," I said. "Camp We-no-kow-to-hawk-naw?"

"Gibberish," she said, letting me in. Her place smelled surprisingly lovely, like apples and rich dark soil, with only a small note of old lady mixed in. "Family that built this place in 1880 got the money for it by selling off a prize heifer. We no cow to hock now. Silly. Sit, sit. I made some brownies," she said, and as I sat on one of her uncomfortable leather and carved-walnut chairs, she put before me a plate full of suspiciously perfect confections. They smelled like chemicals.

"No thanks," I said. "Nice of you, though. Now, what's this about Marmaduke being murdered? And how does nobody know of it but you? A murder's a huge thing to hush up, Hazel."

Hazel shuffled to the hard leather seat opposite mine. When she sat, the googly eyes in the frog slippers rolled and rolled. "Think,

Wilhelmina," she said with a snort of impatience. "Nobody wit-
nessed the murder. They say it was nighttime and it snowed the
night he was killed, covered the bloodstains. People back then were
loyal to the seigneur of the town, and Marmaduke sure was that.
The juiciest stuff is passed along by word of mouth. But still," she
said, pulling with a flourish a manila portfolio out from under some
papers on her table, "some things slipped out into print. Take a
gander at this."

Hazel spread open the portfolio. Inside there was a yellowed,
brittle piece of paper with the *Freeman's Journal* spelled out across
the top in the same old-time font. But this really was an antique
Freeman's Journal, and I looked up at Hazel, surprised. "You stole
this from the library?" I said.

"Big deal," she said, her mouth full of brownie. "They have mi-
crofiche now. Go ahead and read it," and I did, as much to escape
the roil of dark wet matter in her mouth as from curiosity.

᪥ EDITORIAL FROM THE *FREEMAN'S JOURNAL*, ᪥
DECEMBER 6, 1799

*Attention, Templetonians! Look about you with consterna-
tion; guard carefully your vote; keep your wives and children
from hearing facile rhetoric, for among us there is an impostor. A
man who seeks to betray the class he was born into, who seeks to
destroy the underpinnings of this grand new democracy of ours.
A man who came from nothing, who married his first money,
who shrewdly built his land and his fortune until he was one of
the richest men in this new country. For he, of all people, is cam-
paigning for the party that wants an American aristocracy, that
wants to keep the common men under their heels. He, who
should be grateful to the good yeomen of the county for the
wealth they had brought him, is a rank Federalist.*

*"Of whom do you speak, Phinney?" the good reader of this
journal now perhaps asks, rattling the paper in vexation. I
needn't have to pronounce it, but in the small chance one does
not recognize the man in the portrait above, this villain, this
Benedict Arnold, is none other than the landlord Marmaduke
Temple.*

I say his name now with sorrow; Temple was once like a brother to me. For, when I arrived in Templeton in late 1786, I was young and adventurous, ripe for a revolution in my life. I had been for five years a newspaperman and desired greatly to become a man of the land. I had been enflamed by the writings of the Philosophers, and believed the only authentic life was the life of the good farmer with dirt under his fingernails. Odd as it seems to me now, in my late mid-age, the owner of the largest printing company in New York State and this newspaper, in those days I was eager to dig into the loam and extract my living with sweat and blood. Young men are often foolhardy. When I went into the ramshackle office that he used during those hard first years, Temple gave one look at me and raised his great guf-faw. I am, admittedly, very small, and one can see most bones in my body even through my clothes.

"Thou?" he said. "Thou thinkest thou art farming stock? With thy white hands and university pronouncements?" This only enflamed me, this man of my age scorning my abilities. I drew myself up as straight as I could and gave a fiery yes.

To his credit, the landlord liked my spirit and sold me a patch beside the river, which one settler had already cleared for potash and returned to Temple at a higher price. "If thou findest thyself wanting a different profession, Phinney, I should be glad to help thee with its establishment. We need educated men in the village proper," said he, not unkindly.

I wish I could say I lasted a year or even six months on my lot. It took me two months to drag myself back to his office, filthy and ill with a catarrh caught from the leak in my ill-fitting roof. Temple took me to the pub and bought me a few mugs of flip. Over the night, I let it emerge that I had been a newspaperman in Philadelphia, and the next day, as I nursed my illness in the comfort of a rented room, Duke burst in, blazing with excitement, and announced that he had ordered me a printing-press, and had exchanged my lot of land for a storefront beside the General Store. I would produce a newspaper, he said. He wanted it called the Templeton Times. *I named it the* Freeman's Journal.

In those years I did admire the landlord. He did a great deal for the common man, though now it is apparent it was only for his own profit. Where so many other men who tried to conquer and settle the wilderness had failed, he succeeded because he, too, had come from nothing, and he knew what would draw men to stay. Slowly, however, Temple grew ill with the brain fever that arises from contact with money, and began believing himself to be the natural nobility of our land. He built Temple Manor, an enormous, stone monstrosity with its sunbright yellow roof. "No man needs such space," I argued. "Spend your money on improving the town." He simply winked at me. Over time, I began hearing rumors of other, darker deeds. Soon, Marmaduke Temple was courting rich men to do other business deals with him, and as he was moving in the circles of the richest men in our new country, he took on their politics. It was a horrid day when I learned he'd been out all afternoon canvassing for the Federalist candidate for governor. That day I knew that Temple's pretensions had overwhelmed his sense and I could no longer support him.

Templetonians, Marmaduke Temple and I haven't spoken in a year, and in that year I have become certain of one thing. And it is this: that I believe that Temple has so changed from the kind, sensible man he once was that he would cheat and lie to secure his candidates their positions. For he is the judge of this county, the man with the power to take the locked boxes to Albany. Though it pains me to suggest it against an elected official, I do believe Marmaduke Temple would cheat the people, for I have heard, more insidiously, of his bad ways, his shady dealings that are not befitting of a moral man, a man of faith. And in these political times, he should take careful note: so many men hate Marmaduke Temple that there have been brawls in the street, even cane fights among mild-mannered attorneys, and I have heard such oaths against the landlord that his ears should be ringing. If he would listen, I would say for the sake of old friendship that Marmaduke Temple should take great precautions against sudden, unbidden violence.

My friends, one last word: I will be scrutinizing the election like a hawk. If I weren't, if the newspapers weren't being vigilant against the corrupt men of the world, we would be lost. Ours wouldn't be a democracy. And let us only hope for the peace of our beloved village that propriety in this election, and all future elections, will be observed.

Templetonians, be secure in one thing: the Freeman's Journal *shall be watching.*
 —*Elihu Phinney, Editor and Publisher*

I looked at Hazel, whose eyes were bright and whose dentures were truffled with nuts. "Holy crap," I said. "Did Phinney kill Marmaduke, do you think?"

"Maybe," she said. "Either that or this election business served as a foil for, maybe, a more personal sin. Look, he says, '*I have heard, more insidiously, of his bad ways, his shady dealings that are not befitting of a moral man, a man of faith.*' See? There's something bad there, personal venom. Maybe even why the murder—and it *was* a murder, I'm sure of that—was hushed up."

"So you're saying," I said slowly, "maybe old Marmaduke got sneaky with Phinney's wife?"

"Or daughter," said Hazel. "Rosamond Phinney was a great beauty, you know, a great flirt. There was a bit of a scandal about her flirtations, a quick marriage to some distant cousin," and Hazel looked at me now, her eyes dancing. "Remember when I said you were in the right ballpark? Well, Rosamond was the mother of Adah Phinney, the poor girl who had been lost in the woods, you know," she said.

"And Adah was—we think—the mother of Simon Phinney," I said. "Huh. Phinney," I repeated.

I blinked, now thinking of the only Phinney I knew who could possibly have been my father: the great-great-great-great-great-grandson of Elihu, short, bald, and acerbic Frank Phinney, who owned the struggling little *Freeman's Journal*. Frank Phinney! *Oh, hell,* I thought, and with the next heartbeat I smiled a little. I had fetched Frank coffee from Stagecoach Coffee when I interned at the paper in college, and I'd once fallen out of a chair, laughing until I wept at a stupid joke he'd told: *What goes clip-clop-clip-clop BANG! clip-clop-clip-clop?* he'd said, and before I could say *What?,* he'd said, his pink face flushed with glee, *An Amish drive-by shooting.* Frank wasn't so bad—at least he had a sense of humor, and he liked me because I was one of the only people who laughed at every one of his jokes, good or bad. And then, I thought: *Siblings!* with a thrill: I'd babysat his two little hellions, Joshua and Tilly, on family trips to

Hilton Head and Scotland, and I'd always known there was a reason
why I hadn't murdered them then.

"My God," I said, standing. "I think I have to go talk to Vi,"
and without thinking, I swooped down to kiss Hazel's prickly little
cheek. She blushed violently and started, and only from my bent
position did I see poking up from the garbage the ninety-nine-cent
box of grocery store brownies from which the old dear had taken
her treats.

OUTSIDE, EXUBERANT, I steamed up River Street. The Susquehanna
rippled on my right, and Kingfisher Tower was outlined in the mist
on the lake like some elfin castle that flickered to nothing when
you fixed your eyes on it. My head was light, and great bolts of
adrenaline made my limbs sing: I imagined throwing my arms
around Frank Phinney, saying *Dad!,* even picturing a sweet little
picnic on the manicured Opera grounds, with Vi and Frank and
champagne and black-bottom cupcakes and all of us laughing together as the late-afternoon light grew gold and stretched long
around us. Great rolls of relief swept over me: I was done, at last,
with my endless quest; I already loved Frank Phinney, he was a Bud,
and I knew he would make a fun father; I could go back to Clarissa,
pick up my life again in San Francisco, begin afresh.

Soon, though, with every step I took, a flower of doubt bloomed
within me, and by the time I reached the top of the stairs leading
down to Council Rock, I stopped walking completely. I was able to
make my way to the bottom of the steps, to sit, before the joy
seeped entirely from my joints. Before me, the lake in its mist
lapped gently at the bank. I hung my head over my knees, watching
the ripples. It was wrong, all of it.

Wrong: squat Frank Phinney, with his fat thumbs and teacup
ears, in whose reflection I could see none of myself, save a slight resemblance around the chin. And even if he were my father, it was
equally wrong to throw this stick of dynamite—me—into his life.
His wife, Linda, already sharp-tongued, would whet it against him
more, I would confuse his young children, I would make this poor
man, his daily existence already eaten by guilt, feel endlessly guiltier.
I'd add more complication to his life. It would make our friendship
strained, ruin something that was so simple and sweet.

Where I had been elated just minutes before, now I only felt empty, a brown paper bag kicked around by the wind. I tossed a stick into the lake, and it only bobbed once before sinking. I was sick. I couldn't go home.

I had been there for maybe five minutes, stewing, when I caught sight of a pair of big brown boots sidling closer to me on my left-hand side. It wasn't until they were six inches away that I recognized them and, startled, looked up the dark jeans, the leather belt cinched to its last hole, the blue-jay blue shirt. My eyes rested for a moment on the book in the large, worn hand, a glossy paperback of *The Complete Spinoza*. For a long moment I watched the book until I forced myself to look up past the top button, up that throbbing neck, to that jaw, that face.

"Zeke," I said, a slow warmth spreading through me, banishing, for a moment, the new sadness. "Nice to see you."

"I," he said. "Um," and he seemed, for the moment, unable to go on. At last, he flushed, pushed the book into his back pocket, and said, sitting beside me, "I really, really like that dress, Willie. Yellow. Nice. It's my day off. I saw you leave your house an hour ago, and was waiting for you to come back."

"Really," I said, trying to smile, my teeth feeling too-electric in the air. "For what?"

"Lunch?" he said, and his flush deepened. He looked away.

"Hm," I said, and let the seconds collect and puddle between us. The world trickled in: the gulls circling a buoy, traffic behind us on Main Street, the Susquehanna brushing its mossy boulders. And suddenly the day that had become so glum had turned, by means of a luminous yellow dress and Zeke before me, into something lighter, hungrier. A car horn honked; I startled, and flushed hot, and Zeke smiled, his dimple emerging. Watching it, I found myself saying, "Follow me."

In retrospect, I knew what I was doing. At the time, I only watched myself doing it. I took Zeke's hand, and holding it made me send everything else back into the shadows, made me forget everything but his skin's hard calluses, its warmth.

Like this, Ezekiel and I crossed back over Main Street, over the river, went around the gate by the wild riverbank between town and the hospital. There were some late flowers, white and yellow stalks on the bushes, that had a musky scent, and I felt each hair of my skin against my clothes as I walked, I felt each crack in the mud beneath the pads of my feet. We rounded a corner to see the antique stone bridge over the Susquehanna, the Victorian footpath, with its crenellations, blocked off by an iron chain stretched across its mouth.

I stepped over the chain. Zeke followed. I could hear his breath soft in his mouth behind me. We went over the mossy bridge and into the woods on the far side. From one drunken night in high school, I had remembered, vividly, a small cup in the trees, filled with ferns, visible to anyone walking on the path we'd just left and who knew where to look. When we found it, the ferns bobbed and dipped in a small wind. I turned to Zeke, who had closed the gap between us as I watched the ferns, and whose hands were now on my waist, shaking a little.

"Wait," I said. "Are you perhaps the most inappropriate person to do this with at this moment? Is this probably the dumbest idea I've had yet?"

He winced and took his hands away. "Probably," he said and kicked the ground with his big brown boot.

"Great," I said, and reached up. His lips were warm and minty.

AFTERWARD, ZEKE'S BACK cooling beneath my palms, his breath softening into sleep, I watched a blackbird wheel in the sky and felt darkness settle over me again. My imagination over the past month had made this moment with Zeke into something smooth and silky. But it had been all misplaced lips and pine sap, Zeke whispering worriedly in one ear, a fly wailing in the other until I smacked it in midthroe. A pinecone now pushed awkwardly between my shoulder blades. And yet, deeper, beneath my back, I also felt a hundred small shiftings of the plants, the worms, I felt the ground exert its hungry pull on my bones. Inch by inch I slid out from under Zeke's good weight, and dressed. He slept, openmouthed like a boy, blissfully naked, his smooth rear exposed trustfully to the sky. As I crept back across the bridge, I imagined him awakening in an hour to the rustling bowing of the ferns, looking up, a frond pressed to his cheek, seeing himself alone, wondering if he'd dreamed the whole thing. He'd dress and stand, sorrowfully. And then he'd reach into his back pocket to find my hostage, old Spinoza, gone, and, I hoped, understand its absence.

BACK AT AVERELL Cottage, I went back into the entrance hall and shook my head mournfully at great, fleshy Marmaduke in the copy of his portrait.

"You rapscallion," I said. "I think we know your little secret, my old friend." Perhaps I saw the corner of his mouth twitch a little at me; perhaps not. But I was suddenly tired again, my mother's cinnamon bun still unrestful in my belly, and thought of the great white welcome of my bed. I climbed the stairs to my room.

I never did get to take a nap that day.

I was halfway up the stairwell when my heart did a tremendous jig in my chest, and my skin felt swept with a terrible chill. The stairwell seemed to expand, to stretch until it was distorted and immense, the vastness of the lake outside, and then the room snapped back into place and quivered like gelatin around me, until it shook me down so I was sitting on the tread, clutching my temples. There was a great darkness, then, a sucking sound. When I opened my eyes, everything was blurred together, as if my sight had been smeared with grease.

It was only when I stood, wobbly and sick, that I felt it around me. A mass, a heaviness, some alien thing large and terrible; it was only then that I felt the pulse. But the throbbing wasn't in my own heart, and it wasn't in my gut, where I'd so recently believed I held the Lump, either. It was higher, in the muscle between my shoulder and throat, as if it were a second heart, one belonging to a taller person. I wanted to move my hands up to touch it, but I couldn't. My feet would no longer move; my head would no longer move. I had to strain my eyes to peer downward, and I saw how, above my dress, there seemed to be an ethereal fabric moving in an imperceptible wind like cobwebs. On my arms, another dark fabric was shimmying.

My legs moved without me, and I watched them climb the stairs in horror. Foot above foot, so clumsy, as if whatever was in me had forgotten what it was to walk. I felt the eyes of my ancestors, all those pictures, fall on me. As I moved past the guest bathroom I managed a glimpse of myself, and saw my features were dark and veiled. I knew then it was my good ghost, the indirect watcher over my life, that had for now slipped around me. I'd become the yolk in an egg; I'd become one human bone, my body at the marrow and the ghost surrounding it, tense as flesh.

Like this we came into my bedroom, and like this, we picked a random little book off the bed. My alien hands flipped with a hummingbird flutter through the pages until, at last, they stopped. A finger slid down the page until it reached one word. And then my ghosted fingertip scraped at the word until I said it aloud.

Horse, into the wet morning, muffled as if I'd pressed cotton in my ears.

Horse, the ghost tapped again.

Horse, the finger stopped tapping.

I don't understand, I said.

Then the other exhaled a ghostly breath of frustration, though already I had begun to feel suffocated. The book dropped on the bed. Out the door again, down the stairs. Into the entrance hall, into the formal living room, into the dining room with its vast bay windows framing the lake like a gloomy Hudson River portrait, rich with Romantic bluster and poetry in the wet gray wind.

Toward the dining room table I went despite myself, and I took up with two clumsy hands the little horsehair horse on his four ancient wheels. I took it to the glossy dining table and put it down. Stood akimbo looking at it for a while, until I said, smothered, *Yes. A horse.*

That's when the ghost around me stepped forward and began disassembling it.

Stop! I said when it began unbuckling the little tin buckle on the saddle and slid it off. It didn't stop. My own clumsy foreign fingers dug in the leather under the saddlehorn and prised it apart. And there, in the gaping old wound in the saddle, there was a tiny scrap of yellowed parchment, crispy. When I picked it up, the ghost slid suddenly away with a tremendous popping sound and I gasped and heaved until I felt the air burning the bottoms of my lungs. The paper was so fragile that I held it as gently as a petal I didn't want to crush. The ghost moved outward into the room again. I closed my eyes until my lashes made it even smaller, but this tactic didn't work: the ghost still purpled its way in.

At last I was breathing normally, sitting down, still staring at the paper that flapped and flapped in some small wind on my palm. It was brittle, liable to fall apart into my hand when I did touch it. And though it was only a small scrap, it had the heft of lead.

Before I opened the letter, I looked up so quickly that I caught the very thin edge of the ghost and at last fixed on it. It squirmed and throbbed in oil-coated waves, as if trying to wrench itself away. "Who are you?" I said, but the ghost didn't answer and instead slowly turned dark with impatience, then a horrid eggplant blue. I considered the ghost, its goodness, its obsession with cleanliness, and didn't say what I thought, which was *Hetty?* I turned back to the paper and opened it. I saw, in child's script, the words *Guvnor Averell*. And then I read.

Elizabeth Franklin Temple
*Elizabeth Franklin Temple, when young. This
was a miniature portrait on ivory that Marmaduke Temple carried around with him on
his many travels.*

Elizabeth Franklin Temple
*Elizabeth Franklin Temple, at an advanced
age. This is a not-very-flattering watercolor
and pencil sketch, probably done by one of
Jacob Franklin Temple's brood of girls. By
that time, Elizabeth had become a shut-in
at Temple Manor, legendary for saying her
mind at all times.*

Elizabeth Franklin Temple

I HAD HAD a dream of it long before it happened. I was not one for false portents. I am far too Quaker for that.

Every night in my hard bed was this: first the squeak of boots, the hickory-smoke freshness of winter air. Night. Snow sifting down. And somewhere behind, the sound of carousing men, somewhere on Second Street, the crossroad between the Eagle Hotel— the Federalists' bar—and the Bold Dragoon—the Anti-Federalists' Bar. A crowing of victory on one side, and on the other, a fiddle in a reel of defeat. It is only with the swim in my head, the flip souring in my mouth, that I know that I am Marmaduke within the dream, that the vast body at my command is my husband's.

For a moment, there is the maiden three-quarters moon, nailed above the icy lake and powdered hills. And there is the long stretch of the town before me, down the hill to the lake; and behind me, past the boys' academy and the churches into the heifer-rich farms; and to the right, past the Manor and up Mount Vision, where

Davey Shipman's cabin sits; and to the left, beyond the bakery and past the new courthouse and jail. A violent uprising of pride rises in my body, the likes of which I—as a waked Elizabeth—have never before felt.

Then there is a strange sound that I cannot identify, and, sudden, a darker sound within my very head, a hollow thump, like a muskmelon dropping to the ground. The slow tilting of the world as my big body goes loose and falls. The face to the cold, hard mud, a horse-smell. And from there, the trees loom dark over the huddled roofs of Second Street, as if they were menacing the town, and my cheek goes numb against the road. My darkening eyes see a stump in the dirt of the road, a vast old stump from some ancient tree, for-gotten, cut to nothing in the road, and in the very central crack of this stump, the tiniest of saplings has taken advantage of some small warmth from dropped manure, and is springing up its tender sprig. Then something hot pools inside my ear, the sound of the carous-ing behind me fades and is replaced by a series of pulses, beats of a vast and terrible heart, and then there is darkness, and then there is a good release.

I dreamed of my husband's death many times, vividly. The mys-tery has always been who had killed him. He had many enemies, especially with the questionable election that had happened a few days earlier. The recount of the votes was to end that day. He was an intemperate man, my Marmaduke, wrestled too commonly with the pioneers in town, made enemies with his wealth and strength.

But on the night of his murder, I knew who killed him. Even before he died, I knew why.

THE NIGHT BEFORE my husband's death, I had been watching Davey Shipman's cabin, how all through the night the windows gleamed red. Noname was still in labor by morning, for they would have extinguished the light to give her some sleep had she already delivered the child. I, a mother of seven, though only two survived, I knew what the poor child was going through. When the dawn was about to come, I had been fighting against it for hours. I knew even then that the coming evening was the night I dreamt of, the moon, the blow, my Marmaduke's death. Every time I shifted asleep, the dream came, and I awakened, all my hair bristling with fear. Like an animal. At last, I washed myself in my French violet soap, dressed in my lightest gray frock, pinched roses into my cheeks.

And I stole in my softest shoes to Marmaduke's chamber in the west end of the house. In the keen silence, I could hear the dozens of sleeping aspirations that seemed to make the house itself breathe.

I opened Marmaduke's door and entered. It took me a moment to see that he was not sleeping. He was sitting behind his curtains, watching me through the opening. I came to him. He opened his arms, opened the covers for me. Full-clothed, I slipped inside his warmth; I was so small beside him; I had always marveled at this, my size, his, how I was like a child beside him. We didn't move. We didn't speak. I smelled his good smell, his sleep-smell and he kissed me on my temple. How he let off heat like a veritable furnace, and I, who was never warm enough, was now warm to the core.

I thought, I must tell him. It is my duty, so that he will stay home tonight, for the next few nights, allow the danger to pass. I was stalled by something, though, by large fears. Marmaduke did not always do what one thought he would, and I was afraid he would think himself bigger than any risk that could be in the world. Might even go out simply as an act of defiance. I gave myself until I heard Remarkable talking to herself in the kitchen, as she always did in the morning making breakfast. Then I had to tell.

Duke, I said at last, but he kissed me so that I could not say more. No, he said. Can't we just be silent?

Marmaduke, I said, but he sighed, rolled away. His huge hand held my hand for a moment, swallowing it up. We both stared at the canopy above, the dip in the fabric, the thin, strong posts. I was ready to try again, but then there was the tread of Mingo on the stairwell, bringing up Marmaduke's breakfast, and I had to hurry up and out of the bed, hide behind the door as Mingo came in, then slide out as he kneeled over the fire. I took a long look in the doorway as my husband climbed out of the bed. Even in his undress, he seemed invulnerable, and for a moment, seeing his broad feet planting themselves like stumps on the ground, I doubted my dream.

• • •

IT WAS NOT an easy day. I could barely breathe with the strain.

LATER, AFTER DINNER. In the parlor, my little son Jacob was playing checkers with his brother, Richard. I with my book, Marmaduke warming his boots by the fire. Every hour, one of the servants went up to the Shipman cabin to check on Noname and bring Midwife Bledsoe another glass of whiskey. For purposes of cleanliness, the midwife claimed. Though, as Remarkable said, Goodwife Bledsoe must be scrubbed as pink as a baby inside. Every hour, Noname grew weaker. Remarkable came in, licking her lips to smile at Marmaduke, reporting every hour or so on the election recount in the offices of the *Freeman's Journal*. Still counting, Master Duke, she said, shaking her head but not without a gleam of triumph. In the triumph, I feared for my husband.

BY EVENING, NONAME had been in labor for forty hours, and could not be awoken by the midwife. Dr. French went up. By evening, the throng surrounding the *Freeman's Journal* offices had thinned, and only the trails of chimney smoke made the town seem alive. I saw from my window Elihu Phinney as he sat there, counting, recounting, recounting, checking a list. I watched him. He sat there until dusk.

A DARK DAY already, it was tarblack outside by the time Kent Peck knocked on the door. They said he was a handsome man, but to me he was as attractive as a block of wood. He brought with him his manure smell, the scent of new snow. I shrunk a little into my wraps. The man squeezed his felt hat so that the three corners became six before he surrendered it to Mingo.

Phinney has published the results, Duke, he said. Ran a special print. Found forty-three ballots missing from Otsego alone. Even tallied up likely Federalists and likely Anti-Federalists, and found a gap of near eighty. Claiming it's because we pressed ballots into some folks' hands.

We *did* press ballots into some folks' hands. Is that wrong? said Richard, growing furious, purple, tightening his fists into dangerous mallets. My poor Richard, so earnest and good. Something had shifted in him over the past few months, I saw. He was not as innocent as he had once been. Phinney pressed ballots himself, Richard

continued. I saw him. And I rode with the boxes, and I can attest
that there was no wrongdoing on the journey to Albany. That terrible Phinney, that terrible, spiteful man.

A very weighty silence.

The question, said Duke, standing at the mantel underneath the
handsome portrait of himself. The question is not what, if anything, happened. The question is what one does now. There are still
rough men in these parts. If the rumor goes into the streets of this
county, anything could happen to us.

And I in my corner, I who knew Marmaduke so well, knew
from this that he had been guilty of some terrible wrongdoing. I
knew then that he had dabbled in the election, and it would all turn
out horribly wrong.

HOURS, IT SEEMED, they debated what to do.

Peck was for hiding out, calling in the courts of the state to settle it, keeping quiet until the people forgot.

Jacob was for giving that little Scot weasel Phinney a good
thrashing, but he was reprimanded by his tutor that children must
be seen, not heard, and Marmaduke grinned at his ten-year-old son,
who shook his fist at the town through the window.

Richard was for calling a public hearing on the matter, immediately, presenting the case to the people, publishing an accounting of
the Federalist side, insisting on innocence.

Marmaduke was quiet for a very long time, but as the tall clock
in the hall rang, he spoke. I believe, he said in his deepest, loudest
voice, that we must pretend we are not bothered by this. That
Phinney is concocting this out of spite and bad form. We should
celebrate and pretend we are not bothered. Do what we would
normally do after winning an election of this magnitude.

And after he spoke, there was a great silence.

Drink, said Kent Peck, nodding his granite head with gravity and
tapping his pipe three times on his knee, for emphasis. Go to the
Eagle.

Hire fiddlers, suggested Richard. But, Father, is this appropriate?

Wrestle, said Marmaduke, and laughed. I should like to wrestle
that "little Scot weasel Phinney" a good one, and he raised his eyebrow at Jacob, who nodded with vigor.

They stood, Mingo went from the room to fetch the canes and hats and greatcoats, there was a great bustle. No, I thought, this cannot happen, Marmaduke cannot go out. I was about to stand, to tell my husband I must see him, right now, it is an urgent matter, when Remarkable came in, curtseying with haste.

Oh, Mistress Temple, she cried, her eyes darting with great interest at Marmaduke, leaning massive on the mantel. Marmaduke in paint smirked above her head; Marmaduke in flesh frowned at her.

Such news, you never would believe, Remarkable said. That poor, dear Noname, bless her innocent soul, has died in childbirth.

And Remarkable crossed herself, which I do not like to see in my house, a papist thing. But my sympathies were quickened, and even Marmaduke seemed to listen to this news with interest.

Mingo entered. Richard and Kent Peck went to him, pulled their greatcoats from his arms.

And the child? I said. Remarkable seemed to expand, to tremble in her eagerness. She leaned forward to say in an overloud whisper, It is a girl. And perfect. But, Mistress Temple, she is a terribly huge baby. And then, looking at Marmaduke, who had gone still and white, Remarkable spilled in her lilt and brogue, She is covered in red hair. Red. And has blue eyes, unlike any red Indian the world has yet seen.

Satisfied, she leaned back, and the shadow of her nose on her smile was great and made the old woman look horrid, like a witch.

I thought in a moment of the big red-furred baby, and then of my russet Richard, laughing gently with Kent Peck by the door, helping him on with his jacket. But there was no man alive more virginal than he. A mother would know. He had never kissed any other woman than me. His loves were chaste and good; he would marry a simple girl, and be too shy to touch her for the first month of their marriage. I knew all this.

And it was then that I looked at Marmaduke, who had a pallor on his face like wax. He saw me looking, and cracked a small smile.

How wonderful, he muttered, avoiding my gaze. We shall send old Davey Shipman a cask of wine, he said. Then he bowed to us and stepped across the floor to Mingo and the waiting men, ruffling Jacob's hair as he passed him. My small boy's face was pale and stricken: he must have heard, the tutor was bending over him, whispering softly, taking him from the room by the far door. I was standing with Remarkable by the fire, my skirts nearly in the fire, I was watching my husband put on his greatcoat, and it seemed to me that he did it slowly, excruciatingly slowly. A year seemed to pass when one arm went into the coat, and another year passed before the next.

I HAD BEEN blind. I had believed that when I got rid of that Hetty, when I came to Templeton myself, that Marmaduke would be faithful, would adhere to the vows he had taken before God on the day we eloped in Burlington. And to hear that Noname, the innocent little Indian child, had produced a red-haired baby. In that one night, I aged a decade.

BEFORE THEY LEFT, there was nothing in the room save Marmaduke and me. And, between us, the dream hung darkly. The three-quarters moon. The rustle and the muffled thump in the head. The collapse, the sapling, the darkness.

I could have saved him. I could have prevented him from going out. I did not.

MY MARMADUKE, FATHER of this town, important man, husband, visionary, fool. I let him put on his coat. I let him take his stick and his hat. And when he turned to say good-bye to me, his eyes skittered past, beyond my slight form, beyond Remarkable, around the room. I did not find my voice to call him back, to warn him about the crossroads.

True, I did not look for it, either.

HIS BOOTS CLATTERED over the boards of this house he built from nothing, and he was out the door. I watched their small forms struggle down the snowy path, and out the gate to Second Street. From my window, they were indistinguishable from one another, all bending against the wind, the snow. My son could have been my husband, his father the son. They went around the fence, they were gone.

Remarkable turned to me, urgency making her face twitch, rabbity.

Davey Shipman went wild when he discovered the red hair, the
blue eyes, they say, she said. Destroyed the cabin, turned furious,
told Midwife Bledsoe that he was to kill Judge Temple. Went out
with his gun. Chingachgook, too, that old Indian, stared at little
Noname's body until at last he stood, took out his tomahawk, and
when Midwife Bledsoe screamed, only nodded, and went down the
road to the town. The midwife was shaking, half out of her mind
with drink and fear. And with Elihu Phinney, drunk and dangerous
tonight after the election tally . . . she trailed off, gesturing out toward the road.

She left it open for me to send someone to bring him back. To
warn him of his enemies. And, for a second time, I resisted. I only
stared into the black night, the gray snow.

REMARKABLE AND I, alone, in the parlor. At last, I turned to my foe,
my friend.

Something inside me was cracking with a terrible noise, but Remarkable could not hear it, she made no horrified step away from me.

Sit beside me and ring for tea, I said, my voice much steadier
than I could have imagined it. I have never told thee of how I first
truly saw my husband. The story of how we eloped, I said.

There was something in this that Remarkable never expected:
she blinked, and though I could see her desire to crow in the kitchen
about Noname's redhaired baby, this was even more compelling. I
wonder now that her heart didn't burst from all the excitement that
night. She rang for tea, for her knitting, then sat near me and took
my hand.

Ach, Mistress Temple, she said, avid. I'm dying for this tale.

And I told her.

I WAS TWENTY-THREE, plain, and very good. I had known of him
since I was small, as we attended the same Quaker Meeting for
years. But he was a foundling, a runaway from his own overpacked
farm of Temples. He had nothing when he ran away, breeches, and
nothing beneath, a shift, and no shirt. He had no shoes. He had no
hose. He dreamt of carriages, of thick rugs, he dreamt of owning
all of Burlington. He had luck then, as he has always had luck. The
day he ran away, he was adopted and taught to be a cooper by

Phineas Dorley. When I saw him that day, in Meeting, he was nine-teen, and a master cooper already, but also illiterate, a rake, a wild son given to drinking. Given, they said, to an unnaturally strong taste for serving girls. Even I—the fiercely protected daughter of the richest widower in New Jersey—even I had heard of his excesses.

There we were in the Meeting that day, silent, waiting for the word of God to fill us with its light. It was bitter cold, the skin around my nostrils and my eyes was smarting, and the congrega-tion's breath rose from our bodies, tethered to us like souls.

I sat on the women's side, my sister Sarah beside me. How I hated my sister that morning. Hatred like that had never been held behind the stomacher of any other delicate Quaker. Sarah was younger, she was more beautiful, she was light as a butterfly, she was to be married in two weeks to a wealthy Quaker from Philadel-phia, and could not stop speaking of it. Even beside her in Meeting I could feel her dreaming of her wedding. It was I who should have been married, I who had made the trousseau that my sister was tak-ing in its entirety, for Sarah was the younger sister and was meant to care for my father until he died. She was never meant for marriage. I was. When she was secretly courted by her husband and when she said yes, when my father agreed, my world shifted. I became the one who was meant to remain at home with my father. My sour-tempered father, Richard Franklin, wealthy, and mean, and gouty, who soaked himself in Madeira every night, but was not punished for it by the Meeting, as he was rich, and rich Quakers can have peccadilloes with no fear of punishment.

I thought of the sudden desert of my life at that very moment, and the thought sinfully blocked the light of God. Anger rose in me so strong and thick I tasted it, and it was like molasses, like blood.

In my anger, I looked up at the men's section. In the great silence of the hall, filled with the small movements of cold bodies and breath, I looked up and found the heavy, handsome gaze of that rake, Marmaduke Temple, on my face. It was not in my nature to smile back, to flirt, but I believe my rage made me. It was brief, our look. But when, on Monday, I looked up from my novel, to distract myself from my sister, who was counting linens from my trousseau in my chamber, I saw Marmaduke, great and hulking, outside by the oak tree. He was looking into my window, forlorn as a dog.

Such power I felt, and continued to feel as he returned, stood in the cold, every day for a week. The groomsman went out there to give him company, smoke a pipe with him, and came in, chuckling over some joke. The cook stole out with a steaming bowl of soup, and by her walk, I knew that there had been something between them once.

I watched Marmaduke watch for me, and at the end of that week, as my father was in Philadelphia, finishing the preparations for my sister's wedding, Sarah stole out to the oak and spoke to him. Cruel girl—I could hear her laughing when she came in and ran up to her room, and I was not surprised to find him in the parlor for tea the next day.

Overlarge in the dainty chair, vulgar, and how terrible the yellow gloves on his hands. Poor boy. He did not know better. Later, he admitted that the haberdasher only had those gloves that were large enough for his bear paws, those hands so sensitive for casks and rondelets, those work-hard hands. By inviting him, how my sister made such a mockery of him. Of me.

My teacup rattled in its saucer. I could not look. And after an especially bad gaffe of his, my sister could not hold her laughter—she pretended to fetch an album she wanted him to look at, and ran out to laugh. Marmaduke's deep voice, shaking. Thy sister, Miss Franklin, is kind to invite me—but I interrupted.

Cruel, Mr. Temple. She is cruel. She cares only to hurt us. Thou art far too vulgar to be considered and I am not meant to marry. I must care for my father until he is called to God.

Marmaduke, frowning—even then impressive—But thou art the elder sister.

I, raising my hand to stop him, hearing the nearing froufrou of my sister's skirts. Leaning forward, within inches of his beautiful lips. Trembling like a bird in a hand: Marry me, Mr. Temple. And soon.

My sister came back in. The clock on the Anglican church down the street chimed the hour. I could see nothing but the shine in his beautiful boots, the massiveness of those boots in our feminine parlor. And that night, the low whistle at the window. Sarah already in bed, dreaming of Philadelphia, my own candle quick-blown out. Below, Marmaduke with the rented horse. My trunk, my trousseau, pushed down. And then I stepped, my mother's prayer book in my arms, the only thing I have ever had of my dear, dead mother, I stepped and fell through the winter air, clutching my calèche to my head, and I landed in Marmaduke's iron arms. Marmaduke walking beside me on the horse, carrying my trunk on his back, glittering in the moonlight on his back like a beetle's shell, the house growing smaller at my back with the immensity of every step, I imagining my sister's screams when she discovered I was the one married that morning, my father's shouting filling up the town, raising sparrows into the sky, trembling the ground so the cemetery's dead raised their eyelids, my own dead mother spinning her skeleton in her grave, and I was glad. I laughed, then, in the night.

And from that night, Marmaduke and I lived together in our many houses. That first terrible, hasty cottage with its sand floors and cook-stained walls (Marmaduke, seeing the horror on my face, making his jaw hard, making him frown, saying, Elizabeth, I promise I shall give thee a beautiful house someday). Then on to a better house in Burlington, but not much better. Then after a year to a house on the land my father gave us, which he meant for a punishment, for Marmaduke to farm (an insult), but which Marmaduke turned into a prosperous little town (the first Templeton, his first experiment in settling a town, before the second Templeton where we sit, now).

Then on to a fine brick house in Burlington near the size of my father's own, from which Marmaduke failed to carry me off one humiliating day. Later, I was extracted from that beloved house by a letter written in the hand of an adolescent Indian, Cuff. Telling me that wasn't it lovely that the new slave, Hetty, such a pretty girl, was with child. That alone sent me to the last, to this, grandest, the Temple Manor, in which I was just then awaiting the news of my husband's death, shaking with the terrible cold.

BY THE END of my story that night, Remarkable had dozed off. It was very late. The fire in the grate was low, almost embers, and because of the low light, I could see the stars, the three-quarter moon, the snowy street an opal color. I imagined my husband standing, sweat russeling off of him in streams from yet another wrestling victory, clapping his broad hand on the shoulder of his foe. The old settler Solomon Falconer, a man almost as vast as Marmaduke himself, allowing himself to be defeated by the landlord.

I saw Marmaduke draining a tankard to cool himself off, head spinning dizzy, staggering a bit. Richard and Kent Peck laughing together by the fire, men spitting and ringing the spittoon like a bell, Mingo drinking, surreptitious in the kitchen with a pretty cross-eyed cook who would fancy him, if he were only not black. Widow Crogan slamming another tankard before my husband, and he nodding at her, telling her to save it, he needed to cool off first. The noise of the many celebrating men unbearable, the pressure in his bladder unbearable, his conscience heavy with guilt, unbearable: picturing Noname, sleek and naked in the lake one day, stepping up to him in the trees, stepping up to him with a sly little smile, water coursing over her perfect, young body, the kiss, why not, then the dead girl in Shipman's filthy cabin, the redhaired baby squalling in the drunken midwife's arms. Perhaps he thought he would do something to make life easier for her, that poor child, his own daughter, still.

I imagined him walking through the doors into the comparable relief of the night, feeling alone, feeling safe. What he did not see is that in the alleyways huddled separate dangers. The noise of the Bold Dragoon, the Anti-Federalists, riling themselves up with their fiddler for a fight. The Bold Dragoon louder than the Eagle Hotel, where the victors, the Federalists, were. I imagined Marmaduke drawn into Second Street by the hard glint of the moon on the ice of the lake, the cold of the night, the dark, the pride in this, his town, the one he made with his own two hands.

And I knew the moment when the blow was struck. I knew that not just one person did it. It was also I. Through not warning him, through not commanding him to stay home. I, bone-cold in my big house, killed him.

And then I waited for the discovery of the lump of him in the road. How the blood seeped into the ice-packed street and froze. I waited for the men to bring him home, for our bloodhound to boom his sorrow into the night, for Mingo to carry his vast and chilling body inside, to return it to my house, which it never should have left, for my good servant to give him to me, like a present, his eyes to the ground so I wouldn't see the victory in them. I'd keep my own down at the funeral so I wouldn't see the victory in all of the faces, all of those terrible, hating faces. And that night, I waited for the knock, and I opened the door to the house, and let his body in. I opened the door of this house he built, the house he dreamed of giving me. The cooling husk of a husband, a broken and emptied ruin; a husband, in the end, who was never truly mine.

Guvnor Averell

CIRCA 1859. *Family lore has it that Guvnor was wearing white gloves for this tintype and had carefully applied great masses of powder to his face before sitting. Note his wonky eye.*

Rising from the Deep, The Sun, One Breath Beyond

IT WAS ONLY a few hours, but it felt like an ocean of time.

I sat at the kitchen table with my mug of cold coffee, looking at Guvnor's little paper, my brain frozen.

At some point someone knocked on the garage door, and then, giving up, went to the great front door and rang the bell. I imagined, as if in a vision, that Ezekiel Felcher was out there, shivering in the drizzle in his short-sleeved shirt, frowning. I saw every wrinkle in his jeans, every muscle in his back contract and loosen as he walked away.

I couldn't be bothered. Behind me, the great stretch of windows registered the slow close of this wet day, and the room grew dark as the lake grew dark, and then it all grew even darker.

The rain stopped near eight, and the frogs emerged in lusty choir.

I sat in the dark until the headlights pulled up and then the freeze in my brain thawed.

There were voices in the night outside, Clarissa's joyful laugh I could hear even from the table. But before the door opened and they clambered in, I held the paper up to the watery moonlight and read, again, what it said.

⊹⧠ TESTMENT FROM MASTER GUVNOR AVERELL ⧠⧖
ON DECEMBER 24 1799

I seen it Tonite the Death of Marmduke Temple and I cant get Asleep unlest I write it down and thats what Im goin to do and then put it in the Horse I stole from Little Jacob Temple so Ill get it outa me and dont have to worry no more. I wonder if I shoult tell my Father the Mayor the Sherif but no I cant I dont preciate the Temple Way and maybe Marmduke owns the Town (ownt I gess now) but he dont own me.

Was a time I liket Marmduke he give me Coins when he seen me pat me on the Hed but what happent was on one day I look in the Winder in the Harnes Shop and seen the Reflecshin him and me standin there and a suddn I seen Somethin in me looks like him. Seen it and begun wondrin bout my Father Jedediah Averell and I dont look Nothin alike him and thinkin my Mama Hetty Averell was a Sarvent in the Temple Manor afore she was my Mama and I dont lissen Much in Scool but nuff to ken that One and One make Two and I cant look on my Mama no more after that. I got so mad. I uset to go into the Temple Manor at Nite and walk round and I got so mad at the skinny Little Jacob Temple for havein so Much that I stole Little Things from him a Slinshot a Led Solder a Ball made of Leather and Twine and the last thing was the Real Horseskin Horse Ima put this Testment into when Im finisht.

No I dont like the Temple Way and so I have desidet I will not tell. And sides Im only ten years ol and I still can pretend Im just a Little Boy and was too scaret.

Heres what happen Tonite I was out late wanderin because I was mad at my Father he wouldnt let me eat Mamas Trifle at Supper account a the bad Skinnin I done today account a me wantin to go out and play Ball with the Boys who was playin down by the Ise House and I ruint a fine Foalskin. So I was wanderin throwing Iseicles to see them smash sayin to myself my Father coult go to H★★★. And then I was comin up behind Second when I herd the loud shoutin and I remember it is the Election and account a the Eagle shoutin loudest I spect the Fedralists won. And I creep up and am watchin the fine Doins the Fiddler and the Men chawin Tobaccer and drinkin Mugs a Liker and then Marmduke Temple wrasslin with that great Bear for a Settler Solmon Falconer and Marmduke hes ol and he gets beat and there is Mazment for Marmduke Temple never was Beaten afore. And so he gets up and shakes Hands and says he needs some Air and that normally means a Piss and I scramble around the Corner cause I was standin on the fowl yaller Iseblock where the men pisst in the Ally so as I coult look in the Winder and see the Doins on.

But no he means a Breather for real and he goes and stands in the middler Street the crossroads Second and Pioneer and just stands and looks at the froze Lake and the Settlment. Smilin like. And a sudden I see Movment. There was Little yaller Elihu Phiney comein from the Bold Dragoon with his bras-head Cane in Hand. Sneakin up out into Pioneer. Like to kill Marmduke. Dont know what hed a done tho cause there was also Davey Shipman comein out from the other Side near me and Phiney he saw and went back into the Ally by the Bold Dragoon. And dont know what Shipman a done with his long Rifle neither because up silent as Wind swift too comes ol Chingachgook over the Isey Street from Susquehanna way with his Tomahawk in Hand and Davey stops movin five Foot from Marmduke Temple and lets the ol Injun just smash Marmduke Temple on the Hed with the back a his Tomahawk. The ol Man he move unbelievable fast in his ol Blanket. There was a Melon Sound and Maraduke he crumplt like an ol Kwilt and a sudden there was Nobody in the Street. All the Men vanisht Phiney Davey Chingachgook. Jus Marmduke on the Ground a Black Puddle growin under his Hed. A minute or so goes by and Im so suprizet I dont do Nothin Im froze. And then out comes Mingo the Big Black from the Manor and goes shoutin in his Frenchy accent but speakin in posh Words and a sudden theres the whole World in the Street all the men from the Eagle and the Bold Dragoon and the great big Hairy Richard come out and begins to Weep over his Father like a big Babby and Mingo scoops up Marmduke like he wasnt Nothin to carry and takes him oft and all the men follow in this strange Silence save for Hairy Richards Babby cryin. And they all gone away.

And I come out shakin because a Man died afore me and I see the big Bloodstane on the Ise in the Street and it was Much Much Blood. I come Home and cant sleep and so I wrote this. It was the Injun done it. And if what my Mama was whisperin to my Father Tonite about Chingachgooks Pretty Noname Grand-daughter and Marmduke Temple makein that Babby a RedHed when Everyone knows there aint no RedHedded Injun Babbys well I unnerstand why ol Chingachgook done it. My Mama calld the Babby Euphonia, Euphonia Shipman, poor Babby. And Davey too I would unnerstand with Noname bein his Lit-tle Wife and all and that Damd Marmduke takin what int his. Honest since the Day I seen my Face in his I Hate ol Mar-maduke Temple with a Hate so Fierce and tho Im not happy to a been there to seen it Im to be sure glad hes Dead.—G.A.

I put the paper down and took one big breath. Guvnor's words buzzed and flicked in me like bees in a hive, so loud I could barely hear the door open. The light flicked on in the mudroom. I stood in the kitchen and waited.

Then the light snapped on in the kitchen and when I blinked, there before me was Clarissa, so beautiful. Her hair curled on her head, darker, like a cap: her face was flushed with fatigue. Something I'd held knotted within me since the day I'd learned about her sickness unknotted then.

"Clarissa," I said, and stepped to her and hugged her gently. She felt as delicate as a bird in my arms, but squeezed back.

"Willie," she said, but couldn't say any more.

I grinned down at her and said, "I'm glad you're home, too."

And that's when Vi and Reverend Milky came in the door, both struggling with Clarissa's designer luggage, red-faced, puffing. I hugged Clarissa again, my mother blushing under the force of my gratitude, and in her pleasure, she began picking lint from Reverend Milky's shoulder.

FOR MOST OF dinner, Clarissa didn't eat, but, rather, held my hand. Vi bustled about so merrily, and Reverend Milky told such a long, convoluted story about seminary school and the pranks they used to play there (darting his eyes between us, anxiously, as if gauging the rise in his level of coolness with each story) that we didn't have much time to speak. At last, when Milky rose and waddled off to the powder room, I took Vi's hand as she reached for another white-top roll from Schneider's Bakery. Her old eyes narrowed, and she tried to pull herself away, but I gripped her harder.

"Vi," I said, softly. "It's Solomon Falconer, isn't it?"

"What?" she snapped, and looked away.

"Vi," I said, and let go of her hand. I lifted both the excerpt Clarissa took from *Shadows and Fragments* and Guvnor's little parchment paper onto the table and began to speak so quickly my words tumbled over one another like wavelets. I said, "Look, Vi, I figured it out. Here," I said, and shoved Guvnor's paper before her, though her eyes darted away. "Vi, look. Guvnor Averell wrote this on the night Marmaduke died. It says here that the night of Marmaduke's murder, there was a baby girl born with red hair, and because of the red hair, everybody assumed she was Marmaduke's, though her mother was married to someone named Davey Shipman. In seconds, everybody knew Marmaduke had had a child with someone else's wife; that's why he was murdered that night. Listen, the baby's name was Euphonia Shipman. Now, I remembered that name Euphonia Shipman from something else I'd read," I said, shouting by now with elation, and then I shook in front of her Clarissa's excerpt from *Shadows and Fragments*. "Now it says in Charlotte's note at the end of this little piece here, '*Euphonia Falconer, née Shipman, became a devout member of the Methodist choir*' . . . Vi, are you listening? It says Euphonia *Falconer*, née *Shipman*, and that means that she, Euphonia Shipman, Marmaduke's illegitimate daughter, married some old settler named Solomon Falconer. Solomon Falconer! Everybody knows that Euphonia's son was Solomon Falconer; his son was Solomon Falconer, and down the line it goes until Solomon Falconer the Fifth, the Running Bud, my friend, ends up being my *father*. Vivienne Upton, you slept with Solomon Falconer. My *father* is Solomon Falconer."

Reverend Milky, who hadn't yet made it to the powder room, actually gasped like a girl and hurried back to the table. Clarissa's hands were planted over her mouth, and she gazed at me wetly. My mother's eyes bulged. And we all waited, our bodies tense as taut rubber bands, and Vi began shaking. She reached out her hand and touched my face. And then she said, wonder ringing her voice like a bell, "Oh, Sunshine. I can't believe it. I cannot believe it. You did figure it out, didn't you, oh, didn't you."

Ordering the Threads

REVISE THE VISION: Vivienne young, blasted with acne, on a bus roaring home from San Francisco, the peace-medallion flapping on her belly. She was definitely not pregnant. There was no me-Lump anywhere on her person. I always did think it fishy that she claimed I had spent ten and a half months in the womb.

When Vi saw the old lawyer Chauncey Todd and was fondled by his eyes, she was not pregnant. Not pregnant, she missed the funeral but attended her parents' memorial and numbly shook the hands of well-wishers. She was not pregnant as matrons from the town said snide, passive-aggressive things as they held her hands.

Oh, Vivienne, they said. *Your dear mother had such lovely clothing; I am sure you'd be her size if you watched yourself a little bit.* And *Your parents were so eager to see you for Christmas last winter; such a pity you couldn't come home to visit them just once before they passed.* And *What's the scent you wear, darling? Patchouli? How very . . . fascinating of you.*

Though even then they suspected she was pregnant, she wasn't;

she just liked butter and doughnuts, even then. This would help her with her alibi in the years to come.

Winter melted into early spring. Birds flittered into the trees, trailing arias. Vivienne had thrown open the windows of Averell Cottage so the fresh March air blew in. She had a red handkerchief on her hippie head, and those days of painting and stripping wallpaper and sprucing the house up for the quick sale had made her lose some of her flab. She went through a strange sort of drug withdrawal in the last few weeks where she shuddered and couldn't sleep for weeks on end, at which time her acne, miraculously, cleared. Perhaps, she thought, she had been allergic to cannabis. Perhaps she was allergic to not washing her face. Home again, she had fallen into the routine with which she was raised: obsessive tidiness, a sense of order.

With its yen for cleanliness, the dovelike ghost was pleased, showed itself again to Vi, cooed approvingly when she walked by with a washcloth in hand. Its vague feathers accumulated under the beds and its down rolled around her feet like mist when she walked.

Then came a day when Vi rode a wobbly ladder in the entryway, rolling white paint onto the age-yellowed ceiling, singing to herself, *Summ-mer time, time time, whoo-hooo, the living's eeeeasy.* She crowed up there, she cackled. She felt possessed by Gershwin. There was a drop cloth on the floor, so she was not too concerned about drips, but when she looked down, there was a man holding the base of the ladder, and on the crown of his curly red head a splotch of paint very much like a bird dropping.

"Whoops," she said, beaming down at his gray summer wool suit, the necktie tight in a Windsor knot. "Who are you?"

He must not have felt the paint through his thick reddish curls, because he blinked up at her, confused. "Pardon?" he said. Then, seeing how she was waiting expectantly, he said, "I'm Sol. Solomon Falconer. The Fifth."

"Okay," said Vi. Then, "Oh. You mean you're the beer guy. The Heir of Beer."

"Well," said Sol. "Yes?"

The two stared at each other for some time until Vi said, musing to herself, " 'To see him pass conveys as much as the best poem, perhaps more.' "

"Pardon?" stuttered Sol. "I'm sorry?"

"Oh, I'm being rude," she said. "That was Walt Whitman. A great poet."

"Oh, I know Whitman," said Sol. "Haven't read him since college, though. Ages ago."

Vi put her roller down and beamed at Sol below her. "A friend of Whitman's is a friend of mine," she said. "You look hungry. I'm making lunch. I rarely have guests, but I found some really beautiful tomatoes in the grocery store yesterday. I'm Vivienne Upton."

Then she climbed down off the ladder and shook Sol's hand, and he wiped the paint off them with his handkerchief, surreptitiously, as he followed her into the kitchen. "Thank you," he said, surprised. "That's very kind of you to offer. But I'm here to talk business. A business proposition. If you will."

"Business," said Vi, as if the very word tasted bitter. She pulled olive oil down onto the counter and sniffed the dimple of a tomato. "I'm hungry. Who cares about business?"

"Oh," said Sol Falconer. "Well, I went to business school. I mean, I do."

"I don't," she said. "There's nothing less interesting to me," and she frowned a little.

An awkward silence fell between them, and Sol watched Vi slice the tomato neatly into segments. "So," he said. "Should I take it to mean that you're not interested in selling Averell Cottage then?"

"Aha," said Vi, looking up, her eyes dancing. "Well, that kind of business. Maybe I am, after all. First, sit down, though. What the heck, open that bottle of wine. Tell me all about yourself, Mr. Sol Falconer. I want to know the man with whom I aim to conduct my business."

Was she flirting? Perhaps she was: to be honest, Vi's head was a little swimmy from paint fumes, and Sol's hands were sweating too much for him to take much notice. No new addition to Averell Cottage existed yet, no vast glass doors that opened into the glorious early spring world—that would be my mother's big architectural mistake when I was six—so Vivienne escorted young Sol Falconer through the kitchen and directly out into the day and had him sit at an old wrought-iron table, flaking with rust.

"Sit," she said. "Stay."

And she imped back in and imped back out with tomato salads and fresh-baked bread and yogurt she made herself and a great bottle of wine and a plate of her special tuna fish salad that she was careful to garnish with a lettuce leaf frill.

At last, she sat down and drank a goblet of wine in one go. "Now eat," she said to Sol Falconer, who looked upon the meal with hungry eyes—he'd been working all day, it was now three in the afternoon, his father never let him take a lunch hour, only five minutes to gobble half a sandwich, which he hadn't had time for today—and he tore in. He washed each mouthful down with a gulp of the sour wine. After about ten minutes, he had loosened the knot in his tie. After fifteen, he was light-headed, and he suddenly saw the sweet way the cherry trees would, very soon, burst into bloom; he saw this now as if he'd never seen a flowerbud before in his entire life. And, perhaps, he hadn't. Back then, he never had time for joy; he had never joined the generation of love, only dancing alone in his parents' great house to some of its music on the radio, turned low.

Vivienne, drinking happily, watching her handsome guest chew, asked him one question when it seemed he'd slowed down. "So, who are you, Mr. Sol Falconer?" she said.

And that unleashed the torrent. He told her he was a fresh graduate from Harvard, both undergrad and business school, twenty-five years old. His family only came to their old house in Templeton in the summer: the rest of the time, they were in Wisconsin, overseeing the brewery. This summer they came early, and his father decided to make him his own personal toady, and there he was, working his butt off for no money just so his father could teach him the business, but, frankly, a monkey could run the business; beer was not something that people would ever stop drinking; and, besides, he didn't see how fetching contraband cigars from very shady places in Manhattan could count as learning the beer business, but, whatever, he'd do it, if only the old donkey's behind ended up giving him the business when he croaked.

"Oh," said Vivienne, intermittently nodding. The sun sank a little lower, the shadows edged away from where they'd begun. With the sunlight tamped out, the spring day reverted again to winter, and a chill draft rose from the lake. Sol seemed so flushed and warm inside his story that Vi didn't have the heart to ask him to go inside. Instead, she kept drinking to keep her bones from freezing.

Frankly tipsy now, Sol Falconer leaned back in his chair and ex-
pounded anew. Anyway, that old bastard had also put him in charge
of buying up old property in Templeton to make sure the hoi pol-
loi didn't take it over and start ruining it with all sorts of fast-food
restaurants and strip malls and, frankly, when they heard this morning that Vi might be selling Averell Cottage, his father had bellowed
from his perch on his throne—the toilet, Sol-the-Fifth clarified for
Vi, as if she were a child—that no goddamn way was she going to
sell that place to any rank developer because, frankly, it would be
the perfect place for a strip mall, and there was utterly no way that
he was going to allow a strip mall to come into Templeton, no way.
So here Sol was, vowing that he would best any offer anyone would
make for the place, just to keep it from being snatched up.

"Oh," said Vivienne, watching the way the lake had turned an
opalescent gray in the late sun. She sat on her hands, shivering,
yearning to go inside, but her guest was wild now, and the cold
didn't seem to bother him. Now Sol veered wildly off course and
began telling Vivienne about his family. She knew they were the
big cheese around here, but had no idea that they were some of the
original settlers, Solomon Falconer the First coming with Marmaduke Temple the very first time he surveyed and sold the land.

"Some say," whispered poor, drunk Sol, "that Marmaduke even
screwed around with some Indian girl and they had a girl who the
first Solomon Falconer married. Get it? Marmaduke's illegitimate
daughter married Sol-the-First. It's all very hush-hush, but if it's
true, I'm related to the Temples, just like you. How exciting!" Then
he put a finger on his lips and blew to signify the sanctity of the
secret. Vi, suddenly alert, smiling hugely, nodded.

Sol continued, saying they had a history, the Falconers, of marrying in great late age and leaving one son behind. Only five generations of very old Solomon Falconers with very young wives
between him and the original. They were originally farmers up on
West Lake Road until Euphonia Falconer had the brilliant idea to
plant hops when she herself was an old woman. At one point at the
end of the nineteenth century the Falconers were *the* employers in
town, and they even ran a place on West Lake Road, right underneath their mansion that still sat there, a place that housed over
three thousand seasonal workers (way bigger than Templeton at the

time!) and was called Hops City. It had a barber's, a butcher's, a dance hall, a grocery store, a blacksmithy, a bakery, tons of huge longhouse-style dormers, et cetera, et cetera.

"Oh," said Vivienne, and imagined the entire hillside full of twelve-foot hops poles, turning buttery and golden in the August heat.

The rising musk of the hops.

A man twanging a mouth harp as he walked the shadow-ribbed rows.

However, Sol began to relate with a wine-thick tongue, then there was an overproduction of hops for about five years in a row and prices were terrible and then there was a blight and then there was the Great Depression, and his family fortune almost died out once again, but then Solomon Falconer the Fourth (his father) had the idea to open a brewery in Wisconsin of all places, and it took off, and now nobody grew hops around Templeton any more but the Farmers' Museum out at the old Franklin House barns. Sol-the-Fifth was in Templeton that summer, he said, because he had been in love with the town all his life.

"It never changes, does it?" he mused, eyelids heavy with drink. "Incorruptible."

"Oh," said Vivienne, shuddering now. All this talk had thrilled her: it was more conversation than she'd had for as long as she'd been home. It was sweet, a relief. Besides, she wanted to get out of the cold. She put a hand on Sol's thigh. "Kiss me."

He leaned over the wrought-iron table and put his wine-soaked tongue in her mouth. She kissed him back. They fumbled their way inside, and there, on the ancient floorboards of the dining room, floorboards that the beautiful and proud Hetty Averell once scrubbed on her hands and knees, there, on those old boards, I was begotten.

VI FINISHED HER story that night by leading us into the dining room and pointing with great majesty at the exact site of my generation. We stood in a circle and gazed down. It may have been my imagination, but I swear I saw a lighter stain in that place. I had to look away.

"This," said Clarissa, "is just so weird."

Vi sighed and led us away, back into the bright-lit kitchen. "I stayed here," she said, "because he went off to Manhattan the next day and I waited and waited and waited for him to come back and make another 'offer' on the house, if you catch my drift. But he didn't. And then, the next time I see him, I'm four months gone and he has his wife on his arm, and I just *couldn't* tell him. I didn't know that he was going to get married, but I did know, just by looking at them, that it wasn't going to last. So I decide just to ride it out. It would only be a year or so until they broke up, I was sure, and then I'd show up one day with Willie in my arms and say, *just take a look at this little one—she has you written all over her.*" Here, Vi stopped and shook her head. "I think"—she sighed—"I was reading too many historical novels at that time."

"But," I said, "that never happened. You never took me to him."

"That never happened," she agreed. "His first marriage lasted for five years. At first I was a little, well, unhinged. I stalked his wife through the Great American. I got drunk and set fire to his front porch. It was stone, though, and didn't take. By the end, I'd gotten over him. Came to my senses. I didn't want him to know. I don't think he ever knew about who you really were, Willie—I think he thought I was hounding him because I was anticapitalist and taking it out on him. He never knew about you being his."

We sat there, the four of us, for some time, mulling this over. Clarissa took a meditative sip of her tea, and the mug in her bony hands looked so large I had to hold myself back from snatching it up, afraid she'd break her wrists. And then I glanced up at my mother to find her looking at me with a strange glimmer in her eye— merriment? pride? relief?—and I narrowed my own and frowned a little. We stared at each other like this for some time until, with a great watery crash, it broke like three tons of whitewater on my head. Perhaps she'd meant this all along, wily old Vivienne. Perhaps this was her grand plan, the way she would make me heal. She knew me, in and out: she knew my obsessiveness, the way I'd learned as a little kid. She could've told me who my father was easily, but I needed to know the precise weight of what my family carried; I needed to work for my redemption. I wanted to throw something— a vase, a book, Reverend Milky—across the room, but my mother blew a little kiss at me and hid her smile in her mug.

And then there rose a strange squeaking sound, as if some rodent were scuttling over our feet, and I peered under the table to find it. But when I looked up again, Clarissa and Vi were staring at Reverend Milky, whose face was red and cheeks blown out, and eyes squeezed shut, and who was making the little squealing noises. Then he couldn't keep it in and let loose a tremendous roar of laughter, shaking herky-jerky in the chair so it creaked under his weight, letting a tear or two slip down his apoplectic face. Despite myself, I couldn't keep from smiling at the sight of this fleshy wobbly man, at his gasping sobs of laughter and the way his hobnail crucifix danced a jig on his belly.

"You," he huffed at my mother through his peals, "are a remarkable woman, Vivienne. You set his *porch* on fire."

I looked at my mother, and said, "Well, this bodes well. To be honest, I didn't think he was capable of laughter."

She raised an eyebrow back at me. "You think I'd let myself be stuck with a sourpuss for the rest of my life?"

Clarissa seemed as if she was about to say something, her mouth twisted wryly and looking at me in her old ironic way, when she thought better of it and said, "You? Living with a sourpuss? Never, Vi." And there was either a speck in her eye or she winked at my mother, but I pretended not to notice. Instead, I watched Milky wipe his face and chuckle into the bowl of his hand, then I reached over and gave him a clap on the shoulder.

"Frankly, Milky," I told him, "you just warmed the cockles of my heart. You may be okay for my mother."

"Oh, goody," he said. And this set him off again.

33

Teratology: Or, of Monsters in Paint, in Teeth, in Wood, in Sheet-Iron, in Stone, in Mountains, in Stars

The image clings to my mind like a growth.
I sense some riddle in it.
—JOHN GARDNER, Grendel

THE WEEKS AFTER the monster died, it faded from our memories. The film crews slowly slipped away, two by two; the divers went down and came up shrugging; the deep-sea pods circled the murky depths and found no vestige of the monster, no lair, no offspring, nothing; even the children forgot their fears of the water and zipped around on their tiny water skis and in their luffing Sunfish. In the raveling days of late August and early September, Templeton seemed normal, if quieter this summer.

Then, suddenly, when we had begun to forget the sweet monster, it blasted up through the darkness again. Doctor Herman Kwan, he of the blooming sweat-roses on the evening news, put out a sixty-three-page article in the same exact issue of *Nature* as my—Dwyer's—own article. Kwan et al.'s "A New Species,

Genus, Family? What We Know about *Templetonia Portentum"* ended two pages before Dr. Dwyer and twenty-one coauthors' "Archaeological Evidence of Alaskan Human Migration More Than 25,000 BCE."[1]

Head-to-head scientific sensationalism, like dueling banjos.

By far the more interesting was the Templeton Monster's. Cutting through the murkiness of scientific argot and syntax—why, I always wonder, do scientists believe that unintelligibility equals intelligence?—the Kwan article basically stated that the monster of our lake was a unique animal in the history of the world, and went on to list the reasons why.

As it is always good to have an image in mind when discussing abstractions, here is a picture from that report:

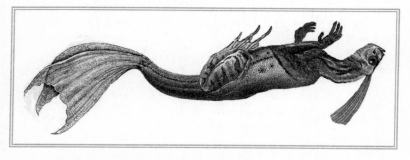

An "artist's" rendition of Glimmey. Sadly, the only "artist" that lives in Templeton is a seventy-five-year-old collagist named Milton Witherbee, who never quite got over his Ernst-inspired surrealism, and creates "art" like this rendition of Glimmey that, let's be frank, has very little to do with the Glimmerglass Lake Monster as he actually appeared. Two weeks after the production of this work, Witherbee set fire to his studio, weeping, and retired to Hawaii, saying, "It is a false art that cannot survive a monster."

---

[1] Could scientific titles be more reductive? It's like calling *Anna Karenina* something like: *In Which a Woman Leaves Her Family for Another Man, Feels Great Guilt and Jealousy and Throws Herself under a Train; Including the Plight of Levin, a Man Who Searches for and in the End Finds God.* Science needs an infusion of art.

ON GLIMMEY, THE LAKE GLIMMERGLASS MONSTER, OR *TEMPLETONIA PORTENTUM*

THE MONSTER OF our lake, the report said, was found by DNA analysis to be a placental mammal of the superorder Cetariodactyla, the same order that gave rise to even-toed ungulates (pigs, hippos, deer) and cetacea (whales and dolphins).[2] But this is where the similarity ended between pigs, deer, and whales, as our monster was apparently a synchronous hermaphrodite,[3] and self-fertilizing, at that. The only other animal known to self-fertilize is a fish called the killifish, so the discovery of a mammal that could do such things was enough to shock the scientific community out of its pants.

Bone analysis found our monster to be over two hundred years old, and the tiny fetus of a fertilized baby deep within its cavernous body found the gestation period to be about twenty years. Twenty years! The little fetus was about ten years into its development and still didn't have eyes: it was the size of a six-year-old child, and, despite its tail and superlong neck, its potbelly and clenched fists were so uncannily human that one of the researchers, the mother of an autistic boy, wept when they pulled it

---

[2] This is so delightfully screwy: imagine that, a bazillion years after the first fish crawled, panting, out onto land, one silly ungulate looked into the water and thought it was a good idea to dive back in. Apparently, this is what happened. Instead of imagining whales as mythical, brilliant alienlike beasts, as poeticized in millions of crystal-and-hemp new-agey stores worldwide, we should simply imagine them as great blubbery goats. Sometimes, the ancients were wiser than we: Proteus, in Greek myth, was, apparently, the herder of Neptune's dolphins. Aka, an underwater shepherd for the underwater sheep.

[3] Hermaphrodite: an organism that has both male and female sexual characteristics; a synchronous hermaphrodite is one that has both sexual organs at the same time. There are also sequential hermaphrodites, when the gonads change throughout life (Tiresias in Greek myth was a sequential hermaphrodite because the Gods changed him to a woman and back again over the span of his life). Humans can be gonadal hermaphrodites, intersexual, but it is rare for either sex organ to be functional. The word came from the son of Hermes and Aphrodite, who was said to have been fused to a nymph, resulting in a god with both sexual traits.

from the raw belly of the beast. From what evidence the researchers found, it was hypothesized that the monster had already given birth at least once. Thrilled calls were made, and the next day the scuba divers tried to touch the bottom of the lake and failed. They called in the ocean-diving equipment, all to no avail. That's when they found Glimmey's nipples were largely ornamental, as there were no milk sacs behind them: Potemkin nipples.

In addition, the monster had rock-hard black teeth, flat, not pointed, and in rungs of three for better chewing the fish and lakeweed that made up its diet. It had huge reservoirlike lungs that held up to three months' worth of oxygen, so that it only ever had to come up four times a year to breathe. It also had such dense fat that sperm whales were comparative lightweights; one ounce of pure Glimmey fat, the researchers found, would burn for fifteen hours, and the small amount of smoke that it let off smelled curious, fresh, like pine and lake water. It must have needed such dense fat, for the winters were terrible under the thick ice of Lake Glimmerglass, and there was a lot of bulk to keep warm.

Glimmey also had four legs and curiously articulated hands, exactly like human ones, but without thumbs. In fact, they were so delicate and beautiful that the artist hired to draw every part of the beast snuck in late after all the scientists went home for a nap and made furtive plaster casts of the hands for further study, using a bulldozer to put them in the back of his truck. Though the monster was never seen out of the lake, it was, apparently, easily able to walk on dry land, though the researchers believe that after a certain point—100 or 150 years of its life—it would have been far too difficult to move such a vast body in the air, and so the monster stayed exclusively in the more buoyant water.

Also, unlike a whale, Glimmey had an unfused malleus in its ear, and such exquisite inner-ear makeup that the researchers hypothesized the monster had the purest, most intricate sense of underwater hearing of any animal in the world. This was what had allowed the shy creature to remain undetected for so long: it could hear with great sensitivity if a human was even within sighting distance, and would, presumably, come up only during the darkest or foggiest nights to fill its vast lungs.

ONE LAST THOUGHT

Here is the image that popped before me when I read the article on Glimmey. I was in my pink little girl's room in Averell Cottage in the twilight, my bags packed all around me, my ghost in a light violet protective ring, and I saw, clearly and in my mind's eye, the monster in a cold cement warehouse, split open like a fruit. I saw cranes digging among the dead flesh, humans crawling on scaffolding around the corpse like Lilliputians across the body of poor shipwrecked Gulliver, the head bent back so the mouth flopped open and three rungs of shining black teeth bared to the ceiling. Offal extracted and studied and photographed, the creamy skin turning black at the wounds' edges.

It was such a terrible image, in such tremendous contrast to the idea I'd held of the monster—the silky white of the beast swimming in the black depths of Lake Glimmerglass, the happiness of limb through water, the joy of the wondering eyes, the hands grasping for a fish—that I put down the journal, and I couldn't keep my eyes from overspilling.

Wilhelmina Sunshine Upton

As a baby. And at her college graduation, briefly and insanely blond, for some reason she still doesn't quite understand. The day after her graduation, she will awaken and scare herself so badly in the bathroom mirror that she will promptly and forevermore dye her hair back to its natural color.

34

On Leaving

THE DAY I left Templeton, I took my father out to lunch. He didn't know he was my father yet and had sounded mildly surprised when I called him up the day before. I waited in the dark, cool cave of Cartwright Café, sipping my iced tea and trying to will the furious flush from my cheeks.

When Sol Falconer arrived it was in definite date attire, a very expensive dress shirt and nice slacks, as if it were natural that a girl half his age would chase after him, and the least he could do was to dress up for her. Apparently, I wasn't the first. I stood, and patted my own dark dress down. I held out my hand, and he looked at it, grinning.

"Ah," he said, shaking it. We had the same hands, I noticed, long nail beds, long fingers, a thumb twisted more to the side than normal. "You're breaking an old man's heart, Willie. I didn't realize this was going to be about business." He folded his great height into his chair, and smiled at me.

"Business?" I said. "Depends on what you call business."

By now, the waitress was standing over us, tapping the eraser of her pencil against the notepad and sighing. She had been a few years behind me in high school, and kept from that era her great garish swoops of green shadow above her eyes, and the gold hoops dangling from her ears to her shoulders. She pretended to not know who I was. "Abner sandwich, please," I said without looking at her. "Side salad, with balsamic on the side. Iced tea with lots of lemon."

He blinked and frowned a little. "Exactly the same," he said to the waitress, and handed her the menus we hadn't bothered to look at. "That's exactly what I always get," he said.

"Makes sense," I said.

"What makes sense?" he said.

"You'll see," I said.

He unfolded his napkin and spread it across his lap. Then he leaned over the table. "All right," he said. "The drama is unbearable. Could you explain the mystery, please, Willie?" he said. "Is this about the college loan? If it is, you know you don't have to worry about it."

I looked around the restaurant to see if anyone could overhear, but it was an hour before the lunch rush, and the only patrons were at one long table, a baseball family all in Mets jerseys, save for one little iconoclast who obstinately sported a Yankees pinstripe. I caught his eye and gave him a little wink. He winked back, and a piece of his hamburger fell out of his mouth.

"All right," I said to Sol Falconer. "There's a story I think I want to tell you."

"Tell away," he said.

"Once upon a time," I said, "there was a young girl who came home to her hometown. She was an orphan, all alone in the world. One day, a very good-looking young prince stopped by, and they began to drink some wine, and one thing led to where such things generally lead if the parties are drunk and young enough. Unbeknownst to the prince, a child was born. That child, at last grown up, decided one day to find her unwitting father." I waited, expectantly, looking at Sol, but I have always been a rococo storyteller, and this story only confused him.

He blinked. "What?" he said. "Prince? Child? Where?" and he craned his head around and saw the waitress leaning over the base-

ball family. "The waitress?" he said, turning back. "Is she some secret heiress or something? This is a very strange story. Why are you
telling me this, Willie?"

"No. Duh," I said. "Sol. Dad."

His eyes opened very wide, and seemed to drink my face in. The
cheekbones that must have seemed familiar, the height, the eye
color, the smile. He passed a hand over his face, and gave a shuddery
sigh. "Willie? I just," he said. "I just don't understand."

"Tell me about it," I said.

"But I *can't* have kids," he said. "Three marriages broke up because I couldn't have kids. This just isn't possible."

"Apparently it is," I said. "I'm living proof. Pinch me." It was a
joke, but he did, and I sported twin plums on my arm for a week
afterward.

"But," he said, "nobody told me. Nobody said anything. I
cheered for you at all your soccer games and track meets in high
school and I didn't even know."

"I didn't know," I said. "Not until last night. My mother told me
last night."

"But I never did anything with your mother. I swear I didn't."

"Hm," I said. "Well, if that were true, we'd all be miracles. But,
sadly, it's not."

"But I didn't," he said.

"But you did," I said. "Just think back. Remember one fine
almost-spring day with buds on the trees. Tomato salad. Wine."

I watched as his face (my face) turned red as his fine nose (my
nose) caught scent of something deep and troubling. He began to
blink, and then he sat back in his chair.

"Wait a minute," he said. "Something's creeping back."

"I have all the time in the world. Dad," I said, smiling so widely
my face felt as if it were cracking at the seams.

Solomon Falconer rubbed his hands over his face and gave a little
twist of his lips. "Oh my God, that's right. This is so, excuse me,
bizarre. I didn't even know what happened that night with Vivienne.
Your mother. I woke up in that house hungover and half-naked. I
panicked. If she ever found out, my fiancée would kill me, I thought,
and I left, and just avoided your mother for a long, long time. Put it
out of my mind. I didn't even know what happened. Holy shit."

"Holy shit," I agreed, "absolutely."

He sat back in his chair and folded his hands above his head. His hair had thinned and grown gray even since I was in high school, when he wore it in wild, gingery curls over his head. Now, he kept it clipped short. It looked nice.

When he looked back at me, it seemed he was having difficulty keeping himself from tears. "You must forgive me for asking," he said. "But I am. I have a lot of. Well, I do have money, and if this is a way to get . . ."

In response, I stood and was about to stalk out when he grabbed my hand. "Stop," he said. "I believe you. I just can't believe it."

"I know," I said.

"This is just," he said, his face suffused with red, "a miracle. A miracle. Willie Upton. I have a daughter."

"And she's me," I said. I squeezed his hand.

"And she's you," he said, shaking his head. "I couldn't have asked for better."

The invisible waitress laid our food down gently, but neither of us ate it. We sat there as the restaurant began to fill, baseball families and Templetonians both. But the people we knew steered clear of our table, sensing something, perhaps, and we could see them at their own tables, heads together, wondering what was going on.

A fourth wife, I think some of them were thinking. I wasn't far from the profile.

At last, Sol Falconer heaved a sigh. "I couldn't have asked for a better surprise," he said, shaking his head and beaming. "I couldn't be prouder of a surprise daughter, Willie Upton. I am just," he said, "well, to put it simply, moved."

I KNEW, EVEN then, what I couldn't admit that I had known: that now that I could lay claim to more predecessors, to more history, it wouldn't vastly change the course of my future. Because before a little humanoid came striding across the Bering Strait, and died and left a tiny smidgen of his existence in the tundra to be dug up by people in the unimaginable future, there had probably been a good number of humanoids before him who had also stridden over those same ancient rocks. Because, even though I now had a father, he brought with him such thicknesses of ancestors that it would be impossible to dig and understand them all, and they would be stamped only in the DNA of whatever future children I could have. It was too much. It was impossible to understand it all.

And yet, we cling to these things. We pretend to be able to understand. We need the idea of the first humanoid in North America though we will never find him; we need a mass of ancestors at our backs as ballast. Sometimes, we feel it's impossible to push into the future without such a weight behind us, without such heaviness to keep us steady, even if it is imaginary. And the more frightening the future is, the more complicated it seems to be, the more we steady ourselves with the past. I looked at my father, Sol Falconer, and felt an impossible relief. It didn't matter, not really, that I had him at last. It didn't matter, and yet, in my illogical, unfathomable heart, it did. I was glad to have his real, breathing self on that long road behind me. I was glad to know he was there.

LONG AFTER SOL Falconer and I shook hands, after an awkward embrace that turned real and warm, I walked up Main Street trying to gather myself. The day was beginning to blaze with bone-melting heat, and already the high school druggies were taking shelter under the huge old oak in Farkle Park, too hot even to play hackysack. Piddle Smalley stood, sweating, ringing a bell, wearing a yellow rain slicker backward and his signature bloom at his crotch. Small children wailed against the heat, cars seemed to have to push through the thickening air, even old Mrs. Pea, sweeping the steps of the post office, had bands of sweat deepening on her blue shirt. As I walked up past old Temple Park, where the Manor once was, I saw someone across the street who made me flush again. I hurried across the road and under the great Corinthian columns of the town library, where Ezekiel Felcher was sprawled on the stone steps in the shade.

He looked good, I saw, when I came closer. He looked great. His thick gut had trimmed into a tapered waist, and I had a wild urge to run my hand up those small muscles marching in rows up his abdomen. His cheekbones had reemerged; he was tan. He saw the way I was looking at him, and he raised an eyebrow, and I laughed.

Then his face changed, and he said, "Queenie," sadly. "Come sit. This marble's the coolest place in Templeton."

"Radical," I said, sitting beside him. It was true: the stone was almost shockingly cold under my rear.

"I meant in terms of temperature."

"I know, Zeke," I said. "I know. You on the job? Towing those cars?"

"Yup," he said. "Slow day." I tried to pretend I didn't feel him watching my profile carefully.

"Ah," I said, and didn't say any more for a moment. Over the bustle of town, the voices of the tourists pouring into the baseball museum, I could hear the slow August course of the Susquehanna, only half as high as it was when I had returned to Templeton only a few weeks before. Zeke sat up again, and looked straight at me.

"I'm pretty mad at you, Willie," he said. "I heard you're leaving today for California."

"Yup," I said. I had stopped by the NYSHA library the day before to give Peter Lieder a copy of Vi's recipe book. I also slipped Guvnor Averell's note to Hazel Pomeroy, though I kept Cinnamon and Charlotte for myself. *Oh, gracious*, the old woman had crowed. *You're going to make my reputation in my old age, Wilhelmina.* I wasn't surprised the news had circled back to Zeke. "I'm taking off in a few hours," I said. "I'm finishing that goddamn dissertation and moving on."

"You going to stay in the Bay Area, you think?"

I shrugged. "Maybe," I said. "Eventually I'll come back here, though, I think."

"That's funny," said Zeke. "Because I'm going out there."

My breath caught in my throat, and I looked at him. "What?" I said.

"I was thinking Berkeley," he said. "But I'm afraid it won't be challenging enough. I hear top colleges like Stanford love unconventional students. Especially ones who got really high SAT scores."

"Probably," I said. "Jesus Christ. What about your boys?"

"Ah," he said. "I didn't say it wasn't complicated. Everything is complicated. The older you get, the more complicated life gets. It's one of those joyful things we have to look forward to, I guess."

"I guess so," I said.

"Could I have a good-bye kiss?" he said.

I leaned over and gave him one small one on the cheek, right where his dimple sometimes emerged. Then I stood. "Shucks," he said. "That's not at all where I was hoping you'd kiss me."

"Bye, Zeke," I said. "Be good. Look me up when you come to San Fran." We held a strange current between us until I began to feel a sort of panic in my gut, a growing feeling that, if I didn't move it I wouldn't, maybe, leave that day. I laughed and broke the moment.

And Zeke's face fell. He said, "Sure thing, Queenie," a little bitterly and settled back on his arms. "It was nice knowing you." He looked away, and bit his bottom lip hard. He looked so young, so wounded, it was all I could do to take a step away.

I went down the steps and smiled up at him, shading my eyes with my hand. "Oh, I think we'll know each other again, Zeke," I said. "Ezekiel. Sexy old Felcher, you," I laughed and I heard his reluctant chuckle all the way down Fair Street to the wide blue spread of the lake.

RIGHT BEFORE MY going-away dinner we had appetizers on the porch, and Clarissa was telling, with her usual wild gestures, a story about an undercover assignment she'd once done as a stripper in a North Beach club. Her shtick, of course, was a schoolgirl dancing to AC/DC, and she made great money on the stage, but always fell into arguments when it came time to do the lap dances.

"Then," she was saying, "the night the city commissioner came in and wanted me to call him 'Uncle Billy' and tug on his tie until he couldn't breathe, that was the end. I gave a little shimmy and was reaching out toward his tie when I planted my foot in his . . ."

I had just gone inside to open another bottle of wine. I'd heard this story before, many times, and so I was already laughing softly when I saw, in the bouquet of mail my mother had brought in earlier, the unmistakably lurid corner of a postcard. My heart did a slow revolution in my chest. My stomach sank, sour. I pulled the postcard out until I could see it whole.

On the front was an overexposed photograph of a municipal building that could've been from anywhere in the country: Redwood City, California; Oshkosh, Wisconsin; Delhi, New York. A boxlike 1960s affair, bland and gray.

I turned the postcard over, and, next to my name and address, was one word: *Sorry*.

For a moment, grief woke and stretched like a cat in me. *Primus*, I thought, and imagined him in his Mr. Toad waistcoat, stealthily slipping the postcard into the mailbox and hurrying away into the California sun. But then I looked more closely and recognized the script. Neat, tight. Architectural. Sully, from his small Arizona town.

I held the postcard and looked outside where Clarissa was miming putting her dukes up for my mother and Reverend Milky, who were laughing, clutching their ample sides. She grinned and shook her finger at her imaginary opponent; their laughter pealed into the dusk. I could've brought the postcard out to show her, put it on her pillow for her to find later; it was, I think, what Sully had intended by sending it; it was what I would've done before that summer. Instead, I spun it across the room like a Frisbee into the trash, where it settled among the wet coffee grounds and soaked brown and unreadable. Then I slid open the vast glass door and stepped through it, closed it behind me. I walked toward Clarissa, who was finishing her story, whose face had a faint flush to it, and I was already applauding.

I left Templeton as the sun began to set in the crown of trees on the West Lake hills. In the rearview mirror, I watched as my mother held Clarissa beside her, and my best friend settled into Vi's kind bulk. Reverend Milky had a plump hand on my mother's shoulder, and this little cluster seemed so right, so good, I almost turned the key and stepped out of the car again, and joined them in the magnificent Templeton August dusk. But I didn't. I put the car into gear and rolled up Lake Street, pinching them small and then smaller in the mirror, until they disappeared.

As my car hummed over the Susquehanna, I had a bright vision of myself coming home. And unlike fantasies, where I am far more glamorous and beautiful than I ever end up becoming, this, I knew, was real: there was a child in my arms, a plumpness swelling in my belly, and it was nighttime, and the lights of Templeton glittered in the deep black of the lake. Some dark shadow beside me was a husband, maybe, and perhaps he was singing, and though I couldn't hear the voice or the words, I know it made me calm.

This stayed in my mind like a song, this vision of myself, as I drove out of Templeton that evening. The air through my windows smelled fresh, pine-clean. I thought of Primus Dwyer, awaiting me in his little office at Stanford, and though I tried to be stern with myself, I couldn't help a tiny little smile from spreading over my face before I tamped it down again. I couldn't wholly swallow that rising knot of badness in me.

But then the road uncoiled long and shaded before me, the good, glorious world in its perpetual rot, in its constant downswing, the whole world before me in its headlong, flaming fall, and I still didn't know when the dark ground would rush up toward us. Just then, I couldn't care. My town glimmered at my back. The asphalt hummed underneath. And the last sunlight sparking off the lake winked through the spinning trees.

35

The Running Buds (Big Tom, Little Thom, Johann, Sol, Doug, Frankie) Yet Again

THIS DAWN, WE all saw it, we have seen it, we know it; we all saw that gold leaf as it fell from the tree. We ran up to it, we ran under it, we ran past it, we fell silent. The arbiter of autumn and we watched its long, slow seesaw all the way to the ground. It is now September, the summer will be over; it was long, it was hard, but soon there will be the geese. Soon, breath in the mornings, soon long sleeves and tights, headbands to protect our delicate ears. The dawns will turn blacker and they will come later, we will skip work for the cold football field, the leaf smoke in our noses, coffee in hand, cheering those young boys who could be our sons but are not, and we will stand there watching for the fun of it, for the game. We will watch their young legs run and cheer them on. Today the dock is being taken out at the country club. The tourists have thinned after the Baseball Museum Induction Weekend, the opera singers have packed themselves into their undramatic little sedans and driven home to Manhattan or Topeka. The

Chief Uncas, the guide boat in the lake, will be withdrawn tomorrow and packed away in a boat hangar in Hartwick. We will settle in, settle down, curtail our runs to under four miles. We will then wait for winter.

Big Tom has his daughter back, detoxing at his camp on the west side of the lake. She won't say where she was, but she is back. Little Thom underwent a bypass, and all looks good; he will run again with us in a few months. We are planning to make tee shirts saying CAUTION: OUR TICKERS ARE TIME BOMBS. Now he meets us at the Cartwright Café and drinks his decaf and laughs at Frankie. Frankie is happier, has gained weight back, has scattered his parents' ashes over the ocean on his vacation. Doug was dumped by his little mistress for a six-foot-eight ex-baseball catcher whose name is being bandied about to be added to the baseball museum. His wife forgave him. The IRS has not, but his jail time will be short, and we will not speak of it ever afterward. Johann's daughter brought home her lover, and she's so funny, so butch she looks like a man, so good with power tools that they've made plans to put up wainscoting in the guest bedroom on their next visit.

And Sol, Sol was the big winner, Sol the childless, three-time divorcee with a sudden daughter, wowzers, Willie Upton, Amherst and Stanford graduate, smart as all get-out, beautiful, a girl who even babysat for us when our own children were small. Who would have thought that all this time, when we thought we knew of all the affairs, the old hurts, the wounds, that Sol could hide something as big as an affair with that old hippie Vivienne Upton? He didn't know about his daughter, of course. But that Willie has restored his faith in his own pecker, his virility, his manliness. No more ground tiger's penis, no more tisanes of strange black herbs slipped to him under the counter at Aristabulus Mudge's pharmacy. That Sol could make a child like Willie was worth three dead marriages, as he said yesterday, unable to contain his grin.

We all hooted, we all ran a little faster. And then yesterday, Big Tom said something that made us all quiet again for two good miles. We ran in silence, in awe. We didn't even spit. We didn't even fart. We were struck with joy that was as big as the

Templeton we were circling on our run, on our loop, spread before us.

Even now, on our run today, we are so glad, we see it as if it had
happened before us: Big Tom's meth-head daughter swimming
alone at three in the morning, sleepless in withdrawal, swears she
went under the dark water once. She opened her eyes. She looked
in the person-size face of a small white monster, staring at her curiously and waving its fish tail. She says it was much like our monster, our vast haul that morning in July, but in miniature. The girl
forgot to tread water, sank lower and lower, and the monster sank
right along with her. The girl looked at the big, bulging belly. The
dancer's neck. The feet with articulated phalanges. The little monster opened its mouth with its inkblack teeth, and Big Tom's girl
swears it smiled.

The girl was so relaxed she almost took a breath. She almost
let water into her lungs and let herself drown. But she didn't, she
kicked up, kicked to the surface, passed that little monster that accompanied her up. She took a big, fresh lungful of air. The monster
swam back with her to the dock, and looked up at her as she
climbed out. She never once felt fear, the girl said. It was not out to
harm her. It just wanted a friend. Before the monster flippered
back to its depths, she reached out a finger and felt the downy skin.
And she was washed with happiness like honey. The monster
grinned its inky grin again, and away it dove.

So. We ponder this as we run. We have a monster in the lake
again, a baby, an offshoot of our old one. We probably should tell
the authorities, but we can't make ourselves, we can't bring back
the divers, the scientists, the media, we can't give it again to the
world. It is ours, Templeton's. We will keep it close.

We will swim on Lake Glimmerglass on the Fourth of July next
summer, take out all our motorboats and float in the lake. Drunk,
we will dive into the water when the sun sizzles out over the west
hills, and the bats flit above, and the brass band at the Firemen's Car-
nival on Lakefront Park will start up, and the smell of cotton candy
will blow out over the lake, and we will gather there in the water as
the launch at Fairy Springs begins to send bright fireworks into the
night sky. We will kick and kick in the water there, run in the water together, watching the bursts reflected on the water around us in

gold and green and red, and we will swim and watch the stars when the fireworks fall, and we will feel good, we will feel glee, because below our feet, there will be swimming a white monster, a beautiful thing, brushing its back on our feet, young and naughty. And it will be Templeton's. It will be ours, and ours alone.

Sagamore *(or Chingachgook; Mohican Chief)*

Uncas *(Mohican Chief)* and Cora Munro

Noname Shipman —— Davey Shipman   Jedediah Averell —— Hetty Averell ——
1785-1799   1720-1799   1760?-1819   1767?-1810

                                     Dot Lippit —— Guvnor Averell *(illeg*
Euphonia Shipman —— Solomon Falconer 1810?-1855   1789-1860
1799-1902   1751-1834

                              Ginger Averell   Cinnamon Averell
Solomon Falconer, Jr.   1832-1862   1834-1908
1835-1862   m. Stokes
m. Aurelie Falconer   m. Starkweather
(secret marriage)   m. Sturgis
1844-1862   m. Graves
                                                m. Dirk Peck in 1862

Solomon Falconer, III
(raised by Euphonia)
1862-1905
m. Lily Little
1883-1904   Leah Averell Peck   Ruth Peck Starkweather
                              1867-1890 *(moved)*   1868-1910
                                                   m. Hiram Starkweather
Solomon Falconer, IV   1860-1908
1900-1977
m. Zina Mix
1923-1964   Claudia Starkweather
                                                   1888-1923
                                                   m. Chuck Tipton
                                                   1887-1948

                                                   Phoebe Tipton ——
                                                   1923-1973

                              Solomon Falconer, V ——
                              1947-

A MASSIVELY REVISED GENEALOGY OF
❧ THE TEMPLE FAMILY ❧

Marmaduke Temple ———————— Elizabeth Franklin Temple *(wife)*
1754-1799   1751-1834

Richard Temple   Five dead children   Jacob Franklin Temple
1775-1834   1789-1851
m. Anna Cox   m. Sophie Randall De Lancey
1812-1834   1789-1851

Flora | Marguerite | Rose | Jasmine | Lily | Lilas | Daisy | Charlotte *(Charlie)*
                                             (twins)   Franklin Temple

1812   1814   1819   1822   1824   1825   1827-1912

(all illeg.; all married important men in America and Europe
and moved)

Philippe de la Vallée *(aka Monsieur Le Quoi)*
1798-1869 *(died in jail)*

m. Monique Bezier *(in 1882)* ——— Henry Franklin Temple *(illeg.)*
1861-1909   1862-1939

m. Hannah Clarke
(in 1909)
1888-1979

Richard Franklin Temple   Saul Franklin Temple
1879-1938   1884-1957
(moved to New York)   *(moved to New York)*

Sarah Franklin Temple
1913-1933
m. Asterisk "Sy" Upton
1895-1953

——————— m. 1951 ——— George Franklin Temple Upton
1933-1973

——————————— Vivienne Upton
1955-

Willie "Sunshine" Upton *(illeg.)*
1973-

Epilogue

ON THE DAY it Dies, the Monster Thinks of:

fish and fish and fish and fish and fish;
the darkness soon lightening, the sun soon opening its eyes;
how it will soon see the wriggly duck-bottoms from below;
*   now the pain rising dark and terrible from the monster's*
deepest parts;
*   and how it will soon see the people legs kickety-kicking up*
there in the bright surface and how it loves to watch the legs
kickety-kick and how it always hopes the people belonging to
the legs forget to go up into the air and begin to sink;
*   how the people sink and scream bubbly underwater screams*
and hurt the monster's ears, and then they stop screaming and
thrashing;
*   how the monster darts like a minnow to the limp and falling*
body, puts out its hand and catches the falling person;

how upon falling into the monster's hand the person's face would soften and the person would stop screaming and thrashing and a peaceful look would come over it;

and how the monster loves them, those pretty unmoving people, takes them and strokes their hair like moss and holds their smoothness to its chest and lets the warmth of those tiny bodies touch the cold of its big body;

now the pain, the searing, the terrible pain;

and how sometimes the little dead people would come untethered from the lakeweed the monster had tied them in so they wouldn't go floating up into the broad air, for even when they turned purple and their flesh fell off, the monster loves them;

and even when their flesh is polished off with water and leaves only their gleaming bones, the monster even still loves them;

now the pain the pain the pain the terrible pain;

and when the monster only has the delicate bones left, it cradles them and carries them to the little shelf near the tower of stones that the men had built only a few heartbeats ago, where the monster keeps its beautiful bones and it sweeps the mud from the many bones and places the new bones beside the other bones and gently presses them into the clay there;

now another rip of pain;

and the monster makes a sound and watches three months' worth of air leave its mouth, watches the huge bubble spin toward the surface to explode;

how the monster has no strength to go the great distance from the dark depths to the bright air for another breath;

now the pain, faster now, deeper, darker;

the nights the monster spent with its ear twenty feet below the surface, listening to the roar of the people of Templeton, breathing and moving and speaking, the fishes and the leaves wiggling in the trees;

the pain, darkest now;

now the monster's gaze is darkening and it is beginning to float upward through the thick water and into the thin;

and one last wrench of pain;

now a tiny blinking thing in a pool of spooling blood, a queer, pale thing with a long neck, with the monster's own hands;

now the vast ancient monster and the small new monster stare at each other;

and the vast monster floats upward, away, and the last thing it sees is the little monster snapping with its black teeth at a little fish going by;

and as the vast monster's membranous eyelids go down, it remembers the music of the surface, that intricate music of wind and human and animal and other;

how with that music the monster was not all alone, not alone, for a while;

how the darkness falls even as the monster floats into the light, thinking of music;

how the darkness falls and the water is pricked with dawn-light;

how it is good
and it is good
and it is good

Acknowledgments

MY DEEPEST THANKS to . . .

all the people at Hyperion and Voice who worked so hard and made this book stronger, but especially my champions, Pamela Dorman, my brilliant editor, and Ellen Archer, Voice's publisher, both of whom believed in this story from the beginning;

Sarah Landis, associate editor extraordinaire, Beth Gebhard, Voice's publicity director, and my own publicist, Allison McGeehon;

Bill Clegg, my agent, who flew to Louisville and won my eternal adoration;

The UW-Madison MFA faculty: Amaud Jamaul Johnson, Jesse Lee Kercheval, Ron Kuka, Judith Claire Mitchell, Rob Nixon, and Ron Wallace;

With a special thanks to Lorrie Moore, who is lovely and wise beyond belief;

My buddies in the program, among whom Steph Bedford, Christopher Kang, Anna Potter, and Rita Mae Reese gave more than I could ever return;

Kevin A. González, a friend in need and deed (indeed);

Yaddo and the Vermont Studio Center, havens for hungry writers;

Anne Axton and the University of Louisville Creative Writing department for the astounding gift of the Axton fellowship;

All my friends whom I neglected when writing took over, especially Katie Harper and Jaime Muehl;

My midnight skinny-dippers Lisa (Senchyshyn) Trever, Meghann (Graham) Perillo, and Jeff Dean;

The original Running Buds: Pat Dietz, Donny Raddatz, Jerry Groff, Mikey Stein, Bobby Snyder, and Bill Streck, whose whip cracked all the way to Wisconsin;

My husband, Clay, gentle giant, first reader, and favorite person in the world;

Adam and Sarah, my siblings (and the fire in their bellies);

Cooperstown, and all the people who live there, have lived there, or loved the village even a little;

And, last and best, my parents, Gerald and Jeannine Groff, for their boundless love, support, and foresight for giving us such a gift of a hometown.